M000190497

Free Me

BOOK ONE IN THE FOUND DUET
**A FIXED TRILOGY
SPINOFF SERIES**

LAURELIN PAIGE

Copyright © 2014 by Laurelin Paige
All rights reserved, including the right to reproduce this book or
portions thereof in any form whatsoever.

This is a work of fiction. Names, characters, places and incidents
either are the product of the author's imagination or are used
fictitiously. Any resemblance to actual persons, living or dead, events
or locales is entirely coincidental.

First edition December 2014.
ISBN: 978-1-942835-72-1

The following story contains mature themes, strong language, and
sexual situations. It is intended for adult readers.

Free Me

Chapter One

I wasn't supposed to be working the night I met JC.

Jana had called me at the last minute to fill in for her. I knew it was serious before she even started talking. Jana never called in sick.

"They said I need twelve stiches. On my chin, Gwen. Jesus, I hope it doesn't scar."

"I'm just glad you're okay." I really wanted to tell her it was surprising she hadn't gotten hurt before this—roller derby wasn't exactly a safe sport, after all—but I managed to refrain from chiding.

"Ah, that's so sweet." Her Long Island/Puerto Rican accent seemed heavier over the phone. Or maybe it was the pain pills they'd given her. "I'm fine, really. I could come in when I'm done."

"Don't be ridiculous. I'll take your whole shift." What was I going to do anyway? Watching *The Voice* with Norma was pretty much the only thing on my agenda, and I could still catch the first half before I had to leave. It was our sisterly bonding ritual as she ended her day and I began mine. Lately, TV night with her had been less than fantastic, though, as if her mind were elsewhere. Which was weird. Where the fuck else could your mind be when Adam Levine was onscreen bantering with Blake Shelton?

But we had DVR. I could catch the rest in the morning before I went to bed.

"Thanks, babe," Jana drawled in my ear. "I didn't have a chance to call Matt, but I'm sure he's cool. I'll pick up your Thursday, that way you can still have your weekend."

I hoped she wasn't too doped up to remember that. I prized my "weekend"—my two days off from the Eighty-Eighth Floor where I worked. Not that I had anything exciting to do with the time off, and not that I really even needed the break. I'd work every shift if the law allowed. But I was the only manager at the club that had secured regular, sequential days off, and I valued what that meant. It meant I was good at my job. It meant I deserved the reward.

It meant there was something in this godforsaken life of mine that was actually worth something.

"You're going in?" Norma asked as I clicked END on my cell. She didn't look up from the papers spread across her desk tray. Norma was a workaholic, and although she tried to put it away on our nights together, it wasn't unusual when she simply couldn't. I didn't resent her for it. Her job at Pierce Industries as a financial manager was earned by hard work and relentless ambition. That was my sister—ambitious to a flaw.

But her ambition got us out of the ghetto. It paid for the high-rise apartment she shared with me. It paid for my brother and his life on the other side of the country. It paid to keep us away from the past we didn't ever want to go back to.

"Yeah," I said, already stripping from my jeans. "Jana's in the ER." I paused as I debated whether or not to inform our general manager, Matt, then decided against it. He was on vacation for the week and didn't need to be bothered with our minor changes. "She's switching me for Thursday. So I'll still have two days off in a row. We could watch *Project Runway* together this week."

Norma lifted her eyes from her work and furrowed her brow, as if looking at a calendar hanging in midair before her. "Uh, I'm not sure Thursday will work for me. I have...something." She disappeared into her work again without even remarking on the part where I said *ER*.

I shrugged as I gathered my clothes and headed to the shower. She probably had a fundraiser or another one of those fancy events she was always going to. Even my older sis of five years had a better social life than I did. So what that it was all related to her job? She still got out.

As the hot water streamed over my body, I swallowed back my impulse to envy and reminded myself that I could get out too if I wanted. I just hadn't ever decided that *was* what I wanted. And if I did decide it was what I wanted, I'd have no idea at all how to go about doing it.

• • •

Working on a Tuesday was odd only in that I kept forgetting what day it was when I went to write it on my paperwork. The Eighty-Eighth Floor was one of the hottest clubs in Greenwich Village. Hell, it was one of the hottest clubs in New York City. We were nearly as busy on weeknights as we were on the weekends. Tonight was especially hopping because of the nearness to the holidays. Colleges were out, people were visiting friends, it was too cold for outdoor activities—though you wouldn't have known that from the outfits most of the girls wore. Everywhere I looked there were breasts peeking over bikini tops and asses hanging below skirt hems. Perhaps I'd feel differently if I were liquoring up and shimmying on the floor, but I was covered and comfortable in my gray slacks and cowl-neck maroon tank top.

Maybe I was just too old for the club scene. Thirty was approaching. Was it normal to prefer a quiet evening on the couch to a night of dancing at this age? Norma had never been a partier, so I couldn't compare myself to her. Our little brother, Benjamin, had lived on the West Coast since he was eighteen, so I wasn't aware of his habits. And friends…well, I didn't really have those.

That was the real problem, of course. I'd probably like clubbing just fine if I had someone to go with. Or maybe not. It was hard to know for sure.

I did like my job. It was steady and rhythmic. Managing gave me the opportunity to be no-nonsense and harsh. It was how I preferred to be. Cold. Hard. In charge.

The night was off to the usual start. All four of our floors were full, and we even had a small line at the door by eleven. The bars were all staffed well. The cash drawers all had sufficient change. Our best bouncer was working head security. It was starting out to be a predictable shift.

I knew better than to settle into the comfort of predictable. It was more important to be prepared. I should have been prepared.

But nothing could have prepared me for JC.

I'd only been on the clock for a couple of hours when I overheard the murmuring of the waitresses. They hushed the moment I came near, which wasn't unusual. I was their boss, not their friend. Normally, I'd ignore that kind of buzz amongst the staff. Most of their gossip was about the hottest new employee or even where to score a quarter, which was not any of my concern as long as their job was done well.

This time, I heard two words that piqued me—*Viper* and *cigar smoke*. Okay, three words. A word and a phrase that automatically sent alarms sounding in my head.

I stepped closer to the women. "What's that you were saying?"

Bethany's eyes went wide. "I have to deliver this." She took off toward the lounge with her tray of appetizers before I could stop her.

The other waitress was still entering her order into the register. She didn't have an excuse to run.

I leaned against the counter next to her, grateful that the registers were off the kitchen in a quieter part of the club where I didn't have to shout to be heard. "Alyssa, what did she mean about cigar smoke in the Viper?" It wasn't that unusual to have patrons mouth the damn things without lighting them—helped with that oral fixation thing that so many people had—but the actual smoking of cigars was not allowed in the club. The Eighty-Eighth Floor was a smoke-free establishment, and if that rule was being ignored, then I had to address it.

Alyssa didn't look up from the computer right away. I saw her throat move as she swallowed. Then she met my eyes, a bright smile on her lips. Too bright of a smile. "Oh, you know. Just talk. I'm sure there's not really any smoking going on."

I narrowed my stare. "Uh-huh." Alyssa was one of the more reliable employees. But like I'd said—I wasn't her friend. "Who's got the room booked tonight, anyway?"

The Viper wasn't really the name of the secluded area that the club offered to elite guests. It was officially called The Deck on our marketing material—the club's official VIP Room. But on all our paperwork, Matt always wrote *VIP R.*, and with his sloppy boy handwriting the R usually ended up closer to the P and soon the whole staff called it the Viper.

Alyssa shook her head, her ponytail swishing with the movement. "No one special. A white collar group." She was dismissive. Then, seeming to realize that tactic wasn't working with me, she said, "I could go check in up there. If there's anything sketchy going on, I'll let you know."

Yeah, like I was falling for that. "How about we go and check on it together?"

Her face fell visibly, but she nodded an agreement and headed toward the spiraling metal stairs that led up to The Deck.

I followed. Adrenaline was already sizzling in my veins as I climbed up toward the Viper. I wasn't scared of what I'd find—we had a good security team, and I'd seen enough in my life to set my fear threshold high. But there was something exciting about the prospect of something different. The thrill that maybe the night *wouldn't* be typical or predictable.

The delicious raising of goose bumps on my pale skin as something inside me wished for the unexpected.

Not that I'd do anything other than correct the off-course situation. I might have longed for variance, but I didn't know how to live with it when I found it.

At the Viper door, Alyssa paused and waited for me to join her. "Maybe we should knock?"

Fuck that. Managers had carte blanche to the entire premises. I wasn't going to give our errant guests a chance to hide their coke and cover their cocks. Especially since I could already smell the Cubans.

I swung the door open and stood in the threshold to survey the scene. What I saw surprised me. Or, some of it surprised me. The smoky air and half-smoked cigars I'd been expecting. And where one club violation was found, there were usually more, so the half-dressed women didn't completely catch me off-guard either. Nor did the three men playing poker in the corner with actual money laid out on the table.

It was the men. The way they carried themselves, the way they behaved like the respected businessmen that their expensive suits said they were rather than a house of drunken frat boys. There were a dozen or so of them—young, single. At least, I didn't see any bands or tan marks from removed rings. The snippets of conversation that passed my ear were intelligent and intelligible, not like the hundreds of twenty-something guys I saw come through the club on a weekly basis, the ones who focused on the waitresses' tits when they ordered and were too wasted to remember where they left their iPhones.

Then there were the women.

A room full of debauchery wouldn't be complete without hookers and sleazy call girls. That was routine. But these women, five in total, were definitely not sleazy. Even as they draped themselves over the men—even though three of them were topless and another was dressed only in a French lace bra and panties—they gave a definite air of refinement. They exuded polish and class. Sexy, yes, but not trashy.

One of the topless women, a brunette sitting on a man's lap, looked up at me. Her eyes lit with recognition. She smiled and mouthed a hello before returning her attention to her fingers as they combed through the man's hair.

My brows pressed together as I tried to place her. Pure shock washed through me when I realized it wasn't from my seedy past that

I knew her, but from school. She'd been a graduate student teaching a commercial kitchen resource class that I'd taken. Now she managed a five-star restaurant uptown.

And she was here? Part of this…this…

I didn't know what this was actually. It was a party that broke the rules, but it wasn't unruly or sordid or out-of-hand. It was naughty and sensual and…enticing. I would lay down the law—of course, I would, how could I not?—but for a moment, I hesitated. For a moment, instead of wanting to admonish, I wanted to join.

"You're welcome to sit." The voice came from behind me. It spoke with insight. As though it understood my conflict. As though it knew what I really wanted.

Which was bullshit. It was just a fucking invitation. Nothing more.

I turned to deliver my *what the hell is going on* speech, until my eyes landed on the man who had spoken. At the sight of him, I lost the words. He sat with his legs stretched out in front of him, his back against the wall behind the door, which was why I hadn't noticed him at first.

But now that I noticed him, I really *noticed* him.

It was impossible not to. Sex appeal and charisma oozed off him as if he'd dressed in both. Well-defined muscles pressed against his snug dress shirt. His dark blond hair was severe—the sides short and the top sculpted to look like a hot Italian mobster from the nineteen twenties. He wore stubble that I suspected helped keep him from looking younger than he was, an age that I put around thirty.

And his eyes…

I couldn't see them clearly in the darkness, but I *felt* them. Felt the way he studied me with earnest. Felt the flicker of yearning in them. Felt the heaviness behind that, where hurt lay, or bitterness perhaps.

Like the slack of a rope that is suddenly tightened and taut, my own gaze was drawn to him. I couldn't look away, and as he continued to peer at me—peer *into* me—a hum began to vibrate through my body, setting my every molecule on high alert. Even my girly parts, which had been hibernating, wakened in his presence—expanding and buzzing, tingling with awareness of him.

This was all for him, I realized. The partying, the entertainment—it was his. Everything was centered on him.

Except, in my periphery, where the others continued with their previous activities, I realized everything really wasn't centered on him.

The party might have been his, but no one was giving him any mind. It was *me* that was centered on him. Centered like the whole room was a ship on rocky waves and this single man was the axis. A solitary point of balance in a space of chaos. It was unusual because *I* was used to being the point of balance in chaos. I was stability. I was order.

Under his intense scrutiny, I was knocked off-kilter. As if one heel had broken and my foot had scrambled for purchase and he had been there to give me an arm. He both tripped me and steadied me all at once.

I don't know when he started talking again. I saw his lips moving before I registered the sound. "Come on. Join us," I think he said.

"What?" I had now completely zeroed in on his mouth—his teeth were perfect, straight and white. His bottom lip was plumper than the top, pale and inviting.

It curved up into a slight smile. "Pull up a seat. Alyssa will get you a drink. Maybe Luke will even give you a backrub. He's great at working out muscles. You're so tight I can see your knots from here."

"I don't...I can't...I'm..." I was flustered. Flabbergasted. He was the mobster asking the cop to dinner. Who even did that?

Plus, he was really attractive. And while really attractive men usually had no effect on me whatsoever, this one did. And that...scared me.

So much for having a high fear threshold.

The man motioned to someone behind me. "Jennie, can you get our guest a chair?"

The underwear-clad woman pushed a chair closer to me, and automatically I sat, my knees pointed toward the stranger like a compass pointing north.

Then, realizing that wasn't what I should be doing, I popped back up. Back to myself. Back to my place of authority where I was the one in control, the one with the poise.

"Thank you," I said, firmly, steadily—at least I hoped firmly and steadily—"but no. I actually have to ask you to clean this act up."

"Clean what up exactly?" His casual demeanor threw me. Again. Usually when a manager busted a patron, the guilty party became apologetic and full of excuses. Unless they were too drugged or drunk to care, and this man seemed to be neither.

Surprised that I was, I tried to keep it together. "There's no smoking in the club. Or gambling. Or stripping. Tell your friends to extinguish their cigars, put away the cards and put their clothing on or they can leave. Or do all those things *and* leave. That would be another, even better option."

While most of the room remained unaffected by my speech, one of the men tapped my waitress on the shoulder. "Alyssa, who is this chick?"

Irritated that Alyssa obviously knew more about this party than she'd cared to share with me downstairs, I gave her a searing look that said both *don't answer that* and *we're going to have to have a talk later.*

Maybe my annoyance was misplaced. Male customers commonly learned the names of their waitresses, sometimes innocently, sometimes not so innocently. Matt had a strict rule that only first names were used at the club for exactly that reason—so that no one could find themselves stalked online or their home address searched for on findsomeone.com. It was a safety precaution that I one-hundred-percent supported.

Still, the way Alyssa exchanged glances with the questioner, it seemed she knew this crowd much better than she'd let on. It dawned on me that they were regulars.

But I wasn't a regular. Not on Tuesdays, so I was more than a little stunned when the charismatic stranger said, "This is Gwen. She's our manager on duty tonight."

"How did...?" I cut off, but not before I'd given myself away. There was no way he couldn't tell how easily he derailed me.

"You're wondering how I know all that." He sat back in his chair, placing his ankle over his opposite knee. One of the topless women came to perch on the arm of his chair and draped a hand around his neck while he spoke, but he didn't throw her so much as a glance as he continued speaking. "I'll tell you how I know. It's my business to look out for my guests, and that includes knowing the staff on duty. Alyssa here informed me earlier you were in charge tonight. She did a pretty good job describing you, too."

My jaw tensed as I wondered exactly how Alyssa had described me—*blonde? Bony? Uptight? A pain in the ass?*

"Though, Alyssa, you were wrong," JC said to the waitress behind me. "You said that she was pretty, which is totally not correct."

My eyes widened with horror. I wasn't pageant material maybe, but I'd never been outright told I wasn't pretty.

JC turned his focus back to me. "No, no, no. You're taking me wrong." *Jesus, was I really so transparent?* "*Pretty* is a complete put-down if you ask me, because you're actually quite gorgeous. It's a unique sort of beauty. A hardened one. Not many people can pull off stony and stunning. But you can. It's your eyes. They're softer, inset like that. They contradict your expression."

I blinked. Maybe I gaped a bit too. The straightforward way this man—this *stranger*—talked about me, about my looks…it should have felt crude. Violating. Not flattering. Not charming.

And it sure as hell shouldn't make my stomach flutter with butterflies or make my pulse pick up. Or make my cheeks blush.

The woman behind him leaned forward, her breasts rubbing casually against the man's ear. "It doesn't hurt that she has nice tits," she added.

This time I did gape. For one, how could she possibly know anything about my tits, which were on the bigger side, yes, but completely covered? And two, had she looked in a mirror? Because if we were talking about nice tits, there were few that could compete with hers, and I was even pretty sure they were real.

"Now, Natalie, that's hardly appropriate." But his eyes moved down to check out my rack as he said it.

Still, I appreciated the attempt at civility.

Then I remembered I didn't appreciate any of this at all. "Flattery is not going to get you anywhere with me. You need to get this out of here. Now." Thank God for the natural rasp in my voice—I used it to hide my unsteadiness.

"I don't do flattery, Gwen." He paused, seeming to want that to sink in before he went on. "And, I'm sorry to be the one to inform you, but I have this room booked to do absolutely whatever I want."

"You may have the room booked. But not to do whatever you want." The room had an explicit lease agreement with definitive rules. He had to have received a copy. He was a regular—none of this could be new to him. And if he thought he could try to take advantage of my unfamiliarity, he had another thing coming.

I clung to that—the rules, the law. Clung to the knowledge that right was on my side.

"Actually, he does have the room booked to do whatever he wants," Alyssa said meekly.

I turned to see her face crumple into an apology. Whether she was apologizing for not telling me about the situation beforehand or for taking his side, I didn't know.

I did know there was no way she was right.

As if reading my mind, he said, "Alyssa's right. I do."

There's really only one person who would have arranged something with that kind of authority, but I asked anyway, dreading the answer. "Says who?"

"Matt." The answer came both from Alyssa and him at the same time.

Then he clarified. "Matt and I have somewhat of an informal agreement."

What was left of my dignity fell away. If it was true—and I had a sinking feeling it was—then I was in the wrong. It was humiliating. And disappointing.

I'd heard rumors about Matt's informal agreements, but I'd yet to see them live and in action. Probably because Matt knew I'd disapprove. Since he was my boss, my endorsement wasn't exactly required. Unless he was worried that I'd go above his head and tell the owner, Joseph Ricker.

I wouldn't do that. Matt was a good boss and I had no interest in taking his job. But I could at least scare him into ending such ridiculous arrangements. "Maybe I should call him."

He seemed to understand what was on the line. He tilted his head and before he even spoke, I knew he'd be a good debater. "You don't really want to do that, Gwen, do you?" He sat forward, both feet on the ground, his hands clasped with his index fingers extended. "I mean, here's how I see it. Obviously Matt doesn't want you to know about me. I've been booking this room now for what—seven, eight months?" He looked around the room for agreement, which several people readily gave.

Then he looked at me. "How long have you been here?"

"Five years." I'd been hired as a manager right before my twenty-fifth birthday. It had been my first real job after I'd earned my dual degree in restaurant management and human resources, paid for, of course, by Norma. I hadn't necessarily intended to stay at Eighty-Eighth, but I'd climbed from part-time assistant manager to second-in-command within three years. The pay was good. The job was comfortable. My boss and my peers respected me.

He pointed his index fingers now at me. "You never work Tuesdays, do you?"

"I don't."

"Because Matt's kept me from you on purpose. Why do you think that is?" His question was patronizing, so I answered only with a hard stare. "No guesses? I have one. I bet you must be the tight-ass around here. The follow-the-rules girl. And the deal I have with Matt, well, the rules are vague. That probably goes against your nature. Doesn't it, Gwen?"

I hated how he said my name, like he had all the power because he knew that bit of information about me. Hated it and loved it. I also hated how his eyes drew up my body, long and slow. Sensually touching my every curve, my every angle.

Hated and loved it. Hated that I loved it.

I sat on the chair that was still behind me, not trusting my legs to keep me steady for much longer. "What exactly is this deal you have? And who are you?"

"I," he paused, "am JC."

I'd never heard of him. "JC...?"

"Just JC." He said it like it answered everything. Two short syllables to put me in my place.

"As in Jesus Christ?"

A few people laughed. But actually, if Christ really had existed—a point I was not sure on in the least—I imagined he'd be quite like the man in front of me. Magnetic, smooth, surrounded by depravity that he didn't publicly partake in.

JC chuckled as well, his expression brash and sexy. "I've been called that. But usually only when my face is pressed between a woman's thighs."

Ew.

Also, *hot.*

It wasn't strange for me to hear such lewd comments. I worked in a club. In New York City. I knew crass.

But the way JC said his inappropriate words made the muscles clench low in my belly. Lower than my belly. In forgotten regions that hadn't been stimulated in years. Hadn't even been thought about in years. It brought the room to a tilt again.

I didn't like it. I didn't understand it. Yes, I was human—a woman with sexual desires just like any other—but I'd learned long ago how to turn those feelings off. They didn't make themselves known without my permission, and they certainly didn't send sparks down my spine that ricocheted out to my limbs and ignited my every cell. I did not like it in the least.

So I decided not to acknowledge it. "And your deal...?"

There was a glint in JC's eye that said he knew exactly what I was trying to hide. Or maybe I was imagining that because he didn't bug me about it, and I had the feeling he was the type who would. Instead, he answered my question. "I get The Deck every Tuesday. I use it to entertain my friends and associates."

"You entertain your associates," I repeated. Ah, I knew what this was. He was the snake charmer. The man who brought the deals into his firm by schmoozing their potential clients with hot girls and liquor. "With strippers?"

"Come on, do you really think these women are strippers? They're my associates too. Don't judge them by their lack of clothing." He eyed one of his guy friends who was currently being straddled by one of the topless girls. "Give it another hour and I bet the men will have undressed too."

I looked around the room again, the idea so foreign to me. Getting paid to disrobe…I could understand that. I'd come from a life where sometimes you had to do those kinds of things to keep yourself fed.

But to break rules just because? That, I didn't get. *What would it be like to be that uninhibited? To be that unrestrained?*

I shook my head. The whole thing was beyond my grasp. It also had me pissed. I felt undermined. And disrespected. When Matt had offered me Tuesdays and Wednesdays off a year ago, had that really been because I deserved it? Or was it simply his way of keeping his dealings outside of my radar?

"This is fucking bullshit," I muttered, my anger directed more at my own stupidity than anything else.

JC raised a questioning brow.

Hell if I was going to explain myself to him. "What is it you do anyway?"

"This and that. Invest in projects sometimes. Hang out and do what I want the rest of the time."

So not the charmer, but one of *those* guys. A trust fund baby that kept up his lifestyle by giving money to other people who did the work while he partied it up and collected.

I couldn't help myself. I rolled my eyes.

"I could also help you with that stick up your ass." JC's tone was serious, but his expression held a glimmer of something more playful. Teasing.

I narrowed my glare. "By what, replacing it with *your* stick up my ass?"

"Ha ha. Funny. I mean, if you wanted to…" He paused as if giving me a chance to jump in and agree. *Fat fucking chance.* "But that's not where I was going with that. I was offering something else. Not *was*—am. I *am* offering something else."

Sure. Something else. Right. "Is that one of the things you do? One of your side jobs?"

"I don't take money for it, if that's what you're implying. No. It's not a job. I just see that you're pretty tense. I think I could help you with that." He was matter-of-fact where I'd been sarcastic. Genuine where I'd been caustic.

It left me speechless, and I couldn't even begin to say why. Because he had the upper hand? Because I'd been thrown off my managerial pedestal? Because the way he looked at me was the most appreciatively I'd been looked at in who knows how long? Like he wanted to eat me up, but also like he wanted to savor me.

Like he knew that there was a very small but very persistent part of me that wanted just that.

"He helped me out," Natalie said. "Honestly, you can't hang out with JC without learning how to chill a bit."

He didn't glance up at her, his eyes still glued to me. I wondered what exactly he'd taught her. What method was used to educate her? Surely it was as shameless and vulgar as I suspected.

"Yeah, no thank you." Not that I was a prude. I was just uninterested in the freeness of character that seemed to be present. I preferred control. I preferred restraint.

I looked around the room again. There was a couple making out on the loveseat and a threesome half-dancing, half-dry-sexing on one of the tables. The woman straddling the guy's lap was now gyrating over his crotch as he bit his lip, lust marked heavily in his expression.

My disgust must have been apparent because JC said, "Hey, don't knock it 'til you've tried it." He studied me for a second. Then he stood and started toward me. "You haven't, have you? Tried it, I mean. Haven't had a good lap dance. Haven't had any lap dance."

He was taller than I'd thought he'd be, his height reaching a good six or seven inches above my standing height, putting him around six feet. And the way he pierced me with his eyes, the way he goaded me with his libidinous undertones, I felt smaller than usual.

Smaller and hornier.

The hairs on my arms stood up and my heart fluttered at his nearness and his hypnotic voice. I stumbled on my response. "I hav-v'nt."

He nodded to Natalie. "Wanna show her?"

"Um, no thanks," I said, standing up before Natalie could answer. Did he really think I'd let her give me a lap dance? No way. I shivered at the thought, though, not entirely sure it was in disgust.

JC shook his head. "Not for you, babydoll. You'd freak. The girls here will show you."

Normally I'd correct him for calling me *babydoll*. And I'd definitely walk out before the insane scene went farther. But I was glued for some reason, my feet planted to their spot as JC pulled the chair I'd abandoned out in front of me. He didn't have to ask anyone to sit there—the girl wearing the French lingerie silently sank into the seat. She braced her arms behind her and spread her legs. Wide.

Natalie took three sultry steps and stopped between the seated woman's knees. She turned to face out and began her dance. Her movements were subtle at first, a slow tilt of her hip to one side, a sensuous slide of her pelvis to the other. Soon she rested her hands on the other's legs and bent her own knees as she twisted down—her ass practically sitting in the lap behind her—then twisted back up.

There was a palpable tension that spread throughout the room, but JC's guests remained in line. I'd expected whoops and cheers to erupt, but none did. The only sounds besides the faint thump of the club music on the other side of the wall were the soft brush of Natalie's thighs as they slid back and forth against each other, the swish of her ponytail, and the ragged breaths of both the girls in front of me.

My own breathing had become jagged and I had to concentrate to keep it quiet. It wasn't easy. Natalie's dance was hypnotic. Her body moved to a definitive beat that no one but her could hear, yet it could be felt. It was seductive. It was foreplay. Watching made my thighs quiver. Made my nipples pebble. Made my panties wet.

A shiver ran down my spine as I let desire spread throughout me. It wasn't just the sexual aspect that had me so turned on. Nor was it the artistic beauty of her movements. It was something else, something I couldn't name, something I didn't quite recognize.

"It's extremely sensual, isn't it?"

I startled, not realizing JC was so close behind me. Or maybe I did know and that was the real cause of my body's simmering arousal. But I didn't know how to answer his question.

It *was* sensual.

And that pissed me off because I wanted it to be porn and not whatever odd thing it was in actuality. I definitely didn't want it to be this thing that flooded me so entirely.

So I didn't answer.

JC seemed to take my silence as an invitation to say more. "You know what makes it so hot? Besides the beautiful naked women and the fluidity of Natalie's movements, it's hot because of what it is. A transfer of power."

He must have leaned closer toward me because now I could feel his breath skate across my shoulder as he spoke. "When you get a lap dance, you can't touch. You want to—*God, you want to*—but you have to let the pleasure tease you and take over while you remain helpless. It seems at first that it may be easy, doesn't it? That it's just about keeping control. Something I'm sure you excel at. But it's really exactly the opposite. It's about giving up the control. The control belongs to Natalie. Lena has given her the power. She's promised to abide by her rules—rules she might not like or agree with. And in return, Natalie gives her the pleasure she's looking for."

He bent in farther, his breath tickling my ear and stirring my blood as he said, "Tell me you don't want to be her."

I crossed my arms over my chest. "I don't. I don't even like regular dancing."

"Not Natalie, Gwen. That's not who you want to be. You want to be Lena. You want to be that free."

My breath caught as unexpected tears pricked my eyes.

I wanted to turn and slap JC. He was cocky and arrogant to think he knew anything about me. He didn't. He was guessing, trying to get in my pants most likely, and with his guesses he'd struck a nerve. Struck it hard enough that, if I were the free person that he clearly stated I wasn't, I would have slapped him. Hard.

But I wasn't upset because he was guessing or even because of why he was guessing. I was upset because his guesses were right. I *did* want to be free. I was a tight-ass. I was boxed in. I existed on routine and missed a whole helluva lot of pleasure.

What he didn't know—he couldn't know—was that I'd chosen to be that way for a reason. It didn't matter what I wanted, this was how I knew how to survive. Fuck him for trying to insinuate that I'd made the wrong decision. He wasn't me. He didn't know.

I didn't slap him. And I didn't say anything. I simply spun around and left the Viper, pulling the door shut behind me. But beyond that slight outburst, I refused to let JC get to me. I refused to think about the choices I'd made and the character I'd taken upon myself. I refused to let myself wonder if there really was any other way I could be.

The rest of my shift went by without me returning to the room upstairs. I convinced myself I could forget about the whole experience. That meant I wouldn't tell Matt I knew about his informal deal.

And I sure as hell wasn't working another shift on Tuesday as long as I could help it.

Chapter Two

"Did I catch you before work?" Norma's voice sounded muffled through my coat collar as I tried to balance the phone on my shoulder and unlock the doors to the club at the same time.

It was cold, and with my gloves on, I'd only just managed to hit the *TALK* button before my phone stopped ringing. "Barely. I'm walking in now."

It was a Thursday, and like many other weeknights, Norma had worked late so I hadn't gotten to see her before leaving for my eight o'clock shift. "Did you get dinner? There's leftover takeout in the fridge if you didn't."

"Yeah, I ate." She sounded distracted. "I'm sorry. I meant to call you earlier, but I was tied up with…meetings."

I pushed through the employee entrance into the kitchen. "No problem. What's up?"

"I heard from Dad's lawyer today."

Dad. One simple word, and I was frozen in my tracks. "And?"

Relax, I told myself. *He's probably just contacting you to wish you an early Happy Birthday.*

Yeah, right. He'd surprised us every now and then with remembering the special events in our lives. But not recently. Not since he'd landed in jail.

"And…" Norma hesitated, which alerted me to how bad her news was going to be. "And he's coming home earlier than we thought."

"Jesus Christ, no." I could barely speak past the ball in my throat. "When?"

"June."

"June?" I repeated it again in my head a few times before I was able to comprehend it. "That's six whole months early! I thought he couldn't get out before December." Dad's sentence had been issued without parole. December would be ten years. It was coming up fast, but at least then I still had a whole cycle of seasons to get through before I had to deal with it. With him.

Now there was only spring between his cell and his freedom. I felt like I might throw up.

"He wasn't supposed to be able to get out early, no. But there's crowding and…it's complicated. They're putting him in a half-way house to finish his term." Norma sounded weary so I didn't make her explain any more. I trusted my sister to tell me what I needed to hear and keep the rest away. She was one of the only people I trusted, actually. "We could try to fight it, but we'd probably not get anywhere. It wouldn't be worth the time or money."

Frustrated, I ran a hand through my hair before remembering I was wearing gloves. The gesture wasn't nearly as satisfying as I wanted it to be, the weird smoothness of it actually irritating me more. I tugged the glove off with my mouth and then asked the most important question. "Have you told Ben?"

As much as Norma and I dreaded our father's release, it was our little brother who would take the news the worst. Which was reasonable. He'd been the most affected by the darkness of our past.

"Not yet. I'll call him. Soon." Norma cleared her throat, and I suspected she might have the same ball of apprehension that I did. "But not tonight. I need to think about how I'm going to tell him."

"Let me know if you need any help." Not that I could do much. Norma was the one who'd always had the soothing touch. My approach was always to say *ouch* and move on.

Really, it was more like say ouch and shove it deep inside the black hole that I half-seriously believed existed in place of my heart. What else would explain why I was so vastly void of any lasting emotion? The darkness ate any real feeling that threatened to take hold of me. Anger and anxiety probably snuck in more than anything else. But even the panic about my father was subsiding already, turning into a dull buzz of irritation. Maybe it wasn't the healthiest way to go through life, yet it had been the way that I'd survived.

Ben wasn't like me, though. Ben would take this hard.

"Man, this really sucks." I started through the kitchen, bracing the phone on my shoulder again as I took off my other glove and stuffed it in my coat pocket.

Bethany looked up from her prep work and stopped me just as Norma started to say something.

"Hold on a sec, Norma." I put my hand over the receiver and nodded to Bethany to talk.

"That JC guy—"

I rolled my eyes and cut her off. "Say no more."

JC was the last person I needed to think about at the moment. He was the last person I needed to think about period. He was arrogant and crass. Ridiculous and entitled.

And every time he crossed my mind, my heart did a flip-flop.

I hadn't seen him since that night a month ago when I'd met him in the Viper, but now that I was aware of his existence, it felt like he was everywhere. I heard him casually mentioned by the staff a few times. Once I saw a phone message from him for Matt. His initials were even on a calendar in the office—how had I never noticed any of that before?

Then, of course, there had been the flowers.

He'd sent some to the club the weekend after we'd met. I'd come in to find them in the office at the start of my Saturday shift. As I'd opened the sealed envelope with my name on it that accompanied the lavish bouquet, I'd been dying of curiosity, and admittedly, excitement. No one I knew would send me flowers. So what the hell?

The message was simple.

"The difference between who you are and who you want to be is what you do."

JC

An array of emotions flashed through me so fast I had no idea which one I was actually feeling. Surprised, embarrassed, annoyed, anxious. Turned on.

Finally, I settled on anger. Just like when I met him, I wondered, who did he think he was? So he could quote Bill Phillips, was he my personal motivational speaker now? How did he think he knew anything about me, anyway? And if he was trying to get me into his bed, this was definitely not how to do it.

Though, wasn't it a little bit flattering that he'd still been thinking of me several days later?

No. It definitely was not. It made me angrier that I'd even considered it. So I dumped the whole thing, vase and all, into the trash next to the desk and tried to forget about it.

I'd still thought about it.

Or, I'd thought about *him*. A lot. Throughout the Christmas holidays, into the New Year, he wasn't ever very far from my mind. He was attractive, yes, and that might have been why his image so easily appeared in my head at the oddest of times. But more, it was the things he'd said about me. He'd said I wanted to be free. He'd said he could help me learn. What exactly did that mean? Sex? Was he serious?

And even if sex could do me some good, could anyone actually break through the prison I lived in?

If anyone could, it wasn't him. That I knew for sure.

"Just wanted to warn you," Bethany said to me now.

Great. Probably another bouquet waiting on my desk. I should have known he wouldn't be that easy to shake.

"Thanks, Bethany," I mouthed then returned to talking to Norma as I continued through the kitchen. "Okay, I'm back."

"I only have one more thing."

"Shoot." I paused to scan the kitchen schedule posted on the wall. While I didn't manage the staff in there, I liked to know whom I was working with before a shift began.

"I don't want you to be alarmed," Norma said hesitantly, "but he asked if he could stay with us when he gets out."

"Who asked? The lawyer?"

"Dad asked his lawyer to ask us."

"Oh, hell no!" Now I was pissed. That was one of the emotions I was able to hold onto for more than a minute. "No way, no how. How can he even have the balls to ask? You said no, right? You damn well better have said no."

"Yes, I said no. I won't even tell him where we live for as long as we can manage that. But I just wanted you to know in case he tries to contact you."

"Thanks. I think." I pushed through the kitchen door into the main part of the club. Then, for the second time in a matter of minutes, I froze in my tracks. "Hey, I have to go."

"Okay. Talk later. Don't let this eat at you, Gwen. We're fine. Everything's fine."

I ended the call, barely registering Norma's parting words. My attention was completely on the man leaning against the bar.

Why, oh why hadn't I listened better to Bethany's warning? I could have gotten Brent or one of the other guys in the kitchen to get rid of him for me.

Once again, I wasn't prepared.

When he saw me, JC's lip curled into a smile. Then he winked. *Winked!* And my stupid body decided to react with a parade of goose bumps. Which only pissed me off more than I already was.

"Seriously? I don't know you exist for the whole year and then I see you twice in one month?" I immediately regretted lashing out. If there'd been even a chance that he hadn't realized that he affected me then it was gone now.

Since the club wasn't open yet, the work lights were still on, and I could see him more clearly than when I'd met him. It was a sight I didn't need to see. If I'd wondered at all that the dim lighting of the Viper might have been overly kind to his appearance, that notion had been killed.

Because now, in full view, he was stunning.

He was dressed much like he had been the last time I saw him, wearing a dark gray two-piece that fit him spectacularly. His hair wasn't styled as severely, and I could see now that he had a bit of natural curl. He still wore stubble, more recently trimmed so that it looked even more enticing to touch. I had to clench my fist tight so as not to reach my hand out to rub against his cheek.

He straightened and put his hands in his pockets. "I know. It should have been sooner. But with the holidays and all…"

"Why should you have been here sooner?" Why I asked, I didn't know. It was a setup to hearing something I probably didn't want to hear. It was just so hard to think in his presence. He was so aggravating and alluring all at once. Should anyone really be that attractive just from stuffing his hands in his pockets?

It was cruel, really.

JC took a casual step toward me. "Because I *wanted* to see you, Gwen." He said it as if it were the most matter-of-fact statement ever. "Normally, if I want to see someone, I don't put it off that long. It's just…I wasn't even in town. I would have sent you more flowers so that you knew I was thinking of you, but I heard that you didn't enjoy them as much as I'd hoped."

"I…" He was doing it again—knocking me off-kilter, pushing me out of my stride. "You know about the flowers?" I closed my eyes briefly, regretting my words. "I mean, thank you. The flowers were lovely. I'm not interested."

But also, how the heck did he know what I'd done with the flowers? *Dammit, Alyssa.* She'd been there when I tossed them. She had to have told him.

Well, so he knew. It was better that he didn't think I'd appreciated them.

Except, it hadn't seemed to get the point across because he was here now.

"That's not fair, Gwen." He took another step toward me. "You should really give me a chance to at least re-extend my offer before you shoot it down."

Suddenly feeling warm, I started working the buttons on my coat. "I know I sound ridiculous because I'm asking question after question, but could you remind me which offer that was?" I was bluffing, of course. I knew exactly which offer JC was talking about. The idea of it—sex with this irritating stranger—it stirred me in places I hadn't realized could stir.

But there was no way I could let him know that. He knew way too much about me already.

My pulse quickened as JC took several fast steps toward me. But he merely circled behind me to help me take off my coat. "You know which offer. The one where I help you loosen up a little."

Now he was close to me, real close. And even as I shed the weight of my coat into his arms, I felt my temperature rise.

I groaned though it sounded almost like a moan to my own ears. "You are so crude." I turned to face him and snatched my coat from his hands.

"You are so uptight." He said the word *uptight* as though it intrigued him. As though it challenged him.

Just what I needed—to be someone's challenge. Still holding my coat, I crossed my arms over my chest. "You don't even know me."

"I don't know you, but I know *that.* Everyone knows that." Again with his hands in his pockets, seeming to mock my more defensive posture.

"Everyone knows that I'm uptight?" My voice sounded shrill. I realized I was only proving his point. I shook my head and mumbled, "This is the weirdest conversation I've ever had with anyone."

"Then stop talking. We don't need to talk." His eyes searched mine. Which gave me the opportunity to search his. They were bright and alive in a way that I was sure mine hadn't been in years—if ever. But beyond that, beyond the laughter and the light, there was the same thing I'd seen that night in the Viper. Something hollow. Something lonely. Something void.

"You two know each other?" Matt's wary tone cut through my focus. I'd been so fixated on JC that I hadn't heard him come in from the office.

Great. Just great.

Now that he'd seen me with JC, I'd have to admit I knew about the rule-breaking deal Matt had set up. And that meant I'd have to either tell on him with the owner or let him believe I was okay with it. I wasn't going to tell on him. I also wasn't okay with it. I liked it better when he thought I was in the dark. More than that, I liked it when I *was* in the dark.

Too late now.

Matt was worried as well. His expression said it all. I bit my lip, trying to decide what to say.

But before I could admit anything, JC said, "We've just met." He cocked a brow. "Gwen, you said?"

He probably wanted me to say something, but all I could manage was a nod. I was too surprised. JC had no reason to hide that we knew each other. Unless he understood the position I was in. Unless he understood me better than I gave him credit for.

The idea made the blood rush from my face and my throat go dry.

"I thought I knew all the managers at Eighty-Eighth. Guess not." JC turned away from me and walked over to Matt. "Anyway, I came by to see you."

I'd have thought that Matt would be relieved to find that I didn't know about his secret dealings with JC. But his voice sounded even more anxious when he asked, "Why? What did you find out? Is there something new?"

Matt's reaction sent a chill down my spine. He was fraught and concerned where I'd always known him only to be mellow and reasonable. That it was JC he was addressing bothered me. Made me interested in their relationship when I'd normally not care in the least.

JC put his hand on Matt's shoulder. "No, no, I'm not here for anything like that. Just haven't seen you for a few weeks. You took that time off and then the holidays—it's been a month."

They'd forgotten I was there, and I let them. It wasn't polite of me by any means. I should have excused myself so they could discuss their private matters. Instead, I slid onto a bar stool and pretended to straighten a stack of happy hour menus.

Behind me, Matt gave a shaky sigh. "I just couldn't be around that week. Not this time. Too many memories."

"I know," JC said. "I understand. Why do you think I spend so much time on the coast?"

I peeked at them in the mirror above the bar. JC's face couldn't be seen, but his hand was still on Matt and now Matt had put his hand on JC's shoulder as well, as if they were comforting each other about what?

"You were still here though. That's tough of you." Matt patted JC one more time before dropping his arm.

JC let his hand fall too, stuffing it in his pocket with a shrug. "I had work to do. It helped distract me."

"Thank you. I appreciate that you're still trying."

Their voices lowered then, and I couldn't make out more of what they were saying. What I *had* heard, though…it was obvious that Matt and JC were more to each other than just business associates. Matt was the type to keep personal, personal and work, work, so this relationship between the two men struck me as odd. I'd known my boss five years and still didn't know whether he had a family besides the wife that his simple wedding band suggested. The whole interaction between him and JC, a man young enough to be his son, was curious and intriguing. And personal. It was a mystery that I knew full well wasn't mine to know.

Whatever was between them, I did know this—it was heavier and more urgent than JC's flirtation with me. Was I not even the reason he'd come to the club tonight? Had he really come to see Matt?

And why did that disappoint me so much?

"Gwen?"

I jumped at the sound of my name but tried to hide my surprise by pretending to be consumed with my work. "Hmm?"

"Matt went upstairs. It's just us."

I looked up again into the mirror and realized it was only JC behind me.

And he was close behind me. "Oh. Okay."

I spun so that I was facing him. "Uh, thank you. For not letting him know that I knew about you." Maybe if I were polite and straightforward, he'd accept my gratitude and leave.

"I should tell you it's purely selfish and that I was just worried that I'd lose my deal." He took a step toward me, and I had to lean back now to meet his eyes. "But that would be a lie."

I swallowed, but my voice still felt weak as I asked, "What would be the truth?"

"I didn't want you to feel uncomfortable on my account."

It was amazing I didn't laugh. I already felt uncomfortable. He was invading my personal space, the heat from his body warming my chest, my thighs, my face, and for a split second, I wondered what it would be like to press myself into him. Against him.

Perhaps I should have shoved him away. I didn't. "Why do you care?"

He closed the distance between us, resting his hands on the bar on either side of me so that I was caged underneath him. "I don't really know, Gwen. I'm attracted to you. I'd be interested in spending time with you. In a bed. I think it could be mutually beneficial and if that comes off as crude, I apologize. But I learned a long time ago that the only way to get what you want is to ask. And sometimes even the things that seem impossible turn out to not be so impossible after all."

His words, his invitation…I should have been offended, and a small voice in my head said that I was, but another part of me, the bigger part of me, wanted to accept what he was offering. Wanted to tilt my chin up and let our mouths meet and explore. My tongue swept along my lower lip as if that kiss that I imagined were inevitable.

His gaze fell to my mouth and his eyes darkened.

This is it, I thought. *He's going to kiss me.*

Instead, he inhaled and closed his eyes, savoring the scent in the air between us. The motion, the way it seemed like he was taking in my very essence, made me feel like the main course in a very long awaited meal. It was almost shameful how the baseness of his gesture turned me on.

"You smell good," he said. He leaned closer, so close that now I could smell *him* distinctly. He had cologne on of some sort and his clothes had a clean scent, but all I could register was Man. All I could think was Sex.

"What do you say, Gwen? Should we try to make an arrangement?"

Somehow my hands found their way to his chest, as if they had a mind of their own. He felt firm and warm beneath my palms. My breasts ached at the thought of pressing against him. It wouldn't be the first arrangement I'd made for casual sex. If they didn't have the habit of getting messy and tied up in feelings, I'd probably pursue more strictly sexual relationships.

But the effort to keep things unattached was so not worth it. And, with JC, I could tell it would be especially difficult. He was the type of guy who liked to be fawned over. He wanted to be special. He wanted to be loved. I couldn't give that.

Even if I could, JC wasn't the guy who would ever give it back. Any relationship with him would be doomed from the beginning. It would be bad. People would get hurt. And I'd never been into causing pain.

There was no denying my attraction to him though. And fighting off his advances took more energy than I wanted to expend. Which, coupled with my frustrating call with Norma earlier, made me more than a little irritated.

With more strength than was probably necessary, I pushed him away. "No, definitely not."

I slipped off the bar stool and spun to him, my back tall as I let gravity give me an anchor that I so desperately needed. "I don't know what you have over Matt, Mr....." God, it was ridiculous that I didn't even know his name and JC was simply too familiar. "Mr. C. But I don't work like that. You're lucky that he's the general manager and not me because there would be no such special favors or blind eyes. I am not the type that makes deals or arrangements of any sort. I'm by the book. So it's best you remember that and keep all your negotiations with Matt."

JC bit back a smile.

"Hey. I'm serious." I felt like stomping my foot, but held back, knowing it would probably not help my case.

He covered his mouth with his hand. When he removed it, all traces of his smile were gone. "I'm sorry. I know you're serious. I didn't mean to patronize you. You're just even more adorable when you're feisty."

"You didn't mean to patronize me, but you just did?" If he wanted feisty, I'd give him feisty. "You know what, Mr. C? I do have an arrangement I'd like to make. I work on Thursday nights and you have the room booked on Tuesdays. How about we agree that I won't come into the club on those nights and you don't come into the club on these nights?"

"Oh, Gwen. I can't make an arrangement like that. That wouldn't give you a chance to change your mind. And as worked up as you are right now—your shoulders tight, your jaw clenched, your eyes tired—

I'm betting that you're going to change your mind. Real soon."

"Don't wager too much. I'd hate to see you in the poorhouse."

He took two steps toward me and reached his hand out to my cheek. It was the first time he'd touched me and it was almost too much. Like a hot coal against an ice cube, I melted under him. Melted into him.

I also wanted very much to drop the coal and jump away.

He sensed my warring reactions. I saw the disappointment in his eyes. But along with the disappointment, they flickered with hope.

"The next move is yours, Gwen." He slid his thumb down my face, following my jawline. "You know where to find me."

That was the problem. I wished I didn't know where to find him. I wished I didn't know him at all.

Mostly, I wished I didn't know what it was like to feel the touch of his skin on mine. The trail he'd swept on my cheek burned for long minutes after he turned and left the club.

Then, it faded and was gone. And I was left alone in the cold of my ice prison once more.

Chapter Three

"Have you heard anything lately from Ben?" I asked Norma as I folded the stocking embroidered with his name and packed it in the tote marked CHRISTMAS. It was Martin Luther King Jr. Day, so even though Norma worked on her laptop most of the day, it was from home.

"Not since I called him last week with the news about Dad." Her words were obscured as she spoke around the spatula handle between her teeth. She'd taken a break to make grilled cheese sandwiches, and I'd seized the opportunity to have an actual conversation. Norma took the flipper from her mouth before going on. "And I got a short email yesterday."

I stifled a yawn and looked at my watch. It was after noon, way past my bedtime, especially when I had to be back at the club by ten that night. But it wasn't often that Norma and I had daylight hours together, and I liked to be with her. In her company, I was less inclined to wandering thoughts of sensual lap dances and a sexy-grinned ringmaster who occupied my mind way too much. Especially since he'd made it clear what exactly he wanted from me. I couldn't give it to him, but as I lay awake trying to sleep, I fantasized that I could while my hand crept underneath the band of my panties and danced around in regions I'd ignored for way too long.

Getting off felt good and all, but it was also a blaring reminder of how alone I was most of the time.

So I put off bedtime as long as I could when Norma was around. Besides, someone needed to get the holiday decorations put away, and if it wasn't me, they'd probably still be up come summer.

"Yeah, I read that email." It was one of the reasons I'd been thinking about him.

"If you read the email, then you know as much as I do about him."

Norma had waited until after my birthday to call Ben with the news about Dad. He'd taken it fairly well. He'd been upset, of course, but he hadn't broken down like we'd expected. After that, he seemed to withdraw. Maybe that was his way of handling it. Or maybe he just wasn't that worried about it, being across the country and all.

But then there was the email.

Norma had left her laptop up and her email open. I'd seen his name, so of course I read it. His four sentences had stayed in my mind like a memorized poem.

Checking in. Don't bother sending more money this month. I'm working overtime this week. I won't need any more.

It was fairly banal, really. Nothing special, but something about it put me on alert. It wasn't the brevity of it—Ben was often a short and sweet type of guy. The message itself didn't necessarily raise any red flags. And Norma regularly supplemented his paycheck from the movie theater that he worked at, so the topic wasn't unusual.

Just, Ben wasn't…strong. I hated to think of him as fragile, but that was a fair description. He'd been better the last couple of years. Not like before. He had his job. He had friends. Boyfriends, occasionally. I supposed I shouldn't worry.

Still, he was far away. It bothered me not to have him closer where I could see him and know he was okay. Especially now that Dad would be out so soon.

I put my stocking on top of Ben's, followed by Norma's. "What did you think about the email? Did it seem strange at all to you?"

"No. Should it?"

Maybe it was me. I felt off. I'd felt off for several weeks. It started the night of my first encounter with JC and only grew more when I'd seen him again, but I refused to give him full credit for throwing me for an entire month. So he'd said some things that wouldn't leave me. So he made my insides twist and turn with want. It didn't mean anything. I was due for a total life examination. That he was there when it began was merely a coincidence.

But just because I was going through something didn't mean that Ben wasn't going through something too. In fact, considering the circumstances, I'd count on it.

"Maybe not." I stood and pulled the ceramic stocking holders off the mantel, wrapping each piece one by one in newspaper. "Do you think it's weird that he asked you not to send any money? I mean, why doesn't he need any extra spending money?"

She buttered the top of the sandwich that was cooking. "He said he has overtime. He must be doing okay."

"Even with overtime…is he not going out? Is he turning into a recluse? Is he not splurging on himself ever?"

"Gwen, you're being paranoid."

"You're right, you're right. I know you're right." But I couldn't let the worry go. I felt an unexplainable anxiety. Like an itch that I couldn't quite locate, I kept scratching at my mind, trying to figure out the thing that was making me so uncomfortable. So uneasy.

I bent to pack the final stocking holder and closed the tote. "We should go visit him."

Norma flipped a sandwich, the butter sizzling as it met the hot pan. "Okay, tell me when and I'll look at my calendar."

This was how this conversation always went. One of us suggested visiting, and the other said to pick a date, and then neither of us would agree on a good week to take off from work. Maybe Norma wasn't the only one of us that was a workaholic.

This time I meant it. I needed to see Ben. I needed the break. I needed…something. But what?

An image of JC popped in my head, which I quickly squashed. It wasn't JC I needed nor anything he had to give. But maybe California for a weekend could make a difference. It was something at least.

I stacked the tote in the corner with the rest of the boxes that needed to be put in storage. There weren't many—our celebrations were minimal at most. Then I crossed to the side of the island counter that was opposite my sister and stretched my body across it and propped my face up with my hands. "Let's really do it this time, Norma. Not just talk about it. Let's really go to San Francisco."

"Of course." She didn't meet my eyes, but she was buttering the next piece of bread, so maybe I was reading too much into it.

The gesture also made me nostalgic. The whole situation did, in fact. It reminded me of days in college with Ben still in high school, both of us living with Norma. She'd cook for us then too. We never really celebrated holidays until it was just the three of us. This year, it had only been Norma and me.

I turned my face so my cheek rested against the granite countertop. "We really should have made him come home for Christmas."

Norma pursed her lips. "He didn't want to, Gwen."

"But we should have convinced him." So we'd had the conversation a few times. It didn't change how I felt.

She removed the skillet from the burner and wiped her hands on her jeans. Then she turned her full attention on me. "He doesn't want to be here. Don't you get that?"

I straightened to a standing position and met her patronizing tone with one that was obstinate. "Then we should have gone to see him."

"You didn't want to miss work."

"*You* didn't want to miss work."

She rubbed her hand over her mouth, and I suspected she was revising whatever it was she originally planned to say. After a moment, she nodded once. "Neither of us wanted to miss work."

"Okay, well, let's both miss work and see him now." I cocked my head and studied her, trying to read her silence. "Why don't you want to go?"

She rolled her eyes. "I didn't say I didn't." She put the just cooked sandwich on a plate and pushed it toward me. "There's grapes in the colander over there if you want some to go with."

I slid the plate closer to me but ignored the topic of food. "You didn't *say* anything. So I had to read your expression and your face said it's not going to happen. Don't you want to see him?"

She met my eyes. "I want to see him. Of course I do, Gwen. He's my baby brother." He was much more than her baby brother. She'd practically raised him. She'd practically raised both of us.

Her focus went to her own sandwich where she picked at the crust, and this time I was sure she was using the food as an excuse. "He doesn't want us there."

"Nah. That's not true." Then I thought about it a second. "Did he say that?"

"He doesn't have to. I can tell." Her voice was tight. Much like me, Norma rarely showed her emotions, and I never knew how to react when she let a bit of sorrow or disappointment slip past her stoic front.

"No, you can't tell." Maybe she actually could. She talked to Ben a lot more often than I did by email and by phone. It wasn't that I didn't want to talk to him, but Norma was the mother figure in his life.

Still, he and I were close. There was no reason I knew of that he wouldn't want to see either of us.

Was there?

A possible reason popped into my head, and I blurted it out. "He doesn't want to have anything to do with the past. Does he? Including us. That's why he's pulling away."

She shrugged. Then she thought better of it and shook her head. "I don't know. Don't listen to me. Maybe I'm wrong."

Her body language said that she didn't think she was wrong. And now that I'd had the epiphany, I realized she was probably very right. I picked at a hangnail on my thumb, mostly so I wouldn't have to look Norma in the eye any longer, but also because the tiny sting of pain comforted me. "We aren't Dad, though," I mumbled. "We aren't the bad guys."

"No. But we remind Ben of him. I can understand that he doesn't want to be here. It's easier to forget about it all without constant reminders."

I wondered if that's what she thought of me as—a constant reminder. Did I make her remember our childhood? Did I make her miss our mother? Norma was twelve when she died. She remembered Mom better than I did. We both looked like her, but I was the one who had her fair coloring—her blonde hair, her blue eyes. Did Norma see her when she looked at me?

Or worse, did I make her think of Dad?

Even if I did remind her—even if we reminded Ben—I wished it wasn't an excuse to break the three of us siblings apart. I wanted us all together. I wanted to protect the little family I had. Wanted to stay close and bonded.

If I couldn't have that, I at least wanted to make sure we were all safe. "If Ben wants to be in San Francisco, then I support that. But I worry about him. Especially when we don't hear from him or when I don't know that he's engaging in his life. He pulled away before, remember? Before he—"

"I know." She cut me off, not wanting to hear me finish the sentence as much as I didn't want to say it. "I know, Gwen. I worry too."

She gathered her brown hair off her back into a ponytail, held it for a second, and then dropped it again. "I'll call him, okay? Let me call him."

And because Norma was the one who always dealt with Ben, I'd let her. "Okay."

FREE ME

• • •

Eighty-Eighth was busier than usual that night. Apparently MLK Jr. Day was something people had decided to celebrate this year. I wasn't complaining—I liked to be busy.

The club closed at four-thirty, and because Matt and I were so fast when we shut down together, I was done with my reports a little after five. I left him in the office to finish up his work while I checked on the floors.

I did my normal walk-through, checking the restrooms for stragglers before crossing the main dance floor to the bar by the kitchen. The place was quiet, but there was a single figure sitting on a stool at the end, his back toward me. I looked around for Alyssa or Greg—the closing staff for that floor—but didn't see them anywhere. They were usually quick at cleanup, so I suspected they were already in the employee room, punching out.

But that made the lone figure more puzzling. "Excuse me," I called, as I got closer. "The club is closed."

The man turned, and my pulse tripped. "Oh. It's you."

JC seemed less surprised to see me, which made sense since it was my work, and I was expected to be there. Still, I didn't have to like it. That he again had the balance and I again was thrown.

His lip ticked up, and I imagined he was pleased to have me off-kilter. "Hey. Nice to see you."

As they always did, his eyes raked down my body, slowly. His pupils dilated as he took in each part of me—my chunky heeled black sandals, my bare shins, my black flared Jersey skirt, my white V-neck ballet sweater, the curve of my generous breasts.

Above that, his stare lingered at my throat, then at my lips.

The back of my neck grew warm, even with my hair pinned up. My mouth watered, my skin felt on fire from just one simple sweep of his gaze. It made me forget the question I should have been asking—why was he here?

Finally he met my eyes. "You look good, Gwen."

The compliment knocked me. Not because he'd given it—men rained compliments on women in my work environment. But because he'd actually looked before saying it. And because it was absent of the sleazy undertone that usually accompanied such words. There were still hints of desire, yes, just it felt less about trying to get laid and more about actual appreciation.

I'd have rather had the lewd ogle. That, I knew how to deal with. This, I didn't. It confused me as it begged me to consider that maybe JC wasn't that horrible of a person, and that wasn't something I was willing to acknowledge.

So I put up my guard and returned his sincerity with Class A bitch. "I thought you said the next move was mine." I wasn't making a move, but, dammit, I didn't want him around tempting me.

"It is." He cocked his head. "Are you ready to make it?"

"Uh, not a chance."

He turned away from me. "Then pretend I'm not here. I didn't come for you."

It wasn't until he'd said that he wasn't there for me that I realized how much I wanted him to be there for just that very reason. Stupid. Because I thought I didn't want him there at all. If I wasn't careful, he was going to accuse me of giving mixed signals. I certainly was giving them to myself.

Just walk away, I told myself. *Do your work. Ignore him.*

I couldn't ignore him. "I guess you probably don't have to leave with the rest of the customers, do you? Another part of your informal deal? It's not Tuesday." Even to myself I sounded childish and snotty. It did nothing to calm the butterflies in my stomach.

JC took it in stride. He swiveled on his stool to face me with his whole body. He had on dark jeans and a dark blue pullover underneath a brown leather jacket. He wore this casual look as easily as he wore the business look. Wore it with just as much sex appeal.

Without a trace of animosity, he said, "You are incorrect about that. It is Tuesday. It has been for…" He glanced at his watch—a stainless steel sports thing—expensive, I gathered, but not flashy. "Exactly five hours and two minutes now."

Dammit, he was right. It was the problem with working the job I did. My days and hours were always screwed up. I wouldn't go to bed until around eleven a.m. and, for me, Tuesday would begin when I woke up later that evening. But, for everyone else, it had begun in the middle of my shift.

He'd trumped me again.

I could either let my mistake make me feel foolish, or I could simply concede. "You're right. It's Tuesday morning." Then, I couldn't help myself, snotty returned. "Still, you don't have the room booked—and all the privileges that go with it—until tonight." *When I'm not here*, I added silently.

Honestly, though I was hard and serious, I wasn't usually a giant dick. But with JC, I felt the express need to protect myself, and since I had no authority over him with his ridiculous arrangement with Matt, bitchy was the only weapon I had in my arsenal.

If he noticed, JC didn't acknowledge it. "Ah. True, true. But I'm not here as a customer right now anyway. I'm waiting for Alyssa."

"Oh." Disappointment gathered in my belly, chasing away the butterflies like a thick storm. I thought he'd been waiting for Matt. *Stupid, stupid, stupid.* Because why shouldn't JC be with Alyssa? She was a pretty enough girl, and obviously she knew much more about the man than I did. Just because he'd made a move on me, did I think that meant he wasn't pursuing anyone else?

And more importantly, why did I care?

I didn't. Of course I didn't. "Well, she should be out in a few minutes. We normally make non-employees wait outside the front door, but since you're already up here…" Really, I wished he'd leave. "Anyway, I'll just get back to…" I couldn't even remember why I'd come down anymore.

Alyssa burst out of the employee room and thankfully cut off my awkward attempt at conversation. "JC, you're here. How was your flight?"

I turned toward the kitchen, not wanting to interrupt them, or maybe not wanting to witness any displays of affection.

But Alyssa stopped me before I got too far. "Oh, Gwen. I almost forgot. You have a phone call on line two."

"Okay. Thanks." The ringers on the bar phones were kept on silent, so it wasn't strange that I hadn't heard it. It was strange that I'd get a call at this time of the morning. I didn't know anyone except the people I worked with. It had to be Norma. She knew I didn't keep my cell on during work hours. Matt had a strict policy of no mobile devices while on the clock—partly because it was more professional but mostly to protect celebrities and other high-profile club-goers from being photographed and recorded in unflattering situations.

But since Norma rarely contacted me at the club, I was nervous as I walked across the bar and picked up the receiver on the other side of the counter.

"This is Gwen." I twirled the cord around my finger and glanced behind me at JC and Alyssa. I wished suddenly that I'd gone to another room to take the call. Since Matt didn't allow cordless phones in the club, I was stuck. He worried they'd get lost, the battery would die, and no one would be able to find them again. Usually I agreed. Right now, I thought that phones that didn't move were ridiculous.

Even more ridiculous was how distracting JC and Alyssa were. The way her eyes lit up as JC told her whatever it was he was telling her… Pathetic. I wondered if he'd told her she looked good. Wondered if his eyes had raked her body as thoroughly as they had raked mine.

"It's me." Norma pulled my focus back to the receiver, her voice tight and low. But she probably hadn't had coffee yet since it was so early.

Still, there was something *too* tight about it. *Too* low. "Are you all right?" Maybe she was getting sick and needed me to bring home soup and lozenges.

"I'm fine. It's Ben." She cleared her throat. "He tried again."

All noise around me disappeared, the laughter of Alyssa and JC no longer registering in my awareness, and all that was left was the sound of my heart beating in my ears and Norma's voice telling me the thing I dreaded most—Ben had tried to kill himself.

Chapter Four

My world went black. There weren't any words that could have punched me harder, even though a part of me had known that something was off, known that something was wrong. It was the fear I woke up with every day—that my baby brother would once again attempt to end his life.

I sank down in a move that was more fall than sit. My ass hit the ground and I tilted my head against the back cabinets of the bar, not caring that I was in a skirt or that the floor was sticky from spilled liquor. Wrapping more of my hand around the phone cord, as if that would give me support, I managed to choke out the question that mattered most—the one that meant everything. "Is he…?"

"Alive," Norma finished with me. "Yes, he's alive," she said.

Now the tears came. Not many—I'd been long ago schooled by my father on how to keep them back. Crying usually only led to more swipes with the belt. But every once in a while, the tears would surprise me, pricking behind my lids, a stray sliding down the side of my nose.

I swallowed past the huge ball in my throat, forced myself to find out more. "And he's okay?" I was fully aware *okay* was relative and that even if his prognosis was good physically, that his emotional state was likely nowhere near that. I hoped Norma knew what I was asking, because I didn't have the power to rephrase.

"He's going to be okay." She said it definitively, as if she were the person who had the power to make it so. I wasn't so sure, but it felt better hearing her say it. "He took pills this time. A bottle of Vicodin, but as soon as he'd swallowed them all, he changed his mind. He called 911 himself. They pumped his stomach. He's in ICU now, but they're pretty sure he's going to be okay. They're watching his liver. That's the main concern right now."

I nodded as she spoke, even though she couldn't see me.

"He changed his mind, Gwen. He wants to live." There was more than hope in her statement. There was blind faith. She believed it like she'd once believed in God. She preached it to me like it was her religion.

"He does. He does want to." I wished I had her conviction. Maybe I did before—when he'd done it the first time—but now that it was a second time, I wasn't as confident.

Confident or not, I wasn't giving up on Ben. I needed to be there for him. "So when are we flying out?" Norma was the queen of organized. She would have had a flight arranged before she picked up the phone to inform me, which was only bothersome if I didn't remind myself that that was who she was.

"Hudson's letting me use his private jet. I'm flying out soon."

I'd never been so grateful for my sister's boss or that her longtime crush on him had made them close enough that she'd be afforded such favors. "I'll come straight home. If I take a cab, I can be there in twenty."

"I, uh…" She paused and I sensed she was gathering strength to say something else unpleasant that I didn't want to hear. "I'm going alone, Gwen."

Damn, Norma and her penchant for martyrdom. "That's crazy. I'm coming too. Let me just get off the phone—"

I started to push myself off the floor, but Norma's next words stopped me. Froze me. "He doesn't want us there. He said it this time. He doesn't want to see us. He was very clear."

"Oh." Whatever strength I had left, deserted me. There were only two people I cared about in the world. Two people that I let care about me. And I needed both of them. Needed them healthy and whole and in equal need of me.

Hearing that Ben didn't want to see us, didn't want to see *me*—it was almost as painful as hearing he'd tried to commit suicide. "Oh," I said again, the single syllable heavy on my tongue.

Norma attempted to comfort me. "I'm only going because I'm the emergency contact person. His social worker said I wouldn't get to see him. They want me there in case…in case…"

She couldn't finish. Norma, the strong one, the one who carried us through everything—she couldn't finish a simple statement.

"You'll need me there. To lean on." Maybe it was true, maybe I could be helpful, even if it felt like it was really me who needed her to lean on. "So I'll come and stay in the hotel. He never has to know that I'm there."

"Gwen, I'm going alone. I need to do this by myself."

I'd flown out the last time. We both had. When he'd cut his wrists with two long jagged marks. The wrong direction, thank God, which bought him time. His boyfriend of the moment had managed to get him to the hospital before taking off, never to be seen again. I'd only been at the club for a year and had just been promoted to full time. Matt understood. Gave me two weeks off.

So I'd flown out with Norma. We'd spent every day with Ben, who'd seemed brighter for our presence. We'd found an outpatient psychiatrist for him. We'd got him help and he'd been better by the time we left.

But four years had passed, and he talked to us now less than he had then. I'd hoped that meant he was building a life besides us. I'd been wrong. Which made it even more important that I be there with him now. To make sure he got better. To make sure that this time he came home with us.

"Norma, I'll buy a ticket and meet you there. You don't need to do this alone. We'll bring him back together—"

She cut me off. "That's exactly why I don't want you there, Gwen. He doesn't want to come home. And I don't trust that you won't force it. He doesn't need that conflict right now."

I opened my mouth to argue, but she had more to say. "Besides, I don't think it's good for you to see him."

I didn't bother to hide that she'd hurt me. "What the hell does that mean?"

"It means you're not quite as strong as you think you are." In the background, the apartment buzzer sounded. "That's my ride. I'll call you later, Gwenyth. As soon as I find out anything. It's going to be okay. I promise."

She clicked off before I had a chance to say more, before I could beg her to change her mind or ask her to explain herself. Before I could even say goodbye.

I sat on the floor for several minutes until my butt tingled from having fallen asleep and the straight dial tone of the phone turned into the buzz, buzz of being off the hook. I was numb. Everywhere. My body, my skin. My lips. My chest. Inside my chest. I was void. I was space. I was a vast universe of nothing, nothing, nothing.

I didn't remember finally standing or hanging up the receiver. Or if I even did. Next thing I was consciously aware of was being in the kitchen.

The place was empty, the cook staff having gone home long ago since we stopped serving food by two in the morning. No one would bother me here. No one would stop me from whatever it was I meant to do. I still wasn't sure what that was.

I scoured the place looking for something, not knowing quite what. My numb mind wouldn't let me hold on to any thought, but several floated through my consciousness, trying to find root. *He tried again. He doesn't want to see me. I want to feel like he does. I don't want him to feel the darkness alone. I wish that it were only me who ever met the back of Dad's hand. I need to feel as bad as Ben does.*

I need to feel.

Then I remembered there were knives in the kitchen. That's what I needed. A sharp blade. I could slice across the surface of my skin. Not to maim, not to end my life. But to feel.

I found the drawer we kept the cutlery in and pulled. It was locked. Of course. And my keys were back in the office. I couldn't go get them without running into Matt, and besides, the journey seemed painfully long. I needed this now. Needed it instantly. Needed to calm the noise in my head. Needed to wake up to the pain.

Alarms rang in the back of my head. I was nearing the edge of a cliff I'd managed to stay steady on for years. I was one of the ones who had it together. I was not this person.

But the compulsion toward harm was stronger than the alert.

I tugged at the drawer again. Harder. As if I could somehow pull it open if I put in enough effort. Even using both hands, it didn't budge.

I let out a frustrated groan. So I was feeling something after all. Irritation. Anger. Blazing hot rage. They struck through the void like lightening in a dark sky. I still wanted those knives. I wanted to hurt something. I wanted to hurt me.

"Gwen? Are you okay?"

I was firm in my nothingness, but I heard the voice dimly in the background, as though the speaker had a scarf wrapped around his face. I turned toward the sound and found JC at the threshold of the door I'd entered through a moment before.

I'd forgotten he was there, but he didn't surprise me. The sight of him was...a relief? No, not that. But he was a substitute for the knives. He could be another option in my attempt to find sensation.

"I called your name out there and when you didn't respond, I followed you in here." His brow creased as he studied my face. "What's wrong?" I didn't say anything, didn't even think. I just started toward him. He tried again as I crossed the long kitchen. "Did something happen? Can I—"

Then I reached him. Instead of explaining or leaning into his arms, which were open and welcoming—instead of doing anything rational, I grabbed his jacket with both hands and pulled him to me. And I kissed him.

I pressed my mouth to his, slipping my tongue in between his lips as he parted them in surprise. I wasn't soft or tentative. I was determined and unyielding, pushing farther into his mouth with each plunge of my tongue. Sucking and nipping on his lower lip.

JC didn't pull away. He didn't pull me closer either. He stood there, letting me kiss him, not touching me anywhere except where our lips were joined. When I broke to breathe, he attempted to say something, but I didn't give him the chance to get any words out before I'd tugged him back to me, attacking him even more aggressively.

I'm not sure when he started kissing me back, but when he did, things changed. Though he'd let me set the mood, he took over, and soon it was *his* tongue licking across my teeth and *his* teeth nipping at my lips. He tasted like coffee and the butter mints we had in small dishes on the bar. He tasted new and different and dangerous.

I wanted more of him.

It was another way to cut myself. Another way to hurt. Another way to access that pain I was so eager to rip into and feel.

I pressed my whole body against him, hoping he'd get the signal. Hoping he'd agree, if he did. I practically sighed in relief when he wrapped his hands around my waist and pulled my hips into his. His hands fondled my ass through my skirt, but it was the stiffening bulge at my belly that interested me most. I wanted to touch it. To stroke it. To have it inside me. In my mouth, in my cunt—I didn't care as long as it defiled me in some way.

By the time I threw a leg around him, he was just as lost as I was. He gathered my skirt at my waist and pulled my other leg up. He hoisted me around his middle, pressing my pelvis tighter against his so I could feel the throb of his erection where I wanted it now. Against my crotch. The pulse of his desire heightened my madness. I squirmed against him, stroking the ache between my legs with his cock.

Our lips never parted as he carried me the short distance to the stainless steel tabletop. As soon as my ass hit the surface, I pulled away long enough to shimmy my panties down to my ankles and then kick them to the floor.

This was my official invitation. If he didn't know what I wanted from him before, JC could have no doubt now. I wasn't looking for a make-out session or even, really, to be touched. I wanted a hard, quick fuck. That was all. I spread my legs, exposing myself to him.

He didn't hesitate, undoing his jeans and removing his cock in record time. I didn't ask about a condom. I didn't care. I was on birth control, and STDs? Hell, I didn't give a shit. It was Russian roulette. It was dangerous and unsafe, and I welcomed the rush of the risk.

When he was ready, I scooted forward and tugged him closer to me until his head was lined up at my entrance. "Please," I said. It was the only begging I was going to do, so I made it count. "Please, fuck me."

I watched him decide. His eyes flickered between *not sure* and *hell yes*. Then, when he decided, he left all his doubts behind, shoving into me with one blunt thrust.

I was wet, but not quite ready for him, so it hurt when he entered me. It was exactly what I wanted—the ache, the bite, the burn. It was piercing agony as he pulled back out and drove in again.

Then my body adjusted to him, my walls relaxing and clenching at him in a different way. It felt good now. The slide of his cock out and then in, touching every part of my insides, awakening every nerve ending with each measured thrust. It felt really good.

And good wasn't what I was looking for. I needed rougher. More painful. "Harder," I urged him. "Fuck me harder."

His eyes glinted with desire as he let go of me to pull first one arm and then the other out of his jacket. He threw it to the floor. Then he grabbed my hips and dragged me into him. His momentum quickened, his thrusts becoming jabs as he pushed into me, pushed so deep that he hit my womb.

This was better. Rough, wild. I bucked against him, spurring him on with my body and the words I kept repeating. Over and over. "Fuck me. Fuck me. Fuck me." I didn't want to come. I fought against the curl of tension gathering low inside me. I bit JC's lip and willed the pleasant hum in my limbs to go away.

He was getting close; I could tell. His breathing became more ragged and his tempo uneven. He was close and then it would be done and I would have done something stupid and unpleasant and I'd embrace how shitty it made me feel.

But the success of my plan depended on my complete lack of enjoyment. And even as JC plunged aggressively and without mercy, I couldn't say there wasn't any pleasure. Then he moved his hand from my hip and buried it in between us, finding my clit with ease. I nearly exploded from the first firm graze of his thumb.

Shit. No. That's not what I wanted. No pleasure. Not for me.

I wriggled my hips back, trying to get away from the increasing pressure of his massage while still remaining joined by his cock, but his other arm gathered around my waist and pulled me closer. So I tried to push him away with my hand.

JC halted, mid-thrust, his expression saying that pausing was difficult for him, but he held still just the same. "I'm not doing this alone." His voice was gritty and tight and while I didn't want it to, it turned me on to see how affected he was. "So if you want me to keep going, you're going to have to come with me."

I'd wanted to feel pain. I'd wanted to feel dirty. I'd wanted to feel bad.

And JC refused to let me.

It scared me. Because the only thing worse than feeling nothing was feeling good. I didn't deserve it. I didn't deserve pleasure while my baby brother was hurting so bad.

JC must have seen the fear in my expression. "It's going to be okay," he said, echoing the words Norma had said to me earlier. "I'm going to make you feel good, and it's going to be okay."

Call it the magic power of the cock, but I actually believed him. I set my hands down on the counter next to me, curling my fingers around the edge.

JC recognized my act of surrender. "Good." His praise was a balm. Confidently, without any trepidation, he resumed rubbing my clit. Expertly. With perfect pressure.

My belly tightened and I felt my orgasm begin to rise inside.

JC picked up his thrusting then, pounding into me with sharp jabs that were less frenzied than before but were deeper, more intense.

"I want to make you feel amazing, Gwen." His thumb continued its play with my nub, and I edged closer and closer to the brink. "I want you to feel so good. Let yourself go, Gwen. Come with me. We'll go together."

I did then. I don't know if I intended to or if I simply got caught up in the poetry of his words. But I let myself go.

The minute I did, my orgasm took over, crashing through me with violence. My whole body shook with tremors that shot down my spine, down my limbs. Tears slipped out of the corners of my eyes. I cried out so loud, I had to muffle myself in JC's shoulder.

But the best part was the release. Not the physical part but the emotional part. The spiritual part. I felt like I was soaring. Or skydiving. Or, rather, I felt like what I imagined skydiving would feel like—thrilling and wonderful and free.

He joined me while I was still quivering. His fingers clawed into my waist as he shoved hard and long with a restrained groan.

Then we were still except for the rise and fall of our chests and his cock still twitching in me.

It took a few seconds for the rush to subside and the "after" to hit full force. Only I didn't quite know what to do with this after. I'd had sex just for sex's sake before, but not ever with a stranger. Also, never initiated by me and certainly never anywhere on the premises of my work. I didn't know how to behave.

I also didn't know how to feel. The soaring sensation had settled and now I felt much more like I was falling. And I wasn't sure if it was a comforting falling, like the way you fall asleep, or a horrific falling, like the kind in nightmares. I'd wanted to feel but not like this. So even though I felt good, I felt shitty about feeling that way, which almost had me where I'd wanted to be originally, but not quite.

Also, now that the kissing and fucking were over, I had a feeling that JC would want to talk.

Well, not if I could help it.

I was the first to push away. I nudged him, and not even gently, until he got the hint and stepped back. I'd jumped off the counter and had retrieved my panties before he said, "Wow. I wasn't expecting that."

"It wasn't planned." I stepped into my underwear and pulled them up, not caring that I was sticky, just wanting to get the "after" over with. Then I walked over to the small mirror above the sink and tried to do something to fix my hair. God, I hadn't even realized he'd had his hands tangled in it. When had that happened?

"Gwen," JC called behind me, but I didn't turn. I didn't meet his eyes in the reflection. "Hey, Gwen. Stop."

His tone was insistent, and I wasn't so much of a bitch that I could ignore him longer. I turned my head toward him.

"Are you okay?"

"I'm fine." Jesus, I hated that question. I looked back at the mirror and returned an errant lock of hair to the correct side of my part and then turned around to find JC staring at me intently. Obviously my answer hadn't been enough for him. But I didn't have more, so I asked, "Are *you* okay?"

It came out harsher than I'd wanted it to. I didn't apologize.

JC, as always, ignored my bitchiness and smiled. "I'm great. Fantastic, actually." Then he frowned. "But I'm worried about you."

"I said I'm fine." I brushed past him to grab his jacket off the floor. I didn't know why I did—there was plenty of room to go around him. I didn't even need to get it for him. But it gave me something to do besides look in his eyes, and it gave me an excuse to touch him again, even if it was just in a rough pass-by.

I turned back and handed the jacket out to him. He was still looking at me, his gaze intense, his expression concerned. I had to give him *something*.

"I'm sorry." It even sounded like I meant it. Which I did. A little.

He gestured between us. "About this? Don't be." He took the jacket from me and then gently grabbed me with his other hand. He traced a soft circle on the skin inside my wrist. "Please don't be sorry, Gwen. This was nice. Don't ruin it for yourself in the aftermath."

I felt myself caving. I didn't even know what I was caving to, but the walls I'd built years ago seemed to tremble and sway. I thought I might cry. Or laugh. Or maybe kiss JC again but not like before. Sweet this time. Slow.

Or maybe I wanted to slap him. Or slap myself. Or maybe I just didn't know what I wanted, and for that brief moment, if JC was willing to tell me what it was, I was willing to let him be right.

I opened my mouth to say whatever I needed to say to make that happen when I heard my name being called from outside the kitchen.

JC stiffened, mirroring the tension I suddenly felt.

"Stay there," I whispered. I crossed to the door, and after making sure JC wasn't in the sight line, opened it slightly. "Yeah, Matt. I'm in here. Do you need me?"

He was behind the bar filling up his sports bottle with Coca-Cola.

"Wanted to tell you everything's done." As he waited for his drink to fill, he ran a hand over his bald head, something he did often. "I got everything locked up. The staff's all gone. Just need your signatures on the paperwork and we can take off."

Even though he probably wouldn't fire me for getting it on in the kitchen with a customer, it didn't seem like something Matt should know. And if he knew I was with JC, I was sure he'd know we were getting it on.

I had to divert his attention. Forcing a smile, I said, "Okay. I'll be right up to the office. I'm sweeping up some ice I dropped." I shut the door and turned to JC, who was still peering at me with apprehension. "If you go out the front, the alarm will sound. The back door is there, on the other side of the kitchen."

"Gwen—"

I didn't let him say more. "Please, turn off the lights back there on your way out. I gotta go."

I left without waiting for his answer, wondering if Norma really was right about me not being as strong as I thought I was. If I were stronger, after all, I wouldn't have run out like that. If I were stronger, I would have stayed.

Chapter Five

I woke up around two that afternoon.

It was early for me, but I'd gone to sleep early too, having passed out as soon as I'd gotten home. I hadn't even managed to finish off more than a glass of Moscato—Norma's favorite and the only thing in the apartment, though way too sweet for my tastes—before I'd sunk my head into my pillow and let the void swallow me whole. Perhaps that was best because I didn't have a hangover now or even a headache.

In fact, I woke up feeling pretty damn good.

Not good as in I'd forgotten what was happening with Ben or what Norma had said to me about not being strong. But good as in I now felt like I had the energy to cope. It was amazing to see what a difference a good night's—er, day's—sleep could make.

Except, as I headed for the shower and felt the reminder of JC in my aching thighs, I wondered if maybe it wasn't just a good sleep that had affected me. As the hot water poured over me and I washed between my legs, I was invaded with the memory of JC massaging my clit, rubbing me toward orgasm. The words he'd encouraged me with to get there.

And I'd been the one to jump *him*.

A wave of giddiness fell over me. And I started to laugh.

Like, hardcore laugh. Like, make-me-bend-over laugh. "I had to put my hand up against the tile to keep me from falling over" kind of laugh.

In the midst of my fit, it occurred to me that maybe I had finally gone mad, but I quickly dismissed it and let myself go in this emotion as fully as I'd let myself go when I'd climaxed that morning. The laughing made sense, actually. I'd done a completely out of character thing when I'd banged JC in the kitchen. And instead of feeling shitty as I expected, or hoped, rather, I felt renewed. And alive. And just plain good.

It was so unexpected, it became funny. Also, maybe I was going a little bit mad.

Whether I'd lost it or not, I had an unmistakable spring in my step as I dried off. I was still wrapped in a towel with my blonde hair bundled in another on top of my head, when the phone rang. Hoping it was news about Ben, I ran to it.

After glancing at the caller ID, I answered. "Norma? You made it there? How is he?"

"Yes, I made it here. I landed a couple of hours ago and came straight to the hospital." In the background, I heard an overhead intercom paging a Dr. So and So. Then heels on a hard floor—probably Norma's. I could picture her pacing as she talked to me on her cell. "Did I wake you up?"

"No, I was awake. And I wouldn't have cared anyway. How. Is. He?" That she hadn't answered that yet worried me.

"He's good." She sighed, which did nothing to ease the tension she was carrying. Her voice was still tight and strained. "I'm sorry. I should have led with that. He's better than good, actually. Physically, anyway. They got to him in time and his liver doesn't show any signs of long-term damage."

"That's great!" I was so relieved that I thought I might start laughing again. The road to emotional repair was going to be hard enough for him. At least he wouldn't be dealing with health issues as well. "So what now? Is he checking out? Have you seen him?"

"He still doesn't want to see me. But he knows I'm here. I wrote him a letter on the plane. I don't know if it will make a difference or if he'll even read it. We'll see."

I definitely had a different outlook than when she'd first called me that morning. This time, instead of being distraught that Ben didn't want to see me, I was more concerned that he didn't want to see Norma. "Ah, sissy, I'm so sorry."

"*Sissy*. You haven't called me that in years." Finally, the stiffness of her tone loosened and took a hint of nostalgia.

"No, I haven't." When Norma had been my primary caretaker, it had felt right. An apt substitute for calling her mom, which in many ways, she really was to me. I could tell it pleased her now, and I was glad to be able to give her that comfort. "Maybe I should call you that more often."

"That might be nice." Her smile was evident through the receiver. "As long as you're not meaning that I'm a coward."

"Never." I wanted to ask what her letter had said, but I knew it was probably private. So I asked the more important question. "What happens with Ben now?"

The softness she'd discovered disappeared and she returned to the harder no-nonsense version of herself. "They want to keep him until we can make arrangements to transfer him to an inpatient mental facility. His social worker has given me some leads, but I'm looking around to find the right place. It might be a couple of days."

"I don't say this often, Norma, but thank God Hudson Pierce pays you so fucking well." There'd been times when I thought her paycheck was extravagant. Compared to how we'd grown up, it really was over-the-top. Not that I didn't appreciate what she did for me. I also made sure I contributed as much as she'd let me. And I saved. A lot.

But right now I was nothing but grateful for her bank account. I knew it would get Ben the best care possible.

"Well, I'll make sure Hudson is aware of your appreciation."

"Yeah, I bet you will." Maybe it wasn't the right time to tease her about her boss fixation, but I couldn't help myself. Besides, she hadn't mentioned her romantic feelings for him in a long time, and as a sister it was my duty to remind her that I knew. "In case you can't tell, I'm waggling my eyebrows."

Instead of getting embarrassed and gushy, she surprised me with her response. "You're in a good mood. What's that about?"

She was deflecting. But I was in a better mood than I should have been and with only one reasonable explanation. "I fucked a random guy in the kitchen at the club. It did wonders for my attitude."

"You should do that more often. It's helped." Her tone said she thought I was joking.

Which was fine. I didn't really know how I'd explain my encounter with JC if she pressed. "Yeah, yeah. I love you too. Anyway." I'd wandered from the kitchen as we talked and now, in the living room, I flopped on the couch and hugged my knees to my chest before returning to the serious talk. "Norma, will Ben even go into a facility?"

"I think he will. It's completely voluntary, but his social worker says it was his idea."

That was a good sign. I picked at the polish on my toenail as I considered the situation. "Maybe that's what all of this was? A way for him to tell you that he needed more in-depth care." It was hard for me to accept that Ben didn't want to live anymore, and I'd grasp onto any other option if given to me.

I knew Norma felt the same. "I hope so," she said. "Personally I think he doesn't want to deal with Dad's release. He obviously feels guilty about putting him behind bars in the first place—"

"Which he shouldn't. Dad was hurting him." He'd hurt us too, but not nearly as badly as he'd hurt Ben.

And I'd known Ben felt that way. He wouldn't have run so far away if he didn't. It was probably why he was so much more scarred by our abusive childhood than Norma and me. Because though we'd all been hit, he'd essentially been the one to finally put him behind bars.

"It's not that simple to say what Ben should or shouldn't feel," Norma said. "He did the right thing, yes. But it's natural that he feels responsible. And I'm sure that he's worried that Dad will come after him now. I assured him in the letter that the parole terms won't let him leave the state. I'll make sure whatever facility we check him into will be secure, and I'll hire a bodyguard when he gets out if that's what he needs to feel better."

"You told him all that in the letter?"

"Yeah."

It was overwhelmingly reassuring to discover the lengths Norma would go to for Ben. I knew she'd do the same for me. She loved us wholly. She cared for us in ways that our father never did and our mother never could. She tried harder than she needed to make up for them. Often, I worried who was making it up to her.

Today, I tried to be the one who was her comfort. "He'll read it, Norma. It will help. And when he does, I bet he'll even want to see you."

"Maybe." She cleared her throat, and like I always knew with Norma, I could sense she was about to say something I didn't want to hear. "Gwen, I know you were kidding about the guy in the kitchen, but maybe it's not such a bad idea. You really need something to unwind you."

And I was right—I didn't want to hear it. It was bad enough when a stranger called me out on being uptight and I could deny it, or fuck him, as it turned out. When it was my sister, someone who knew me well, it was not as easily refutable.

My pleasant mood plummeted, and I was no longer concerned about consoling her. "I hadn't realized my personality was so bothersome to you."

"Don't do that," she scolded. "Don't try to make it seem like I don't love you just the way you are. You know that I do." She softened now.

"Your personality has never bothered me in the least. Your unhappiness, on the other hand, has. I always worry about Ben, but you should know I worry about you too. At least Ben knows that he needs an outlet. It might do you some good to find one as well."

We hung up after that, and I immediately felt lonely. Again, I considered buying a ticket and going out to San Francisco just to be there with her. Just to be with someone.

But I didn't want Norma more upset than she was. And she hadn't told me the name of the hospital Ben was at, anyway. On purpose, I was sure.

So I stayed home. It was the first Tuesday evening in a long time that I'd spent alone, and that made me more restless than usual. I couldn't find anything that would occupy my mind enough to settle down. No matter what I tried to do—reading, surfing Pinterest, cleaning—my thoughts kept returning to Ben and Norma and Dad.

I thought about JC, too. I guessed he was at the club while I was sitting on my ass watching Netflix, trying not to worry about my family or my own need for an outlet. I considered going to Eighty-Eighth. Considered finding something revealing in my closet, doing my hair and my makeup. I could show up in the Viper and take Norma's advice—try to unwind.

But it would be weird to show up like that. Clingy and annoying. JC and I had clearly had a wham, bam, one-time thing. He'd probably have his horde with him again, anyway. Half-dressed women ready to respond to the snap of his fingers. He didn't need me. And while I'd been bold when I'd dropped my panties that morning, that didn't mean I was ready for an orgy.

Oh, and Alyssa was working. He'd come to the club that morning for her. I hadn't forgotten that. Shame on me for making the whole thing a potential sex triangle in the first place. I refused to encourage it.

That didn't mean I couldn't fantasize about him again. Home alone with my vibrator, it seemed the thing to do.

It wasn't until I'd woken up on Wednesday afternoon that I remembered—we hadn't used a condom.

• • •

I got into a walk-in clinic that afternoon only to be told that it would be at least two weeks before any STDs could potentially show up. It would be longer before I could test for HIV. I was offered a morning-after pill, which I declined. Instead, I asked the nurse practitioner to check to make sure my IUD was still in place. It was. I left with an appointment to come back in a month.

A whole month. A month to worry. A month to regret. Needless to say, any bounce I'd had from my screw in the kitchen was long gone by the time I showed up for my shift on Thursday night. I was the closing assistant, so I didn't actually need to be on the clock until ten, but I'd come in at eight-thirty, tired of being alone and fidgety at home. The main doors didn't open until nine, so when I came in the back door, I stopped by to check on the kitchen staff before heading out to the office.

Maybe I just wanted to see it again—the cold, sterile room made alive by the bustling of prep cooks and wait staff. The place I'd stripped myself of my sanity and my panties. The place I'd let myself go. As the head chef, Brent, barked an order regarding the proper angle to julienne carrots, all I could hear were JC's words to me. *I want to make you feel good.*

Even with the nagging worry about the health risks of my behavior, the memory brought a pleasant blush to my cheeks.

"Hey, pretty lady," Brent said when he noticed me. He was one of the few staff members at the club that I could really get along with. Partly because I wasn't his superior. While I was the first assistant manager of the club, Brent was pretty much the first assistant manager of the kitchen. We were equals who both reported to Matt.

But I had a feeling Brent and me would get along even if one of us outranked the other. He was as demanding of excellence as I was, as orderly and organized, but the air about him was less severe. He laughed more than I did, for one. And he could joke around without losing respect. His kitchen always ran smoothly, but he never showed the stress that I felt when I finished a perfect shift.

I envied him in many ways but not enough to resent him. I knew he was who he was and I was who I was. I recognized that those parts of him that I coveted didn't live in me.

Tonight, though, filled with the thoughts of the unexpected tryst I'd had the other morning and Norma's insinuation that I should unwind, I wondered if maybe there was a hidden vitality in me after all.

I pretended that there was, that I could access it just by willing it. I flashed a brighter than usual smile. "Hey yourself."

"Now that's what I'm talking about. You need to show those pearlies off more, Gwen-Gwen. They make your whole face."

"Oh, Brent, try as you might, you aren't going to get in my pants." It was a joke that made us both laugh. Not only was Brent twenty years older than me, but also one-hundred-and-ten percent gay.

But along with being humorous, it was also surprising. I hardly ever made jokes let alone let myself laugh at them after.

Brent pushed up the chef hat that I suspected he wore for fashion rather than function. He eyed me. "You're frisky today. Might I guess it has something to do with a man?"

I rolled my eyes, yet I felt my cheeks reddening again. Which was silly because Brent couldn't know anything about JC. Unless…were the security cameras focused on that part of the kitchen?

I casually scanned the ceiling for the cameras as I answered. "If I'm anything it's tired. I'm not sleeping well. My brother's had some problems and my sister flew out to take care of him. And I don't sleep well when I'm all alone." Whew, the cameras weren't pointed directly at the table—*our* table. Maybe if someone watched it they would make out the very edge of us, but no one ever watched the tapes unless there was an incident, and they only stored for a week at a time anyway.

"Ah, that's a bummer. I'd hoped your fella had gotten a hold of you by now. Seems like you don't have to be alone if you don't want to be." He winked at me.

Dammit. He *did* know about JC. But how? And what, exactly, did he know? "I don't have a fella, Brent. What on earth are you talking about?"

"You didn't see the message for you yet?"

"Where? Who from?" I hadn't been anywhere but the kitchen and there was nothing waiting for me here. And the second question was one I didn't have to ask.

"There's one taped on your locker in the break room. There might be another in the office. The guy wouldn't leave a name. Said you'd know who he was."

God, "the guy" was cocky. But I did know who it was. Of course I knew who it was.

Brent moved to the stove to check on his soup as he talked to me. "He was here Tuesday. Came right in here like he owned the place and asked Matt when you'd be working again. Funny, Matt didn't get on him about strolling through *my* kitchen, but he wouldn't tell him when you worked either. Seems our boss cares more about protecting your goods than mine. Anyhoo." He turned back to me. "The young man called again yesterday, and I happened to answer."

"Did he leave a number?" I sounded eager, a stupid hormonal response. My whole body was tingling at the knowledge that JC had come looking for me. How could he do that? Turn my entire nervous system on without even being present?

"Yeah. It's in the note. And, Gwen, I hope you don't get offended by this, but damn, was that guy cute."

"He's a customer, Brent. Nothing else." I wasn't fooling either of us by the way I was already heading to the break room, a place I rarely went and at a speed that could only be called a run.

My locker was in the front of the room, a perk of having been a staff member for so long. I kept a box of tampons and a pair of sneakers in there for days that were too icy to head home in heels. Seemed like I couldn't go a week without a waitress asking to borrow one. It never failed to amaze me how unprepared people could be. Periods came regularly. I mean, even I had feminine products on hand, and I didn't get my period anymore.

The note was taped on the metal, not even folded over. Simply the words *Call this guy* followed by a phone number scrawled in Brent's handwriting. I traced my fingers over the numbers, memorizing them unintentionally, or maybe intentionally, as I wondered why JC wanted to get a hold of me so badly. Was he worried that I'd gotten in trouble? Was he worried about the state I'd left him in? Did he want to see me again?

And if he did, did I want to see him again?

I'd thought about it. Hell, besides Ben and Norma, it was all I'd thought about the last two days. I'd ruled it out completely before we'd banged, and all the reasons I'd listed then still stood. But now that we'd been together, it felt like I needed to rethink. JC was obviously a playboy—if I hadn't figured that out from the night I met him then I knew it now. Who else bagged a girl he barely knew simply because she came on to him?

But if I didn't care about romance—which I didn't—then did his playboy status really bother me? It had been good sex. It had been great sex. More importantly, it had made me feel better than I had in a long time. And he hadn't gotten all mushy about it after. Which was a plus.

So what was stopping me from giving him another go?

Well, the fact that I had no idea how to ask for another go was one obstacle. And two, I wasn't sure he did want to see me again.

And three, there was no way in hell I could call him. I wouldn't even know what to say.

Behind me, the employee door swung open, bringing me back to my surroundings. I'd gotten in early, but I could still start on my pre-opening work.

I spun to head out but froze when I came face-to-face with the person who'd just entered.

It was JC. And he took my breath away.

He was wearing a suit again. It was tailored and expensive and suddenly I understood why so many women went ga-ga over a guy in a three-piece Armani. He looked rich and yet not pompous. Sort of like a rock star that had dressed up for the Grammys—a suit wasn't what he belonged in, but oh, could he wear it.

Adding to his devastating sex appeal was what I knew about him now. That he fit my body like he fit that suit—tightly and with no give.

I didn't bother to ask him how he got in before the club had opened, just like I hadn't asked him how he'd gotten in the last time. And even if I'd really wanted to ask, I was too blown away to find any words.

He looked as surprised to have found me as I was to see him, but after a moment, the shock slid into a grin. "I've been looking for you."

His voice was smooth and sincere. It poured over me like a nearly-too-hot shower—both wonderful and abrasive. I didn't know if I wanted to luxuriate in it or step away and wait for it to cool. Didn't know if I wanted to press closer to him or turn away.

I stayed put. "So I heard. The staff left this for me." I held up the message I'd just read, amazed that I'd been able to make any sense with the way the heat of him jumbled my thought process.

His brow furrowed and I wondered if maybe I hadn't really made sense after all. He pulled his cell phone out of his pants pocket and checked the screen. "That's funny. I haven't missed any calls."

For the second time that night, I laughed. "I *just* got your message. I haven't had a chance." He was easier to talk to than I'd remembered. Or maybe easier to talk to than I'd *realized* since I hadn't had much occasion to actually speak to him as of yet.

"You wouldn't have called anyway."

I lowered my gaze, not wanting him to see the truth in his guess. Hating the way his guess was, as always, right. I'd forgotten how he liked to point out perceptions that normal people ignored out of politeness. Maybe he wasn't as easy to talk to as I'd just decided he was.

Or maybe it was me that wasn't easy to talk to. I decided to put forth some effort. "I don't know. I might have called you. As soon as I figured out what I was going to say."

"You don't know how happy that makes me to hear that." He stepped closer and now there were only a few feet between us. The air around us felt charged, and as afraid as I was that he would close the distance altogether, I was more afraid that he wouldn't.

So, of course, I broke the connection first, dancing to the side in what I hoped didn't seem too obvious of a move.

"How did you know I'd be here tonight?" Trying to appear cool, I smoothed a hand over my hair, wishing it were down and that JC's fingers were tangled in it instead.

No, I didn't wish that. I wished he'd leave and never return.

"Deductive reasoning. You had two nights off. You work full time. Unless you were on vacation, you should be here tonight. I took the risk." He met my eyes and I tried to hold his gaze.

But I found myself trying to read him even though I didn't think I wanted to find out anything his eyes might be telling me, so I looked away quickly, moving my focus to his hands. "What's that?"

He had a paper in his hand, folded into thirds. "Oh, it's for you. I figured you'd want to see it as soon as possible." He held it out to me, and I took it, careful not to let my fingers brush against his as I did.

Immediately, I admonished myself for not taking the opportunity to brush against him, because what if I never had that chance again?

But now I had this piece of paper in my hands, and the strangeness of whatever it could be was compelling enough to center my thoughts.

I unfolded it and scanned over what looked like some sort of report. "What is this?" But I didn't have to wait for his answer. As I read further, it was clear what it was. I studied it closer now. *HIV Early Detection—negative, HIV—negative, Chlamydia—negative, Hepatitis B—negative, Hepatitis C—negative, Herpes Simplex 1—negative, Herpes Simplex 2—negative, Gonorrhea—negative, Syphilis—negative.* Each horrible and terrifying word followed by another word that erased all the fear of the one preceding it.

My shoulders felt the weight of a huge boulder fall from them.

"This is your medical chart."

"Part of my medical chart. The page I thought would interest you most."

"It does. Thank you." I looked at him now, wondering about this man who I knew nothing about. I'd made judgments about him, I realized. Sure, he was probably still a playboy. But while he'd been unsafe with me, his test results indicated that he at least had been safe with others. "This makes me feel a lot better."

He nodded once, an informal *you're welcome.* "I knew it would. That's why I was so eager to find you. I'm sorry you had to wait the last couple of days for it. I would have gotten it to you sooner if I could."

I felt the now familiar stab of irritation at JC's ability to read me so well and had to bite my lip to keep from making a caustic remark about it. Besides, as much as it irritated me, it also fascinated me. How did he know me so well? And why did he care so much that I knew that he did?

Whatever the reason, he'd gone to the trouble of getting me information that I otherwise would have had to wait a month for. "I appreciate that," I said, handing him back his medical report. "Honestly, I probably deserved a couple days of sweating it out." It would certainly teach me to not use a condom again.

Though, now that I knew JC was clean, no condom with him wouldn't be a problem.

Nope, nope, nope. Do not go there.

JC rubbed his chin while I tried not to imagine the tickle his stubble would give on my own hand. Or thigh. "You never do things like that, do you?" he asked.

Again, with his unfailing perception. "You know I don't."

"Good."

I wasn't sure he meant good that I didn't sleep around or good that I didn't sleep around without a condom, and I was about to ask when he answered my question for me. "I mean, good that you don't normally put yourself in that sort of risky situation."

"I don't," I said, but the shaking of my head that accompanied my response was at my continued awe of his ability to predict me and not to emphasize my statement.

He caught my eyes and this time he held them for several long seconds. I'd been avoiding them because I knew when I finally fell into his gaze, I'd be lost there. I saw, again, the traces of hardness and sorrow that I'd seen the first time I'd met him. There was a hint of recognition too, as if he knew that I saw that in him, as if he expected it of me. And also I saw genuine fascination.

It was that last thing that kept me in a daze. He looked at me with interest. Not my body, though he'd definitely stolen several glances at my curves, but *me*. It made me stand up a little taller. Made my smile a little easier. Made my heart a little less heavy.

Just about the time that I thought I'd either have to kiss him again or combust in flames, JC frowned and said, "Look, I hate to ask this, but… birth control? Do you…? Or the morning-after…"

He was nervous, and I had to stifle a giggle. It was hard to imagine JC ever being anything other than completely cool, even as I was witnessing it in front of me. "We're good. I have an IUD."

It was subtle, but he relaxed. "Good."

"I don't get periods anymore either because of it." I reddened. "I don't know why I told you that."

"That's good to know as well." He chuckled, and I could tell he was laughing at himself as much as at me. "I didn't realize how worried I'd been about it. Not your period but the birth control. I'm just usually really careful about being protected." He leaned toward me—how were we suddenly only a foot apart?—and added. "Also, periods have never been something to scare me away, but it's much more convenient to not have to worry about them."

Goose bumps ran down my arms as I tried not to infer too much from his statement and yet wanted to all at once. "Well, like I said, we're good. On both counts."

"Awesome."

I pulled at the hem of my shirt, suddenly not knowing what to say, half fearful I'd blurt out something else that was unnecessary or embarrassing. "Oh. I'm clean too. I haven't had a test in a year, but I'm scheduled to get one next month and I can get it to you, if you want."

"No. That's fine. I'm sure you're clean."

It struck me as odd that he cared so much more about an unexpected pregnancy than a potentially life-threatening STD. Did he really fear children more than disease? Typical guy.

Then a horrible thought crossed my mind. "Are you saying I couldn't have had sex in the last year? Is that why you don't need to see a report to know I'm clean?"

"No! No. Of course not." He was closer now, and he reached his hand out to brush my cheek. "I'm saying I trust you."

His touch on my skin felt so right. The only thing that stopped me from leaning into it, begging for more, was the impact of his words. They equally affected me. "Thank you."

"You're welcome." One side of his mouth curled into a sneaky smile. "And it's also likely you haven't had sex in the last year."

I started to say something—something not very nice—but he stopped me with a finger to my lips. "Hey, hey, not because of anything except that you're denying yourself for some reason."

My frown remained but I settled somewhat.

"Look, Gwen, you could have your pick of any guy. I have no doubt of that. You just don't pick any. It's not a put-down. You're a very controlled woman." He brushed a strand of hair off my face, sending another buzz of awareness through my body. "That's admirable. A lot of people—most people—would kill for that skill. Control is the solution to weight loss and keeping money in your wallet. It's something to be proud of no matter what anyone tells you. Me included."

They were the words I'd been wanting to hear—words that assured me that I was okay like I was, that I didn't need to change as Norma seemed to think I did. I was flattered and grateful and moved.

But I also sensed an undercurrent of something else to his tone. Condescension, maybe. Arrogance. Or maybe it was simply that I realized that JC's compliment wasn't really that complimentary. Because even if control were remarkable, even if other people would kill for that skill, I worried that if I didn't find a way to sometimes let it go, my control might kill me.

So I was thrown. Again. Caught between being the person who'd banged a stranger in the kitchen and the person who alphabetized her spice cabinet. Caught between wanting JC to say more things like he just had and wanting him to take them all back.

Caught between wanting to tell him to go away for good and wanting him to never go away.

Confused and frustrated, I did what I often blamed Ben of doing—I ran away. I pushed JC out of my personal space, and in case the physical act wasn't enough, I pushed JC away with words too. "By the way, I'm sorry I derailed your plans the other morning."

If he was disappointed by my withdrawal, he didn't let on. "My plans?"

"With Alyssa." I could barely say her name without it catching in my throat. "You'd said you were waiting for her." God, I sounded like a jealous girlfriend when I meant to sound exactly the opposite—like someone surrendering, not clutching on.

"Alyssa? You thought I was with Alyssa?" He chuckled. "I didn't have plans with her. She wanted the number of one of the guys from last week and I dropped by to give it to her."

"Oh, I assumed." My tone was cold. While I was more relieved than I'd wanted to be that he wasn't with Alyssa, I didn't much appreciate being laughed at.

Before I had a chance to react, JC grabbed me with one hand at the waist and spun me against the lockers. He leaned close, his mouth inches from my lips, his body caging mine in. "Don't assume, Gwen. It doesn't become you."

"You know you're kind of an ass." Damn, I wanted to kiss him. And then smack him. Then possibly kiss him some more.

"Yes. I really am." His breath tickled against my lips and I held my own breath, waiting for him to move in. Waiting for his mouth to cover mine. Instead, he kept talking. "Mostly, Gwen, I just don't want you to think you have anything to be jealous of. She is definitely not who I want."

I didn't know what to say. Or do. But as the seconds ticked by, it became apparent that he wanted me to make the next move. He wanted *me* to kiss him.

I wanted to—I so, so wanted to.

But I just couldn't. When I'd jumped him before, I'd been half-crazy with grief and worry. I had an excuse for acting irrationally. Now, I didn't. Now, if I kissed him, if I made a move of any kind, well, it would be a conscious choice. And while I'd flirted with the idea of more with him, I didn't know if I could actually make that firm of a decision.

He sensed it in me. His eyes fell first, and I thought I might have caught a flash of disappointment in his expression, but perhaps I was flattering myself. Then he stepped back, setting me free from his all-male prison. "Well, that's all I had. I should let you get back to work. If there's anything, ever, that you need…"

It was the last invitation he'd give me. I don't know how I knew it, but I knew it clear as crystal. And I ached inside, wishing I had the strength to be someone else. Wishing I was the kind of person who didn't think too much or too hard or too long.

Wishing I could do more than watch him leave.

He was almost gone when it happened. I called after him. "JC!"

I waited until he spun back toward me before I went on, mostly because I had no idea in hell what I was going to say. When I spoke, the words were automatic. "Your offer—did you mean it?"

His brow furrowed questioningly.

"You said before that you could help me. Help me be less tense." My words fell out in a rush partly because I was suddenly full of adrenaline and partly because I was afraid I would stop myself if I slowed down. "Did you mean it?"

JC smiled in a way that was half-taunting and all hot as hell. "Gwen, if you're asking if I'm willing to pop your cork again, the answer is yes, I very much am. Additionally, I'm willing to help you relax."

"You'll help me relax with fucking?" *Norma would be so proud.*

"And other things." He grinned like a man who had caught his long-hunted prey, and my pulse kicked up from both fear and excitement. "Did I mean it when I offered it? Yes. I did. I do. Is it something you'd like to talk more about?"

"I think I would." I wanted to sound surer than that because I *was* surer than that, so I corrected myself. "I would like to talk more about it."

"I'll take you to lunch tomorrow." His tone was final. He may have been tentative before, when I'd still been indecisive, but once I'd admitted my interest, he took control.

Surprisingly, I liked that. It was strangely comforting to not to have to worry about something even though it also felt foreign. But this was what I wanted. So I'd let him make our plans.

Except for one thing. "I don't do lunches." If JC were going to be in my world, it would have to be on my schedule.

"Of course you don't, I wasn't thinking. That's fine. We can work with that." His tone suggested he was talking about more than just the date we were currently planning. "We'll do breakfast. I'll pick you up here at six."

He left then, and in complete opposition to the morning I'd heard about Ben when I'd felt numb and frozen, I was overwhelmed with emotions. I couldn't decide if I wanted to scream or squeal or laugh or cry. I felt like a pressure cooker ready to burst.

For better or worse, I'd done it—two impulsive things in less than a week.

Somehow I had a feeling this was just the beginning.

Chapter Six

I had no idea what JC meant when he said "I'll pick you up," and I half-feared he'd show up in a car and take me someplace fancy. That wasn't what I wanted from our meeting. I wanted a conversation, not a date. Also, I didn't want anyone at the club seeing me leave with him and starting rumors.

But I needn't have worried. When I walked out the back door, JC was standing a few yards away, casually leaning against the side of the next building and not at all appearing to be waiting for me. He was dressed in jeans now, and a tailored gray wool coat that fit him so perfectly it made my stomach flip-flop. He nodded at me inconspicuously as I said goodnight to the other closing manager who took off in the other direction toward the subway.

Then I headed over to meet JC.

We didn't say anything as he led me a couple of blocks down to Café Angelique. It was cold and still fairly dark, but between our brisk pace and my hyperactive hormones, the temperature barely fazed me. By the time we arrived at our destination, my cheeks were flushed and my heart was beating, and I was grateful to be able to blame it on our walk.

At the café, we ordered breakfast—quiches and coffee—and found a table in the back. I waited until we'd stripped our coats and gloves, noting that the blue of JC's sweater brought out his eyes, before diving into conversation. "So…your offer."

With a smile, he shook his head. "You can't even enjoy five minutes of just hanging out before jumping in, can you? No wonder you need me."

Actually, it had been closer to ten minutes, twelve even, if you counted the walk over. I pursed my lips, trying to decide if I should correct him or not. Also, there was the irksome *you need me* remark. It was the latter that I addressed, borrowing a variation of the words he'd said to be earlier. "Don't be so cocky. It doesn't become you."

"Touché," he said with a grin. "But, really, I don't think it bothers you very much. My *cocky*, I mean." He emphasized the *cock*, which was totally juvenile, but also sort of cute.

I bit back a smile. "Somehow I don't think you're using the term in the same way I was."

"You are like one-hundred percent uptight, aren't you?" It was amazing how he could say something like that without coming across as a total douche. He was abrupt, yes. He was bold. But it was evident his motivation was curiosity, not cruelty.

So instead of snapping back at him—my first impulse—I attempted humor. "Ninety-nine percent. I wouldn't be here if it weren't for that small window."

"Thank God for that."

His serious response, paired with the intense heat from his stare, shook me. I shivered, not feeling chilled in the least.

His eyes blazed at my reaction. All night as I'd worked my shift, I'd wondered what our meeting would be like—friendly, banal, sensual, or flirtatious. It was in this moment that I realized that whatever happened from then on, whatever else occurred between us, my encounters with JC would be nothing if not electric.

As far as I was concerned, we were here to discuss a repeat of the other morning. Now I knew there was a very probable chance that the repeat would happen before *this* morning was over.

The epiphany was exciting. And it strangely relaxed me.

JC looked away first, taking a bite of his quiche. I followed his lead. He watched me while he ate, studied me. I couldn't be so bold, so I snuck in my glances. His eyes weren't just blue, I realized. They had flecks of gray and I imagined the prominent color shifted with what he wore. When he put the coat on again, I wondered if they would seem less blue.

Mostly, I wondered about his body. I'd only ever seen him covered, but his outfits so far had been tailored and fitted to him. He was obviously fit—I just didn't know how fit. He'd carried me easily when he'd lifted me to the table in the kitchen. I suspected he was impressively toned underneath his clothes. Just imagining how toned brought a flush to my skin that I hoped he'd attribute to the coffee I was drinking.

It wasn't until we'd completed nearly all of our breakfast that he finally dabbed at his mouth with his napkin and said, "Okay, my offer to help you be less tense. Are you ready? It's simple." He spread his arms out like it was obvious. "Spend time with me."

"And?" Because I'd expected his offer to be something more explicitly carnal.

"And that's it."

I wiped at my own mouth and took another sip of my coffee, trying to decide what it was that bothered me about his offer. Then I figured it out. "That sounds a little like dating."

"No." He drew the "o" out, shaking his head. Admittedly, it was nice to see him worked up for once, instead of vice versa. "Definitely not dating. In fact, no commitments."

"Because you're a commitment-phobe. How cliché." Not that I cared. In fact, I counted on it. Just, somehow, sitting there with JC, poking and teasing came easier than usual. Maybe he was right that spending time with him was the answer to all my problems.

"No, not because I'm a commitment-phobe, though that's not entirely inaccurate. But this is about helping you let loose and commitments are designed to do just the opposite."

I couldn't argue with that. "Okay. So I just spend time with you. Not dating. No commitments. I'm cool with that."

"Good. Look at you. Loosening up already." He ignored the scowl I shot at him. "Now, we both have weird schedules so we'll need to set up a time for a standing date. Or not-date."

"Isn't a standing anything a flat-out commitment?" I'd been the one to initiate this…whatever this was between us, and now I was the one who kept coming up with arguments. I heard myself doing it. But it wasn't like I was looking for an excuse for the "whatever" not to happen. Just, I'd been burned before in a casual arrangement. This time there was going to be no doubt about the terms going in.

"I knew that was coming. And, yes." He pointed in the air with a long finger. "It is a commitment. But it's the only commitment we'll have in this. And either of us can always cancel."

I rolled my hands along the sides of the coffee cup, busying myself, steadying my nerves. "I'm listening."

"So, I don't actually live in New York. I live in L.A."

My eyes flew up to his. "Oh. I didn't know that." I tried not to sound disappointed. He had the Viper booked every Tuesday, but I supposed that didn't mean that he was actually present every week. So how often *was* he in town?

As if reading my mind, he said, "I'm here every week. For work. I take a red-eye to New York on Monday, and Thursday night I take a red-eye back."

Thank the Lord. While I was curious about what he did for a living that had him working on two coasts, it was another part of his statement that struck me. "But today is Friday."

"I skipped my flight last night."

My stomach flipped. "Why?"

"For you."

I felt the color leave my face. There was no denying the rush that came from his admission, but another part of me, the smart part, was ready to take that adrenaline and run. I wanted casual. I wanted strings-free. I didn't want changing-my-routine-*for-you.*

JC leaned over and placed his hand on mine, sending a mess of tingles shooting through my body. *Red alert,* my rational side screamed. *Take your recently rediscovered sex drive out the door and head to the Pleasure Chest to pick up a new dildo.*

Not for the first time in my life, it occurred to me that there was probably something very wrong with me. Besides being completely uptight. Because, what girl in her right mind wanted her sexual relationships to be only physical, no emotion?

Yet that was exactly what I wanted. I was hardened. I'd accepted that long before. There was exactly enough room inside me to love my brother and my sister and nothing else. *No one* else. Everyone else I'd ever felt strong emotions for had beaten me, left me, or died. Of course I knew that my past experiences didn't dictate my future. The next person I cared for *might* not disappoint me—of course I knew that; I was a smart woman. But I wasn't ever going to take that chance.

And emotional involvement from one party in a duo and not the other was messy. I'd been there, done that. Wasn't doing it again.

JC gently squeezed my hand. "Gwen, stop freaking. I'm horny, not in love."

I narrowed my eyes, studying him, trying to ignore the burn of his hand still covering mine. "So you skipped your flight in order to get laid?" It was hard to believe he couldn't just as easily get laid in L.A.

Unless it was specifically me who had him turned on.

"Pretty much."

It was me then. Well. Wow. I couldn't help smiling. So it was over the top to stay for me, but not the craziest thing I'd heard a guy do for sex. And as long as it wasn't wrapped up in touchy-feely, I could live with it. "Very well then. Carry on."

JC seemed mildly surprised that I was so easily convinced. "Okay. Now we're talking." He removed his hand from mine to gesture as he spoke. "So if this is going to work, there are a few things we have to agree on up front."

"Right." Still dizzy from his warmth, I pulled my hand from the table to my lap. If I left it, I was afraid he'd realize how badly I hoped he'd touch me again. And this time not just on my hand.

He seemed oblivious to what was going on with my libido, which was crazy since it was exactly what we were discussing. "First and foremost, we're just spending time together."

"Time that involves sex." The space between my thighs was beginning to itch. I wanted to get through the talking and get to the actual doing.

"Well, yes."

That tiny acknowledgment made my stomach quiver, deep and low.

Then he was back to hammering out the details. "There will be no relationship stuff. No boyfriend/girlfriend. No getting attached. Are you with me?"

"Yes. I'm completely with you. I have no interest in attachments of any sort." I hadn't expected anything else from a guy like JC, but after his earlier remarks that had sounded to the contrary, the confirmation was a relief.

"Are you sure? I really don't want you falling in love with me. It wouldn't be pretty."

Again with the arrogance. Why did he make hubris look so sexy? "Rest assured, JC. There is nothing you could do to make me fall in love with you." I had very few emotions I indulged in. Romance was definitely not in my repertoire.

"Good. I just wanted to be clear up front. Now I'm going to propose something that might seem extreme, but bear with me. The no commitment will be easier if we keep what we know of each other to a minimum. First names only. Exchanging phone numbers is okay, maybe, but no home addresses or Facebook-friending. Are you good with that?"

I paused and let the idea rattle in my head. It *was* extreme, and there was only one reason I could think of for him to insist on that. "Ah, Jesus

Christ. You're married, aren't you?" While that made him less likely to get attached, I did not do infidelity.

Except maybe I had done infidelity, since I'd already fucked him. *Ah, fucknugget.*

But JC was already protesting. "No, no, no, no. I am not married, Gwen. Not. Married. I swear on whatever you think is holy that I have no wife, fiancée, girlfriend. Nothing. I'm a non-commitment guy all around. Come on, do you really see me any other way?"

I could almost imagine it—could see him as a protective caretaker and a doting partner. He'd shown those qualities to me in our brief interactions and it wasn't a stretch to envisage him doing that for someone he loved.

But then there were the other parts of him. When it came down to it—even though he could be sweet—no, I did not see him as the type to commit. At all. Ever. "Then why so secretive?"

"Not secretive. Anonymous." He lowered his gaze, seeming to be unsure that I'd like what he had to say next. "Detached." He raised his eyes again to meet mine. "Is that a deal-breaker for you?"

It probably should have been. If he wasn't married, he had to be hiding something else, even though I couldn't fathom what that might be.

On the other hand, didn't I want the same thing? I didn't want him to know about my life—about my father, about Ben. Maybe he had his own family secrets. Did I really want to demand transparency on his part when he could turn around and demand it of me?

"No, it's not a deal breaker," I said in earnest. "In fact, I think it's a great idea."

"It is, isn't it?" He leaned closer, his voice just above a whisper. "It's also really kind of hot. To not know anything about each other except what matters. The things we learn naturally. Through our own discovery."

His words were full of innuendo, but as other times when he'd said such things, it didn't feel sleazy. It felt sensual.

Also, he was right—the anonymity and mystery was quite a turn on. Which made me even more anxious to get on with the whole set up. "Anything else we need to work out?"

"Yes. The deets. Are you done with this?" He gestured to my half-eaten quiche.

Since I'd lost my appetite for anything but skin on skin, I said yes. He took our plates to the dish bin and returned, continuing where he left off as he sat back down. "Here's what I'm thinking. You get up around what time on Wednesdays? Afternoon? Evening?"

I was impressed that he'd remembered my schedule was unusual. "Six-ish. Sometimes seven."

He nodded as he took in the information. "Perfect. I usually work until around then. Let's say we meet at seven on Wednesdays at my hotel. Then we'll plan to spend those nights together. There's our standing date."

"Don't expect me to sleep. I don't sleep at night." I felt stupid as soon as I said it. He already knew.

"We won't be sleeping," he said, his lids heavy. "Also, I rarely sleep. So we're good."

My breathing suddenly felt heavier and my neck warmed. I wanted this. I did. But I was so unused to giving myself things for pleasure, and more, I was not in the habit of trusting other people. This deal with JC, with a man I knew nothing about, took me out of my comfort zone in a big way.

But my comfort zone was, as Norma implied—as everyone around me implied—a tightly wound cocoon. Surely even the caterpillar had a bit of trepidation before breaking out of his cocoon.

Besides, we could cancel at any time. It was part of the deal. "Wednesdays, then."

"Wednesdays." He narrowed his eyes. "Is this making you nervous?"

I shook my head but said, "I'm not sure."

"Well. That's probably a good thing." He rubbed his hands together as if warming them, or as if he were also a bit apprehensive. "Honestly, I'm a little unsure too. Not about you. Not about this."

"Then what about?"

"Everything else."

His vague answer made me want to dig, but I could tell from his expression that he wouldn't say more. And maybe that was okay. I didn't want to talk about my reasons for trepidation. This was better. Mystery could be good.

There was something I thought should be said, though. About me. "Um, JC, about the other day…in the kitchen. I should explain."

"No, you most definitely shouldn't. No life details, remember?"

I wasn't planning to tell him about Ben or anything specific, but he had to know that I'd been acting out of character. I didn't want him to have the wrong idea about what to expect from me. "You need to know I'm not usually like that. I had—"

"Don't worry." He cut me off. "I know. Whatever drove you to act outside yourself that morning is none of my business, and I don't want to make it my business. I'm grateful I was there. Right place at the right time has never worked out better for me."

Funny, I'd been thinking he was in the wrong place at the wrong time. But I smiled, and by now I'd lost count of how many times he'd made me do that. Smiling was also out of my character. Perhaps JC just brought that out in me.

I took another swallow of my coffee, finishing it off. "All gone," I said, hoping that would indicate I was ready to go.

If JC got my hint, he ignored it. "How many men have you been with?"

I was taken aback. The question was surprising enough, but especially with no lead in to it. "I thought you didn't want to know anything about me."

"I don't. But this is relevant."

Yeah, right. Relevant. Or did he just want to figure out how easy I was going to be to impress in the bedroom.

I wasn't usually ashamed about my number of bed partners. JC, however, had infinitely more experience. I knew it without asking, but since he'd put me on the spot, I turned it back on him. "How many woman have you been with?"

He shook his head dismissively. "That's *not* relevant."

I snickered. "That's the kind of answer you give when you're embarrassed with the truth."

"I'm not embarrassed." He considered for a minute. "You want to know? I'll tell you, but I don't know if you'll like it."

I thought about that. How many women would he have to sleep with to give me pause? I couldn't come up with an exact number, but it occurred to me that whatever that number was, it would lead me to either feel inadequate or overwhelmed. "You're right. I don't want to know."

He didn't hide the satisfaction from his face. "But I do want to know how many guys you've been with."

I let him wait in silence for a few seconds before I gave him what he wanted. "Three."

It was JC's turn to look nervous. "Oh shit. Are you sure you can do this without getting attached?"

This time I couldn't ignore his pretension. "Do you have some sort of narcissistic disorder? I'm not going to get attached. For your information, only one of those three men was a boyfriend. One was a drunken night in college. One I banged for fun."

His eyes lit up like I'd taken off my shirt. "You banged a guy for fun? We're further ahead than I assumed."

"I did. Judger." Actually, I'd banged him because the activity had given me a place to hide. An occasional sanctuary from the trial and the emotional effort it took to survive the aftermath of Dad's arrest. At first, anyway. Then it became a habit.

"So let me ask this—when's the last time?"

"That I got banged? Three days ago. In my club's kitchen." I knew what he meant. I was stalling my answer.

He didn't even crack a smile. "Before that."

"A couple years ago. Maybe three. Or five." It was more than seven, actually. The last friends with benefits had been before Ben had taken off for the West Coast.

"Uh-huh." Like before, I could hear the doubt in his voice. "Why did you stop fucking him? The last one."

The last one—Marcus—had been a nice enough guy. He'd been a student at Pace University. We'd never felt the romantic spark for each other. In fact, when we'd first met he'd been crushing on another girl in our Accounting 101 course. I was simply someone to shag while he waited around for her to notice him, and I liked the escapism sex provided.

Then things changed. "I realized it was easier to get myself off," I said to JC. "A lot less work, a whole lot less emotion involved."

"Then you did get attached."

"Not me."

It took a moment for him to process that. "He fell for *you*. And you cut him off." JC's expression eased. "Wow. Brutal, Gwen. Brutal." Yet, he seemed pleased. "Had you set guidelines beforehand? Told him you weren't interested in more?"

"We didn't set guidelines like this, but he knew." Long before he'd moved his crush on Chelle—was that her name?—to me, I'd told him I only did sex for fun.

JC shook his head. "He liked you from the get-go. He probably hoped he'd change your mind about wanting something else through the power of fucking."

I would have disagreed, except I'd wondered the same thing. Wondered if Chelle was an excuse to get me to spend time with him in the first place. Now I wondered how JC could be so perceptive. "If he did, it didn't work. In case you were having any ideas about changing my mind about anything like that."

"Um, no. You don't have to worry about that." He laced his fingers and cupped them behind his head. "So three priors. And you don't have a problem with no condoms."

It wasn't a question, but I interjected with an answer. "Oh, no. I do have a problem with that. We're using condoms." Even though I'd entertained for a moment the idea of not using them when he'd shown me his clean report, I had since realized the folly in it.

JC scowled. "We've already gone bareback. We can't go to condoms now. That's moving in the wrong direction."

"It was one time, and it was a mistake. I can't have sex with someone who's sleeping around and not use condoms." I gathered our empty cups and headed to the trashcan.

"You think I'd sleep around when I'm with you?" JC followed after me, his statement raising the eyebrows of a lady sitting at a nearby table.

I pushed the cups into the trash and turned to face him. "Isn't that your M.O.?"

"No. It's not." He was irked. "We do this, I'm with you and no one else." The sincerity of his statement was evident in his intense expression.

My chest fluttered. Monogamous sex was what I preferred. Even if I wasn't interested in romance, I was still a girl. I got insecure and compared myself to others. Sometimes I got jealous.

But while I wanted it, the question was, why did he? I was leery. "That's commitment number two in our no commitment deal."

"You're going to be a hard-ass about this, aren't you?"

"That's my M.O., remember?" At least my teasing made him drop the serious expression.

The sound of a throat clearing made me realize we were still blocking the trash. "Sorry," I said to the man waiting to get through. I grabbed JC's shirtsleeve and tugged him back to the table where our jackets still sat waiting for us.

"Okay, yes," JC said as soon as we'd sat. "It's commitment number two. But I think we can both agree that this is an important one."

"We could just use condoms." But the fight was waning in my tone. Even with clean health reports and an IUD, I usually preferred the double protection. But we had already gone condom-free. And if I were truly learning to chill-the-freak-out, then maybe this was a good place to start relaxing my rules.

There was only one issue keeping me from giving in entirely—could I trust JC to be faithful?

JC's persistence also diminished. "We could. I'd prefer not to. Whether we do or not won't change that I'm only going to be with you."

It was weird how I believed him in my heart. He connected with me there, knew how to say things to cause a leap of faith.

But my head still had doubts. "You'd be willing to have sex only once a week? For however long this goes on?"

"Yes. I would. For however long this goes." JC tapped his palm on the table. "And correction, I'd be having sex only one day a week. I guarantee you it will be more than one time."

The ball of want in my belly doubled inside. It didn't matter if my head was convinced anymore—my heart believed him enough to win the ruling. Even if I didn't say it now, I knew the next time he was inside me he would again be bare. By my choice. Not only because it was the laid-back way to be, but because I wanted him like that. I wanted him that close.

The realization shook me. Scared me. Thrilled me. "You get to me when you say things like that. You know that, don't you?"

"I don't know it." He lowered his voice. "Now tell me how."

"How what?"

"How I get to you." His words were heavy and molten.

I was paralyzed with heat, captured in his piercing stare. "It...it turns me on."

"How exactly?" When I didn't respond he wrapped his foot around my chair and pulled me closer to the table. Then he leaned in, as if to tell me a secret. "Does it make your heart race? Does your breath feel heavy? Do I make you wet?"

His breath edged across my ear, but it was his words as much as anything that sent a buzz straight to my core. I wanted to answer. I wanted to tell him, *yes, all those things*. But my voice was stuck in my throat.

He turned his head and nuzzled the upper edge of my lobe with his nose. "See, that's a problem, Gwen. How can I give you what you want if you aren't able to tell me what that is?" His mouth brushed my skin, and I gasped, waiting for him to lick me, to suck me, to bite me.

But he didn't do anything to me. Instead, he sat back, leaving me yearning and keyed up. "We'll work on that," he said.

"This time you can't convince me that you don't know exactly what you do to me."

"No, this time I can't." His smile was slight, like he was appraising his meal. "But I mean it—what you want, you need to ask for. If you asked, I'd get you off right here at this table."

"Well, that is not on my list of wants." Though, now that he'd mentioned it…would I ever be able to do something like that? Let a man touch me, stroke me to orgasm in a public setting? The idea was terrifying.

And really, really hot.

Who the hell was this guy? And how the hell had he ended up in my life? "Seriously, JC. Why would you cease your fuck anyone, anytime lifestyle to shag one girl?"

"There you are assuming again about my lifestyle."

"Am I wrong?" The look he gave me said that I wasn't. It also said that he was serious about changing that. For me.

I had to know. "Why *me*?"

"Maybe you have a magic pussy."

"Come on. Unoriginal." I wasn't letting him skirt around this one.

He shrugged. "Sleeping around gets boring. It's work. I'm tired."

"I don't believe a word of that."

"Too bad." He stood and pulled his coat off the back of his chair.

Panic surged through me. Was this pushing him too far? Was this the end of the deal or was he signaling it was time to go together? And even if it was the latter, could I give in without finding out this answer?

No, I couldn't. I could live without knowing anything else about him but not this. I had to understand this one thing.

He put his coat on and looked down at me still sitting. With a sigh, he sat back down. He ran a hand through his hair. "I don't know why, Gwen. But I want to do this with you. Maybe because I like a challenge. Maybe because I can't stand seeing someone who's as potentially brilliant as you shine so dully."

Maybe I didn't want his answer after all. "You really need to work on the compliments."

He caught my eyes. "Maybe because I know that you don't put out easily, and I like the way it feels to be the guy who gets you."

I melted. I was an ice queen, and with just one line, I felt a layer of cold dripping away. And for a second, I found myself imagining what it would be like to actually get attached to someone like "Just JC." I imagined that I might be a person who could do just that.

Then I stopped with that line of thinking. Because if I could get attached, I didn't want this. And I wanted this. I wanted him to *get me*. I just had to be clear exactly what was allowed. "Gets me in bed, you mean."

"Yes. In bed." He grinned. "And on counters. And all around town, if I have anything to do with it." He waited for me to smile before going on. "You're fun, Gwen. And you don't know it. I'm looking forward to being the person who shows you that. Also, magic pussy."

I laughed now. The real joke was that he already was the only guy to *get me*. No one else had ever broken through so many layers of my armor to make me smile so easily, to laugh so quickly.

And whatever if it scared me. It didn't mean anything other than that sex with JC was going to be fun. Fun was what I needed.

So when he asked, "Speaking of magic pussy, do you want to get out of here?" my answer took no thought at all. "Yes. Yes, I do."

Chapter Seven

This time, as we left the café, JC took my hand in his. I was giddier about the gesture than I wanted to be, which I hated. I also hated that we both were wearing gloves. I wanted skin on skin.

We didn't have to walk far before we caught a cab. JC gave instructions to the driver to take us to the Four Seasons Hotel. Then he chatted for a few minutes about the traffic and the Mets. After a few minutes, he sat back and removed the glove from my right hand and the glove from his left hand and entwined his fingers through mine.

The ride was about half an hour—not long considering it was rush hour now. Neither of us talked. We'd said all we needed to at breakfast. With words, anyway. Now we spoke through the juncture of our hands, his thumb caressing across my skin, our fingers squeezing where they were laced. It was active fondling, the pressure increasing and decreasing as our hands clenched and unclenched. With his touch, he told me what was in store for the rest of my body. I could tell exactly how he'd grope me, how he'd massage me, how he'd pump me.

It was the most erotic foreplay I'd ever experienced. By the time we arrived at our destination, I was aroused and primed for what would happen next.

I slid out of the cab first while JC paid. He'd paid for breakfast as well. When he joined me on the sidewalk, I said, "I know you have money." We were at the Four Seasons, after all. "But I can pay for things too." I didn't want to offend him—if he was the type of guy who expected to be responsible for the bill then there was no arguing it. I'd met those guys.

If he wasn't, then we needed to decide how the expenses would work.

He scowled at me as he took me by my elbow and steered me through the doors. "I'm sure you can pay for things. That bothers me though. If it's important to you to pitch in, I'll try to deal. I don't want you to feel like you're being paid for services or anything."

I thought about it while he led me to the front desk. There was a couple checking in ahead of us, so I had time to give him my response. "It doesn't bother me. And I don't feel like a hooker, if that's what you're suggesting." I'd been offered the role before. It was a rite of passage where I came from. I knew the difference between being paid for something required to survive and enjoying the benefits of a lover's deep pockets.

JC chuckled. "Good. Because you're definitely not a hooker. I would have gotten at least a handjob on the ride over if you were." The couple moved away from the desk, but before nudging me forward, JC whispered in my ear. "Besides, the handjob I *did* get was even better, if you ask me."

Then he felt the same about the foreplay. *Awesome.*

The hotel desk clerk addressed us, disturbing the clouds of my buzz. "And what can I do for you, today, Mr.—"

"Uh, uh, uh." JC cut him off quickly. "What's with the Mr. stuff? You know we don't do that, Joseph."

The clerk smiled in a way that went beyond customer service. "Sorry, I forgot you asked me to call you JC. What can I do for you this morning?"

I wondered if anyone was immune to JC's charms. Did he befriend everyone he met? It was so unlike me. It always felt like such an effort to be friendly, but JC made it seem so easy. Made it actually look like an attractive way to live.

JC half-leaned against the counter so that he was facing me. "Well, Joe, I'd like to introduce you to my good friend, Gwen. She'll need to be added to my room and be given a key."

"Certainly. Gwen, do you have a photo ID?"

I handed the gentleman my ID. After typing a minute into the computer, he handed me my card back, plus a room key. "Enjoy your day," Joe said, and JC once again took my hand to lead me through the lobby.

The arousal that had waned to a hum while we'd dealt with adding me to the room notched back up to a buzz, spurred by my palm against his. "That was close," I said as we waited for the elevator. "I almost heard your last name."

"No kidding. Joe almost killed all the fun. I'd have had to get him fired then. Would have been too bad, too. He knows where to get the best Cubans."

"At least now he can identify me if I go missing. In case you're a serial killer or something."

"Why do you think I had you check in now instead of later? I didn't want you to worry."

I hadn't been concerned that he was going to hurt me, even though that was probably stupid. I'd been making a joke. JC, on the other hand, was trying to relieve any fears I might have. Again. For someone so laid-back, it was admirable how good he was at thinking of all the details. It was funny how seriously he was taking the task of helping me relax. Really, all I needed was the sex.

Also, it was kind of cute.

The elevator arrived and we stepped in. JC pressed the button to the forty-ninth floor, and something else began niggling at my thoughts.

We leaned against the railing and watched the numbers as they went higher. *Six. Seven. Eight.*

After we'd passed *Ten*, I couldn't hold it in any longer. "He thinks I'm a high-priced call girl, you know. The desk clerk." I really didn't think I was a hooker, but that other people thought I might be one was a little less easy to swallow.

JC shook his head but didn't look at me. "He thinks you're my girlfriend."

"No way." Besides the fact that anyone who knew JC at all would know he didn't have a girlfriend, I definitely did not fit the bill of who he'd be with if he did.

"He really does. I know he does."

I looked to see if he was pulling my leg. His expression was completely serious. "How can you be so sure?"

"Because he sees me come in and out all the time. And I've never introduced him to any of my girls before."

The elevator came to a stop, which seemed appropriate since my heart stopped for half a second at JC's statement. The doors opened and I followed him out numbly as I tried to gather myself. *My girls*, he'd said. How many had there been? What number was I in his vast universe of starlets? I wasn't comfortable standing out, but I didn't know if I was comfortable being that anonymous. It also reignited my fears about JC and his decision to be monogamous. Could he really manage that? Could I trust him if he said he did?

But while I wondered at being a drop in a very large bucket, he'd also admitted that I was the only one he'd added to his room, and that was the worst part about what he'd said. That *did* make me feel special. Made me feel wanted for more than a night. Made me feel good about myself in ways I didn't want to feel good about myself.

Made me want to reconsider my decision to be in a hotel with this man, heading to his room, and for very different reasons than fear of his infidelity.

I wondered if I could convince myself the doubts and the compliment canceled each other out. That could work, right?

By the time we reached his door, my palms were sweaty and my anxiety was beginning to outweigh my desire. He turned to me, concern in his eyes. "Are you still good?"

I bit my lip and nodded, afraid that if I tried to speak I'd say something I didn't want to say. Like, *I'm totally fine.* Or worse, *I need to go.*

"Let's make sure your key works." He winked at me, which helped to ease my fears. A bit.

I pulled the card that Joe had given me from my pocket and handed it to JC. He slid it into the slot and the light turned green. "We're a go," he said.

He turned the knob and began to push the door, but before he'd opened it very far, I placed a hand on his arm to stop him. "JC, have you ever done this before?"

"Done what?"

I wasn't quite sure what it was I meant by my question either, what it was that I was looking to glean from his answer. I knew he'd bedded other women, I knew he'd made at least one—the one that had spoken out at the club the night I'd met him—feel better because of her time with him. But the whole situation—the arrangement part, the monogamy—was that new? And how did I ask that exactly?

I had to figure it out because I was on edge. And I knew, somehow I was absolutely certain, that if JC gave me the right answer to my question, I'd feel better.

So I tried to explain it as best as I could. "A committed sexual relationship that really wasn't committed at all, I guess is a good way to put it."

His expression grew serious, but he kept his eyes on mine. "No, Gwen, I have not."

I hadn't known it until he'd given it, but it was the answer I'd been looking for. And when he took my hand once again in his, I felt a surge of arousal and confidence and comfort. It overcame me instantaneously, the way a light goes on with a switch, and I knew that whatever happened between us wouldn't be inconsequential.

And that would be fine.

My smile came easily. "Then I guess we'll be virgins together."

He chuckled, pushing the door the rest of the way open. "Hopefully not for long."

Inside the room, JC took my coat and hung it in a closet by the door alongside his. Then he placed the *Do Not Disturb* sign on the outside knob. I took the opportunity to look around the room. There was a couch and a couple of armchairs and an oval writing desk pressed against a floor-to-ceiling window that looked out over Central Park.

"Where's the bed?" I flushed as soon as I said it, sure I sounded eager.

Thankfully JC didn't make a big deal about it. He nodded down a hall. "Bedroom, bathroom, terrace—all that way." He didn't pull me that direction, however, leading me instead to sit on the couch. "You don't mind if we hang out in here, do you?" he asked as he sat in an armchair across from me.

"Not at all." What was I going to say? *No, I want to get on with the fucking and I'm only comfortable fucking in a bed,* wasn't going to be believable. Or true. But, God, I hoped that he didn't want to spend another hour talking. Because I was ready to get it on.

I crossed one leg over the other and bounced my knee.

JC studied me, his arms stretched out comfortably on the chair's armrests. He seemed like a king on his throne. And what did that make me? "Gwen, relax. You look so tense."

"It's why I'm here, remember?"

"But you just got a hundred times tenser as soon as we walked in here. What can I do to make you feel more comfortable?"

I deliberated what to say. "Honestly? I'd feel better if we just got on with things." He had told me I should ask for what I wanted.

He smirked, and I was afraid he was going to chide me for my impatience like he had at the café.

He didn't. "Okay, we can do that. Tell me something—do you ever touch yourself?"

"Like, get off by myself?"

"Yes."

My shirt was a long-sleeved silk peasant, but suddenly I felt bare. "Of course, I do." Not a lot, but I did. And as much as I hadn't wanted to admit it, I also didn't want him thinking I was a total prude. Though maybe my answer made me sound like a perv of some sort. I rubbed nervously at my neck, already warm from blushing.

"Good." JC seemed to like my response. "I want you to show me."

I almost choked on my own saliva. "Show you? Like…you mean… right now?"

"Yes. Now. Right where you are. Show me." He sat back into his chair, and I no longer thought of him as a king but as a judge.

A judge who wanted to watch as I played with myself.

"Um. I'm not sure I'm cool with that." Except, I wanted to be cool with it. The idea was hot. It just required someone less inhibited than me to pull it off.

"Then don't worry, you don't have to do it. But I think that you want to. In fact, I know you do. You're flushed right now and your breathing sped up as soon as I suggested it. Maybe some of that is fear, but fear isn't very far from excitement. So if it's something you want to do, then this is the perfect place to do it. Because you're safe with me. I won't judge."

He leaned forward, his elbows on his knees. "And if it makes any difference, I *want* to see it."

A shiver ran through me. "Why?"

"Because you have to be truly relaxed to climax with someone watching you. More selfishly, I already know how beautiful you look when you come, and I want to see it again."

I couldn't say exactly what it was that convinced me, and I never actually said yes, but there I was a minute later with my pants unzipped and my hand stuffed down my panties. I rubbed at my clit, and while my body tingled from the effort, I couldn't get any further than that. "This isn't working."

"No, it's not."

I shot JC the evil eye. "Fuck you."

"Not yet." He ignored the second scowl I gave him. "Is this how you usually do it?"

"No. Usually I have my vibrator." *And no one watching me.* Though, the last few times I'd done this, it had been JC I'd thought of. Only in my imagination, he wasn't sitting across the room, not touching me.

This was too strange. Too detached.

Was this what he'd meant by a detached arrangement? Because if so, then it was going to be a deal-breaker after all.

Maybe I was overreacting. I wasn't ready to give up.

JC frowned. "You never do this with your hands?"

"Not in a long time." Not since I'd discovered the magic of Lelo pleasure objects. *Talk about magic pussy.*

"Shame." He shook his head. "Okay. Anyway. Take off your pants. That will help."

I didn't think it would make a difference, but I did as he suggested, unzipping my long boots first, then pulling off my socks before standing to pull down my dress pants. When I sat again, I leaned into the cushion behind me and slipped my hand inside my panties. I still felt awkward. More so, now that my legs were bared. And I was a long way from an orgasm. I threw the back of my hand over my eyes and concentrated. Or, rather, tried to figure out how long I needed to keep going before faking an O would look convincing.

And honestly, it wasn't what I wanted to do anymore. Well, it was and it wasn't. I wanted to be sexy and unbridled. But I didn't want it to be hard. I wanted to be the woman in the porn movie that could get off with just a flick of her clit. I wanted to come instantly like that and then move on to the next part where JC pulled out his cock and we played with that instead.

"Gwen, you aren't trying."

I let out a frustrated sigh. "Then you do it."

Next thing I knew, he was perched over me, his arms braced on the back of the couch, caging me in. "Okay, then. I will."

His mouth closed over mine. I'd been too immersed in my own grief the last time I'd kissed him to pay much attention to the actual kissing. His lips were softer than I'd remembered, but his touch was firm. His tongue moved confidently against mine, licking me with aggressive strokes that made my belly flip-flop and my panties damp. Made me twist and turn as I tried to take everything he had to give. Made me forget what I'd been doing and the failure that I'd met. Made me forget myself all together.

JC cupped a hand around my neck and wrapped a hand around my waist. With some expert move that was lost on me, he sat down on the couch and pulled me into his lap, straddling him. All without breaking our kiss. I liked this position. I could cling to his shoulders for support and squirm against the bulge in his pants while he worked at my bun until my hair fell loose around my face. Then, with one hand tangled in my locks, his other hand stroked my clit through the thin material of my panties.

We made out like this for long lost moments. He didn't ask to take off my shirt. He simply tugged at the hem until I broke our kiss long enough for him to pull it over my head and toss it aside. Then, while he kissed at the skin above my bra, he unhooked the back—expertly, I noticed—then pulled that garment off me as well.

He pressed his palm against my chest and gently pushed me back so he could look me over. I watched his eyes as they feasted on me. Saw his pupils as they dilated with lust.

"Gwen, you have spectacular breasts. So beautiful. You hide them away behind your shapeless clothes. Are you simply being modest or are you uncomfortable with how gorgeous you are?"

"Uh…"I didn't know if I was supposed to answer. If I was, I didn't know what the answer was.

Not seeming to care that I hadn't responded, he cupped a hand over each mound and squeezed, hard enough to really feel it. He kneaded his fingers into my skin then pulled at my nipples until I let out a soft cry of pleasure.

"Grab your breasts, Gwen." He moved his hands out of the way so I could put mine in their place. "Yeah, like that." He covered my hands with his and together we massaged and rubbed my sensitive skin. "Jesus, that's so hot. One day, while you touch yourself like that, I'm going to slide my cock between your tits. Would you like that?"

"Hmm," I moaned. It was the only sound I could make out. I was too turned on by his talk and the way he was touching me—the way *we* were touching me. I thought I might be able to come from this alone.

"That's not good enough, Gwen. I need you to tell me. With words."

"I would like it," I gasped.

"You'd like what? Say it."

I'd heard dirty talk, but nothing quite like the way JC talked to me. And certainly I'd never been expected to reciprocate.

What's more, I never knew how much I wanted to reciprocate. "I'd like you to fuck my tits."

JC rewarded me with a bruising kiss. "I'm going to," he said when he pulled away. "Not today, but sometime soon. I promise."

Christ, the idea practically made me explode. It was so base. So primal. So…naughty. It was exactly what I wanted.

There was something else I wanted. Wanted now. "You too," I said, my breathing labored. "Your shirt off too."

JC seemed pleased, if with my request or with the fact that I had stated it out loud, I didn't know. "You want my skin touching yours?"

I nodded more vigorously than I needed to, eager to have him reveal a part of himself when he kept so much else hidden.

"Then let me make that happen." He took his sweater off. Then the white T-shirt he wore beneath. He stilled to let me study him.

As I fondled my breasts, my eyes raked across his torso. He was trim and sculpted, not overly toned, but still sporting a washboard. His pants hung low on his hips. I couldn't decide what to focus on first—the creases that shot down in a V below his waistband or the tattoos that decorated his skin. One on his bicep, a compass just above the pit of his elbow. Another, words written in a grid on his opposite forearm. A third, Chinese lettering running down one side of his ribcage.

Before I'd gotten a chance to examine much of him at all, he turned me so that I was laid out on the couch. Then he climbed over me. "I love the way you look at me, Gwen. And I hope to give you more time to explore all of me later on. But I'm playing selfish today. Today I'm exploring you."

With a hand on each side of me, he held his weight so that he could brush his chest against me, back and forth across my nipples, which burned and stung from the too-gentle touch. I pushed my breasts closer together, trying to get better contact with his skin.

"That's so good, Gwen. So hot. Now keep touching yourself like that, okay? I need to suck on you." He pushed himself back on his knees and lowered his head to my breasts and drew a taut nipple into his mouth.

I sighed at the near brutal way he sucked and tugged at my tender flesh. His total attention was on this one breast, his hands cupping it as he worshipped it with his lips, his tongue, his teeth. Subconsciously, my fingers mimicked his ardor on my other nipple—pinching it to a peak, pulling it to the brink of pain.

I didn't even realize I was gasping until he said something.

"I love those little sounds you're making, Gwen." He licked a trail from the breast he'd been feeding on, down the valley in between, and to its twin. "I need to hear them louder. Can you make them louder for me?"

As he gave the same attention to my second breast, I tried to be louder. It wasn't easy for me. I wasn't in control of them in the first place, and now that he'd called me out, I felt awkward.

Fortunately, JC was patient. He worked me up again, kneading me with his hands, devouring me with his mouth until I was panting noisily.

When his lips eventually left my chest, he returned to my mouth for another deep, urgent kiss. He stretched his legs out behind him, settling between my thighs so that I could feel the stiff ridge of his erection through his pants against my crotch.

"Ah, fuck, I'm so hard for you right now. I'm steel." He ground his hips into me. "Can you feel that?"

"Yes, yes. I feel you." My voice was tiny and quiet, so I bucked my pelvis up to let him know how well I could feel him, how much I wanted to feel him more, in case he didn't make that out from my small statement.

"Now I want you to put your hand in your panties. Rub yourself like you did before." His tone gave me no room to deny or to question. He wasn't demanding or even coaxing. He simply held the command, and I wanted to do what he said.

I slid my hand down where he wanted it. Immediately, he covered mine with his, and together we massaged my clit, circling and pressing until my entire nervous system was on fire.

"Yes, that feels good, doesn't it? Can you let me know how good it feels? You don't have to use words this time. Just let me hear your moans."

The sound fell out of my mouth without any thought, followed by another. Sounds that were part groan, part sigh, part gasp. As each one left my body, I felt like a weight had fallen from my back. It was like crying—cathartic and releasing.

"Yes, like that," JC encouraged me. "Keep rubbing yourself like that. Keep letting me hear you."

JC's hand left mine, but I kept stroking my nub as he'd instructed while he sat back on his knees and tucked his fingers around the elastic band of my underwear. When he gestured for me to lift my hips, I did, and he pulled my panties down my legs and tossed them behind him.

I was naked now. Completely revealed. My instinct was to curl in— hide my most private parts from his gaze. But I fought against inclination and kept one hand caressing my breast, the other rubbing my clit, my knees parted so his view wasn't obscured.

He inhaled appreciatively at the sight of me exposed. Before our encounter the other morning, I'd neglected things down south. There wasn't much need to trim and shape. Then—after—I decided to tidy up. I pretended it was simply time, but in all honesty, it was because I'd wanted to be ready in case of a moment like this one.

I hadn't gone completely bare. Close though.

JC pushed my hand away so he could see me better. "This is nice, Gwen." He ran a finger over the small patch of hair I had left, sending a jolt down my spine, even as he danced around the spot that yearned for his returned attention. "I have to say, I didn't mind before, but this is even sweeter. I can see you better. I can see your clit right now, and it's so swollen and pink. I can't wait until I suck you off there."

Please, I begged inside my head. I'd lost my voice again, too paralyzed by his stare, and all my invocations remained silent. I could almost feel his lips on my skin, just from the way he looked at me. Could tell how he'd go down on me. Could imagine it so vividly that I was already writhing from the pleasure.

Despite his words, he didn't move to take me in his mouth. Instead, he shook his head. "Not right now, though. And not because you won't ask for it, but because I have other things in mind." He took one of my legs and raised it so my ankle was on the back of the couch. Then he nudged my other farther apart so that my foot touched the floor, spreading me wide. "And also because you won't ask for it. If you want me to lick you there, Gwen, you'll have to learn how to tell me."

He sat back on his knees and swept his eyes over every part of me. "Jesus, you're gorgeous. Don't stop touching yourself, Gwen."

He slid a finger down my slit and circled the rim of my hole. He repeated his circle one more time before plunging it inside me. I was wet. Embarrassingly wet, but JC didn't seem to mind in the least. He dragged some of my moisture up to help me swirl against my clit and then dipped back down, adding two fingers this time. He finger-fucked me like that, bending his stroke just so that it hit me in exactly the right place.

I could feel my orgasm on the horizon. Like how the sun casts a glow around the land before it hits with his full rays. I had that glow. But I couldn't quite get the rays.

JC continued to work me. And as he worked me, his other hand undid his pants and released his cock. It was thick and hard as steel. A bead of pre-cum lay on the tip. I watched him as he took his hand from inside me and rubbed my juices down the length of his shaft. Then he returned to probing me while at the same time he began to pump his cock with long strokes.

It was so hot, so intense, so unbelievably erotic. Watching him pleasure himself as I pleasured myself. Knowing that the thing getting him off was the sight of me. Knowing that I wouldn't be dangling on the edge like this if it weren't for him.

Still, I couldn't fall off the cliff. Couldn't let my orgasm overtake me. It stayed at bay no matter how hot the scenario was. As JC started to pump himself in earnest, I started to fear he'd get there before me.

But, as always, he guessed my thoughts. He met my eyes full on. "You can't imagine how hard it is for me to keep control of myself. But I'm going to do it. So you don't have to. I'm going to hold all the control so that you can let go. Let go, Gwen. Let me hear you. Let me see you. Let everything go for me."

Then, there it was. It came on so easily, as if it hadn't been hiding at all, streaking through my limbs until I was white-hot and shaking. Every cell, every fiber of my body glowed and shone, my every molecule quivered with the brilliance of my orgasm.

I was only somewhat aware of JC coming with me. He groaned and twitched, his knees knocking against my thighs as his cum shot onto my lower belly and trailed down to where my fingers still shook against my clit. I felt him fall sideways against the sofa, and I briefly wondered if he was as devastated as I was before my mind drifted into the oblivion of my climax.

I kept my eyes closed as I recovered, unable to look any longer at the man who'd brought me to such a state of wreckage. He was magnificent—was that the climax talking?—and the stars that shot across my closed lids seemed fitting after staring at someone so bright. Someone so penetrating that he could see right through me, right into me. See what I needed, what I so desperately wanted to be feeling.

He didn't even know my full name. Yet, he knew *me*. A part of me, anyway. A part that no one had bothered to try to know for quite a while.

When I settled, I lay limp and boneless, a smile tickling my swollen lips. He'd done it. He'd relaxed me. He'd taken away the tension and eased the constant knot that resided in my stomach.

JC had unwound me so completely, in fact, that I didn't even let it bother me that he stirred other emotions in me too. Emotions that I hadn't bargained for. He made me feel beautiful. He made me feel wanted. He made me feel something other than boring.

He made me feel. Period.

Chapter Eight

Three days later, I was still thinking about my morning with JC. The memory clung to me like expensive cologne that loses its scent until a breeze stirs it up again. I'd forget that it happened. Then something would trigger me. An image or a phrase would float into my mind and suddenly I was hit with vivid flashbacks. *The touch of his skin against mine. The effort written on his face as he held my control. The bold words he'd used.* With every recollection, I became flushed again and dizzy. Even with the club to keep me occupied, I found myself counting the minutes until Wednesday when I'd see him again.

As I came home from work around six on Monday morning, though, it wasn't JC I was thinking about, but Norma. She'd returned from L.A. the night before during my shift, and I was eager to see her before she went to the office. Not only because I wanted to hear every last detail about Ben but also because I was glad to have her back.

Maybe I'd even tell her about JC. I hadn't decided yet.

"Morning, Kev." I nodded to the doorman, and he let me in the lobby of our Uptown high-rise. He was my favorite of the doormen, older, probably nearing retirement, and despite my preference to remain anti-social, he always had a greeting that drew me out of my shell.

He tipped his hat as I walked by. "That's two pretty Anders ladies in less than half an hour. It's my lucky day."

I stopped, puzzled, and turned back to him. "Norma was down here?" I tried to remember if we had milk and coffee. There wasn't any other reason I could think of for her to venture out this early.

"She got here in a cab about five-thirty."

"Huh." If she'd gone for groceries, she would have walked to the corner store. I'd have to ask her about it.

I waved goodbye. Then, not wanting to wait for the elevator, I hurried up the three flights of stairs to our apartment. Norma wasn't in the living room when I went in. I passed by the kitchen and smelled coffee brewing but didn't find her, so next I headed for her bedroom.

Her room was empty when I got there, but I heard the shower going in the master bathroom. Anxious to see her, I sat on her bed and surfed the net on my phone until she finished.

"Good morning," I said when she walked out ten minutes later in the silk bathrobe I'd given her for her last birthday.

She jumped. "Jesus, Gwen."

Laughing, I hopped up to give her a hug. "Sorry, I didn't mean to scare you."

"I don't know what was more surprising—seeing you when I didn't expect to or the fact that you're hugging me without me initiating it."

Her comment made me try to wiggle away, but she managed to hold me an extra couple of seconds. "What can I say? I missed you." I had missed her. I hadn't realized how much until I saw her.

"Maybe I should go away more often."

No, I didn't want that. I liked having her around. But I already felt too gushy with the hug so I didn't say anything. Instead, I climbed back onto her bed to watch her get ready for work.

As I curled my feet under me cross-legged style, I noticed something. "Your bed hasn't been slept in." Which wasn't like Norma. She usually left that for the housekeeper. Had she not slept at home?

"Oh." She paused, her back to me as she reached in her underwear drawer for a pair of panties. Then she turned to me and waved her hand dismissively. "You know, I was so tired last night, I fell asleep on top of all the covers."

"Wow. You must not have moved at all. It still looks so freshly made."

"I straightened it this morning." Not looking at me, she stepped into her panties and pulled them up. Then abandoned her robe to put on her bra.

I might have made more of a deal about the bed, but now her underwear distracted me. While I'd never been big on spending money on frivolous things, I made sure to always have nice lingerie. If a woman feels good in her underthings, she'll feel powerful in her world, and all that bullshit. Norma never needed those kinds of head tricks. She was powerful and confident wearing cotton whites.

So when had she splurged on silk?

"You did some shopping," I said, as she fumbled with her bra clasp.

"They look great."

She met my eyes in the mirror above her dresser. "A few months ago. I ordered from Faire Frou Frou. Decided to see what all the fuss was about."

"And?"

"They're nice. I like them." She spun to look at me directly when I gave her a skeptical frown. "What?"

"Nothing. I'm just glad you're finally treating yourself to something nice." Also, I was beginning to suspect there was something up. "Did you go out before I got here?"

"Today?" She pulled out some pieces from her jewelry box.

"Yeah. Kev said you came in soon after his shift started. Did you go someplace?"

Norma was never as easy to read as I was. Yet her expression seemed even more unreadable than usual. Like she was trying harder to remain aloof.

After a few seconds, irritation replaced her stoicism. "Geez, Gwen. I expected Twenty Questions when I got in but about Ben. Not me."

"Sorry. I'm simply making conversation." I stood to help her fasten her necklace.

She held her hair up for me. "Thank you."

But I wasn't letting her off the hook that easily. "Also, I was curious."

She let her hair down and straightened the jewel on her neck. "I went for a run, okay?"

In the winter, Norma usually kept her workouts to the apartment gym. I didn't mention that. "Then you got tired and took a cab back?"

"I guess the trip to L.A. wore me out more than I thought it had." She was hiding something, and that irritated me.

But I could tell that if I pried any more, we'd argue, and I didn't want to fight when she'd just gotten home. "I'm sure the whole thing was exhausting. Do you have any new information? About Ben?"

I'd talked to her every day so I doubted she had anything left to tell me, but she managed to give me a few details about my brother that I hadn't yet heard. The facility she'd checked him into wasn't in San Francisco but rather Marin County. It was voluntary and he could check out at any time. His care providers, however, would make recommendations about his continued stay. Ben had still refused to see Norma, but he agreed to let his progress be shared with her.

She sat on the bed next to me to put on her stockings. Thigh highs with a garter belt. I was about to make another remark about her suddenly awesome lingerie when she said, "I met Ben's boyfriend."

This threw me. "I didn't realize he was seeing anyone." It was the one thing Ben was usually open about—his sex life. He always told me who his latest bang was, usually someone he hooked up with on Grindr. Where I had shut myself off from sex, Ben had thrown himself into it, both of us for the same reason—no interest in interpersonal connection.

"I didn't either. They hadn't been together long, and I guess Ben tried to push him away before he took the pills. The guy—Eric—is sticking around, though. Says he's here for the duration. I think he's good people. I feel better about leaving Ben with someone who loves him." Norma attached one garter and began on the other stocking.

I stretched my legs out behind me and propped my face up with my hands. "Hmm."

"What's that mean?"

"I don't know. I'm just not sure that Ben will ever really settle down." Just like I would never settle down. That notion had been beaten out of us. *Love's a fairytale*, our father would tell us. *You think you're going to grow up and live happily ever after? That's a fucking myth.*

Sure, I'd learned that my dad didn't have the secrets to anything, let alone how to live happily, but he'd certainly taught us well about love by his relationship with us. We'd loved him. He'd hurt us. He was right—love was a fairytale. One I knew that Ben did not believe in. "Hope this Eric guy doesn't get burned."

Norma stood up and scowled. "Right now Ben isn't in any position to burn anyone, Gwen. And I think you're wrong. I think Ben is very much ready to settle down, and that thought spooked him. That's what I think led to his attempt."

I didn't agree. Also, it was surreal to be scolded by my sister when she looked like a pin-up doll.

And here we were again on the verge of an argument. "Maybe."

But since I was never really good at making peace, I added, "Mostly it was Dad's upcoming release."

"That too," she agreed. Kudos to Norma for being the bigger person.

She disappeared into her walk-in closet. While she was gone, I kicked myself for being so combative. It wasn't very nice in general but especially under the circumstances. Norma had dealt with an emotional issue, returned home late on a Sunday, and was up at the crack of dawn for work. I needed to show her more compassion.

Besides, I had something I wanted to tell her. It was maybe not fitting considering our conversation topics so far that morning, yet I was suddenly very eager to share. I walked over to the closet door and leaned against the frame. "I took your advice."

"About?" Norma tucked her sleeveless black blouse into her gray suit skirt.

"I loosened up. Or I'm trying to." Except with the way I was nervously biting my lip, I probably didn't look very loosened.

Her face wrinkled as she tried to figure out what I was talking about. Then her eyes widened when she remembered. "You got laid?"

"You don't have to sound so surprised."

"But I *am* surprised. You haven't been interested in getting laid in years." She was right but she didn't have to remind me.

I rolled my eyes, but I couldn't stop the smile that played on my lips. "I guess I probably had everyone convinced I was secretly a nun."

"Not a nun. Your mouth is too foul." She grabbed her suit jacket from the hanger then started out of the closet. "Walk with me while I pour my coffee. Tell me all about him."

"He's just a guy. And it's only happened once. Well, twice." I tagged behind Norma, feeling very much like the little sister who was spilling her guts about her latest crush. While I didn't want her to get the wrong idea about JC, I couldn't *not* tell her about him now. And I still wanted to tell her. Wrong impression or not.

"What's his name?" Norma set her jacket on the counter, pulled a travel mug down from the cupboard and poured half the pot in before asking, "Want some?"

"No, thanks. I'm about ready to go to bed. And his name's JC." I realized as I said it that she'd probably ask me what JC stood for next. Or what his last name was. Dammit, I hadn't really thought this through. "But that's all. I'm not telling you anything else about him."

"Not sure if it's serious yet?" She leaned her backside against the sink and took a sip from her mug.

"It's not." Frankly, I was surprised that she would think I'd ever be serious. She knew I was anti-relationships. I'd always thought she understood that, but there were the Ben comments she made earlier and now this.

Obviously I needed to remind her of my position on the matter. "He's not a boyfriend. He's an…arrangement."

"Tell me more." Despite her skeptical frown, she seemed genuinely interested.

"We're meeting up on Wednesday nights to *spend time together*." I blushed at the thought of the last time we'd spent together.

Norma put her mug down, her eyes bright. "I'm guessing that's code for 'have wild monkey sex all night long?'"

She seemed like a teenager in that moment. Enthusiastic and ready for details and not my thirty-five-year-old surrogate mother.

For some reason, it embarrassed me more. "Something like that," I said, playing the whole thing down. "That means you'll have to watch *Law and Order* without me." It was her show anyway. I was more than happy to miss it.

"Fine. I'll DVR it for you. But I'm not done asking about JC." God, she was practically giddy for me. "I'm all fine with sex for sex's sake, but you don't think that something more could happen between you?"

The idea felt like a spider crawling on my skin. I shook it off with a visible shiver. "No. Oh, no. I'm not looking for that. You know that."

She shrugged and her tone suddenly got serious. "No one's ever looking for it when it hits them."

"Well, if it hits me, I'll hit it right back. Whatever it is." I shivered again and not just for dramatic effect. The notion was *that* disturbing.

"Whatever it is?" Norma's whole demeanor seemed offended. "It's love, Gwen. Don't you want to fall in love?"

"What's that?" I wasn't harsh, but I was resolute. "No, seriously. Fall in love? There's no falling that I know of. I love you, Norma. I love Ben. I love what I remember of Mom. In some weird obligated-by-blood way I love Dad, even. That's about all the love I need. It's about all I can handle too."

"Gwen…" She looked at me with what seemed like pity. Then she sighed and I *knew* it was pity. "The more you love and the more you are loved, the more strength you have to handle everything else. You know that, right?"

"Eh. I'm not so sure the proportion of pain to reward works out in love's favor."

"Oh, honey. You're going to end up alone with that attitude."

"Never. I have you, sissy." I put my arms around her waist and clutched onto her dramatically. This was easier than a real hug—it gave the pretense of being insincere, yet it was still a way to get the reassurance I craved.

She ran her hand through my hair, soothingly, like she used to do when I was sick. "You can't always rely on me to be your companion, Gwen. I want more than this. I need more than just sitting around watching shows together."

I had two choices—I could be hurt by her words, or I could accept that she wanted different things from life than I did and realize it had nothing to do with me.

At another time, I might have played the offended card. Right now, our family still felt too fragile. So I said the thing I knew she wanted to hear. "I know. And you'll have it." Maybe not with Hudson Pierce, like she wanted it, but she'd find someone.

When I thought about that, it scared me. Partly because I didn't want to disrupt the status quo. Didn't want to be without her in my daily life. But also because after the last few days, the idea of a guy in my life didn't seem quite as unappealing as it once did.

And I had no business thinking those kinds of thoughts. Especially when I'd promised JC I wouldn't get attached.

It's just sex, I reminded myself. Sex stirs hormones, hormones think they're emotions. That's all. It wasn't like the real emotions I had for my siblings. That I had for Norma.

I couldn't shake the feeling, however, that things were changing between us. Couldn't shake the feeling that at least one of us was slipping away toward something else.

• • •

I barely slept on Wednesday, too nervous about seeing JC again. He'd pushed me at our last encounter, and I had a feeling that was only the tip of the iceberg. While I kept thinking that we were only going to be about getting off, he seemed to be serious about the notion that he could help me loosen up. And so far, he'd been right. Orgasms in general were relaxing, but the methods he'd used to administrate my last one had left me relaxed well beyond when the hormonal effect had worn off.

Besides being anxious, I was eager. I had to force myself to not speed through my shower. Thankfully, the acts of regular feminine upkeep delayed me a bit. Still, I arrived at the hotel a whole hour earlier than I was expected, and I debated about hanging out in the bar or going straight up to his room.

I settled on the bar, but after killing thirty minutes and a glass of Merlot to ease my jitters, I changed my mind and headed up.

The apartment was silent when I went in, and dark, so I knew I was alone. I took off my coat and turned to hang it in the closet. There was a note on the door.

> *Gwen,*
>
> *Make yourself comfortable. In other words, get undressed.*
>
> *JC*

I laughed out loud, a response that was as much a sign of nerves as it was a reaction based on humor. *Get undressed.* It was a subtle command and such a naughty way to expect to be greeted. My hand trembled at the hem of my sweater. The idea of being naked in his hotel room, even without him there yet, brought on a new flurry of jitters. I left my clothing on.

Not that I wouldn't do it. Just…I needed a moment to warm up to it.

Since I still had time before I was supposed to arrive, I took a few minutes to check out the rest of the suite. I'd been in the bathroom on my last visit but not beyond that. After our session on the couch, he'd had to leave to catch another flight to L.A. and the bedroom was left for another occasion.

I went in there now finding nothing remarkable. A king-size bed. Two nightstands. A dresser. An armchair. I peeked in a closet and found it full of clothes—*his* clothes. An unexpected giddiness came across me, and I had a strange desire to bury my face in them, see if they smelled of him. But that was creepy, so I quickly shut the door.

I wondered briefly if women's clothing had ever hung there. Wondered, if I searched his drawers, would I find traces of past lovers? How would I feel if I did? Surely it didn't matter who he'd hooked up with before if I was the one he was hooking up with now.

But thinking about it gave me a different kind of anxiety. It brought on a feeling of possessiveness that I was unaccustomed to. I didn't like it.

I wasn't a snoop, anyway. His stuff was his stuff. Whatever secrets his belongings held about him, they were theirs to keep. Just like how we didn't tell each other our full names. How we didn't share our ages or our personal history. It was all information and details that, when shared, bound people together. And that wasn't what either of us were looking for.

So I made my way back to the living room without looking any further.

JC walked in about three seconds after I returned. My pulse kicked up immediately, and my breathing hitched. As if I were Pavlov's dog. Just his presence made me excited and aroused.

And happy. There was that too. And there were very few times in my life that I let myself feel that. Here, with him, I didn't even think about giving myself permission. I just did. I just was. Happy.

He already had his coat off, and he hung it in the closet while he eyed me with a narrowed stare. "You're still dressed."

"I just got here." Even in my defensiveness, I grinned.

The look he gave me made me think he knew I was fibbing. It still wasn't seven, so he had no reason to think I'd be here so early. Had he seen me come up? Had he been in the lobby somewhere, watching for me to arrive and then waiting the amount of time he thought it would take for me to follow the instructions he'd left?

The thought gave me an unexpected jolt. I liked that he might have been as anxious for me to arrive as I was. I didn't like that I liked it.

If he really doubted me, he didn't contradict me. "Then I'll cut you a break and let you remove your clothes yourself."

I stifled a nervous giggle. "As opposed to?"

"Me ripping them off."

Another comment that was so naughty and unexpected. Was it strange that I almost preferred that than undressing willingly?

A satisfied smirk played on JC's face. "Don't worry, my plan will still be good. Strip."

I couldn't argue with the soothing authority in his voice. I bent to unzip a boot when he stopped me. "Not there. Over by the window."

I didn't move immediately. I was not an exhibitionist in any way, and parading naked in front of others was never something I'd feel comfortable with. No matter how freeing it might feel.

Except, I trusted JC. Strange, since I didn't know him enough to trust him. Strange, since I never trusted anyone. But, I realized now, that trust was essential in any arrangement I expected to have with him. To give him my control, I had to trust. There also seemed to be a correlation in trusting and relaxing. Letting down my guard went a long way toward relieving tension I didn't even know I carried.

I walked to the window to look out. We were forty-nine floors up, the sun was going down, and the park was across the street. The likelihood of anyone seeing me was slim to none.

"It's pretty private." Goddamn, JC could always read my thoughts. Was I that transparent? "But it doesn't feel private. It feels exposed. Doesn't it?"

I nodded.

"Even if someone happens to look up and think they see a body at the window, they won't be able to tell it's naked. They certainly won't be able to tell it's you."

I wasn't so sure. But, trust.

JC removed his suit jacket and laid it on the back of the couch. "Now. Undress."

There would be no more thinking about it. I handed him the reins, then. I did as he said, first taking off my boots. Then, with shaking hands, I removed my sweater, followed by my jeans.

When I was only in my lingerie, JC inhaled sharply.

I paused my undressing to bask in his appreciation. Silently, I thanked Norma. I didn't own a garter belt, but I did have thigh highs, and the sexy way she'd looked the other morning wearing hers had inspired me to wear my own under my pants. I'd debated it at first, unsure if my thoughtful preparation would give the wrong message. I still hadn't been sure when I'd left the apartment with them on.

JC's reaction now made me glad I'd chosen as I had, even if he only saw me in them for a second. The rising and falling of my chest grew more pronounced as my excitement—and my confidence—flourished. It was exhilarating to be able to arouse someone else so easily, in turn, inciting me.

I took off my bra next, watching his eyes spark as my breasts tumbled free. Then I removed my panties. When I got to my stockings, I paused. "Should I leave these?"

His *yes* was more of a hiss than an actual word.

I was very glad for my decision indeed. Naked now, except for the hose, I stood proudly for him, my back exposed to the city behind me.

JC loosened his tie. Slowly, but with more assurance than I'd had, he began unbuttoning his shirt. God, it was erotic to watch him undress. To watch him peel away the layers that the rest of the world saw, revealing the parts of him he only showed to me. Provocative on so many levels.

I pressed my thighs together to try and relieve the growing ache.

His smile told me he knew the effect he had on me. He removed his shirt and laid it on the couch and began working on his belt buckle, his eyes never leaving me. "You're so turned on," he said with not an ounce of question. It was fact. He *knew* I was turned on. "Touch yourself."

I hesitated, waffling between giving him complete control and letting him know what I wanted. He'd been adamant that I tell him before. And I wanted to be quick to learn his lessons, unlike the insipid heroines of Norma's bodice ripper novels she thought she read in secret.

So I spoke up. "JC, I don't want to do that this time." I would do it again. It had been amazing, and if he squashed down my request, I'd give in willingly. But I needed to let him know what I was thinking first.

His eyes widened, and with his belt now in his hand, a bolt of paralyzing fear ran through me. After years of having one slapped across my back, a man with a belt would always cause a stirring of trepidation. This moment was worse, especially since I'd just been contrary. And I was naked, which made me feel more vulnerable than usual.

He seemed to sense my fear. "Hey, Gwen. Relax." He dropped the belt, and his eyes followed mine as I watched where it landed on the floor. His brow wrinkled in confusion, and then, as if he understood, he kicked it away from him.

I was afraid he'd ask, but he didn't, and I was grateful.

"Thank you, for telling me what you want. Or don't want." He toed his shoes off as he spoke. Then bent to pull off his socks. "You don't have anything to worry about. I won't hurt you and this won't be like last week. You'll still get off. But this time, I'm going to be inside you when it happens."

Whatever fear there had been in me a moment before vanished at his sensual promise.

He unzipped his pants and pushed them to the floor. "So I suggest you touch yourself. You need to get yourself wet because I'm not planning on staying in control this time. Once my hands are on you, you better be ready to fuck."

Moisture pooled between my legs at his words. I was ready to fuck now. I had been since the minute he walked in the door and cast his possessive gaze over my body. So when I pinched a nipple between my fingers and ran my other hand between my legs, I wasn't priming myself for him.

I was showing him that I was already primed.

JC groaned. He rubbed his hand over his crotch, and I watched as his semi hardened. "You really are breathtaking, Gwen. You have no idea, do you?"

I shook my head. I hadn't ever cared to be breathtaking until I was with him. Now, not only did I *want* him to be turned on by me, I also felt that he *was* turned on by me. Felt like I was that exciting. Felt like I was that beautiful.

"It's part of what makes you so amazing to look at. Because you're so unaware." He stripped off his boxer briefs, and my mouth instantly watered at his impressive erection. I couldn't take my eyes off it. It was big and thick and exquisite in a way I never thought a penis could be.

Not a penis—a cock. Penis was a term that turned me off and made me cringe. But nothing about JC's cock did that to me. It made me feel just the opposite. Turned me on ferociously. Made me want to open up and invite it in.

It drew me so magnetically that I started to step toward him.

Then JC directed me otherwise. "Turn around, Gwen. Press your body against the glass and let the city see how beautiful you are."

My fascination with his cock faded as my unease with the window returned. Like he'd said before, probably no one would see me, but it *felt* like they could. And now that it was about to happen, the idea of being watched was actually more thrilling than I'd first thought.

I spun in and pressed up against the window, the cold glass a stark contrast to my heated skin. I continued to touch myself, playing with my clit in earnest. I spread my legs, wanting him to have a better view of what I was doing.

Was that unlike me? Yes. Was it dirty and naughty and completely empowering? Yes, yes, and yes. I reveled in the naughtiness. I reveled in the power.

"Tell me, Gwen." JC's voice was tight and I pictured him stroking himself behind me as he spoke. "Did you wear those stockings for me?"

I bit my lip as I considered. I'd thought I'd worn them for *me*. They were part of my confidence-building undergarment ensemble to make me feel more seductive than I was.

But now, when he asked, I knew that I had worn them just as much for him.

I didn't answer fast enough, and he asked again. "Did you dress this evening with me in mind? Did you put each stocking on, thinking about how I'd later roll them down your thighs? They seem quite versatile. The things I could do with those—tie you up. Bind you. Would you like that? Tell me the truth."

I'd had a boyfriend once who'd tried to tie my hands. With a belt. I hadn't liked it at all, but now I thought it was perhaps the material he'd used, because my answer in this moment was entirely different. "Yes."

"Yes, what?"

The satisfaction in his tone and the fact that I was facing away from him made it easier for me to admit more. "Yes, all of it." My sentences broke as I pushed to speak through the growing tension in my belly brought on by the ministrations of my hand. "Yes…I'd like it. Yes, I wore them…for you…so you'd look at me like you're looking at me now."

I could still feel his gaze on me. Then I realized, if I looked up at the window, I could see him in the reflection. See him looking at me. I met his eyes there. "I wore them because I wanted you to think I was sexy."

He didn't tell me that he was coming for me, but I saw him as he did. And, as he'd promised, the minute he put his hands on me—one gripped my hip, the other one snaked around to grab my breast—he also put his cock inside me.

He thrust in me with such force, I cried out. I cried out again as he pulled back slowly, letting me feel every inch of his length as he drew back to his tip.

"You're the most goddamned sexy thing I've seen in years, Gwen," he said at my ear. "With or without the stockings. But, fuck…" He jabbed in again then held himself still. "You don't know what it does to me to hear that you thought about me while you were dressing. It makes me so hard. Can you feel how hard it makes me?"

His cock twitched inside me, and I swear it grew thicker, pushing against my walls even though he was motionless.

"I do feel you," I gasped. "You're so hard."

"I am," he agreed. "So hard."

He began to move then, in rhythm, but slowly. He leaned his forehead against the back of my head, and I could tell he was watching where we were joined. Watching his cock as he pushed in and out of my swollen pussy.

Knowing what he was looking at drove my excitement further. Combined with the feeling of being watched by the entirety of Central Park, I knew I wouldn't last much longer. I braced one hand against the window and reached my other hand through my legs to graze his balls as he thrust inside of me.

"That's good, Gwen. I like that."

I continued my play, alternating my attention from my clit to his balls. Then his tempo picked up and he moved both his hands to grip my hips. I needed both mine on the window now to brace myself. Our bodies slapped together as he pounded into me.

"Tell me how you feel, Gwen." When I couldn't formulate words, he prompted me. "Do you feel good?"

"Yes."

"Does my cock make you feel good?"

"Mmm...yes."

He had to know how good he made me feel; I was clenching around him, my body ready to explode with pleasure. He liked to hear it—I'd learned that from him in our short time together—but also, as he questioned me this time, I heard something else hiding under his words. He didn't just like it; he needed it. As though he, with all his command and confidence, needed reassurance. As if he longed for an intimate connection that transcended touch and entered into thought and feeling. As if what he really meant to ask wasn't *does my cock make you feel good*, but *do I make you feel good?*

He did. He did make me feel good, and I suspected even as my orgasm gathered and grew, that the good he made me feel also went beyond the physical. So when my climax ripped through me, stiffening my limbs and stealing my breath, I answered him. Answered his true question, the one he couldn't really ask. "Yes...Yes...Oh my God, yes."

He shoved into me harder, deeper, lifting me to my toes as he chased his release. The lamplights in the now completely dark park below streaked across my vision as his invigorated efforts spurred another orgasm. JC followed right after, groaning as he spilled into me. He collapsed over my back, yet somehow his hands now wrapped around my waist were the only things keeping me from falling to the ground. I was wasted in bliss. My strength was gone, and all that existed was his strength in its place.

I was still blinded and panting when he spun me around to face him minutes later. He studied me as he stroked the hair from my face. Then, he kissed me. Sweetly. Luxuriously.

Yet, there was a hint of hesitation to this intimacy. A distinct taste of holding back. There were secrets on his tongue that went beyond his full name and birthdate.

For the first time it occurred to me that I wasn't the only one of the two of us using sex as an escape. Only, what exactly it was that JC was escaping from, I had no idea.

Chapter Nine

Eventually we discovered the bed.

After we did, we stayed there all night. The next Wednesday when I arrived, he was there waiting for me, and with hardly any words at all, we headed straight to the bedroom. There wasn't any place I'd rather be. I'd never had sex like I did with JC—primal and heated and unrestrained. He pushed me to make noise, to be heard, to free my voice. He continued to question me, continued to beg for reassurance in his subtext.

I gave him what he asked for. I answered, I cried out. He even made me scream once or twice. After only a handful of nights, I knew him in ways I'd never known another person. Knew his body, knew what turned him on and off. Knew when he wanted me to beg. Knew when he wanted me to bend.

And I still didn't have the slightest clue what the initials JC stood for.

Overall, our arrangement was working out pretty well. Though I was wrong about one thing—I did fall asleep. Not the first night we spent together, but the next. It was February, and I was fighting a cold. Plus, I was still worrying about Ben, who seemed better from the reports that we received, but still wouldn't talk to us.

Those were my excuses for nodding off, but truthfully, JC had worn me out. He'd fucked me until we were hungry and needed to order room service. Then, after we'd finished eating, he'd fucked me until I slipped into sweet oblivion.

When I woke, I found my body exquisitely sore and the bed very much empty.

I waffled, trying to decide if I really wanted to get up and look for him or if the warmth of the covers was too enticing to move. His voice drifted in from the living room, and my ears perked up. But he was too quiet to be talking to me, so I decided he must be on the phone. I glanced at the nightstand clock—it was almost three. Was he ordering more food?

Then I noticed his tone had an edge to it that I'd never witnessed in my carefree lover. A mixture of curiosity and concern pulled me to investigate.

Still naked, I crept out of the bedroom, not wanting to disturb him, and stood back at the mouth of the room. He'd thrown on his boxer briefs and was pacing the room, his ear pressed against his cell. I could hear the faint buzz of the other person on the line—a man—who was doing most of the talking. Occasionally, JC would interject with an "Uh-huh." Even in those short syllables his irritation was evident.

After a few seconds, he stopped suddenly and said, "Yeah, I'm pissed." It sounded like the response to a question. Something like, *Are you mad?* "And no, it's not because you called me at three in the fucking morning, though that isn't helping."

I knew I shouldn't be listening. Despite my guilt, I couldn't move. I was frozen—captivated by this glimpse into JC's other world. The world that was his real world and had nothing to do with me.

The other guy said something to which JC responded, "People don't just vanish without a trace. And I'm paying you a shitload to keep an eye on him."

A chill ran through me. Where I could usually separate myself from interest in JC, I suddenly was very intrigued. Who was he paying? What was so important to disturb JC in the middle of the night? Who was JC watching and why?

The questions maybe should have made me fearful of the man I'd been sharing a bed with once a week, but oddly they didn't. Whatever JC was involved in, it had nothing to do with me. But now I had a glimpse of the reasons he needed to escape from his life. The reasons he came looking for me.

Most of all, I could tell he was upset. And I had an overwhelming desire to make it better.

"Listen," he said into the receiver now, his voice eerily low and controlled. "I don't want to hear any more excuses. Whether there's enough to hold anything against him means squat if the guy is MIA. Either you track down the motherfucker or I'll find someone who can."

He didn't bother pushing the button to end the call, but the call was over. For a moment, I thought he was going to throw his cell. Instead he swept an arm across the desk and knocked the ceramic lamp and a clear vase with flowers to the ground, where both shattered.

I jerked in surprise.

That was when he noticed me.

His eyes met mine, his hands in tight balls at his hips, his chest rising and falling as he tried to get control of his anger. Fortunately, it didn't appear as if any of his rage was directed at me.

The light on the floor flickered on and off. On again. Then off for good. I took a step into the dark room, now only lit by what came through the windows. "Wanna talk about it?"

He shook his head.

"Do you want me to leave?" I didn't want to go. I wanted to tug him back into the haven of *our* bed and help him forget whatever was bothering him. Just like all the times he'd done that for me.

But that wasn't what we were supposed to be for each other. We weren't comfort—we were distractions. And if a distraction wasn't what he needed right now, I would respect that.

The lamp on the floor flickered back on suddenly. JC said nothing, just continued to stare at me, his eyes wild in the blast of light.

He suddenly looked as sad as he was angry. As tormented as he was frustrated. Again, I had the urge to soothe him. It pulled at me from deep in my chest, much higher than the region of my body that feelings regarding JC usually originated.

It unnerved me more than anything else I'd seen or heard in the last few minutes. And with JC's continued silence, I made the decision myself. "I'll go. Just give me a minute to—"

"I have another idea," he said, cutting me off. He stepped over the lamp and found the jeans he'd abandoned on the floor earlier in the evening. "Get your bra and panties on. And grab one of the hotel robes from the bathroom."

"Okay. Why?"

"We're going on a little field trip."

When I came back from dressing, JC had put his jeans on but was still shirtless. It was a good look on him—his boxers peeking out, the deep lines at his hips that disappeared beneath his pants, the trail of light hair that dusted his perfectly taut abdomen. He wasn't wearing shoes, so I didn't bother with any either.

Without a word, he opened the front door and led me out. We often spent time with each other without speaking, but the silence between us was never tight and tense as it was now. I wasn't sure he really wanted me with him. I wasn't sure that I even *was* with him. I walked right next to him. I matched his stride. But not once did he look at me. We could have been strangers who happened to be going down a hall together.

In many ways, that's exactly what we were—strangers.

I should have gone home. What was I even doing with this guy in the first place? I didn't want to be wrapped up in his drama, which he obviously had, but I also didn't like being purposefully left out of it.

Usually, he made me feel wanted. Right now, I didn't feel that in the least. But what I did feel—the reason I followed him despite the tension radiating off his body—was needed. He needed me. Maybe only for tonight, maybe only for this hour. But I knew that sure as I knew anything.

We took the elevators down but got off on the meeting rooms level. The corridor was empty, but I still felt strange walking around the hotel half-dressed. I wrapped my robe tighter around myself and read the signs as we passed by—*Salons A&B, The Sutton Room, The Boardroom*. We went through another set of doors and turned left into a pre-function room. At the Madison Suite, he stopped.

JC tried the door handle. It didn't turn. Then he pulled his hotel keycard from his back pocket and slid it in the seam of the door.

My entire body went rigid. "What are you doing?"

"A trick. This door has a faulty lock so if you—" There was a click, and this time the knob turned. "There we go. Come on." He opened the door and stepped aside for me to walk in.

Tentatively, I stepped inside. JC flicked one of the switches on the wall and a single row of lights illuminated enough of the room that I could now see. It was a fairly small room with nothing much in it except for a baby grand piano on the far wall.

I heard the click of the door behind me and turned to see JC had shut us in. My heart was pounding, my palms sweaty. "Did we just break into a meeting room at the Four Seasons?"

He shrugged as he walked past me, heading toward the piano. "I wouldn't call it breaking in exactly. Nothing got broken that wasn't already broken."

My pulse quickened. "JC!"

"What?"

"We aren't supposed to be here!" If it was possible to yell and whisper at the same time, that's what I was doing.

JC, however, talked at a normal volume. "Relax. It's fine."

Relax. As if. I was a rule follower. And this? This was definitely breaking the rules.

JC had reached the piano now. He pulled out the bench to sit on it then he looked back at me. For the first time since I'd found him on his mysterious phone call, he really *looked* at me. The way he usually did. With lust, with desire. With camaraderie. With intimacy. "Come on," he coaxed. "Trust me."

Always with the *trust me*. He had me with those words.

I crossed the room to him without another question. At the piano, I leaned into the curve and tried to settle my nerves by rationalizing the situation. Nothing was going to happen. No one was going to discover us. And if they did, what kind of trouble would we get in? JC was a valued client. He'd get a slap on the wrist. That's all.

I managed to calm myself. Until JC pushed back the lid over the keyboard and played a few notes on the high end. "Oh my God, what are you doing? Someone will hear you."

I detested how I sounded like a complete stick-in-the-mud. It wouldn't have surprised me if JC were more than a little irritated with me about it.

He met my eyes, and I braced myself for his chiding. Instead, he gave a reassuring smile. "Gwen. Calm down. I've done this before. It's fine. The walls in here are pretty thick. They're designed to keep noise in. And if anyone does hear, they never complain. People like the sound of a faint piano in the background."

He was so confident, so sure of himself. "You have permission to be here, don't you?" I asked. "You're trying to push my boundaries."

"No. I don't. I just want to play the piano. So sit down and shush so I can."

It wasn't his commanding tone that convinced me. It was the hidden plea underneath. I heard the need in his words. It echoed the unspoken need that kept me with him. Whatever had upset him from the phone call, this was how he needed to deal with it. This was his coping mechanism.

And for whatever reason, he needed to share it with me.

It shut me up. "Okay."

I sat down on the ground and hugged my knees to my chest as JC started to run his fingers up and down the keyboard. Basic scales, but they were rhythmic and smooth and I suspected he had good technique despite not having a clue about what good technique was.

"I didn't know you played." I didn't know anything about him. Why this specific thing I didn't know was surprising was beyond me.

JC shrugged, even as his hands ran meticulously up and down again and again. One scale after another. "Rich parents who liked to occupy their child so they didn't have to spend time with him."

His response had been unexpected. He'd never shared anything about himself. I felt like a child clinging on to a beloved kite string in a windstorm the way I clung to this tidbit of information.

I wanted more of it. Tentatively, I pushed him. "They gave you lessons so they could ignore you?"

"*Shh,*" he said. But he nodded.

I might have said more, but his scales transitioned then into something familiar. A melody I knew inside and out. The piece was haunting and stirring and reflected so much from my past that it was hard to put it in context in the present. I closed my eyes and let the dark notes fall over me. Let them drown me in memories.

Her. Young. Happy. I could still picture her doing dishes while the cheap tape recorder played a collection of her favorites. It was her most cherished possession. Her only possession.

I hadn't listened to the music in a long time now, but for a while, after her death, I listened to it all the time. Playing it until the tape had worn and long stretches of silence interrupted what had been her favorite sounds.

This song was equally bitter and sweet. Hearing it hurt as much as it healed. And JC, playing it now—I recognized it was the same for him. The way his back bent over the keys, the way his dynamics grew and subsided organically. He *felt* as he played. He felt deeply.

By the time he'd finished, I'd forgotten my anxiety about our whereabouts. He too, seemed lighter. His shoulders relaxed and the tension about him was almost gone. He took his hands off the keys and placed them into his lap.

He didn't look at me for several seconds, for which I was glad. He'd played brilliantly. He was obviously a very skilled musician. And I needed the time to focus on those aspects of his performance instead of what the piece had done to me.

Finally, when he snuck a glance my way, I was ready. "That was stunning, JC. Truly."

He nodded once, and I realized he was uncomfortable with praise. So strange. He deserved so much praise.

But if that wasn't what he wanted, I'd have to connect in another way. I swallowed the lump in my throat. "Philip Glass." Specifically *Metamorphosis II*. I hadn't known the names of the pieces when she played them, but I'd learned them when I bought a CD for Norma as a Christmas gift years later.

His head turned to me, his eyes surprised and pleased. "Very good. Not many people can identify him."

There weren't any solo piano pieces I could identify *except* Philip Glass. "My mother loved all his music. She was obsessed."

"Was?"

I didn't usually answer questions about my mother. But he'd given me a piece of his past when he'd mentioned his parents. It seemed only fair to return with a piece of my own. "She died when I was seven."

"Died how?"

"Complications due to pneumonia." I didn't tell him that the main complication was that she'd had her lungs kicked in by my father when he was on a tirade. It wasn't mentioned on her medical chart either. No one looked into it. No one asked. It was the norm in the area I lived in. The poorest hospitals didn't often spend much time on the cases of patients who couldn't pay for their care.

JC didn't press. I was surprised he'd asked for any information at all. The funny thing was that, now that I'd started talking, I actually wanted to keep on talking. I never talked about the past. But now, if he asked, I would have told him everything.

But he didn't ask. So I didn't tell. I moved up to the bench to sit beside him. "Play me something else."

His hands perched on the keys, but he didn't play yet. "More Philip Glass?"

Since we weren't going to talk about her, I didn't want to think about her anymore either. "No. Anything but that."

I recognized the piece he performed next but couldn't name the composer. It had the same haunting, hollow feeling of the Glass piece. It wasn't as simple—his hands danced nimbly across the notes, his arms stretching past me to reach the higher end of the instrument.

He played beautifully. Exquisitely. Incredibly. I was lost in the sound. Lost in the movement. It occurred to me he was telling me more about himself without words during the course of playing that song than he had the entire time I'd known him.

When he finished with the movement, he shut the cover to the piano and stood up.

I followed him to a standing position. "Show's over, I guess."

"Yeah. Show's over." He stepped away from the bench and turned away from me as he shook out his hands, and I wondered what it was that he was hiding from me. What he didn't want me to see on his face.

It wasn't my place to pry. But maybe he wanted me to ask, just as I'd wanted him to ask. I opened my mouth to do that, not quite sure what I'd say, when I heard a noise coming from the far side of the meeting room. Or more accurately, on the other side of the wall on the far side of the room.

JC cocked his head. "It's the cleaning crew," he said. "They vacuum on Thursdays for the weekend."

"That's our cue to go."

I started toward the door, but when I turned back to see if JC was following, I found he hadn't moved. "Come on. Let's get out of here before we're caught."

He took a step in my direction, his head cocked. "I don't think so."

"What? You're joking. We have to go." I laughed, but it was a nervous laugh. He was teasing me. I was sure of it. And I didn't like to be teased.

He met my giggle with a somber expression. "I think, Gwen, that this is a perfect opportunity to try something else. Push your boundaries, as you said earlier."

"JC, I'm serious." But the shiver that ran through me was as much excited as scared.

"So am I. Come here."

I went to him because, hell, that's what I did. I came when I was called. When I was close enough, he reached out, wrapped his hands in my robe and tugged me up against him. Hovering his mouth above mine, he whispered, "How quiet can you be?"

After he'd taught me to be loud? "Not that quiet," I whispered back. "Besides, if you're suggesting what I think you're suggesting, I'm not interested."

"I haven't suggested anything yet. And I think that you're wrong. I think you'll be very interested." He licked my lower lip, teasing me with his tongue.

Suddenly, he drew back and picked me up. He carried me over to the piano and set me down on the closed lid. "Lean back," he said, at the same time pushing me gently until I lay flat on the piano. The instrument was solid and cold, even through my robe. It was a stark contrast to my jittery nerves and the heat that pulsed through my veins. I knew where this was going. I knew I'd soon be stripped and fondled. I knew that we could be caught.

Yet, I did nothing to stop him.

I didn't protest as he pulled my panties down and dropped them on the bench behind him. I let him pull me forward so my ass was directly at the edge of the instrument. When he bent my legs to prop my feet on either side of me, I didn't fight. I was opened wide for him, my pussy exposed. And I did nothing to cover myself.

JC sat on the bench. I could feel his scorching gaze on my sex. "Perfect height," he said, his tone coarse and strained.

The vacuum started up in the next room, reminding me we weren't alone. I panicked and sat up enough to prop myself on my elbows.

"No, Gwen. Lay still." His voice was hot and chocolaty. It melted over my apprehension, covering it in sweet luxury that made it almost impossible to remember what I'd been concerned about to begin with.

Almost.

I didn't lie back down, but I stopped trying to get up.

"They make you nervous." JC nodded toward the cleaning crew. Then he trailed a finger down the seam of my sex. "But let me worry about them. Let me worry about you."

"And what will I worry about?"

"You'll worry about trying not to scream." He bent forward and swiped his tongue across my clit.

I bit my lip trying not to cry out.

Even with all the nights we'd spent together, JC had never once gone down on me. He'd mentioned it that first day in the hotel room, said that one day he'd suck me off, but after that, he seemed to lose interest. It was the same with blowjobs. Once, when I'd moved to put his cock in my mouth, he'd subtly directed me elsewhere. I'd gotten the hint. Oral was out, for whatever reason. I'd assumed it was too intimate. Or maybe it just wasn't his thing.

Tonight, he'd changed his mind. Tonight, he seemed to want to make due on his promise.

He swirled his tongue again around my nub, massaging it with light strokes followed by a long, lush lick. He repeated his pattern, his tongue seeming to move in the opposite direction—I couldn't be sure. I was too consumed with how good he was making me feel to really be able to discern.

Besides being overwhelmed by the physical sensation, I was also lost in the visual one. I was enrapt. Watching him like this, with his head between my legs, his eyes glued to mine as he cherished my most private parts with his tongue—it was the sexiest thing I'd ever seen.

He glided his tongue down farther this time, playing at my entrance. "Do you like watching?" He grazed his teeth across my sensitive flesh.

"Yes," I said on an inhale.

"I've been saving this, did you know?"

I shook my head. I had no words.

"I've wanted to please you like this for so long." He was so close to my cunt, I could feel his breath skate across my moist flesh. "Wanted to suck on you and lick you. Wanted to taste you. Do you know why?"

"Why?" I wanted to know if he'd confirm my silent guess. But I also wanted him to stop talking altogether and return to what he'd been doing.

"Because you've never asked. I told you I wanted you to ask."

Oh. That. He had said that, hadn't he? Maybe I was the one who had avoided it because of the intimacy level.

"But now I can't wait any longer. So I'm giving you a pass."

I started to say thank you, but was distracted by another lick. Then he spread my folds with his fingers and sucked at my clit.

Fuck, it felt insane. So fucking good. Like a fire had been set directly to my nerve center and now I was aflame.

I fell back on the piano, unable to stay up any longer. I gasped and moaned and wriggled. When I tried to push back, to get some relief from the overwhelming sensation of pleasure, he gripped my hips and held me closer. A storm gathered underneath his lips. I grew wetter with each pass of his tongue and the muscles of my thighs tightened as my climax made its impending arrival known.

My foot slipped off the piano, and JC threw it over his shoulder. He drew back to speak again, but this time he replaced his mouth with the expert attention of his thumb. "With as vocal as you've become while being fucked, I'm sure this is very hard for you right now." He spoke evenly and controlled, the exact opposite of how I felt. "But now that you have to work to be quiet, you're going to be surprised at how amazing it's going to feel when you come."

It *was* hard. I was already struggling with it, my moans having turned into soft, jagged cries.

"If you need to," he suggested as a finger now dipped lower to circle my rim, "bite down on these." He dangled my panties in the air. Still holding my underwear up, he bent back down to suck on my, clit simultaneously plunging several fingers inside of me.

I snatched the panties from his grip and stuffed them into my mouth to stifle my scream.

I was vaguely aware of the vacuum in the next room turning off. But it was background noise. Irrelevant. The only thing that mattered was the growing ball of tension inside of me. It tightened as JC stroked and licked me. Tightened and stretched until there was nothing for it to do but burst.

My back arched and rose off the piano as the release slammed through my body, shaking my very core, igniting every cell in my being. My jaw clenched around the muzzle in my mouth as my pussy clenched around JC's fingers. I was spinning, dizzy. Overwhelmed.

Even as I came, JC didn't relent. He continued to fuck me with his mouth, with his hand, and while my first climax hadn't quite ended, I could already feel another building. It was too much. I wanted it to end. Wanted to cry out and beg for him to stop.

And I wanted him to never stop. Wanted to die in the exquisite pleasure of this moment. Felt sure that when he let me finish, I'd be reborn as something new and wild and strong.

Stars burst across my vision as my next orgasm took hold.

Then the whole room flooded with light.

It took a second to register what was happening, especially since my head wasn't exactly in a place where thought came easily. But JC made it clear. "Shit. We have to go."

Disoriented, I sat up and, after blinking a few times, realized that the brightness wasn't from my orgasm but from all the lights being turned on. I spun toward the doors we'd come in through. They were open. A woman dressed in the uniform of the hotel's cleaning crew was pushing a vacuum through it. She saw us immediately. "Hey, what's going on over there?"

I didn't look to see if she came after us. I was too busy hopping off the piano and running with JC out the door closest to us. We fumbled blindly through The Boardroom and out into the corridor, where we sprinted to the elevators.

JC pressed the call button repeatedly, as if it would make the doors open any faster, while I kept glancing behind me, sure that we'd been followed.

But the doors opened and we slipped in before anyone came after us. Inside the car, we looked at each other. Then burst into laughter.

"Sorry," I said, when I realized we weren't alone in the car. That was also the moment I realized I had left my panties behind. I tugged my robe tighter around myself and elbowed JC.

He peered over at the couple sharing our ride. Then angled back toward me. He pulled me close—so close that I could feel the ridge of his hard cock through his jeans—and spoke low at my ear. "You were such a good girl. I promise I'll finish you off in the room. In fact, now that I've tasted you, I don't think I'll be able to keep my mouth off you, whether you ask for it or not."

Though his voice was quiet, I felt certain the others could hear him. I didn't care one bit.

I grinned, leaning in to nuzzle his neck. Immediately, he stiffened. I pulled away, puzzled. I'd just let him bring me to climax with his tongue and his lips, yet he couldn't let me caress him? Couldn't handle the intimacy of my hug?

I studied him, looking for an answer, but he turned away, suddenly intrigued by the changing numbers on the elevator panel. When the door opened on our floor, he took my hand and pulled me out behind him without looking at me.

I tried not to let his demeanor disappoint me. It wasn't what we were to each other, I reminded myself. We weren't intimate like that. We weren't personal. I knew what I'd signed up for.

The problem was, I was changing. JC was changing me. Little by little, he'd been tearing down my walls, letting me out.

But his walls stood just as tall and strong as ever.

Chapter Ten

I didn't fall asleep with JC again until more than a month later.

This time it wasn't a little catnap, either. I'd dozed off somewhere around two or three, and when I woke up, the sun was streaming in brightly from the terrace.

I sat up with a panicked feeling similar to sleeping through an alarm. "Oh, shit."

JC bolted upright beside me, his hair messy and eyes seemingly bleary. "What is it?" He'd obviously been sleeping, too, which was almost stranger than me having nodded off. One thing I'd learned in our weeks together—the man hadn't been lying when he said he never slept. Even though he was on a different schedule than me, he always managed to make it through our time together without a hint of tiredness.

I glanced at the clock on the bedside table. Nine-oh-seven. This was the time we usually parted. I'd get dressed, not bothering to shower, then take a cab back to my apartment where I'd fall into bed, exhausted, until it was time to wake for work on Thursday night.

This change in our well-established routine was awkward.

It was also overwhelming. Because despite everything we had done with each other over the last several weeks, waking up together in the morning was at the top of the intimate list. I didn't smell good and my mouth felt gross. It was *too* intimate. JC had trained me well that intimate was not in the contract. I pulled the sheet up over my naked body.

"I'm sorry," I said.

JC rubbed his eyes then stretched his arms over his head while he yawned. "About what?"

God, he still looked delicious in the morning. He could throw on some clothes and walk out of the hotel and look fine.

It pissed me off. Especially since I never woke up well without coffee.

"What are you sorry about?" he asked again, clasping his hands behind his head.

He even smelled good. Musky and manly. Not fair.

"Sleeping," I said with a sigh. "Dammit. I wasted our whole night." I fell back on the bed and covered my eyes with my arm. "And now my schedule's going to be screwed." I was scheduled to be at work at ten that night, and I wouldn't get home until six the next morning. It was going to be a long shift.

Plus, I really did feel bad about wasting our night. I enjoyed our time together way too much to not treasure every minute. And I'd slept through practically four hundred and twenty of those minutes.

Dammit!

I groaned at the lost opportunity as I turned to bury my head in the pillow.

"How did I guess you weren't pleasant in the morning?" JC was as mellow as ever.

"I don't know. Maybe because I'm never very pleasant." The weight of the bed shifted as he got up. I peeked to find him heading to the bathroom, completely confident in his nudity. He kept the door open, which was also too intimate, even though he wasn't visible from my place on the bed. Even though I'd seen and touched his cock plenty of times now.

When he finished, he stood in the doorframe and looked at me. "I don't think that's true." Before I had a chance to form a comeback, he added, "But I'll order coffee if you'd like."

"God, yes."

"I didn't realize it was so easy to elicit that expression from you. I've been doing it wrong."

I chuckled. "You haven't been doing anything wrong. Trust me." Even my aching thigh muscles praised JC's techniques.

He sat next to me on the bed to dial room service. I forced myself to not freak out. It was...nice, I told myself, having him sit so near, chatting about mundane things, doing ordinary tasks that weren't at all related to foreplay or midway-through-play.

But it was also unnerving. Confusing. I didn't know how to react to him. My body was aroused, as it always was when I was near him, yet my desire was background noise rather than the only sound I could hear. The music in the foreground was something new and strange and a little bit wonderful.

JC ordered breakfast along with the coffee then shifted down so he was lying on the bed between the edge and me. He propped his head up with his elbow and brushed my sex-snarled hair out of my face.

Way too intimate.

With as standoffish as he'd always been, why was he letting this cozy morning happen after all these weeks? Was it a test? Or a change of heart? Or was I simply reading things wrong?

"So what will you do for the rest of the day?" he asked. "Stay up?"

I couldn't think about the rest of my day—I could barely figure out what I'd do now. I turned so I was facing the ceiling, which helped me gain a smidgeon of personal space. "Yeah. I guess so."

Honestly, I needed to get up, get dressed and get home. Same as always. I'd figure out what next from there.

But now he'd ordered breakfast…

"Take advantage of your morning and maybe just get a quick nap in before you have to go to work," JC suggested. "Is there anything you were needing to get done?"

No coffee, awkward situation, naked guy next to me—did he really expect me to be able to answer his questions thoughtfully?

Okay, I can do this. I closed my eyes and pinched at the bridge of my nose. So, my day. I'd eat breakfast with him since that's what he expected. Then do something with my morning. Take a nap later. Go to work.

I opened my eyes again. "Actually, that's not a bad idea."

I scooted up so that I was leaning against the headboard and thought out loud. "Tomorrow's Norma's birthday. I was thinking it would be nice to make her breakfast before she goes to work. I should go to the Greenmarket and get some fresh veggies to make her an omelet."

"Who's Norma?"

"My sister." I still hadn't decided what I should give her for a gift. Norma so efficiently took care of herself—it was hard to get her anything she actually wanted.

I'd had one idea that had a low likelihood of coming through. Knowing that any messages I wanted to send to Ben at the hospital had to go through Norma, I'd had to find other methods of reaching him. Fortunately, she'd left his boyfriend's number on the counter. I'd texted him, told him her birthday was coming up, and let him know how great a present it would be for her to hear from Ben.

It was a selfish present. One I wanted for myself as much as I wanted it for my sister.

But since I'd heard nothing from Eric but a confirmation that he'd received my message, it was looking like I needed something else. So I added, "And I need to get her a present of some sort."

He nodded, his eyes narrowed as if deciding something. Finally he said, "Sounds boring. I'll go with you." Then he stood up and went to the dresser.

I sat up with as much shock as when I'd awoken to sunlight. "You will? You just said it was boring."

"If I'm there, it won't be boring. So yes, I'll go."

"You really don't have to." Then, because that might have sounded rude, I corrected myself. "I mean, don't you have to work or get a flight back to L.A.?" Immediately, I worried about how that sounded too. Did it seem like I wanted him not to go? Because it wasn't that. It was just... we'd never done anything together outside of the hotel room, minus the adventure to the piano in the Madison Suite.

He pulled on a pair of boxer briefs before turning back to me. Which was actually a relief. It made the level of intimacy less awkward. "My flight's tonight," he said. "And all I usually do on Thursdays lately is catch up on my sleep."

If I'd known that we could have been catching up together instead of me going home to sleep alone...

Could have been. But not *should* have been. Sleeping apart was best in a non-committed relationship. Also, not spending entire days with each other outside of the bedroom.

He opened another drawer now and pulled out a pair of jeans. "But since I slept all night with you, I'm now free."

Huh. I bit the inside of my lip as I digested his sudden interest in outside-the-hotel-room-togetherness. Would it really be that bad? Marcus and I had been friends beyond our sexual relationship. We'd gone to movies, hung out. And then he'd fallen in love with me.

JC, though...he wasn't the falling in love type. He barely let me in past the outer grounds of his fortress. Which was why it was weird that he wanted to be with me today. Maybe he simply wanted company. Was I overthinking it?

"Would you rather I not go?"

I looked up at JC from the random spot I'd been focusing on while I dazed. That was the real question—did I want him to go with me? The answer was not what I expected. "I'd love to have you. Otherwise, as you said, boring."

"Awesome." His grin alone was worth the decision I'd made. It made my belly flutter, but also higher, my chest warmed.

I smiled back, and for once, it wasn't merely a grin of seduction. Though, I was feeling that too.

"Why don't you jump in the shower? I bet breakfast will be here by the time you're out. I'll grab a shower after."

"O…kay." I'd half-expected to shower together. We hadn't done that yet, but it sure sounded more fun.

JC met me at the side of the bed with the robe. I stood and slipped into it. When I turned around, he tugged me to him.

"I'd suggest we wait for the food then take a shower together," he whispered at my ear, "but you and I both know that if we did that, we'd never get out of here." He nipped my lobe. "So get in there before I tell you not to even bother."

This was more like the JC I knew. Seductive, naughty. Except that normally he'd not care about leaving the room. He wouldn't have even cared if I'd made it to the shower—he'd have pounced on me before I made it two feet toward the bathroom door.

So what was this?

I took the time alone in the shower to regroup. I had only a few choices—I could ask him point blank what was up and probably get brushed off. I could tell him I'd changed my mind and decided to go home after all. Or I could go with the flow and stop questioning it.

In the end, I chose the latter. JC had been teaching me to let loose, after all. Maybe this was just another one of his lessons. If he wasn't going to worry about our rules, then I couldn't think of a single valid reason I should let them bother me.

• • •

My errands had us trekking across town to the Meatpacking District. Considering Norma's newfound love of lingerie, I decided to buy her a gift certificate at La Perla, one of my favorite splurge stores. The trip was a quick in and out, but even that was enough time for JC to get his kicks.

"How about this one?" he asked, holding up a barely-there red bra and panty set.

"I don't really think it's your color."

The sales clerk chuckled at my response.

"But *you* look amazing in red. Almost as amazing as you look out of red."

Speaking of red, I was now blushing at the forwardness of this conversation. "JC, there are people present."

"So there are. I can ask their opinion too." He brought the item up to the woman who was helping me. "Don't you think this would be perfect for Gwen, here?"

"That is a favorite piece, sir. Lots of women like to pair it with garters." She batted her lashes at JC, which I suspected was less about making a sale and more about how irresistible he was.

Admittedly, it boosted my ego that he was with me. Not *with me* with me, but with me for the day.

"Now we're talking. I'll take it all." When I started to protest, he said, "Where I come from, it's customary to give the sister of the birthday girl a present too."

I didn't know if I should argue or not. It was an expensive gift, but I knew he was the type who liked to pay for things. And I wanted to wear the outfit for him. It made me wet just imagining him stripping me of the garters.

So I played back. "Where exactly is it you come from?"

"*Shh*. I'm not allowed to say. Remember?"

"Fine. It's your money." I placed the gift card for Norma in my purse and started toward the door, careful not to be around to see the last name on his credit card.

"You'll wear it, though?" he called after me.

I peered over my shoulder, my finger to my lips in a *shh*. "I'm not allowed to say." I smiled the rest of the way out of the store, proud of my flirty banter. It wasn't like me to be so playful. It felt good. It felt liberating. It didn't even feel all that unnatural.

"Where to next?" he asked when he joined me outside with his bags.

"The closest Greenmarket open on Thursdays is in Port Authority." I'd looked it up while he was still inside.

JC glanced at his watch before stepping toward the curb to hail a taxi. "And is that the last stop for the day?"

"Why? Do you need to be somewhere?" It was our last stop, but I'd sort of thought we'd spend the afternoon together as well. I suddenly worried he'd changed his mind about hanging out. Did he decide it wasn't a good idea after all?

At the same time, I realized I was a mess of expectations and wants. First, I thought the idea was too intimate. Then I accepted it. Now I was having fun, and part of me wanted it to never end. It was exactly the reason I'd frowned at the plan in the first place. It was too hard to keep things casual outside of the bedroom.

"Only place I need to be is back in the hotel room." He held up the La Perla bag. "And not because I'm tired."

I swallowed, grateful for the cab that pulled over so I didn't have to respond.

The driver was chatty, and JC entertained him the entire way to the market. I admired the way he could joke so easily. How he could make friends with a total stranger. Yet, except for what I knew of him physically, I really wasn't much more of a stranger to him than the cabbie. He had that appearance, I realized, of being an open book while really he held more secrets than I did.

Neither of us had been to the farmer's market at Port Authority, and we had to ask directions. It was smaller than the one I usually went to with Norma, but they had the vegetables I needed. And, again, JC easily found amusement.

"What size is good, Gwen?" he asked me as I tested the avocados.

I turned to find him holding a skinny cucumber in front of him. Low, in front of him. Crotch level.

"This size?"

I waved him away. "Stop it."

"This one better?"

I couldn't help myself—I glanced back at him. This time he held a fat stubby one. I laughed. "Definitely not."

"How about this?" This cucumber was more of a...*familiar*...size. JC shifted the La Perla bag under his arm so he had both hands free. Then he stroked the vegetable up and down. "It's long and thick. You like that, don't you, Gwen?"

My cheeks were flaming now. I looked around to see if anyone was watching us as I scolded him. "JC. Stop it. You're making me—"

"Embarrassed?" he finished for me, questioningly.

"No." I lowered my voice. "I was going to say *hot*." It was silly, probably, and honestly, it wasn't that he was being particularly sexy. But he was being…him. And he was fun. And he was frisky. He made me feel fun and frisky simply by proxy. And that turned me on, not just to him but to life in general.

And also onto him.

But not onto cucumbers. I qualified immediately. "That doesn't mean I want you bringing vegetables into the bedroom."

"Maybe we'll save it for our next trip to the Madison Suite then. Since the bedroom is out." He winked as he threw the cucumber into my basket.

I rolled my eyes, but I didn't hide my smile. "Oh, grab some yellow squash, will you? Norma loves those."

JC picked out two and brought them to me. "Is your sister older than you or younger?"

"Five years older. But we're still really close. Though sometimes she's more like a mother than a sister." I'd said more than I should, more than he'd asked, but I'd become so comfortable with our outing that the conversation seemed natural. At least it was info about my sister and not me.

"And she's turning—?"

My heart sped up as I realized he was asking so he could figure out my age. I pretended to examine a tomato as I took that in. I'd tell him, if he wanted. But we'd been good about never sharing things about ourselves before this. He'd been adamant about it, and I'd…well, I'd thought it might help keep things unattached.

Now, I wasn't sure if it mattered. I did know that if we started this—shared our personal life—we couldn't take it back later. It would be out there. It would be a bridge we could never uncross.

I let go of the tomato and turned to face him. "Do you really want me to answer? I know how you feel about the no-details rule."

He waved his hands in the air as if to erase what he'd said. "You're right. Don't tell me."

I shifted my attention back to the tomatoes, forcing myself to ignore the bite of disappointment

"Except…"

My head shot back up. "Except what?"

"Except I'm kind of curious. About you." His expression was wary, as though he wasn't sure I could accept that.

Which almost made me laugh since I'd wanted to talk to him about me for a long time now. But he didn't know that, so I played it nonchalant. "I knew it would happen eventually." Once again, I was proud of my banter. I liked this me. I could get used to this me.

He laughed. "Sassy today, aren't you?"

"But, seriously, how could someone not be curious about all this?" I swept my hand down, gesturing at myself.

"Honestly, that's a question I ask every time I see you." While I'd been teasing, JC's expression was serious.

It made me feel funny. Warm and giggly. And confused. I wasn't sure what he meant by it, really. Did he mean that he couldn't understand why other people weren't more interested in me? Or did he mean he couldn't understand why *he* wasn't more interested in me?

Or did he mean that he *was* interested in me, and he couldn't bring himself to ask?

Whichever, it threw me, and I didn't have a quick comeback. "She's five years older. I turned thirty in January." Cautiously, without trying to sound cautious, I asked, "And you?"

"I'm thirty-five in July."

"Ooh. You're old!" I teased.

"Hey, people usually say I look younger than that."

"You do. Like a baby." I'd thought he was younger myself, though I also wasn't surprised to find I'd been wrong. "How do you manage to do any sort of business with such a baby face?" Now that I'd gotten the hang of this teasing thing, I couldn't stop.

"Ha ha." He looked up at his reflection in the security mirror and rubbed a hand over his scruff. "The face helps, actually. Not when I first approach people, but when they realize I know what I'm talking about, they seem to appreciate the things that my face can get."

"Like girls who will voluntarily take their clothes off and do lap dances in public places?"

He shrugged.

But all I could think was, *he's thirty-five. I know something about him, and he's thirty-five.*

And I wanted to know more about him.

"What exactly is it you do?" I asked as I made my way to the bins with potatoes. In case he was hesitant to tell me, I added, "It seems only fair that I know that, considering you know what I do." Funny, I hadn't thought of that argument before.

JC answered without any pause at all. "I'm an investor. People give me their ideas, and I invest in them." He raised a questioning brow as he held up a bunch of carrots.

I shook my head and nodded to the peppers. "Like what kind of ideas?"

"Okay, like one I'm working on now. I found a kid—he's barely legal but brilliant as all fuck—who came up with this new social network idea we're developing. It's sort of like Linked In and a little like Facebook, but solely for businesses and organizations to interact for the purpose of cross-promotional opportunities." He set a green pepper in the basket. "It's not very interesting."

"I think it's very interesting." God, I hoped that didn't sound too eager.

"Trust me. It's not. Anyway, the kid heads up the work. Runs a team of people to get it off the ground. I pay the salaries. Eventually, when the site gets monetized, I'll receive a large percentage of the profits."

"So you come in town every week to check up on how the work is going?" I was beginning to understand the travel.

"Among other things. Yeah." He pointed at me with a bundle of celery. "But back to you. How did you end up nightclubbing?"

"Both my bachelor and master's degrees were in restaurant management. There was an opening at Eighty-Eighth after I graduated. I took it." Talking like this felt amazing. Almost as amazing as sex. His genuine interest in me was palpable, and I stopped worrying whether or not I sounded eager and instead simply rode the exhilarating wave of information sharing.

"A bachelor's and a master's? Look at you go, Ms. Smartypants. And before you ask, I don't even have a bachelor's. I dropped out when I made my first multi-million dollar investment. I was twenty." He was cute when he was bragging. Like he thought he had to impress me. Like I wasn't already impressed with everything about him. "Do you ever want to work anywhere besides the club? Or are you happy there?"

"I'm happy. Why, will you help me fund my own nightclub if I ask?" I'd stopped even pretending to look at produce.

JC stuck his hands in his jean pockets and shrugged. "If you've got an innovative concept, sure."

"I'm not that kind of innovative. I'll stick where I am. The club's the best in town. I can't think of any reason why I'd leave." And because I hoped that maybe he'd give me more information on his relationship with my employer, I said, "And Matt's a good boss."

JC turned to look at the onions, even though we'd already picked out what we needed. "You'd only want to work at a club?"

He'd skipped over Matt completely. Well, it had been worth a try. "I think so. I know the business. And I've always been a night owl." I moved to stand next to him, my shoulder grazing against his.

Even through my coat and his, the brush of our bodies made my blood start to simmer.

"I don't know." He bumped his arm lightly against mine. "I'd call you more of a panther than an owl. I've heard you screech like a wildcat in the night." He turned toward me, a single finger on his chin. "Come to think of it, I'm sure I've also heard you purr."

I met his eyes. "Only with you."

"I'm okay with that." His eyes were absent of the lust that I would have expected, which made the comment more intimate than he'd probably intended.

Even if it was giving away too much, I meant it when I said, "I'm okay with that too."

We didn't say anything else until I'd paid for my items. While the grocer bagged up my vegetables, he said, "You know, it's nice to see you in a different atmosphere. You're less uptight than you used to be."

"Your mad plan is working," I said. He was right, of course. I was much less uptight, but it had more to do with being with him now than it had to do with the sex we'd had. "And you knew that. You've seen me loose."

He took the bags from the clerk and tucked them inside the La Perla bag. "I have indeed. I didn't know if it extended outside of the bedroom."

I was surprisingly not humiliated that the clerk had heard the statement. I thanked her then stepped out of the way so the next person in line could check out. We had our vegetables and could leave, but I was too caught up in my next thought. "But isn't the bedroom the only place it matters?"

"Hardly," JC said. "Your life is the only place it matters. The bedroom's just a gateway." He spotted something behind me. "Oranges. I didn't see those."

He walked over to examine the fruit. I trailed behind, considering his statement. It brought on another round of confusing emotions. Had he always intended to eventually make this more than just about sex? Because if so, I had to call a time-out. I could do non-commitment fucking. I couldn't do non-commitment real life. I knew that about myself. It was why I made sure I didn't spend time with many people in the first place—so that I wouldn't have anyone to get attached to.

Maybe I'd misunderstood. Maybe he meant that what we did in the bedroom was supposed to spill over into my daily life without him and spending time together today was just a fluke.

I knew I should clarify.

Except…

The word rang in my head the same way his "except" had rung in the air when he'd spoken it. Except I didn't want to clarify. I didn't want to find out that today was just a fluke. I didn't want to put an end to spending personal time together outside the bedroom.

I didn't want to *not* get attached.

Because, honestly? I was pretty sure I already was.

Shocked by my realization, I looked up from the oranges and happened to catch his gaze. There, I saw a flash of something. Something unfamiliar but engaging. Something that called me to move toward rather than pull away. Something that seemed more like an open door than the brick wall that JC always met me with.

It was only a flash.

Then it was gone.

"You know, we should test how far you've come." His voice had the edge of naughtiness that it did when we were naked together.

It made my skin prickle with awareness and my heart pound with nervousness. "What do you mean? Do you want to bang over there behind the market banner?" I hoped he'd say, *no, but let's go bang back at the Four Seasons.*

"Actually…" He shifted to study the banner I was referring to, as if considering it. Then shook his head and turned back to me. "Well, good idea. But that wasn't where I was going with that. Though I like the way you think."

"I *don't* think that way. I was making a joke."

"Ah, see? We haven't come as far as I'd like then. If you were truly more relaxed, you would have been serious."

"I…" I didn't finish my sentence. I realized that it was pointless to argue with JC about this. There was certainly a difference between being uptight and having a reasonable appreciation for propriety, not to mention the law. Surely a person could be laid-back and chill without having to lose her sense of decency.

But since it wasn't something he was pushing, I let it go. "Whatever. Fine. What was it you had in mind?"

"How about a little mischief?" He tossed an orange up in the air and then caught it again.

"I can't even begin to imagine where you're going with that." Because I was even more opposed to an orange in the bedroom than a cucumber. Unless he was planning to squeeze it and lick it…

Okay, maybe oranges were okay.

But apparently he had other plans. His expression turned impish, and he did a rather obvious sweep of his surroundings. "Ever did any shoplifting?"

"Oh, no." I mean, I had, but no. This was not on my agenda for today. Or ever.

"Come on. It will be fun." He scanned the crowd again.

"Have *you* ever shoplifted before?" I was not going to teach him. Was *not*. Was definitely not.

"Nope. First time." He practically did a full turn this time as he looked to see if anyone was watching.

"That's not…" I put a hand over my eyes and peeked through my fingers as JC began stuffing an orange in his pocket. "Oh my God. You're embarrassing yourself. That's not how you do it." I grabbed the orange from his pocket and stuffed it back in the crate.

"How do you do it, then?"

"First of all, you can't look around like that. That's how you alert other people that you're doing something that you don't want them to see. You have to be coy. And look straight at the person closest to you and smile while you're dropping it in your bag. In the bag you already have. Not your pocket where it will stand out for everyone to see."

"That's brilliant. How do you know this stuff?"

I hated how much I adored his praise. "It's not brilliant. It's logical. And I know because I've done it."

"You've stolen fruit?"

"Well. Yes." Farmers' markets were one of the easiest places to get food. But there were other places we'd stolen from. Convenience stores.

A restaurant once.

I occupied myself with straightening the oranges—straightening oranges, really?—while I explained. "We were poor and sometimes my dad forgot to feed us. So we got good at this. And we never did it just for fun."

"Then this will be your first chance. You can teach me how to—"

He reached for another orange, and I blocked him. "No way." It didn't matter how much I loosened up, I refused to steal again.

But when he tried to reach over me to grab another, the whole crate, which was on the end of the table, fell to the ground. Oranges spilled everywhere, rolling under the tables and out into the walkway.

"Oh. Fuck," JC said. "Now what do we do?"

"Run!" I don't know why I said it. Obviously, the best thing to do—the responsible thing to do—was stay and help clean up the mess. Explain that it was an accident.

But the unexpectedness of the event paired with the general naughty feeling I had anytime I was with JC, not to mention that I *had* stolen in the past, made me automatically feel guilty. And I reacted by bolting.

JC was on my heels, the La Perla bag full of scanty underwear and vegetables for my sister's breakfast banging against his leg as we ran through the long halls of Port Authority. No one followed us. No one even called out after us, but we kept going until we were out the doors and around the corner.

The cool air of the March day perhaps was all I needed to knock some sense into me. I stopped running and leaned against a cement pillar to try to calm my breathing. JC put a hand on the pillar to steady himself.

He met my eyes and we burst into laughter.

We laughed like I'd never laughed before, and I knew that the cause was much more than the knocked-over bin in the Greenmarket. It was from a lifetime of not laughing. A release of all the crap that had been my childhood and the parts that had followed into adulthood. I'd always thought I grew up in a drama, but now, in this moment, it felt more comic than any sitcom I'd ever watched on TV.

It felt like letting go. And it was exhilarating.

Next to me, JC laughed just as hard and just as long, and if I hadn't figured it out before, I knew now that he must have the same sorts of hurts built up that needed as much of a release as mine. I wondered about them as I wiped tears from my eyes. I wondered how it had been so easy for him to recognize them in me and why it had taken me longer to figure out the same about him. I wondered how he knew that spending the day with me was exactly what we both needed. How he knew to ignore our non-attachment rules and connect instead.

I glanced at him doubled over, the La Perla bag dropped at his feet, and suddenly I had a revelation. It might be what he needed, but it wasn't what JC wanted. Just like me, he hadn't wanted to get intimate. He hadn't planned to take me out into the world and test my boundaries. He hadn't planned to ask me questions about my personal life. He hadn't planned to look at me with an emotion that was so much more than want. And when he had, he panicked. Stealing the oranges had been his way of trying to regain his composure. It was his reminder that the world could fuck off. It hadn't been for me at all. It had been for him.

And it hadn't worked. Because behind the amusement in his eyes was the same emotion he'd tried to hide. More vibrant now. More pure.

So a minute later when we'd finished laughing and we'd somewhat found our breath again, it wasn't a complete surprise to find him moving toward me and me toward him. Our lips met and locked.

He cupped his hand around my neck and brought me closer to him, holding me firmly. As if he were frightened I'd pull away. Gently, he kissed first my bottom lip, then my top. Then his tongue swept in, teasing me. Tasting me. With sweet surrender, I opened for him. Sweeter still, he opened for me.

We kissed with the exploration of a first kiss. Tentatively at first, then with complete and utter focus. Because even though we'd had our mouths on each other before, it had always been in the context of sex. And while there was enough passion in this embrace to lead there, it wasn't the reason for it.

We lingered in this kiss. We lavished. We luxuriated. I wrapped my arms around his neck to draw him nearer, then clung on tighter to support my weak knees. I fell into him. I melted.

And he melted into *me*. Filling my spaces, smothering my emptiness. Making me whole. Making me free.

Chapter Eleven

This time, in the cab back to the hotel, JC didn't chat with the driver. He gave directions then turned to look at me, his eyes burning and blazing with want and affection. And I, usually one to buckle up and pray during a taxi ride through the city, climbed into his lap, straddling him. Again, our lips met. His hand tangled in my hair and my hands cupped his face as my tongue traced love notes along his. The ante was upped now. No longer was this kiss not about sex. Now, it was foreplay. The most tender, sweet foreplay that I'd ever experienced. Even with the cabbie shouting obscenities at the road behind me.

JC's hand wandered first, slipping up my shirt to push my bra up and caress my breast. His thumb brushed over my nipple until I was gasping into his mouth. He slid his hips forward, and I pressed my pelvis tightly to him so I could grind against his erection. When I couldn't get the pressure I needed through my jeans, I stopped worrying about me and reached down to palm him through his pants. The feel of him—so hard, thickening further in my hand—I wanted more. Then JC bucked into my touch and that was all the encouragement I needed.

I slid off his lap to the floor, barely fitting in the tight space, and unzipped his pants. It was a delightful surprise to find he hadn't worn underwear and his cock stood upright and proud.

He leaned down to whisper in my ear. "What are you doing, Gwen?" His hushed tone wasn't worried for himself. He wasn't concerned at all to have himself exposed in the back of a taxi. It was me, he knew, that would feel uncomfortable in this situation.

Funny thing, though. I didn't feel uncomfortable at all. I felt excited and naughty, and wow, naughty was a lot more awesome than I'd realized.

I answered JC with a pump of my hand down his length.

"Gwen," he said my name quietly, reverently. "You don't need to do—" He cut himself off with a strangled breath in as I sucked the tip of his cock. "Jesus. That's…you should stop. Ah, don't stop."

I didn't plan on stopping. I didn't think I could. I licked along the thick vein and then opened my mouth to take the whole of him in. He squirmed. He moaned. He was, for once, off-balance because of me instead of the other way around.

None of it was typical behavior for me. I recognized that as equally as I recognized that I didn't care. The only thing that mattered at the moment was having JC as close as possible—having him *in* me in any way that was possible. And since stripping out of jeans and riding his cock wasn't exactly the easiest task in a moving vehicle, a blowjob seemed a little bit more manageable.

Besides, I relished the effect I had on him. I adored his sounds and the tensing of his thighs at either side of me. More, I craved the emotional exchange that occurred as he put his hands on my head and guided me. The way he looked at me as I peered up at him, even while I fisted the base of his erection and slid his cock in and out of my mouth, continued to portray so much more than lust. When I flattened my tongue and sucked his length, my need to pleasure him was not only out of carnal desire, but also out of fondness. When I drew him in until he touched the back of my throat, it was because I suspected he'd become fond of me as well.

He was getting close when the cab pulled up at the curb. I was so entranced with making JC come that I hadn't realized we'd stopped moving. But then he was pushing me away, tucking his erection in his pants as he fumbled with the cash in his wallet. I slid out of the car and waited for him, not even bothering to check out the driver's expression. He could be annoyed, disgusted, turned on—let him. I didn't care in the slightest.

The walk through the lobby was the longest of my life followed by a never-ending elevator ride. The sexual tension between us was so thick, so palpable. If it weren't for the family with young children sharing our car, we certainly would have continued making out. We tried to make up for it with our hands, joined together between us. We squeezed and caressed with our fingers, much the way we had on our first trip to the hotel.

The family got off on the same floor we did, but even when they turned down the opposite hall, JC and I remained connected only through our hands. Each step toward our door piled on another layer of tension, and by the time we made it inside the room, I thought I might explode.

And then I did.

When JC dropped the La Perla bag at his feet and we came together, it was like an explosion of the grandest fireworks. My lips ignited and flamed against his as he worked me out of my coat. My blood roared in my ears and burned in my veins. Then he pulled my shirt over my head and when his fingers brushed against my skin, sparks shot through my nervous system. My bra came off next, and my nipples stood up under his gaze, erupting from my smooth skin like perfect pink buds.

We moved as we undressed. Except for my panties, I was naked by the time we reached the bedroom doorway. JC lost his pants in the threshold then lifted me up and carried me to the edge of the bed. He set me down, tenderly, but not too gently. His every kiss—in fact, every caress—was thoughtful and affectionate but still rough and demanding the way I'd come to expect from him. The way I liked it. The way I loved it.

The way I loved him.

I jerked as the thought penetrated through the haze of passion and landed with a thud in the spotlight of my consciousness. I loved him. Goddammit. I completely loved him.

JC lifted his head from the spot he'd been sucking on my neck. "Are you okay?"

My stomach was twisting and my heart was racing and my skin felt like it was on fire. "Yeah. I think that maybe I finally am."

He smiled, accepting my answer easily as he pulled my panties off of me. He pushed my knees apart and bent down to the floor. Then he buried his head between my thighs, swiping his tongue along my folds and around my clit. His hands massaged up and down my calves as he continued to work me, teasing me to the edge of orgasm, taunting me until the world began to tilt and spin.

Just as I started to fall under, he stood and scooted me back on the bed. He studied me as he stroked himself. I could see the gleam of pre-cum already on his cock, and I wanted it on me. In me. Wanted him to mark me and take me.

Because I was his now. Already. Completely. All he needed to do was claim me.

As he lowered himself over me and pushed into my wet channel, I pretended that he was doing just that. I pretended that it meant everything

I wanted it to mean. Whether it did or didn't, I couldn't know. So as it was happening, I pretended that I *could* know. Pretended that I *did* know exactly what he meant with each thrust that rammed into me.

It was beautiful. It was poetry. The way he moved and touched me. The way he took care of me. The way he kissed me—God, the way he didn't stop kissing me.

He didn't question me the way he usually did. Didn't push me to tell him how I felt or how he made me feel. I was telling him anyway— without words—with my mouth, with my body, with my eyes, with the soft sounds of pleasure that sang in the back of my throat. *Yes, you feel good inside me. You fit my pussy so perfectly. You make me come so hard.*

And I did come so hard. Hard and long, clenching around his cock, milking him. Then he was the one who told me, "God, you feel so good, Gwen. Squeeze me like that. Just like that." His movement stuttered as I tightened, but he grabbed my hips and found a new rhythm. "Again, Gwen. Let's go together next time."

I pulled my knees in and wrapped my ankles around his waist so that he could drive deeper. The shift in angle let his cock hit me in all the right places, let his pelvis grind against me with just the right pressure. But it wasn't only the new stimulation that sent me soaring toward my next climax. It was his eyes, locked with mine. As open as my body was to him at the moment, it was JC's soul that was open to me. He spoke secrets in that look. He told me things I wasn't supposed to know. He told me that I wasn't what he planned. He told me that I was everything he needed. He told me that he wasn't fucking—that he was making love.

I'm sure I said all the same things back. I'm sure I said more. And when I went again, it was with him, my orgasm crashing and mingling with his so completely that I couldn't tell which sounds were his and which were mine. Couldn't tell if it was my heart pounding in my chest or his pounding against mine. Couldn't tell whether it was me sobbing into his skin or him sobbing into mine.

But what I did know was that we'd flown together. He'd loosened me before this. Today, whatever fetters had caged him, they'd been released as well, and we met there in the sky, wild and free, two birds that had been imprisoned too long.

• • •

He held me long after we'd settled, sweeping light strokes down my back with his fingers and intermittently kissing my forehead. Our legs tangled together and our chests fell and rose in tandem. We never cuddled after sex, and while it hadn't been awkward before, this was the easiest we'd ever been.

There was a part of me that was tempted to analyze the situation, wonder what the day meant for our future and try to interpret whether or not I was okay with the change. Whether he was okay with the change.

But I didn't let myself fall into that. Maybe JC's efforts to teach me to let loose had really taken a hold of me. Or maybe I just didn't want to face the possible reality of our relationship. Either way, I let myself linger in his touch, in his scent, in his embrace. Let myself enjoy the exploration of my lover that he'd never allowed before.

"What does this say?" I asked after a while, my hand dancing across the tattoo on his torso. "It's Chinese, right?"

"Japanese. 'The current age is but a brief moment in the greater scope of existence.'"

"Um…what?"

He chuckled and I liked the pleasant way my nipples rubbed against his chest as he did. "It basically means *live for today*. It's Buddhist."

I put my hand on his chest and rested my chin on it to look up at him. "Are you Buddhist?" It seemed like I'd have figured this out already if he were. Like, shouldn't there be tantric sex or something? That was a Buddhist thing, wasn't it? Maybe that's what we'd been having. I was so ignorant about Eastern religion.

But he shook his head. "No. I just liked the sentiment."

Live for today was the epitome of my relationship with JC. "It fits you. That's for sure." I couldn't see the image on his bicep in the position we were in, but I asked about it next. "And the compass? What made you get that one?"

He raised his arm and looked at the black etched compass, as if he'd forgotten what it looked like. "Don't you think it's cool?"

"Actually, it's rather hot." I'd never known I liked tattooed men until I'd seen JC strip, but now I realized that inked men hit my buttons.

Or maybe just JC hit my buttons.

He returned his arm to my back and smirked. "I can live with hot."

I wouldn't doubt that he'd earned the attention of plenty of women with both the positioning and choice of image. Yet, I doubted that he'd gotten it in hopes of hooking up. He didn't need skin art for that.

I tapped his chest playfully. "But does it mean something? Why did you get it?"

He groaned as if he didn't want to tell me. After scrubbing his hand over his face, he said, "Honestly? I don't know. I was drunk."

"You drunk-tattooed?"

"It's why I don't drink anymore. I do crazy things and have no recollection. Once when I was drinking, I remember wanting street tacos. Next thing I know, I was waking up in a cantina in Mexico."

His eyes sparkled when he talked, and I bet that mine sparkled with his. "You woke up with a compass tattoo?"

"The compass was another drunken event." His tone said he was still embarrassed about it. "I'd never even considered a compass before it showed up on my arm."

"At least you didn't pick a flower or a MOM tattoo. Drunk JC has good taste."

"I can't even think about what I could have gotten. Like I said, no more alcohol for me."

"You don't drink?" I was asking so many questions. Too many probably, but it felt so liberating to finally get them past my lips. And his answers…I drank them up like they were the only water on a deserted island.

"I'll have an occasional glass of wine, but nothing harder unless I want to lose several hours of my life and end up as the real life study for the next *Hangover* movie."

"Hey, those are good movies." I ran my fingers across the grid of letters on his forearm. Four rows that spelled out a date—December seventeenth. Had he flinched as I touched it? Or was that just my imagination? This was the tattoo that interested me the most. The one that I was sure shed the most light on the man I'd unexpectedly fallen for. "Is this one also the result of overindulging?"

"No. That one's not." He brushed against a spot on my back. "What's this from?"

"What?" I looked over my shoulder, but I already knew what he was talking about. I hadn't thought about it in a while, and since it was under my blade, I didn't see it all the time to remind me of its existence.

"This mark." He leaned up so he could see it better. "Is it a scar?"

"Yeah, it is." But I wanted to know more about his tattoo. "So what's important about December seventeenth?" He'd said his birthday was in

July, so it wasn't that. What kind of a date would a man mark on his skin? Someone else's birthday. An anniversary. A date that he fell in love. Like I could so easily have today's date tattooed on my body. It would already forever be tattooed on my heart.

I couldn't help but think his date had to do with a woman.

But maybe that was only because I was a woman and because my imagination was limited. Or I was looking for a reason to be jealous.

JC completely ignored my question, which only made me more convinced it was about a woman, and asked his own. "How did you get your scar?"

I wondered if we were playing a game of bluff. Who would tell the story they didn't want to tell first? Except he'd already told me the story behind two of his tattoos. It was probably my turn. Quid pro quo and all.

I bit my lip then said, "I did something stupid."

"What was that?"

"Made my dad mad." I'd been wearing a bikini to sun in the yard. I'd known he wouldn't like me doing it, but I'd done it anyway, hoping he wouldn't catch me. But he did. I was twelve and he'd accused me of dressing like a prostitute. He'd picked up a loose board from the fence, not realizing there was a nail in it. Or maybe not caring. When he smacked it across my back, the nail caught in my bare skin and pulled a deep gash. It should have had stitches, hence why it had scarred so badly. I'd been lucky to not get tetanus, because he never took me in to have it looked at.

It wasn't something I told people. I didn't like the pitying looks I got when they found out my father beat his kids. Worse was when they could no longer look at me at all. It's surprising how many folks can't deal with other people's tragedy. Like it's contagious or something.

I wasn't sure I wanted to JC to know either. But he'd asked, and I wanted to be honest with him more than I wanted to hide the ugly parts of me. Wanted to show him that he could be honest with me.

"Your dad did this?"

I tilted my head up to meet his eyes. "Yeah." I prepared myself to answer more.

But JC surprised me. Putting two fingers under my chin, he leaned up and kissed me. It was the kind of kiss that said what words couldn't say. It said *I'm sorry this happened to you*, but it didn't come off patronizing. It said *Let me make it better*, while doing exactly that.

It was the best balance of compassion and understanding that I'd ever received in regards to my past abuse.

I was so grateful and moved by it that I quickly let it grow. I slipped my tongue deep into his mouth and shifted my body on top of his. His gentle caresses turned rougher, more desperate, as he sucked and nipped at my lips. His cock stiffened under my belly, and without breaking our kiss, I drew my knees up to straddle him. Still wet from earlier, I slid down, sheathing him easily.

I pulled away from his kiss, sitting back to ride him, my palms flat on his chest. This position was outside my comfort zone, and it took a few minutes for me to establish any sort of a rhythm. JC had been right when he'd guessed that I liked to hand over the control in the bedroom. But maybe he needed that from me sometimes too. Even if he didn't need it, I wanted to show him that I could be versatile. For him. That I could give as well as take.

It was different being in charge. I had to shift a few times before I found the angle that hit where I liked when JC usually found it immediately. With me on top, he could touch me in ways he normally couldn't. As soon as his thumb landed on my clit, the pressure began to build, low and warm. Spreading over me and through me, gathering momentum until it felt like I could soar.

Suddenly he sat up, burying his face between my breasts. "Oh, Gwen…"

I slowed as he kissed around one of my nipples. Then his eyes fastened to mine, and he said, "I can't decide if you came along at the best time or the worst."

He tugged my knees higher, forcing my ass to sit back so I sat more firmly on his cock. Gripping my hips, he took over, knocking my clit just right as he rocked me against him. "Right now, I'm just glad that you came along."

His words were all I needed to spur my climax. It hit me, bowling me over, as though it hadn't given me any warning, despite the fact that it really had. Much the way falling in love with JC had hit me. All the signs had been there. Still, I'd refused to see it coming on.

And what could I do about it now? Nothing except ride the wave the same way that I was riding the crest of my orgasm. It shattered through me. It wracked me and wrecked me. Yet in the end, as I dug my fingers into JC's shoulders and felt him pound through my resistance, I was better for it. I was calmed and pieced together. I was made new. I was made whole.

• • •

We slept after.

We dozed away the afternoon, wrapped around each other.

When I woke up, the room was dim and JC wasn't in the bed next to me. I sat up and felt better as soon as I found him in the armchair, fully dressed, watching me. He sat with his legs outstretched, ankles crossed, like when I first met him. Yet his back was straight and his shoulders tight.

Before any words were spoken, I could tell things were different.

"What time is it?" I asked, hoping my half-asleep state was causing me to misread.

He smiled, and while it was sincere, it was weak. "Almost eight," he said. "I was just going to wake you."

"Yeah. I need to get home and get ready for work." I'd have just enough time if I didn't have too much trouble getting a cab. *Focus on that,* I told myself. On the responsibilities I had. I didn't have time to dissect what was going on here.

"I called a taxi for you." How he could always read my mind, I'd never know.

It struck me that if he had called for a ride before waking me that he'd either wanted to make sure I got as much sleep as possible or he'd wanted as little time with me as possible. I hoped it was the former. But, from the awkward distance between us, I feared it was the latter.

"All your things are there." He nodded to the bottom of the bed where he'd laid out my clothes. Was the gathering of my things a kind gesture or a hint? "I'll let you get dressed." He stood and left the room, shutting the door behind him.

I dressed quickly, knowing if I slowed down I'd have time to analyze, and I was afraid I'd be emotional and jump to conclusions. Just because he seemed distant now didn't mean I'd imagined how things were earlier. And it didn't mean he regretted it either. It could simply mean he knew I needed to leave. Knew that he'd be a distraction if he didn't give me space.

Still, shutting the door seemed like such a blatant statement. Impudent, even. Separating me from him. Shutting himself off. Shutting himself down. It stung, and my eyes blurred with tears.

Say ouch.

I blinked them away.

When I came out of the bedroom, JC was leaning against the back of the couch. Waiting for me, it seemed. Waiting for me to leave maybe. I spotted his suitcase by the door. "Are you still going to L.A. tonight?"

He gave a short nod. "My car will be here soon. I'll be right behind you."

"We could share an elevator."

"I'll catch the next one."

So his bags were packed and his ride was coming, and yet he wasn't going to ride down to the lobby with me. Had I done something so wrong that he couldn't even spend another few minutes with me? If he had something to do without me around, he could just tell me. This distinct coldness was brutal.

At least he saw me to the door. I paused, my fingers wrapped around the handle, to search his face. So badly I wanted to see the man I'd spent the day with. When I really studied his eyes, I thought maybe I saw him.

Maybe.

He sighed. And when he did, he softened. Then for sure I glimpsed the guy I'd made love to all afternoon. He shoved his hands in his pockets and leaned back against the closet. "We broke a lot of rules today, Gwen."

It occurred to me that maybe he didn't realize I was okay with the change. "Rules were made to be broken." I winked, trying to adopt the lighter character that usually belonged to him.

He smiled weakly. "Some of them."

My chest sank and I wasn't able to hide the disappointment from my face.

He rushed at me, cradling my face in his hands. "Don't, Gwen. We'll sort things out next time, okay?"

I leaned into his touch, and all doubts quieted when he brushed his lips against mine. We didn't usually part with a kiss. It was a sign. Things were okay. All was well.

He was probably just overwhelmed. Like I was overwhelmed. We didn't have a chance to figure out what should happen between us next. What did I expect? That he'd fall at my feet and profess his love in the fifteen minutes we had before I needed to leave? I certainly wasn't about to.

So.

Like he'd said, we'd sort it out next time. Right now he was still trying to get a handle on the concept of us. Whether love fit into our carefully constructed non-attached worlds. Whether we'd met at the best or the worst time.

To be fair, I was still trying to get a handle on it as well.

Best or worst time. For me, it would always be the worst time. But did it even matter? Somehow it seemed to matter very much. To JC. Mattered that it wasn't the best time. That it wasn't an ideal time.

So despite how upbeat I tried to be, when I walked out of the hotel room, alone, I couldn't help but wonder if it might be the last time.

Chapter Twelve

Interesting thing about being in love—it brightens a dimly lit world and puts a pleasant pink hue on everything. Which was probably why I woke up the next day feeling more optimistic about JC and me. Because I was head over heels. I was as sure of it as I had been sure it wasn't what I wanted. And welcomed or not, whether it changed anything between us or not, whether he felt the same or not, I was pretty certain it was an emotion that was sticking around.

Thankfully, the club had been busy. It kept me emotionally and mentally occupied through my shift. When I'd gotten home in the morning, I'd made the birthday breakfast for Norma, which had gone well despite the bubble of distraction in my chest. We made plans to meet at her office at seven so we could have dinner and I could give her the La Perla gift certificate before I had to be to work at ten. Then she was off. By the time I'd cleaned up breakfast, I was exhausted. I collapsed into bed and fell asleep with only a minimal amount of fixating on JC.

Since I'd gone to sleep much earlier than usual, I woke up much earlier. After getting a solid eight hours, I was wide-eyed by a little after four in the afternoon and in a fairly good mood. An excellent mood, actually, even before coffee. I felt like Cinderella the day after the ball—filled with hope instead of the gloom that she could so easily have adopted about her impossible situation.

That was how the story of Cinderella went, wasn't it? I was so out of touch with fairytales.

The text I found on my phone from Eric only made the day better: *Ben can call you at three our time to wish Norma Happy Birthday. Does that work?*

Three his time was six our time. Thank God that my schedule was screwed, or I would have slept through the whole thing. I responded with a yes, feeling as much like the fairy godmother as I did Cinderella. I was about to make someone else's wish come true. I practically sang as I got ready to surprise my sister with the gift I knew she wanted most.

I was almost out the door when it occurred to me that Norma might have meetings. I'd been just planning to show up early and surprise her with Ben's call, but occasionally she was tied up right until the end of the day—even on Fridays. I checked the clock. It was five. Maybe I could catch her assistant before he left for the weekend.

I practically squealed when he answered. "Boyd! I caught you. It's Gwen."

"Good evening, Gwen. I haven't talked to you in awhile. Nice to hear your voice."

Boyd was younger than I was—twenty-five, if I remembered correctly. I'd been a little stunned when Norma hired him more than a year before. Sure, he'd had an adequate resume, but he was fresh from college and young. Really young.

And Boyd was good-looking.

Not in the sharp, confident way that JC was good-looking. Not even in the brooding, classy way that her boss, Hudson Pierce, was good looking.

No, Boyd was a different type of good-looking. The boyish, nerdy type. His hair was floppy and he wore dark-rimmed glasses that didn't do much to hide his large chocolate brown eyes. He was nice. Sweet. An all-around decent guy. Honestly, if I hadn't been the type to not date, I might have tried to get his phone number. Except that might have been weird considering his superior was my sister.

Besides, I wasn't really that attracted to him. It was more like he was the type of guy I *should* be attracted to and just never was.

Plus, I had a feeling he was probably gay. No man kept his hands that well-manicured without being rich or homosexual.

And I didn't date. So there was that.

But now that I was humming with feelings of love, the idea of dating wasn't all that awful. In fact, going out sounded quite lovely—as long as I was going out with JC. For the first time in our arrangement, I wished for more than our one night a week. I wished he wasn't across the country. Wished he were joining me for Norma's dinner. Wished he were with me for everything.

Boyd's questioning tone drew me back to the present conversation that I'd somehow managed to forget I was having. "What was that?" I asked, forcing myself to focus.

"Norma's on the other line. Do you want me to leave her a message?"

"Actually, no. You were who I wanted to talk to. I'm meeting her for dinner at seven. Does she have anything scheduled right before that?" I held my breath as I waited for his answer.

"No. She's done with her appointments for the day. Do you need me to schedule something?"

I didn't want Norma to have any hint of the surprise, so I said, "No. Just wanted to make sure she wouldn't be running from somewhere to our dinner reservation."

"Got it." After I thanked him, he added, "It really was nice hearing from you, Gwen. Don't be such a stranger next time."

Huh. Was Boyd flirting with me? Or was he simply trying to be an involved assistant? He had become Norma's right-hand man, so he possibly thought connecting with her sister was part of his job.

Yeah, I was going with that.

I was running late when I got to Pierce Industries. Traffic had been a bitch and I cursed myself for thinking a cab would get me there at this hour of the day in any reasonable amount of time. Then again, there wasn't a straight shot of the subway from our place to Norma's office, so I was pretty much screwed no matter what.

I was checking my watch as I got off the elevator onto Norma's floor—it was a quarter to six—so I didn't see Hudson Pierce in front of me and bumped into him. We'd never met, but I knew who he was. It was the first time I'd seen him up close. He certainly was attractive, and I could see why my sister had fallen for him.

But his eyes—they were so empty. As though they were missing something. As though *he* were missing something. Something vital. That nothingness made him seem eerily cold, despite his polite smile as I delivered my apology and headed toward my sister's office.

It was strange how I felt like I recognized that emptiness I'd seen in Hudson. Not like I'd seen something missing in my eyes, but I'd felt the missing thing inside. Like there was a hole in my chest that sat vacant. Waiting. Was that what JC saw when he looked at me? The same blank stare that I'd seen in Hudson? And if he did, how could I hope that he'd ever find any sort of connection with me?

Except, he did connect with me. I knew that. It wasn't up for debate. I'd felt the surge of electricity pass between us, and it was vital and fierce. And when we did connect like that, I didn't feel that hole. I didn't feel empty. I didn't feel unlovable. I felt…loved.

The thought stopped me in my steps. It was one thing to acknowledge that I was in love, but to imagine that JC might return the feeling was going too far. If I didn't quit it now, I'd end up hurt.

I shook the notion off and continued down the hall.

Boyd's desk was empty when I got there. It was after hours and the whole place felt like a ghost town, so that wasn't unusual. But Norma's door was closed too, which was a little odd. I worried for a moment that she'd had something come up last minute, but then I heard music coming from inside. Instrumental music. She'd spent the most time with Mom and had been the one to adopt her musical tastes. This particular piece was loud and vibrant. *Carmina Burana*, maybe. I wasn't that good at identifying much besides Philip Glass. Whatever it was, she didn't hear my knocking.

I tried the handle. It wasn't locked. "Hey, I—"

My words cut off when I saw her. She was bent over her desk wearing nothing but a garter belt, stockings and heels with her ass front and center—bare. And red. Red with palm prints.

Boyd, stood behind her dressed only in his trousers. And he was spanking her. Not gently, either, but full-on slaps. They sounded like they had to hurt, but from the moans of pleasure that came with each swat of his hand and the way that Norma rubbed her thighs together, I had to guess she was enjoying it.

Boyd was too. Without a doubt. And from the evident bulge at his crotch, two other things became immediately evident—Boyd was hung and he was definitely not gay.

"Oh my God," I gasped and immediately regretted it. Until then, they hadn't seen me. I could have snuck out and they'd never have known I'd been there.

Now, they knew.

Both faces snapped to peer at me. "Gwen!" Norma cried, her face turning as red as her behind.

I couldn't look away. Partly, I was processing. This was the first time I'd walked in on my sister doing anything sexual, shocking in its own right, and then to realize she was involved in kink?

It took a moment to regroup.

Apparently, they were as stunned as I was because neither of them moved from their positions. Finally, I came to my senses. "Um, sorry.

I'm so sorry." I closed my eyes, as if that could help at this point. As if I could un-see what I'd seen. "I'll just…take your time. I'll be out there. In the waiting area. No rush."

I shuffled out as fast as I could with my face covered, and when the door was shut behind me, I practically fell against the wall.

What. The. Fuck.

Everything clicked into place. Why Norma bought the lingerie. Why she'd been working later recently. Why she no longer talked incessantly about Hudson Pierce. Why she'd been all pro love and relationships.

Why she seemed happier than I'd seen her in a long time.

But there were just as many questions that rolled in. Like, how long had this been going on? Why hadn't she told me? Was it just sex? Or was it, as I strongly suspected, something more?

They were answers I wouldn't have until I talked to her—and I was already planning a serious interrogation—so in the meantime, all I could cling onto was *holy shit.*

I stumbled to her waiting room armchair in a daze saying that over and over. *Holy shit. Holy shit. Holy shit. Holy. Shit.*

My phone rang, knocking me from my stupor. Suddenly remembering why I'd come to the office in the first place, I sat up and pushed the TALK button. "Ben?"

"Hey, big sis."

"You'll never believe what just happened to me." The words came out in a rush but I didn't wish them back. Because Ben was the only person who would understand how shocking the experience was. He was the one person I wanted to share it with more than any other. "I just walked in on Norma banging her assistant."

"Oh my God." His gasp sounded much like mine had.

Like sister, like brother, I thought. "That's exactly what I said."

"Banging her assistant where? In her bedroom? On the couch? On the kitchen table?"

Oh, damn, I'd left out one of the most important details. "No, at her office! On. Her. Desk." I emphasized each word, still not believing it myself. "And he's young, Ben. He's your age!"

"Oh my God. Is he cute?"

"He actually really is. I think you'd approve." We fell easily into conversation. I'd worried there'd be a strain between us. And there may have been, had we not had such a luscious piece of gossip to devour together. "Ben, it was kinky!"

"Tell me. Every detail."

I gaped for a few seconds, not sure if it was cruel to bring him further into this knowledge about Norma or cruel to leave him out. "Do you really want to hear? This is your sister I'm talking about, remember."

"And I'm forever holding this over her. Tell. Me."

I loved hearing his voice so much. Loved hearing his enthusiasm for something. It was exactly the opposite of the somber mood I'd attributed to him in my thoughts for the last few months. It was hopeful and excited, and it kept me talking about the image that I wanted to block out. Actually, it had been a hot scene—the spanking, the garters, the dominance. Yeah. Totally hot. That was, before I really realized what I was looking at. Or, more specifically, who.

"Oh my God, this is absolutely hilarious. And he was spanking her? With his hand or a belt? I have to make sure I have the mental image right."

"His hand, you perv." But I laughed. Ben had always been like that—the one able to make me laugh. It was why it always surprised me that he suffered so much inside. He was jovial and carefree. How could he be hurting so bad?

"So he was spanking her like he was punishing her?"

"Yes, but she was enjoying it. Trust me." I could still hear her moans in my head. They were so raw and primal. I had to admit I was a little jealous.

"Maybe he was giving her her birthday spankings. Thirty-five of them. And one to grow on. Though I bet it was him doing the growing."

I laughed again, this time with a groan thrown in. I cut off sharply when I heard the sound of the office door creaking open. "Hold on, Ben. I think they're coming out."

I started to put my phone down but heard Ben talking so I put it back to my ear. "Please, please, please put me on speaker phone," he begged. "I want to hear every word of this."

I pressed speaker and dropped my cell into my lap as Norma walked toward me. Boyd hung back by the door, his eyes cast down, but my sister's head was high and I guessed the flush of her cheeks was still from their previous activity.

"So." At least she was as speechless as I'd been.

"So. Is Boyd joining us for dinner?" I felt bad for not addressing him directly since he wasn't that far away, but I couldn't look at him yet, much less talk to him.

She glanced back at him before answering. "He wasn't planning on it."

I wasn't sure if that disappointed me or not. On the one hand, this was supposed to be my private birthday dinner with my sister. On the other hand, every dinner we had together was private and I wanted to know more about this secret relationship of theirs. "It seems he should at least get a free meal after that."

"Gwen! Don't be a bitch," Ben chided me from my lap.

Norma recognized his voice immediately. "What was that?"

I beamed as I held up my cell phone. "Happy birthday."

Norma grabbed the phone out of my hand and put it to her ear, even though it was still on speaker. "Ben?"

I heard him say, "Happy birthday, Sissy," before she found the button to turn off speaker. Then his side of the conversation was lost to me, but I didn't need to hear it. Norma's face said everything. She was beaming and glowing and I was sure it was from more than her sexcapade.

Boyd tried to slip out of the office quietly behind us, but he stopped when he saw the tears spilling down Norma's face.

"It's Ben," she said, covering the mouthpiece.

The smile he gave her read genuinely heartfelt. She didn't have to tell him who Ben was, and that's when I knew for sure her relationship with Boyd went beyond simple fucking.

I turned to him and forced myself to meet his eyes. "Boyd, join us for dinner."

He smiled again, and I noticed a dimple I hadn't seen before. "I think Norma needs to be alone with you right now."

I took that to mean she planned to do some heavy explaining. I could live with that. But I did want to get to know the man who meant something to my sister. "Another time, then?"

He hesitated, stealing a glance at Norma who was laughing and grinning like I'd never seen her. "Sure," he said. "If that's what she wants."

He caught her eye before he left, and the sizzle that I saw between them practically knocked me off my feet. If I hadn't been convinced before then I was now—Boyd was definitely what she wanted.

• • •

The host wasn't even out of earshot before I burst. "All right. Spill."

It was amazing that I'd lasted as long as I had. After Norma had finished talking to Ben, I'd taken another turn with him, followed by a final speaker round. Then, when we'd hung up, I'd figured that we needed to get everything out about our brother first. We'd done that as we walked the couple of blocks to the restaurant, sharing what we'd said and he'd said and telling each other how good he sounded. How much better. How much stronger.

"He's checking out of the facility next week," Norma had said. "And he's moving in with Eric. Having a boyfriend has really been the best thing for him. I think it's going to be good now."

It seemed a little trite to say that maybe a boyfriend was all any of us needed to heal from our past. Yet it also felt a little right. Like maybe love really did make everything better. Or maybe it was the rose-colored glasses talking. If it was, Norma seemed to be wearing a pair as deeply tinted as my own.

Now she put her napkin on her lap and spread it carefully. "Spill what, exactly?" But she gave me a teasing grin.

"Don't toy with me. I intend to hear everything, Norma. I mean it. Ev. Ry. Thing. And go."

"Um." Her eyes danced around as if she could visually see her story in the air and she was flitting from one chapter to another. From one highlighted passage to the next. "I don't know where to start."

"How about start at the beginning? This wasn't the first time, was it?" There was no way this was the beginning. No one got that naughty on their debut run.

"Not our first time." She paused while the waitress set down our water glasses and took our drink order. When we were alone again, she said, "First time in the office, though. We're usually quite good about not doing anything there."

I couldn't decide if I believed her or not. Norma was ultra professional, but after what I'd seen, I had my doubts. "Come on, isn't that the hot factor? Naughty assistant getting reprimanded by the boss?"

She flushed. "It's not really like that."

"Actually, I already gathered as much." It was Boyd doing the spanking after all. And while I'd never have guessed it before today, I was certain now that he'd always be the one doling out the punishments and never the other way around.

"Yeah. Anyway." She nervously straightened her silverware as she talked. "Like I said. Not usually in the office. But it was my birthday, and I'd wanted to play naughty assistant, as you called it. Only I was pretending to be the assistant."

"I don't want to know. I mean, I kind of do, but I really don't." I took a swallow of my water while I decided the things I wanted to know for sure. There were four. "How long has it been going on?"

"About nine months."

Her answer surprised me. Until I really started to think about it. It explained things like the nights her bed seemed to not have been slept in and the distraction that had seemed to occupy her mind for the last while. I'd thought it had all been about Dad. I was strangely relieved to find it wasn't. It felt like permission. Like if Norma could live her life and not worry then so could I.

But I already had been, hadn't I? Without her permission, even. Hadn't I been living and not worrying with JC?

Well. Like sister, like sister, then.

I moved on to my next question. "Is it always like that? Role playing and everything?"

"It's…" She pressed her lips together as she searched for her answer. "It's a lot of things. He's always dominant. But sometimes it's role playing and sometimes it's bondage and sometimes it's just really hot sex." She put her hand up to halt me from speaking. "And before you ask, no, I'd never done any of that before him. He completely introduced me to the world, and I don't think I could ever go back."

That hadn't been one of my questions, but now that she'd mentioned it, I was glad to know. Otherwise I'd be scrolling back through all her past boyfriends in my mind, imagining them as Doms, and with some of them that was simply not a good idea. It was hard enough to imagine my strong, tough-as-nails sister as submissive.

Yet, seeing her as she talked about it, I could tell it was the real deal. My next question was really unnecessary, but I asked anyway, wanting to hear it from her lips. "Is it just sex?"

"Not in the least." Again she halted while the waitress delivered our wine and took our order. Lucky for us, we dined at this Italian bistro enough to know what we wanted without looking at a menu, because we hadn't even taken a peek at one.

After the waitress left, Norma took a swallow of her Chardonnay,

LAURELIN PAIGE

her brow creased in thought. "It was just sex in the beginning, maybe. But even then, not really. Not for Boyd anyway. He always treated it as more. I got on board soon enough."

I'd already realized their relationship was more than casual, but this was when I realized how much more. "You love him."

She peeked up coyly under her lashes and nodded.

"He loves you too. I saw it on his face."

She nodded again.

Then it wasn't just unrequited love. They'd talked about it. Discussed it. Probably made plans and commitments with it.

Which brought me to my final question. "Why didn't you tell me?"

"I should have. I'm sorry." She shook her head as if reprimanding herself internally. "Management isn't allowed to date their staff. Punishable by termination. I know that you wouldn't tell on us, but it seemed the best solution to keeping us private was to adopt total secrecy. No one knew. That included you. I'm really sorry."

"Stop it." I waved my hand in the air, feeling bad that she held so much guilt about something that obviously gave her a lot of joy. "I get it." I wouldn't have told me either, if I were her. Especially back then. I would have given her a hard time about it. Would have told her it wasn't worth the risk.

Now, I said, "Hudson would never fire you."

She didn't need to consider this at all. "No, he wouldn't. But he'd make me fire Boyd. Or, at the very least, transfer him. I can't do that right now. He keeps me together. I need him."

"I'm glad you have him." I sighed and it turned into a bigger sigh than I'd intended. I meant what I'd said. I *was* glad she had Boyd. I also knew I probably wouldn't have been glad if it weren't for my own feelings about JC. I would have been jealous of the time Boyd had with my sister. I would have wanted to keep her to myself.

And I couldn't deny that I was envious about something else—that Norma's relationship with Boyd was out in the open to each other despite not being open to the world. Could JC and I have that? That thing where we both knew how we felt, and we owned it and didn't doubt it?

I wouldn't ever know unless I declared the words to JC, and I wasn't sure I should be thinking about that in the middle of my sister's birthday dinner.

Norma kicked my shoe under the table, pulling me from my thoughts.

"Hey. Why aren't you making fun and scoffing? Is this some sort of birthday reprieve?" Her eyes widened as if she'd just had a realization. "Oh. You're in love too."

"How——? What——? Why would you even…?" I'd lost my ability to form sentences. "Goddammit." I probably should have appreciated that there was someone who knew me as well as Norma did. Even when JC seemed to read me, it was only guesses. We still had so much to learn about each other.

And I did appreciate it from Norma. It was also frustrating. She'd kept her secret for so long, and I couldn't manage to keep mine for a day.

Now that the cat was out of the bag, I might as well acknowledge it. "Yes. I'm in love. Is that ridiculous?"

"With the guy that you're 'spending time with?' JC?"

"Yes," I groaned. "Yes. I really think I am."

"Why sound so miserable about it? He's done wonders for you. I've never seen you as happy as I have the last few months."

I was elated that she'd noticed. Also, scared. Because if she'd noticed, what had JC noticed?

"I don't know, Sissy." I focused on a couple at a table across the room as I let the not quite formulated thought take shape into words. "I guess I'm afraid I'm the only one who wants it to be more. Because I'm not sure what this is for him. He hasn't said he wants anything other than the arrangement we have."

"Have you asked him?" She said it as if it were the most reasonable idea in the world.

It probably was reasonable, now that I thought about it. It was our relationship that wasn't reasonable. We'd both known it, too. It was why we'd been so wary of it when we'd started out.

So, if we'd both been smart enough to understand that we couldn't dictate what happened emotionally, then why had we gone through with the plan in the first place? Was it all about lust? Or had we both been using the whole deal as an excuse?

I didn't have the situation worked out enough to explain it to Norma. "We're getting there," I said, which was at least partially true. *I* was getting there, anyway. "Things…changed…yesterday. And I'm sure they changed for him as well as me." I thought about the way he'd looked at me as we'd made love, the heavy longing in his tone when he'd said he was glad I'd come around. "Maybe he's even willing to admit it."

Except there had been the distance at the end. "I don't know. Maybe I'm wrong. He has some secrets."

"We all do."

"Crazy thing is I think I'm handling mine better than he's handling his." I hadn't thought it until I'd said it out loud, but now that I had, things clicked. There had been distinct events in my life that had shaped and defined me. Things that made me withdraw from people and disconnect from life. Those were the reasons I'd sought a no-strings relationship.

So why had JC? Sure, maybe he just wanted things simple. But wasn't it safe to suppose that he might also have had events in his life that led him to be emotionally reserved too? I'd already let my guard down with him. He, on the other hand…he kept his guard tight. Was his past more tragic than mine?

The idea broke my heart in places I didn't think were possible. It also gave me a clarity I'd lacked before. With a tremble in my lip, I met Norma's eyes. "I don't know if he can do this."

She reached over and squeezed my hand. "Oh, sweetie, you won't know until you give him a chance."

I wanted to believe it was that easy. As the waitress set the food on the table, I let myself pretend that it might be. Let myself believe that I had the strength to put myself out there. Let myself believe that I had the character to be what he needed in a support system.

We ate several minutes in silence while I mulled things over. Norma was the first to speak. "Do me a favor—don't sell him short. I might not know him, but if he knew how to break through to you, I think he's a guy worth keeping around."

I liked what she had to say too much. It made me hopeful. If Norma could see a real relationship between JC and me then it felt more possible.

Possibilities scared me. So I tucked her suggestion away and feigned insult. "You make it sound like I'm so unapproachable."

"Aren't you?"

"I don't know. I guess I am." *Of course I am.* Or I was. "I think I'm changing. Maybe not. A little, though?" If I were really changing, I should be able to tell JC how I felt.

"You're changing. I see it. Everyone can see it."

"Thank you." This time I let her words really hit me. I soaked in them. I celebrated in the truth of them. It was amazing to have the accomplishment acknowledged. It was even more amazing that the accomplishment happened in the first place. So whether I told JC how I felt or waited to see what happened next between us, I'd still progressed as a person. That was what counted, wasn't it?

"All of us are changing, I think," she said, a bit whimsically. "You and me and Ben. We're all learning to let love in. We're letting our wounds heal. And you know what I think? It's about goddamned time."

It struck me as ironic that for as long as our father had been in prison, we'd been locked up as well. We were supposed to be the ones who'd been freed by his incarceration. Yet we'd each gone with him into captivity.

Now, for us to be liberated ten years later…

Yeah. It was about goddamned time.

Chapter Thirteen

The next week, JC canceled our date.

I'd still never given him my phone number—strange, he hadn't asked for it either—so I had to find out in a call from Alyssa.

It was almost seven on Wednesday morning, and her name on my caller ID surprised me. I might not have answered except I was too curious. "Hey. JC was in last night," she said, not bothering to say hello.

"Uh…and?" Of course he'd been in. It was the night he had booked in the Viper. But why she was telling me about it was beyond me. JC and I had kept our arrangement—our whole relationship—completely off the radar.

"He wanted me to get a message to you. Said he's not going to need to book tonight. Said you'd know what he meant."

"Oh." It was cryptic yet clear. My heart fell to the bottom of my chest with a sickening thud. Yet now that it had happened, I couldn't believe I hadn't thought it might be a possibility. If I'd had any doubt that we'd truly connected the last time we'd been together, it was gone now. We *had* connected. He'd felt *something,* even if it hadn't been to the same extent that I had. He had to have. Otherwise he wouldn't be running now.

Or maybe I was jumping to conclusions. Maybe he had a good excuse.

"Did he say why?" After I asked it, I realized it was probably a weird question when he'd framed his cancellation to seem like he was cancelling a room at the club. Which meant I had to let that go unanswered. "I mean, did he say he wanted another night instead?"

"Nope." She inhaled deeply—smoking a cigarette, I assumed. Or a joint. I really didn't know her that well.

I also didn't really know JC. And while I'd never asked or wondered about his evenings in the Viper, I suddenly wanted to know very badly. I hated that Alyssa got to see him in that environment and I didn't. I hated that he felt comfortable enough for her to be his messenger. I hated that he felt comfortable enough to give her *that* particular message.

I hated that he was giving that particular message at all.

I knew I was potentially making a fool of myself, but I asked, "Did anything…unusual happen last night? With JC, I mean."

"Nope. Same old, same old."

Which meant…? "So he seemed…*okay* then?" I pounded my fist against my forehead, realizing how stupid I sounded but not able to control myself.

"I'm not sure what you're asking me. He was JC. Same as always. Do you have a thing for him, Gwen? He's hot-to-trot, but I have to tell you—he's not the guy for a girl like you."

"What does that mean—a girl like me?" I tried not to come off too offended. But the whole conversation had me turned around. Alyssa wasn't usually this relaxed with me. This straightforward. This blunt.

And I wasn't usually so off my game. So easily defensive. So desperate and needy.

"I mean that you're the type who expects fidelity. The type that would want commitment and monogamy in a relationship." Another inhale. When she spoke again, it sounded like she was attempting it while holding her breath. "Am I wrong?"

Until I'd met JC, I'd been the type who didn't want relationships at all. And it had been him who had insisted on monogamy. The idea that he was fooling around with others bothered me, and not just because we hadn't been using condoms.

I didn't know how to respond to her question.

When I didn't speak, she did. "But if you don't mind being a flavor of the month, go for it."

I knew I shouldn't ask. It was the worst thing I could know. "Have *you* ever been his flavor of the month?"

She laughed. "That's very funny," she said, as if I'd purposefully cracked a joke.

Except I hadn't. I truly wanted to know. Now even more so. Did she find my question humorous because she would never go for it with JC or because she had and everyone knew so why was I asking?

I wanted to dig further, but I couldn't figure out how to do it without seeming like an idiot. And I already felt like an idiot. I'd been dumped for the night, after all. Through a messenger.

"Anyway," she said. "I'm about to crash. Just wanted to give you the heads up."

"Thanks." But I wasn't grateful in the least.

The next week, I got the notice that JC canceled on Monday. I'd been melancholy and moody since the call from Alyssa, but when I saw the note on my locker as I came in for my shift, my disposition plummeted to something akin to despair. I didn't have to read it to know what it said.

I read it anyway. *Have to cancel. Something came up.*

He didn't even sign it, which incensed me. He couldn't even bother to write his initials? Was my heartbreak only worth twenty-seven letters of his time?

Really, I didn't care about his signature or the goddamn twenty-seven letters. I wanted *him*. In person. Wanted to see him and touch him and kiss him and tell him I loved him. Even if he were only going to tell me he wasn't going to make it on Wednesday, I wanted him to tell me to my face.

I knew in my gut that face-to-face wasn't happening. Just as sure as I knew that he was done with me. Done with us. How many notes would I get before he stopped leaving them all together? How many phone calls from Alyssa? How many missed dates before he felt like I'd gotten the hint?

But Norma had said to give him the benefit of the doubt. And while I hadn't entirely decided to follow that suggestion, it was the best choice I had. What else could I do? I wanted to lash out. I wanted to mourn. By keeping me in limbo, he made those options seem rash and unfounded.

All I could do was hope.

Well, and I could check in at the club the following night.

I never went in when I wasn't working, but I staged it this time by leaving my phone in the office so that my appearance on a Tuesday wouldn't seem odd. Of course, after I'd retrieved it, I still hadn't seen JC. I lingered at the first floor bar, looking up at The Deck. Going up there wasn't an option. I hadn't seen Matt, so it was possible he was up there. If I walked in on him with patrons breaking the rules then he'd know I knew about his deals.

And even if he wasn't, JC could be. And he'd know why I was there. He'd know it was for him.

I went up anyway. Climbed the stairs two at a time and burst into the room like I belonged. There was a group of men drinking and playing cards. Smaller than the time before. Only a couple of women. Everyone was dressed. Matt wasn't around. Neither was JC.

"He's not here tonight," Alyssa's voice came from behind me.

I turned to find her with a serving tray of appetizers. "Who isn't?" Like she'd fall for that. We both knew who I was there for.

She smiled with that gleam that said she wasn't going to play that game. "He has the room booked every week, but sometimes he sends his people without him. Nice making a move, though. You should probably wear something a little more…" she eyed my jeans and T-shirt "…accessible…if you're going to try again."

I rolled my eyes and stormed out. It was silly to be so mad since she was so wrong about what was going on with JC and me. But she was right about one thing—I was not dressed to get the guy. I should have planned that a little better.

As for JC's absence, I was torn. I hadn't thought through what I'd say to him if I saw him. Mostly because I just wanted to see if he'd be there, not confront him. Finding out that he wasn't made me feel… better? Like maybe something really had come up, and he wasn't even in town.

But also, he could have guessed I might have shown up and so he'd stayed away.

Really, I hadn't learned anything. And I really didn't have any reason to be mad at him or not trust him. So I'd take Norma's advice and give him the benefit of the doubt.

For as long as I could justify it, anyway.

• • •

By the following Wednesday, I hadn't heard from JC at all. I barely slept that day, trying to decide what that meant. I wanted to assume it meant we were still on. But it could also mean that he thought that's all it would take to dissuade me.

He couldn't think that. Because he knew, he *knew* me.

Which made all my debates pointless. I'd go, and he'd know how I felt whether I told him or not. I'd go, and if he let us be like last time, if he let me in and held me there, then I'd know how he felt too.

I put on the underwear from La Perla. Plus the garter. And the stockings. I blew out my hair and did my makeup. Sultry eyes, mascara. Light lips. I found a coat in the closet that was light enough to wear on a warm April night but long enough to hit my knees. I put it on over the lingerie, slipped on some strappy high heels, and took a cab to the Four Seasons.

I was late when I got there; still I lingered outside the door for several long minutes. What if he wasn't there? What if tonight was the night he officially ended our deal?

What if, what if, what if.

What if he'd gotten scared, tried to back away, and realized he couldn't? What if he was on the other side of the door waiting for me with as much trepidation as I was on this side of the door? What if I walked in there and he took me in his arms and loved me? What if it was wonderful?

I slid my key in the slot and went in.

He wasn't in the living room, but when I walked in a few steps, he appeared in the doorway to the bedroom. He wore suit pants and an undershirt. A wife-beater. I'd always hated them, not only because of the name, but well, no, mostly because of the name. But there was nothing I hated about the way JC looked, his forearms resting on either side of the frame, his muscles tensing from the pose. He looked surprised to see me. And relieved. And worried. And maybe a little lost.

I read every single emotion with clarity because they mirrored how I felt exactly.

A stream of heartbeats passed with our eyes clinging to each other, our bodies frozen while we took each other in. It was like physically touching, the way his gaze skimmed over my skin. Like he was caressing my every inch. Embracing me. Stroking me. Adoring me.

I saw the exact second that he saw them. His expression had been soft and searching, then, as he scanned down my legs and registered my stockings, it turned dark and carnal.

"Take it off," he said, his voice scratchy with barely contained desire.

I tugged at the tie at my waist, my focus never leaving him. My arms tingled and I couldn't decide if I felt a flash of warmth or a flash of cold as I dropped the coat to the floor.

JC exhaled heavily. "Turn around."

I spun, slowly, letting him see me in the underwear he'd purchased for me. Letting him see how perfectly they molded to my shape. He visually devoured me and it turned me on. Set me to flames. By the time I'd made it all the way around, I was wet and needy. A glance at his tightly bulging pants only made it worse. I yearned for him to touch me. Ached for it.

It only took him three strides to cross to me. But when he got there, he didn't reach for me. Instead, he circled me, drawing a perfect perimeter around me. As if he were setting his boundaries. *Here,* his confident saunter said. *This is the farthest I'll be from you tonight.*

It sent sparks down my spine that ricocheted and traveled to my very core.

"I think," his tone was rough and raw, "that we," every word purposeful and promising, "should push your limits."

A thrill shot through me that was equal parts fear and excitement.

"Follow me."

Goose bumps shot down my arms as I tailed him to the bedroom. It was so sexy how he commanded me. How I obeyed.

He stopped at the edge of the bed and turned to me. "Take off your bra. And your panties. Leave everything else."

Each word was thick and raw. They fell on me like little grenades, exploding on impact and annihilating my composure.

I trembled as I complied, nearly sick with anticipation. He'd yet to touch me. I was dying to have his lips on mine. I was hot and horny.

I was also afraid. Because besides the silent exchange we had when I'd first arrived, we hadn't addressed the last time. I still didn't know where we stood. And while his aloofness was provocative as fuck, I feared it was purposeful.

So when I'd finished undressing—naked except for the garter, stockings, and shoes—I couldn't stop myself from moving toward him, seeking his embrace.

He stopped me before I reached him. With a curve of his lip, he said, "On the bed. On all fours."

I hesitated for the briefest of seconds. *It doesn't mean anything,* I told myself. *This is the game tonight. Follow where it leads.*

And because it was a game I fiercely wanted to play, it wasn't hard to do as he said.

I climbed onto the bed, on all fours. It was a vulnerable position. I was exposed to him, my cunt on display, the slick evidence of my arousal plainly visible. Even more vulnerable because I was facing away from him and couldn't see if he was looking at me or not. If he were pleased with what he saw. I had to trust.

"Very nice," he said, and I beamed inwardly. He began to strip. I heard his zipper. I heard his belt buckle as it fell to the floor with his pants.

Now would he touch me? I hoped. I prayed.

"Crawl to the edge of the bed."

I moved forward, and as I did, I felt the weight of the bed shift. I shivered with apprehension. Wondering. Waiting.

His hands settled on my hips just as his tongue slid up my seam.

I gasped, and he immediately did it again. This time, he dipped into my pussy. He licked a circle around my hole, rousing my nerves as he passed over them like the wave at a baseball game. I fought the urge to squeeze my thighs together. Let the pleasure build and tease as he taunted me with his attention.

As he serviced me, his palms moved to knead my ass. It was heavenly and unexpected. He'd gone down on me plenty, but he usually focused on my clit. This time, all of his treatment was on my pussy, and while it was fucking fantastic, the swollen bundle of nerves above throbbed and begged for a turn.

But when JC's tongue left my cunt, it traveled in the opposite direction—to my ass. He nibbled along my crack, burying his face between my cheeks. As he grazed his teeth against sensitive skin, I whimpered. As he licked around the perimeter of my hole, I wrapped my fingers tightly in the bedspread and fought back a curse. Because... shit...what was he doing? And why did it feel so goddamned brilliant?

He pulled away, and his mouth was replaced with his hand.

"Has anyone ever touched you here, Gwen?"

"Uh, no." And no one was going to. Well, except he was already touching me there. The swirl of his finger around my rim traced the path his tongue had taken, and as it dipped in, pushing just the tip inside, I felt myself grow wetter.

The warmth of his finger disappeared suddenly. Disappointingly. Then a second later it was replaced with something else—something cold. It twisted outside my hole then slipped farther inside.

I tensed.

"Do you remember when you first touched yourself for me? How strange it felt? How foreign? And then you relaxed. How did it feel then?"

"Amazing." I glanced back at him over my shoulder. He nodded so I went on. "It felt…*I* felt beautiful. Because I could do that to myself. I could make myself feel good, and you could see it. Which was the best part. The way you enjoyed watching me."

"Remember that. This is going to feel foreign to you at first, too. But if you relax, it's going to feel beautiful. It's going to make you feel good. And I'm going to enjoy that very much."

His words held promise and allure. They also alarmed me. How could they not when there was an unidentified object pressing against my back door?

I twisted my neck to try to see what he was holding.

JC pushed my head forward. "Don't look. It will frighten you, and I don't want it to."

"Hearing that frightens me even more."

"Don't let it." He pushed the object a fraction deeper into my ass and rolled it around the sensitive walls. "I promise you that it isn't going to hurt. If we do this right—*if you trust me*—there will only be pleasure. Do you trust me?"

God, my legs were quivering just from this.

Yet, even on the edge of pleasure as I was, I didn't know if I could go through with it. I was also starting to worry that JC wouldn't give me a chance to say no. That amped my anxiety.

"I don't know," I managed, my voice breathy. "I mean, I do trust you. But I'm not sure about this. I don't know what I'm supposed to do. And that makes me nervous."

"I understand, and I'm going to help you with that." With the plug still partially at my hole, he leaned his body over my back so that his mouth was at my ear and his erection poked into my asscheek. "Let me tell you what's going to happen, Gwen. I'm going to put a lot of lube onto the plug so that it's really slick. Then I'm going to slide it into you. Slowly. As I do, I want you to push out and relax. When it's inside, you're going to feel your nerves wake up. It's going to make you nice and snug so that when I fuck you, your pussy will wrap tightly around my cock and you'll feel me everywhere. And all those nerves that have woken up will be on fire. Then you're going to come harder than you've ever come in your life. Multiple times. You'll barely be able to stay on your knees and I'll have to hold your hips while I pound into you. You're going to feel so good. You're going to be beautiful. And I'm going to enjoy that."

Words. Words! The man had me with his beautiful, filthy words. I was more turned on than I'd ever been in my life.

He nibbled on my earlobe. "Does that sound okay to you?"

My yes was more of a grunt than a syllable. Partly because I was already there, already halfway to orgasm where speech became less and less intelligible.

But also there was the part of me that was wary. Not because of what he was going to do or how he was going to fuck me, but because of the giant chasm that had formed between us. We were touching, we were connected by skin, but emotionally, he'd closed himself off. There wasn't a doubt in my mind that he'd positioned himself behind me so that our eyes couldn't meet. So that he would make sure that as he slid in and out of me, as he stroked the most private parts of me, he'd still never actually let me reach the most private parts of *him*.

This would be sex for sex's sake, he was telling me. Like we'd agreed. It would be good sex. Amazing, mind-blowing sex. And that's all. Nothing more.

If I didn't like it, he'd given me the chance to say no.

And I didn't. Because as much as I didn't like it—as much as I was falling apart inside—my body was completely fine with the situation. It was humming and buzzing and wet and greedy for whatever JC had to give me. I was like a crack whore who would do anything to get her fix, including giving up the things that were most important to her. The things she really cared about. I was desperate for my high.

And, damn—as he slid the lubed plug into my ass, as I pushed against it, relaxing, opening up, as the nerves I'd never known about came alive and sang—it was easy to forget a little heartbreak.

The plug felt wider as it passed my tight rim. Then it seemed to narrow, and I wondered if it was all the way in. I tested it, squeezing my cheeks around it. It felt good.

"Fuck, you're so hot like this, Gwen." JC rubbed the base of my spine. "There's one more ridge to go. How are you feeling? You're doing great." He was gentle and patient, yet his excitement was evident.

It bolstered my own excitement until it overtook the last of my anxiety. All that remained was a ravenous want and desire. "More," I groaned, bucking back into him. "I want more."

He half laughed, half moaned. "Hold on, baby." He reached a hand through my legs to massage my clit, and I focused on the thrum of pleasure instead of the squishy way my chest felt after he'd called me *baby*.

His fingers slid along my slit and jabbed into my cunt. "You're dripping, Gwen. Do you like how it feels to be this tight?"

I didn't want to talk. I was teetering on the edge of orgasm and all I wanted was my release. I opened my mouth to tell him, but what came out was a blissful sob. Because, right then, while he continued to rub and play with my clit, he pushed the plug the rest of the way in.

I came.

My orgasm shocked me with its sudden appearance, making my thighs quiver and my arms shake. I fell to my elbows as it thundered through my limbs.

"Ah, Jesus, that's beautiful. I'm so hard, Gwen. I'm stone." He was done being patient. He was past being gentle. I could hear the ragged edge in his voice.

Which was just fine with me. I was reeling in my own ecstasy. And I was ready to be fucked.

JC nudged my knees farther apart and a bolt of electricity shot straight to my core as the new position tightened the plug in my ass. Then he grabbed me at my hips, positioned himself, and entered me on a merciless thrust.

I practically screamed as another orgasm split through me. JC didn't give me any reprieve. He pulled my slack body tighter against him and pounded into me. Each drive touched me everywhere, stroked me everywhere. His tempo was rigorous, and with each staccato jab, his pelvis knocked against the plug, sending sparks shimmying in all directions. I couldn't tell anymore where the sensation was coming from. My pussy, my ass—all of it burned. It was impossible to recover. I was a waterfall, constantly falling, constantly hitting the rocks below, constantly creating a splash.

Soon I was begging. Pleading with a jumble of sounds and syllables that didn't make sense. I didn't even know if I was asking for him to stop or go on. Just. Just, please.

Then, without pulling out of me, JC wrapped an arm around my waist and pulled me up so my back pressed against his chest. My hands flew behind me to clutch his neck—I didn't have the strength to support myself without holding on. He put a hand on my breast and squeezed, his other returned to my clit. It was too much.

It was exactly what I needed.

The flames spread, licking up, up, until every cell in my body was ignited.

Then I burst.

My vision dimmed, blood whooshed in my ears, my entire body turned rigid and tense with the explosion. It wrecked me. Destroyed me.

JC's voice wove through the decimation, praising me, cursing me. "Good girl, Gwen. Fuck, you're killing me. You feel…Jesus. I'm coming. I'm coming."

He pulsed into me, deeper, deeper, growling as he spurted out his climax.

I didn't register finishing. Didn't really notice when he pulled the plug out. I couldn't feel anything anymore. I was numb. Exhausted. I was the ash after the fire. I was devastated. We fell—me facedown on my stomach, he on the bed next to me—sweating, out of breath. Worn down.

Satisfied.

JC came out of the haze first. "That was incredible. Holy fuck, this is the best arrangement."

Then the haze cleared for me too. Because with those words, I remembered. Remembered it was all a lie. Remembered it was a quick fix. Remembered it was without strings, without commitment, without love. Remembered the chasm between us and the walls he hid behind.

I turned to my side, facing away from JC, and closed my eyes. Tears spilled out the corners, and I couldn't decide if they were brought on partly from the amazing orgasms I'd just received or if they were entirely from the piercing stab of pain in my chest. How was it possible to have the best sex of my life while my heart splintered into pieces?

I was the type of woman who could be with a man without feeling anything for him, without feeling anything from him. But could I be with a man and feel something for him without the feeling being returned? Could I settle for whatever he had to give—the world's best O's and rare moments when our eyes would link and we'd fuse and feel?

Or would I insist on all or nothing?

It seemed like a harsh ultimatum, but now, as the afterglow of coming hard faded, and I was left with no touches, no kisses, no embrace, all or nothing seemed quite reasonable. Because this ache, this painful excruciating loneliness, was far worse than the ache he'd eased to begin with. It was trading one misery for another, and I didn't know that it was worth it.

The bed shifted behind me as JC got up. I heard him in the bathroom. A few minutes later, he returned. "Gwen?"

I didn't say anything. I was afraid if I spoke I'd end up sobbing or saying something I'd regret. This was supposed to be a no-strings thing. There weren't supposed to be tears. So I kept my eyes shut and feigned sleep with deep even breaths.

He sighed, and I felt the weight of it as if it were a heavy blanket that he'd covered me with. Then another sigh. As though he could expel me from inside him with enough exhalations. He moved around for a bit. Then he left the room, and I let myself cry.

I didn't overindulge—my cheeks were wet and my makeup smudged, but my eyes wouldn't swell. I'd learned how to covertly cry growing up. For the times when saying *ouch* simply didn't cut it.

When the tears subsided, I wiped away the evidence and realized that the hotel was quiet. Too quiet. I peeked in the bathroom and found it empty. He wasn't in the front room as well. I would have heard him if he'd opened the doors to the terrace, but I checked there anyway. No sign of him anywhere. And he'd left no notes, either.

I'd felt lonely before, but this was worse. This was abandonment. The sting that had eased with my weeping now returned with a burn that made my previous ache seem dull. Perhaps I was being overemotional. Perhaps I wasn't being emotional enough. I wasn't schooled enough in the processes of love to have a grip on what was the appropriate amount of feeling involved.

What I did know was that I couldn't wait around. Fuck, I'd been waiting around now for years. Ten of them. More. My whole life. I couldn't escape one prison only to be chained in another.

I forced myself to clean up and dress. Even as I wrapped the coat around my near-naked body, I hoped he'd return with a good excuse. *Hey, I ran down to get some champagne.* That could have been delivered. *I needed a breath of fresh air.* There was the terrace.

I couldn't figure out how to…be…with you when we weren't fucking.

Ah. Now that one. That one would be honest. And if that was his excuse, there'd be even less reason to stay. At the door, I considered leaving my room key. It wouldn't mean I couldn't ever return—my name was at the desk. But it would be a message. When he saw it, he'd know something about my state of mind when I left.

In the end, I kept it. He'd left me clueless with no note. I'd leave him wondering as well.

I made my way to the elevator with as much stoicism and confidence that I could muster. Inside, I pressed the Lobby button then, on a whim, hit the button to the floor with the Meeting Rooms.

I didn't hear him until I was just outside the Madison Suite. He was right—the walls were thick. The melancholy rolls of Philip Glass's *Opening* slipped through the cracks at the door. I leaned my head against the wood and let it float over me. Into me. Let it simultaneously hold me and set me free.

It was gorgeous. Heartfelt. Not as sad as the songs he'd played for me before, and I wanted to believe that was a sign that, perhaps, JC wasn't in as much despair as he had been. I twisted it into a daydream, as I tried not to breathe, afraid of missing even a single note. Pretended that this melody was the one that had demanded to be played. Because it was Philip Glass, which reminded him of me. Because it was hopeful and not forlorn.

But it was only a fantasy. And while I felt less abandoned now that I'd discovered where he'd gone, I didn't feel any less alone. That man in there, the one lost in the sweet intoxication of his instrument, he was out of reach. Even if I went in and interrupted him, and he put me on the top of the baby grand and made me scream and writhe with his mouth and his cock...even then. Even then, he'd still be out of reach.

And I'd still be alone.

I listened until the end of the piece. Then I kissed my palm and placed it on the closed door, holding it for the space of a prayer before I pulled my coat tighter around myself and went home.

Chapter Fourteen

I'd begun to measure my life in Wednesdays. Every episode of my inner television show revolved around them. I filed the titles in my head: *The Wednesday I Fell Asleep. The Wednesday He Canceled. The Wednesday He Canceled Again. The Wednesday I Tried the Butt Plug.* That episode was broken into two parts—the second was called *The Wednesday I Snuck Out.*

This one was *The Wednesday I Stayed Home.* It wasn't a decision made on a whim. I'd pretty much known as I walked out of the Four Seasons in the *Snuck Out* episode that I wouldn't be back. On Monday, I'd given a note to Alyssa to deliver to JC. It felt shitty and gutless, but he'd set the precedent.

The worst part was Alyssa's smug expression. "You're going after him with a note?"

I'd thought of several comebacks after—*Wouldn't you like to know?* Or *Please, I don't have to go after him.* But I'd felt too guilty, so I'd lamely said, "Just give it to him."

Then I spent the next two days curled up in a ball in my bed trying not to cry. On Wednesday night, Norma stuck her head in after work. "You still not feeling good? Are you not going out tonight?"

She'd been so happy the last week, going on and on about Boyd now that she could finally talk about him with me. I hadn't wanted to kill her buzz with my stupid boy drama. "Yeah, I'm no good. I canceled."

"Oh." She frowned. "I was planning on staying with Boyd tonight since you weren't going to be here. But I can tell him I need to stay home and take care of you."

Her kindness was salt in a wound. My days off were salt in the wound too. Basically, I was an open wound and everything pressed against it and rubbed against me in a way that made my breath trip and my chest spasm. Maybe Norma could make it better—distract me with a hot bath and instrumental music and make me peppermint tea like she used to when she'd come home from college and find me bruised and sore from my father's latest rampage.

Except this pain was in the inside. And instrumental music would only make me think of JC at the piano, giving his soul away to an empty room. And I didn't want to ruin her date with the person who finally seemed to take care of her.

"No, Sissy. I'm fine. I'll probably sleep the whole night anyway." I wouldn't sleep. I'd toss and turn and relive every minute I'd had with JC. It was exactly what I hadn't wanted with him. I'd wanted freedom and fun and a reason to feel alive.

Instead, I was restrained and confined.

I'd get over him. Of course I would. I was tough like that. But that would be another episode. This episode I would wrap the chains around me like a blanket, clinging to the corners of my prison like an animal that had yet to realize that its cage door had been left open.

• • •

I'd half expected JC to show up at the club on Thursday night. Especially since the last time I'd seen him, I'd left without a goodbye. It seemed reasonable that he'd wonder what was up and come looking for answers eventually.

When he didn't, I swallowed the lump in my throat and took it as a sign. He'd fought for my interest before. Now he was done. It made it easier to give the note to Alyssa the next Monday. And the next. The problem was trying to decide when notes were no longer necessary.

When Alyssa's vacation came around and I had no one to deliver my message, I figured it was time. It had been the fourth Wednesday, anyway. He should have gotten the hint by now, but if JC wondered at all whether or not we were finished, he'd know when I didn't show up this time. Without a formal cancellation, he'd know we were over.

That became my mantra, in fact. *It's over, it's over, it's over.*

It's over, as I went into work that Thursday night.

It's over, as I checked out cash bags to the bartenders for their registers.

It's over, as I finished my opening tasks and climbed the stairs to the Viper to set up for that night's bachelorette party.

It's over, as I opened the door to the room and found him sitting in the same pose as when I'd first seen him. His legs stretched out in front of him, his arms casually at his sides.

I froze in my tracks, but my blood...my blood ran hot. Like I'd suddenly walked into a sauna, except the steam was on the inside. It was hard to get a breath, and when I did, all I could smell was *him*—half real, half remembered scents of sandalwood cologne, sweat, and sex. With my heart thumping and my stomach swimming and my senses on overdrive—yeah, this wasn't over.

This wasn't over by a long shot.

He's here.

Through the lust-inspired haze, excitement spiraled through me that had less to do with his ability to carnally intoxicate me and more to do with the empty pit in my chest that was only filled by his presence. That center part of me that recognized him as the guy I wanted. As the guy I loved. That hum was harder to silence than the ache between my legs. And oh, how I wished for that hum both to quiet and to crescendo. How I wished I could simultaneously drown out even the faintest whisper of the emotion and yet sing it full out at the top of my lungs.

I needed to be strong. I needed to not want him. I needed to not get sucked back in.

I needed to jump in his lap and beg him to let me ride him.

No. Not that. Not ever that again.

Besides, what if he wasn't there to claim me as I secretly yearned he was? What if he was there to make our ending official and final? I clung to the disappointment that bubbled up at those thoughts and let that be my guide in our interaction.

I suppose I didn't cling quite enough, because my voice was coated with desire when I found the strength to speak. "I wonder if I'll ever stop being surprised at your ability to show up in this club when the doors have yet to be opened."

Actually, I was pleased with my greeting. I thought it made me sound laid-back even though every muscle in my body was tense.

He smiled, and I swear I went wet.

"I hope you're not. I like to be able to surprise you." His eyes narrowed. "Your surprises though...I'm not really sure I like those."

I swallowed, not sure I wanted to go where he was going. "My surprises?"

"First surprise was an empty bed after I'd left you in it. The second surprise came when you no-showed on me last night."

Yep. Definitely didn't want to go where he was going.

Which was admittedly naïve because what did I expect? More to the point, what did I think I wanted him to say? That he wasn't bothered by my brush-off? That he hadn't noticed I'd ducked out on him? That everything was hunky-dory?

No, I wanted him to be bothered because it meant he cared. So I'd have to take it, whether I liked confrontation or not.

"Okay, well." I bit my lip as I gathered my words. "The first time shouldn't even count because *you* left the bed before I did. Excuse me for thinking maybe my presence was no longer wanted." I'd come off a little bitchier than I'd meant to, but I didn't regret it. He needed to know I was bothered by what he did too.

"Yeah. Because I've made it so obviously clear how much I don't want you." His sarcastic retort made me scowl.

But it also made my heart trip. Silly, really. I already knew he wanted me. Of course I did. Hearing him say it, though, when he wasn't seconds from pushing inside of me and I still had all my clothes on—it felt different. It felt like he was saying something more than he was. It messed me up.

Feeling out of control, I turned away from him. "You disappeared. I took it at face value." I busied myself with making sure the chairs were arranged around the tables the way the party had requested instead of with studying JC's expression and trying to analyze its meaning.

Behind me, he let out a frustrated sigh. "I was downstairs. You fell asleep. I figured you needed your rest, so I went down to play a bit. It hadn't ever been a problem before."

I spun toward him. "You'd abandoned me before?"

"Don't make this bigger than it is." He pulled his legs in and leaned over, his elbows resting on his thighs. "I'd slipped out a couple of times before, yes. Like I said, it's never been a problem."

"You couldn't leave a note?"

"I could say the same to you."

He had a point. At least when he'd left, he'd intended to come back. I hadn't.

But I was hurt. I was mad. I was self-righteous. "Hey, I'm not going to feel bad about leaving that night. You were closed off from the minute I walked in the door." My words were heavy and bitter on my tongue.

"Really, I guess you didn't abandon me since you were never really there."

I despised everything coming out of my mouth. They threw blame, and worse, they gave me away. I preferred that he didn't realize I had feelings for him. There was no way I wanted to be accused of breaking our deal by falling for him. In fact, if he confronted me about it, I'd probably deny it. And I'd look more foolish than I already did because it was so obvious that I felt a lot.

Yet I couldn't stop myself. I kept saying the girly, emotional blackmail-y shit that I hated saying almost as much as I hated feeling.

"I have no idea what you're talking about, Gwen. I was there." He didn't meet my eyes, though, and I felt justified. Because it reinforced my belief that he'd been closed off on purpose.

Didn't that mean he really had felt something for me? Why else would he try to hide himself? And if he'd felt it for one day, why couldn't he feel it again?

Maybe I was being too obstinate. If I gave him time, if I was patient with him, perhaps he could become more comfortable with the emotion.

On the other hand, what if I just got further wrapped up in him and he never came around?

His gaze found mine. As always, he saw right through me. Saw me debating. He took advantage of it. "You remember. I know you do. Or should I remind you what happened that night? Should I tell you what we did?" His eyes were dark now. "We had a pretty fantastic time, if you'll recall."

I didn't want to talk about the *fantastic time* we'd had. I was already wavering, and for whatever ridiculous reason, our argument had only elevated my desire. My core was wet and tingling and thoughts of fantastic times were not what I needed.

I turned back to the chairs, shifting them gruffly. "You know what? Forget I said anything. I left because you were gone. You didn't try to reach me after, so I assumed it hadn't been an issue."

"I figured you needed your space. I'd pushed you that night. Sexually." He was still teasing, trying to push my buttons. Trying to get my thoughts where he wanted them—on our physical connection. On how good we were together.

It didn't work. That he'd thought it had been about sex actually made things worse. *Fucking asshole.* My irritation notched up, when I should have been relieved that he hadn't called me out on emotional involvement.

And if I really hadn't been fine with the kink, as he said he'd suspected, then shouldn't he have been more concerned about checking in on me?

"Whatever," I said, more to myself than to him. I couldn't talk about that night anymore. Thinking about it was starting to rub at me like the itchy fabric of a wool sweater. It looked good, but it also scratched, scratched, scratched.

I had to get rid of the sweater.

I spun back to him with false bravado. "Anyway, the second surprise shouldn't have been a surprise either. After three weeks, I figured you'd get the hint."

His posture tensed. "Get what hint?"

With his eyes on me, it was harder to say it. Even though I'd practiced it all day. *It's over.* I opened my mouth to say it. Nothing came out.

JC bolted out of his chair and closed nearly the whole distance between us, his face hard. Harder than I'd ever seen it. "Get what hint?" he asked again.

I shrunk back, unable to speak or look away. Doubt trembled down my spine. I'd done this wrong. In this moment, I realized my actions had felt shitty because they had been.

He read the guilt on my expression. "Are you ending our arrangement, Gwen? Because I think that I at least deserve the courtesy of getting that kind of news face-to-face."

I pushed past the lump in my throat. "I'm sorry. You're right. You did." God, I felt small. And tired. And out of my league. "I thought that..." *That if I'd shown up to break things off face-to-face, I'd never go through with it.* I couldn't tell him that. "I don't know what I thought. I was wrong."

He held his arms out to the side in a grand gesture. "Finally. We're getting somewhere." His hands fell to his side. "Now. Why?"

"Why what?" I should have prepared myself for this conversation. I'd been stupid to think I would never have to have it, and I didn't have believable answers at the ready.

"Why do you want to end things? Did I hurt you? Were things not working out? Have you found someone else?"

"No!" I had to pick a lie, but none of those were fair. "No, to all of that."

"Then what?" He exhaled as he asked, his relief evident. "Come on. We're good together, Gwen. You can't say that we don't have chemistry."

"It's a lot of things." I went back to the chairs, using my movement around the table to distance myself from him.

He followed. "Like?"

"Like work. It's been busy."

"You still have Wednesdays off. Don't say you don't. I stopped by last night looking."

He looked for me. It hit me in the gut. While I'd sat at home convinced he didn't care in the least about our end, he'd come to the club to find me. Had he wanted to see me that badly? Was he giving himself away too? Was this proof that he was also emotionally involved?

I couldn't let myself think that way. It was a slippery slope, and I was already close to saying *fuck it all* and that I'd be there next week. "Yes, I still have Wednesdays off. But I have other things to do with my free time."

"Like what?"

He stayed at my heels. I could feel him like a wall of warmth. If I leaned back, let my body fall into him, would he put his arms around me? Would he help me feel secure? Would it make up for the other things he couldn't give me?

"I don't know…th-things," I said, stumbling over my words. "Family things. My sister needs me. And my brother. My father is being released from jail in a few weeks and that had a big impact on—"

JC cut me off. "So you're a little stressed. So what?"

I swung toward him, unable to decide if I was more peeved at his disinterest or his condescension. "If you'd let me actually tell you something about myself, maybe you'd see why I'm more than a little stressed."

"That's not us. That's not who we are to each other."

In his straight inflection, I heard the truth. I heard him convincing himself as much as me, and again I saw the potential relationship we might have if I only had patience. If I only had the grit to stick it out and wait for him, one day possibly we could be *that* to each other.

But I was gutless.

"That's not us," I said. "You're right. We have an arrangement to be carefree and fun. And now we're arguing. Over our commitment-free relationship. Over sex. That's not what I signed up for."

My throat tightened, and I had to clear it before I went on. "Anyway, my point is I don't have time for this right now. I have other things going on."

Back to the chairs. Focus on the chairs.

JC hesitated, and I thought I'd finally gotten to him.

But then he was at my side again, his demeanor light and yet tenacious. "And that's exactly why you need what we have right now. You need the release."

You need, you need, you need. It struck me as a strange argument. *You should because you need.* Why did he care what I needed? What did he need?

I spun toward him. "Why are you even here, JC? Aren't you supposed to be on a plane?"

"I moved my flight."

"Until when?"

"Tomorrow night." He slipped his hands into his pockets, and while I liked that pose on him, I recognized it was one of his less confident stances.

It was my turn to take advantage. "Why?" I could play the same game he had with me. The push, push, push. It wasn't that hard when I was motivated. "Why did you change your flight?"

He shrugged. "I wasn't ready to leave town."

"Because of me?"

He ran a hand through his hair, unable to look at me. Unable to answer.

I had him on the edge, and it thrilled me. Because I could only get to him this way if I already got to him in other ways. I pressed on, sidestepping a chair so there was nothing between us. "Why can't you say it? Because of me, right?"

Abruptly, he grabbed my upper arms and pulled me to him roughly. "Yes, because of you. Of course, because of you. I need..." His lips hovered above mine—tempting, taunting—and I couldn't decide if I wanted him to kiss me or to finish his thought.

He exhaled, his breath dancing across my mouth, his body relaxing as he pressed into me, hot and inviting. "I need a distraction. I have things on my mind. I want my mind on you. I want my hands on you." He brushed my arms with long strokes. "I want my mouth on you."

I was the addict again, on the brink of giving in to the sweet pull of his temptation, not caring if there was anything real behind his drug. Eyes half-closed, my skin burning up from his touch, I gave a last-ditch effort to save myself. "There are a hundred girls out there who could be your distraction."

"No, there's not. There's only you."

My breath caught. I would have sunk to my knees if he weren't still holding me up. And yet, he still wasn't kissing me, his lips still flitting only inches above mine.

I lifted my eyes to his. He regretted saying it. I saw it plain as day, his face having fallen with the slip. Or the wrong choice of words. I didn't know which. Only saw that he wished he could erase it.

It gutted me.

He shut his eyes tightly, and in those next few seconds, all I could think was *why doesn't he let me go?* When he opened them, I expected he'd take it back. I waited for it. I prayed for it because while I cherished his admission, whatever it was he meant by it, I couldn't bear it. It didn't make it better. It only made it worse.

When he spoke again, it was carefully. Controlled. "I don't want to push you," he said. "You're right that we agreed this was going to be casual. It still is, for the most part. But you've come a long way. You seem happier. And I…I like spending time with you. I'd hate to see our arrangement ending just when I think you need me most."

Every other word he said made me melt. The words in between pissed me off. And he needn't worry about losing the ability to surprise me because none of what he'd spoken had been expected.

He trailed his hands down the length of my arms. "I know you have to work. I'll let you get back to it." He laced his fingers through mine. "But I'll be at the hotel tonight. I'd love it if you came by after your shift. Think about it." He let me go, and after one last lingering look, he headed toward the door.

I glanced at where he'd held me, sure I'd see burns on my skin from his touch. Sure that he'd left some sort of a scar.

I wondered if I'd marked him at all in return. "And what about you, JC?" I asked, my words landing on his back. "Do you need me?"

He stopped, but he didn't turn to me. "That's not us, Gwen. That's not what we have." His statement wrapped its cold arms around me as he started out again. In the threshold, he pivoted back to face me. "But I came here tonight, didn't I?"

• • •

When I slid my key card in the door lock, I could no longer say what was going on between us, nor what I thought would happen next. I only knew I had no other choice. I had to be there. Even if he never said anything more meaningful than, *"There's only you,"* even if he never fought more than he had by showing up at my club, I would be there for him.

He was dozing in the armchair, but his eyes flew open when I walked toward him. As if he could feel me as he slept.

He cleared the sleep from his voice. "You came."

"Not yet."

His lip curled up slowly into a wicked grin that was both familiar and arousing. "Is that a challenge?"

I barely had a chance to nod before his hands were on me. Within minutes, he'd released his cock, removed my panties and pulled me into his lap. I was wet but still tight as he ground into me. I screamed from the mixture of pleasure and pain and wrapped my arms around his neck while I begged him for more.

He delivered, pounding into me at a feverish pace. He was hard. He was merciless. He was punishing me for having stayed away, handling me rougher than he ever had as he bit at my nipples and dug his fingers into my hips.

He spoke as he fucked me. This time, instead of asking me how I felt, he told me. "I make you feel good. You like this. You love the way I feel inside you, Gwen. You feel me now. Feel me." He was reminding me. Making sure I didn't forget. Making sure I would remember this before I thought of ending us again.

I came. More than once. By the time he'd released, my voice was hoarse and my thighs ached. My dress felt hot and heavy on my sweaty skin. And though my center continued to hum with thoughts of *more*, I was content. Even when he gently pushed me off. Even when he didn't meet my eyes.

I knew then, and I accepted. This was how it was going to be between us. We'd meet. We'd fuck. He'd put up walls between us. And I'd love him.

Chapter Fifteen

"Do you want me to file the workman's compensation form for Dean's claim?" It was usually something Matt did, but I was running out of work to do. If I didn't keep busy, I would probably fall asleep. That was the hardest part about the floor waxing days—staying awake. They were scheduled quarterly and could only be done when the club was closed. The team that came in took around four hours to do all the floors, and two managers had to be there for safety reasons since the cleaners were contracted laborers. It was now just after nine in the morning, and they'd been there since six. Since Matt and I had closed the night before, we were the two sticking around.

"Hmm?" Matt seemed to be paying more attention to the radio than to me. He'd had it on all morning, tuned to an all-news station. The current report was about an arrest made in a four-year-old murder of a local woman.

It gave me a chill. I hated the news. Any of it. All of it. I had enough drama in my own life. I couldn't deal with listening to tales of murders and rapes and kidnappings and drug busts. They were all really the same story—pain, pain, pain. I'd had enough pain. I didn't need more. All it did was make me dwell on my abusive past and on my father who had been released from jail only the week before. I hadn't seen him, and I didn't want to. I didn't even want to think about him.

"Matt, why don't you go on home?" Then I could turn on something with a beat. Something not depressing. And daydream about JC without anyone in the room to question what I was thinking about while I stared absently into space.

It was what I did with much of my free time lately—relived my nights with JC. It had been six weeks since he'd asked me to keep our agreement going. After that, our relationship had maintained a status quo. He was never again as cold as he had been the night I'd woken to an empty bed and never again as open as the day we'd spent together in the real world. I took it as an acceptable compromise. Really, I didn't have another choice. I was sure that he felt *something* for me and I didn't want to give up on that. Besides, whether he did or didn't, every night we spent together I fell deeper into love with him. Ending things was no longer an option. I wanted to be with him, whatever his terms.

Still, I dreamed of more. *If I'm patient,* I'd tell myself, *maybe it could be more than just a dream.*

A monotone voice reporting the *"current speculation that bail will be denied"* was not a part of my JC daydreams. Since Matt had yet to answer me about going home, I got up from my desk and went to stand in front of his.

I snapped my fingers in front of his glassy stare. "Hey, Matt. I think you're dozing over here. Why don't you go home?"

He blinked a few times then seemed to wake up from his stupor. "I'm sorry. I guess I am in a bit of a daze." He looked at his watch. "I'll make it. Paco should be done soon."

"Exactly. Paco should be done soon, so there's no reason for us both to hang around."

He smiled. "You know I can't leave you here alone."

We always followed the two manager rule. I didn't think this one time would be too much of a problem.

"I won't be alone. I'll be with Paco. And you and I both know that sweet old man isn't going to do anything to me. So go on. Get out of here. I don't usually go to bed until noon so I'm still wide awake." Or I would be as soon as I could get some Sia playing.

Matt didn't seem convinced.

"I'll walk you out, and we can see exactly how much more he has to do. Come on." I nodded for him to follow as I headed to the door. When he didn't, I went back to him and grabbed his arm and tugged. "Come on, you stubborn oaf."

He groaned. But he stood up with a smile. "I'm not agreeing. We'll check on Paco and then decide."

"Okay. But bring your things because if he's almost done, you're leaving."

He muttered something about me being bossy and reminding him of someone else he used to know while he grabbed his keys and wallet from the safe where he kept them while he worked. As soon as we walked out of the office, we heard the whir of the wax machine and found Paco just starting on the main level. He always worked top to bottom.

"See? He's almost done. Out you go." I walked Matt to the employee entrance to be sure he actually left and to grab a bottle of water from the extra fridge designated for the staff. As I was about to start back to the office, there was a knock on the door.

Protocol was to check the security cameras before letting anyone in, but Matt had just left. It had to be him. "Did you forget something?" I asked, as I pulled the door open.

It wasn't Matt.

"Daddy," I stepped back automatically, a reaction from years of training to cower in his presence. It was a mistake. I should have shut the door in his face. Now it was too late because the man who'd threatened me for as long as I could remember was already crossing the threshold.

"Gwenyth." His grin was lopsided and dark. "Look at you. You grew up all pretty." He was thinner than when I'd last seen him. More wrinkled. Harder. His eyes had never had any light in them, but somehow they'd now lost their color, leaving two pools of black. His dark hair was peppered with gray. He had scars. There were several on his face and neck, remnants of prison fights, I assumed. There was a particularly angry line under his right eye that extended to his jaw. I couldn't help but cringe at it, the pain it must have inflicted obvious from its ugliness.

Serves him right.

He threw the door closed behind him but didn't use enough force for it to latch.

I took another step back into the kitchen. My heart raced, pounding against my chest so strongly I was sure it was audible to him as well. I told myself not to panic. Not yet. Maybe he just wanted to see me. He'd be stupid to hurt me when he'd just gotten out of jail.

Not that my father had ever been very smart...

Somehow, I found my voice. "What are you doing here?"

"Now is that any way to greet your father?" He put a fist on his hip and looked around the room. "A kitchen, huh? I thought this was some sort of a music club."

"It's a nightclub with food service." I wasn't sure why I was explaining. I was trembling, my thoughts shaking as much as my body. "You aren't supposed to be here. It's employees only. You need to leave."

My eyes darted everywhere. Over his shoulder at the door not quite closed—could I make it past him if I ran? Over my shoulder toward the room where Paco was—could he hear me over his equipment if I screamed?

This is all learned response, I told myself. *He hasn't threatened you. He won't threaten you.*

"Don't worry. I won't stay long. I only came to give you the news."

He wasn't the sort of person who could calm me with a *"don't worry."* I swallowed. "What news?"

"I got out!" He threw his hands up in the air in *ta da* pose. I jumped at the sudden gesture, which only seemed to make him grin wider.

He was playing games. Of course, he'd gotten out. He was standing in front of me, wasn't he? It was a statement meant to throw me off-guard and make me lose my wits. It did both.

I gaped, not knowing what to say. Not knowing what he *wanted* me to say.

He squinted one eye and tapped a finger to his chin. "Oh, yeah, that's right. You knew that. You told my lawyer you didn't want to have anything to do with me when I was released. I couldn't believe that when he told me. I had to check it out for myself."

My gut twisted with the old familiar feeling of being in trouble. "I didn't say that." My voice sounded thin and unsure. I took a breath and steadied myself. "Norma just told the lawyer that we didn't have any place for you to stay. And we don't. It's only a two-bedroom apartment." That was a lie. It was three bedrooms—Ben had stayed in the third room when he'd lived with us. Now it was Norma's office/storage room.

My father glowered. "I could have stayed on the couch. I can pretty much sleep anywhere after ten years of a prison cot."

I bit my lip, looking for excuses. "That wouldn't work. We have odd schedules. You'd never get any sleep out there with us going in and out. Don't you have to be in a halfway house or something, anyway?"

He shrugged. "Only for a little while. When they let me out of there, I'll need a place. Surely you could find a spot for me in that posh high-rise of yours."

"It's Norma's apartment, Daddy. She said it wouldn't work. You'll have to ask her if you want her to reconsider." I didn't feel too bad throwing Norma under the bus. He hadn't gotten abusive toward us kids until our mother had died, and since Norma was older then, she'd received little of it. She wasn't under his thumb the way Ben and I were.

She'd stand up just fine in a confrontation with him, unlike me.

Problem was, Daddy knew that.

"Cute. I ain't gonna go talk to Norma. She's never been fond of me. Did you know that bitch didn't even send me a Christmas card once while I was in jail?"

His last comment was actually a dig at me. I'd sent one the first couple of years, when I still believed I might have love for him. I'd since realized that all I ever had for him was fear. Funny how those emotions could be mixed up so easily when they were nothing alike.

I dug back into my repertoire of ways to calm him. *Apologize.* He always liked to hear that. "I'm sorry I didn't contact you more. It seemed like it would be easier—for both of us—to keep our distance."

"Easier. You really believe that or are you talking shit to protect your ass?"

I wanted to say that I was trying to be nice. That I wasn't worried about protecting my ass because I hadn't done anything wrong.

But I was scared, and I was protecting my ass. "I did believe it, Daddy. I do believe it. Anyway, you're out now. So everything's good." Just like when I was younger, I didn't know what to say or how to say it. It felt like playing Russian roulette with words. Which one would please him? Which one would set him off?

"Yes. Everything's good. Except now I have to get some income. The more money I make, the sooner I'm out of that place. Do you know how hard it is to find a decent job with a criminal record?"

I shook my head, afraid to speak, praying that Paco would finish up and come find me soon.

"Well, I got something."

"Good! Congratulations!" I was too eager. My smile was too bright. He didn't say anything. He studied me with cold eyes.

A chill ran down my spine as I suddenly realized something. Norma hadn't bought her condo until after he'd gone to jail. He was well aware of her address since it was the one on file for all of his next-of-kin paperwork. He must have scoped it out after his release. Or else he was guessing because of her location that it was *posh*, as he'd said.

But there wasn't anything on file saying where I worked. Norma had always been very good about making sure both Ben and I remained sheltered from him, even when he was behind bars. It was to make us feel safer, she'd said. Now I realized she'd been planning ahead. Been planning for this very situation.

It was never good to question him, but I needed to know. "How did you find me anyway? Who told you I was working here?"

"My lawyer did. A while back. He happened to come in here one night and saw you working. Kudos, Gwen. Managing a big club in the city. Pretty big stuff for a poor Anders kid from Jersey. I didn't think you had it in ya like your sister. I sure as hell know your faggot brother doesn't have it in him."

My jaw clenched at the mention of Ben, and for the first time since he'd moved across the country, I was glad. There wasn't any way our father could get to him.

"Anyway." He scratched at the collar of his button-down. "I was taking a chance when I came by today. I'm guessing you usually work at night but I can only be out in the world during daytime hours. Lucky break that I found you."

"Yeah, lucky." At a time of day that I was almost never at the club, on an occasion that I was the only employee in the building, on the one fucking time I didn't look at the cameras before opening the doors. Real lucky.

"Look," I said, feigning control, "I have to get back to my work. My boss is going to come looking for me soon. So you need to go."

He ignored my bluff, either not believing me or not caring. "It's not gonna cut it, Gwen. My job. It will take a long time to get out of that house and into a place of my own with the kind of wage they offered. And I can't stay there that long. You don't know what that place is like."

"I can't let you stay at our place, Daddy. I told you, it's—"

"Up to Norma," he finished with me. "Then let's see. If that's not going to work, maybe we can discuss some other ways you can help me." With eyes half closed, he rubbed his neck, his long hair shaking as he did, reminding me of a dog scratching at an itch. "How about you just give me the cash directly?"

Yes. He was a total dog.

"H-how much?" I stuttered as my fear neared its threshold. He was setting me up to have to say *no* to him, and I tried never to say *no* to him.

"Hmm." He looked at the clothes I was wearing, my shoes. They weren't Bergdorf Goodman quality, but with Norma paying most of my bills, I was able to splurge on a few nice things. I felt guilty now as I remembered the kind of life we'd had growing up. My shoes could have paid for groceries for a month.

So I shouldn't have been surprised when he named his amount. "Twenty-five thousand ought to do it."

"I don't have that kind of money." My words came out breathy and thin. He hated any response to a request that wasn't *yes, sir.*

"Come on. With that pretty building you girls are living in? I'm betting twenty-five k doesn't even cover half a year's rent in that place. You can't spare six month's rent to help your old man get out of the hellhole he shares with a bunch of filthy addicts?"

"It's not me who has the money. I told you. It's Norma. I barely make enough to contribute to the utilities." More lies. More pointing at Norma. She'd take care of him, though. She'd know what to say to make him back down, while I...just...didn't.

He made a clicking sound in the back of his throat that was more menacing than it should have been. "You can get it. I know you can."

I shook my head fervently. "I can't."

"Ask Norma for it." He came toward me as he spoke. "She'll give it to you. Do it for your dear old dad. To make up for all that time you didn't do shit for him." With each step he took, I took one backwards until I was up against the stainless steel worktable with nowhere else to go.

I braced my hands on the hard surface behind me and quickly tried to plan my next move. If I told him that I'd get it, would he go? And then what? Would I have to give him the money? Would I have to go into hiding? He couldn't be charged with anything. Growing up, we'd had home visits from the cops and social services a couple of times, and my father had made sure we showed them what he wanted them to see— food on the table, toys in the house. He was always able to cover up his crimes. Especially when half of them were merely mental games. Games that didn't leave marks or bruises.

This was that type of game. If I didn't give him the money, he'd hurt me. I had no doubt of that. It would be nice to believe he'd changed over the years—I had—but prison never softened anyone. If anything, he was probably harder. I wondered if he hit harder too. If he hit me, if he physically touched me, the law would step in. It was too much to hope it would be enough to put him back behind bars, but was getting smacked around worth it to get a restraining order?

It was. But I didn't think I could provoke him like that on purpose. It went against a lifetime of training. I obeyed. I tried *not* to get hit.

Except…

Something triggered in me. Something besides fear. Rage. Because how dare he? How dare he come into my work, my life, and demand compensation for the time he spent in jail because he'd beaten his children? How dare he have beaten us in the first place? It had taken years to let go of the constant ball of worry in my stomach and even longer to gain any sort of confidence. How dare he take it from me now?

"Well?" He took another step toward me. We were less than an arm's length away now.

Gathering every bit of strength I could muster—more than I knew I had—I straightened my back and said, "No."

"What did you say?"

"I said no. I'm not going to get you the money. Not because I don't think Norma will give it to me, but because I don't want to. It's not yours. We don't owe it to you. I don't owe you anything."

Smack. The back of his hand across my cheek. I heard the distinct sound of it before I registered the burn, the shrieking pain. I'd half expected it and yet, as his knuckles made contact with my bone, it stunned me, stole my breath, sent green specks across my field of vision.

I gasped, raising my palm to my face, as if that could stop my skin from stinging. As if it could protect me from another strike.

"You fucking bitch. You've always been so fucking ungrateful." He lifted his hand again, and I closed my eyes, bracing myself for the next one.

It never came.

"Don't you fucking lay a hand on her!"

At the sound of JC's voice, my eyes flew open. He must have come in the unlatched door. Now he was behind my father and gripping his forearms, pulling him away from me. They were similar in height, but where JC was fit and trim, my father was bulky and buff. It wasn't a fair fight. My father could crush him.

"What the—?" Dad was as surprised as I was to find we had a guest. "Get your hands off me," he said, shrugging out of JC's grasp.

JC rushed to me. "Gwen, are you all right?"

"I think so." *Now that you're here, yes.*

He wrapped an arm around me but didn't pull me too close, tilting my chin up to examine my face. I could tell by the way he cringed that I was already bruising.

"Jesus, did he do that?" JC's eyes grew dark and hard even before I nodded. He turned back to my father, his arm pulled back to punch.

That's when I saw the knife.

"No!" I grabbed JC's arm, stopping him before he hit. "He has a knife."

He followed my glance to see the knife in my father's hand. It was a rusty old pocketknife. Something he'd probably bought on the street. I doubted he was allowed to have weapons in his house. It would just be another thing I'd report to the police later.

JC stepped forward, blocking me. Protecting me. "What do you want from her?" I clutched onto the back of his shirt, and he wrapped an arm behind him to pull me in closer. It made me feel exactly the way I'd always thought a parent should make you feel—the way my father never made me feel. Warm, fiercely guarded, defiantly loved.

The man who'd donated his DNA to my existence looked past JC, his eyes landing directly on mine. "Gwen knows what I want."

My gaze flicked down to the knife and back to my father's face. JC tensed further under my hands, and I knew he'd fight for me. I couldn't let him do it. He was smaller and unarmed. There's no way he'd win, and the thought of him getting hurt...

My throat tightened.

"I'll get it," I said, lying through my teeth. "I'll get the money for you. Just go."

Dad didn't even look at JC, as though his presence didn't faze him in the least. "You see that you do. I'll be back on Thursday. Same time." He took a couple of steps backward then added, "You know I trust you, Gwen baby. Don't let your father down."

With a final nod, he went out the door.

JC followed to shut it after him, making sure it latched properly this time. I, on the other hand, ran to the sink, where I proceeded to dry heave.

• • •

JC got me a Sprite from the bar and had me sit on the worktable and drink it to try to calm my stomach. He took care of Paco, signing the paperwork that said the floor work was complete, and made sure the door was shut and locked after he left.

I watched him do my job, wondering if he thought I was helpless or if he was just being nice. I wasn't helpless. I'd picked myself up after many attacks. This, though. This sweet attentiveness and concern—it was nice.

When JC disappeared back into the main part of the club, I called Norma.

"Are you alone now?" my sister asked after I'd told her everything.

"No. JC's still with me."

"Perfect. If you don't stay with him, make sure he takes you home. Our apartment is secured, so you'd be safe there. I'll talk to some people and see what our best options are from here. We'll have to talk to the cops later, though. Are you good for now?"

I hadn't cried, but now I felt like I might. "Mm-hmm," I said, holding back the sob. "Thank you, sissy."

JC returned as I clicked END. "I turned off all the lights and locked up the office."

I nodded, not trusting my voice.

He nodded once in return. Then, taking a towel from the rack of dish linens by the sink, he asked, "Are you sure we shouldn't have called the police?"

"Yes, I'm sure." Memories of red and blue lights arriving at our house flashed through my mind. The rare occasions that the neighbors cared enough to call them because of sounds of domestic distress. Each time they were there to rescue us. Each time Dad made his excuses—scared *us* into making excuses—and they left us to be hit again.

I took another sip of my Sprite and explained. "I've never had a good experience with police. I'd prefer to let Norma handle all of it. There are security cameras in this room. I'll give her the tape, she can take it to whoever. She'll make sure we do this right so he gets put back behind bars."

I was still worried. My father had always been violent, but he wasn't an idiot. He had to know I could report him. Did he think I was still so under his thumb that I wouldn't?

"I don't like this," JC said, dropping a handful of ice from the bin into the towel.

"I know. Thank you for doing it my way." From the look he gave me, I wasn't so sure he planned on continuing doing things my way. I wouldn't have been surprised to find he'd already called them while he was getting my drink.

But then, as he wrapped the towel up to keep the ice from spilling, he sighed. "I've been let down by the law before too. I understand doing things your own way."

I pressed the somewhat cold drink to my aching cheek and stared at him, more grateful than ever for his presence, and only a little bit distracted by the realization that the last time I'd sat on this table, I'd had his cock inside me.

He walked over to me then and took the drink out of my hand. He set it on the table next to me and gently pressed the ice pack against my cheekbone. "This should work better."

I hissed at the sting. He winced with me. "I'm sorry."

"It's fine," I said through gritted teeth. "It will get better as it numbs." I spoke from experience, but I bit my tongue before saying anything else on the matter, conscious of how much personal information I shared.

We were quiet for a few minutes, JC dabbing at my face while I tried not to wince. Then I realized, "Oh my God, I didn't even say thank you! I would probably look even worse right now if you hadn't come along when you did."

He kept his eyes on his task. "I just wish I'd gotten here sooner. And you could never look anything related to the term *worse*. You're breathtaking. As always."

My stomach squirmed at his compliment. It was weird how he could make me get all shy and flustered from only a few words after all the things he'd seen me do naked. I looked down at my knees, hoping he thought my flush was from the cold of the ice. "How did you know I'd be here, anyway?"

His mouth turned down at the edges. "I didn't. I was coming to see Matt."

"Oh. I sent him home." It was silly to be disappointed. He'd been there for me all the same. It didn't matter if he'd come for me or not.

JC's brows drew in. "I can't believe he'd leave you here alone like that." His words were terse and barely controlled.

"It's not Matt's fault. I shouldn't have opened the door." It had been a stupid mistake. My father was only one of the many bad situations that could have met me. *Stupid, stupid, stupid.*

JC lowered the towel from my cheek and looked me directly in the eyes. "No, you shouldn't have." His scolding completed, he returned the pack to my now-frozen face. "But trust me, Matt's going to get an earful from me as well."

The moment felt vulnerable and fragile, and though it might have only been me that was really vulnerable and fragile, it seemed like JC was as well. "You and Matt have a lot more between you than just your rental of The Deck, don't you?"

His eyes flicked to mine then back to my cheek. "Yes."

"But you don't want to talk about it."

"No."

So much for vulnerable. All I ever got from him was walls, walls, walls. He'd shown up like my knight in shining armor, and I'd wanted to believe that it meant something. That I was someone he wanted to save. That I was worth fighting for.

But how could he think I was worth anything if he wouldn't tell me even the simplest of details about himself?

It was impossible. I had to wake up and smell the coffee once and for all—he was never going to open up to me. I was never going to needle my way in. A relationship built on anything more than sex was never going to happen between us.

I wrapped my arms around myself, new tears pricking at my eyes. At least, if he asked, I could pretend they were for my father rather than JC. Though I doubted he'd even care if I said they were for him.

I sat up straighter. "I got this." I reached to take the ice pack from him, ignoring the buzz that surged through my body as my hand touched his. "Sorry you had to deal with this. I'm sure I can take care of myself now." Norma had told me to stay with him, but I couldn't deal with the pain of rejection on top of everything else that had happened that morning.

He chuckled, not relinquishing the pack. "I'm not leaving you."

"It's fine. Really. This goes far beyond what *we are*." It was bitchy and uncalled for, but I couldn't help myself. I was hurting in so many ways. Lashing out felt good.

JC put the ice pack down and tilted his head to look at me. "Gwen, don't." The two words alone in that serious tone—they bit into me. Made me feel childish. Made me lose some of my bravado.

Some. Not all. "Don't what?"

"Don't belittle us."

I scoffed. "I'm not saying anything you haven't said."

He placed his hands on either side of me, leveling his gaze, caging me in. "You're right. I said it. It was complete bullshit then and it's complete bullshit now." He waited a beat. "You know I have feelings for you."

My breath got caught in my lungs.

"You do?" It came out as a whisper, barely audible over the sound of my heart thump, thump, thumping in my chest. Maybe my father had hit me harder than I thought, and I was imagining this whole scenario.

JC smirked at me tenderly—was that a thing? Could people smirk tenderly? Because that's what he did. "Don't act like that surprises you. I know you know that I do."

My breathing was back now, fast and shallow. I pinched my hip to make sure I wasn't dreaming, which never works. If I really wanted to be sure, I needed to ask him to pinch me. Since my face was starting to sting again without the ice to keep it numb, I decided that was proof enough of my consciousness.

I played it cool, as if I weren't completely floored by the conversation. "I'm surprised that you're admitting it." That only lasted half a second. "Why *are* you admitting it?" *And why couldn't you before?*

Because he was right—I *did* know that he had feelings for me. It was the only thing that made it possible to go back to him week after week. He'd had feelings for quite some time, just as I had. So why was he only telling me now, out of the blue?

God, I hoped it wasn't out of pity.

"Honestly, I don't know." JC let go of the table and ran his hand through his hair, his focus somewhere beyond me. "I got some news yesterday that I've been wanting for a long time. News that should have made me very happy. And yet all I could think was, *I wonder what Gwen's doing now*. And when I walked in and saw that assface about to hit you, I'm going to be honest, I wanted him dead. Even more when I found out who he was. That he was your father. Someone who'd hurt you before."

He reached a finger out to trace the hem of my skirt across my kneecap, sending a smattering of goose bumps down my skin. "I thought that I could keep anything with you away from the rest of my life." His voice was quiet now. Raw. "That I could lock it in the space of our hotel room. But you're everywhere. You've permeated everything I do, Gwen. It's problematic for several reasons. But I think I'm just going to have to figure it out, because I can't pretend it's not happening anymore."

He looked up, his eyes lost and pleading.

My heart lurched. "Christ. You *are* married, aren't you?"

He laughed. "No. I'm not married." His expression settled and his gaze went back to my cheek. He picked up the ice pack and was silent for several seconds, dabbing it against my cheek before he said, "I was engaged."

"When?"

He shook his head once. "Not now. Before you. Several years ago. Her name was Corinne."

"*Was*? Is she—?" I didn't know how to finish my statement without sounding brash.

"Yes," he said, his voice careful. "She's dead. And the things I'm dealing with, the things that keep me from being everything I want to be with you, are related to that."

"And you don't want to talk about that either."

He sighed. "I…I can't. It's not fair, I know."

I shrugged, trying not to feel bad. This was progress, wasn't it? Then why did I still feel so shut out?

"Gwen." It was the same tone he'd used before. The *don't*. I felt him saying it now with his body, with the plea in his voice.

He set the ice pack down again and gently brushed a stray hair off my face. Then he traced his thumb along my jaw, the side that was uninjured. Swept it tenderly across my skin. "I didn't want to love you, Gwen. Not just because it wasn't the right time, but because I didn't want it to be possible to lose that much again."

My pulse picked up, the hurt from a moment ago already erased with his new words. "But you do? Love me?"

Shit, I sounded eager. And hopeful. And happy.

"I do." He dropped his hand. "That's pretty much all I can give you right now. I can't tell you the things you want to know. I can't let you in on the rest of my life. Not yet. But I love you. I can give you that. Is that enough?"

It was honest and heartfelt, and for as many walls that he had surrounding him, I could still feel his earnest desire to connect. His sincere want to be with me. His utter and truthful love for me.

Was there anything else I really needed from him?

"It's enough," I said, my hands trembling in my lap. "For now, at least. I've been sticking around for a lot less. Not that really great sex is anything to scoff at."

"Really great sex?" His smile was boyish, reaching all the way to his eyes. "Not just great sex but *really* great sex?"

I kicked him in the thigh then threw his own words back at him. "Don't act like that surprises you. I know you know it is."

He laughed, then cupped his hand behind my neck and pulled my face to his. He gave me one gentle, restrained kiss. "I want to kiss you more than this, but I'm worried I'm going to hurt you."

"My mouth is completely fine." Even if it weren't, I would have endured the pain, because I needed to kiss him. Needed to feel his words in action.

"Thank God." His words became muffled as he crushed his lips to mine. As gentle as he'd been with my face, he was equally rough with his kiss. He bruised me. He marked me, and I let him.

When I threw my arms around his neck and wove my fingers through his hair, I remembered how we'd kissed that day in March. How I'd felt free and light. How that glorious kiss had turned into something sad and empty when he'd turned me away. I'd realized that as liberated as he made me feel, I was now shackled in a new way, bound to JC with all my heart.

Which was only a bad thing if he went cold like he had before.

The thought of it brought a dark cloud over me. I pulled away.

JC didn't let me go, one hand still at my neck, one around my waist. "What's wrong? Did I hurt you?" He searched my face.

I tried to shake it off. "Nothing. No. I mean…" I decided to be honest with him. "I'm scared you'll push me away again."

He lowered his eyes. "I'm sorry I did that." He lifted his gaze back to mine and stroked my good cheek with his fingers, so sweetly. With love. With adoration. "I was an asshole. I was falling for you, and I got scared. I didn't know what I should do."

Was I an idiot to believe things would be different this time? When I could still taste the pain of his rejection on my tongue?

"I still don't know what I should do," I said. But I knew what I *would* do—anything he wanted. He was my warden. I belonged to him.

"Well," he fingered the collar of my shirt. "Do you love me?"

"I know that you know that I do." I grinned a little too widely and gasped as the ache reignited in my face.

JC promptly returned the ice pack to my cheek, concern etched on his features. I covered his hand with mine. Then, because I hadn't said it yet and I didn't think it was fair to not let him hear the words, I said, "I do love you. Very much."

His eyes brightened, but his face remained somber, serious. Desperate, even. "Then come be with me. Stay with me today. Tonight."

"But it's Tuesday."

Now he smiled. Lacing his free hand through mine, he said, "I know what day it is. Be with me every day."

And so I would.

Chapter Sixteen

When we got to our hotel room, JC fed me pain relievers and water. Then we stripped to our underwear and headed straight for the bed, where I promptly fell asleep. He held me as I let oblivion overtake me, kissing my face and neck every so often, and almost every time I stirred, I found him still there. The day's events had exhausted me, and I slept until almost ten at night. But when I awoke, I felt refreshed and new and cared for.

Breakfast-slash-dinner greeted me. "I tried to order eggs and bacon," JC said, bringing me a tray with a sandwich and fries. "The grilled cheese and bacon was the closest I could get until the Owl menu at eleven."

I sat up against the headboard and took the tray. "I don't think I've ever had coffee with grilled cheese." I added a sugar substitute and took a sip from the mug.

"Should I have gotten something else?"

"Nope. This is perfect." It was comfort food. And I was starving. I'd already eaten half of a sandwich by the time JC got into bed beside me with his tray. He'd ordered the same, minus the coffee.

After we were both settled, he handed me three Advil from a bottle on his nightstand. "How are you feeling?"

"All right. This will help." I swallowed the pills. "Actually, my body almost aches as much as my face." I must have really tightened up when I realized Dad was going to strike. I was out of practice.

JC shifted so he could knead the tension in my shoulders. "God, you're all knots. I'll run you a bath when you're done eating."

"Just me? Or will you join me?" The attentive boyfriend was sweet, but it was unfamiliar and somewhat awkward. And with the bruises from my father marking my face, his treatment felt a little like pity. I'd never sensed it from him before, and I hoped a little time together, slippery and naked, would fix that. "Because I hope you'll join me."

"You don't have to ask me twice." His fingers slid down my back and around to tease my nipple.

I moaned, leaning back into him, my hand finding him semi-hard in his boxer briefs. I squeezed playfully.

JC put a hand over mine, stopping my exploration. "Uh uh uh," he scolded. "Not yet."

I pretended to pout, or actually only half pretended since there was a part of my pout that was real and stinging from the rejection.

As always, JC read me and eased me.

"Soon," he said, then licked along my earlobe. "I should warn you— you're going to need more energy than you have to keep up with me tonight, Gwen." His breath tickled where he'd left my skin wet. "So eat your dinner like a good girl, and then you'll wait until I say before we start to get naughty."

Now that was the man I'd fallen in love with. "Then let me go so I can."

He laughed, removing his hands from me. We ate the rest of our meal in silence, exchanging flirty glances as we did. When we finished, he put our trays on the room service cart and rolled it into the other room. He came back and stood next to the bed, studying me intently.

I'd lost the sheets while I was eating and was naked except for my panties. In our time together, JC had taught me how to enjoy his gaze. I'd learned to love it. Tonight, it was harder. I had yet to see my face, but its constant ache made me feel unattractive and uninspiring.

I forced myself not to cower as he looked at me. Forced myself to sit proudly.

After several long seconds, he let out a heavy sigh. "Look, Gwen—"

"Ah fuck, is this when you're going to do the pulling away bit?" It was pathetic to be so insecure, but unease lay just underneath the surface. I was wary and vulnerable.

"No." He seemed offended at the suggestion. "I told you I'm not doing that. You have to trust me." He moved closer and put a finger under my chin. "Do you trust me?"

Trust had never come easy to me. And, yes, I trusted JC with my body, with my pleasure—but with my heart? I wanted to. I just wasn't sure.

He sat on the bed next to me. "Come here." He pulled me into his arms. "My life is complicated right now, and believe me, it would be easier if you weren't in it. But, like I said earlier, you're in it. I'm not pushing you away." He kissed the top of my head, and I nuzzled against his bare chest, listening to him. Letting myself believe him.

"Okay." It wasn't very confident, but it was a start.

"We'll work on it together. I know you don't have a reason to believe me, yet you're still here. I'll try to give you reasons." He stroked his hand along my arm. "What I was going to say before is that there are some things that I can tell you—and I want to—but would it be okay if we wait just another day for that?"

Of course it was okay. Just, with the way he was holding me...I couldn't see his eyes, and it made it easier for me to be direct. "Can I ask you one question before I answer?"

"Yes. Maybe. What's your question?"

Secrets were human nature. I had mine. There were very few people that I told about my father. I lied about my scars. I lied about my home life. I respected JC's secrets because I understood what it felt like to have to hide.

But I couldn't help wondering what he was hiding and why. How could I not? It was human nature, too. So, while I said I wouldn't pry—and I meant it—I had to know, "Will you ever be able to tell me everything?"

He wrapped me tighter in his embrace. "Yes. Definitely, yes. And the minute I can, I'll tell you it all."

I didn't know if the thing preventing him from telling me his secrets was real or imagined, but ideas popped into my head. *Federal agent? Undercover cop? Hiding from the law?* Really, it didn't matter. He'd tell me when he could. I believed that. I guess I did trust him after all.

I shifted so I could see his face. "Then take as many days as you need. As long as you love me—"

"I do."

It was my turn to cup his cheek. "That's all I ever really needed from anyone, JC. Was to be loved. I told you it was enough. I meant it."

He stared down at me with what I could only call awe. "Has anyone ever told you how absolutely fucking incredible you are?"

"No," I said, a little giddy, a little embarrassed. "No one ever has."

"You are absolutely fucking incredible. I will do my best to say it more often." He stood, pulling me up with him so that we were face-to-face. "And tomorrow we'll say more. The basic stuff. The stuff I *can* say. I want to know you. I want you to know me too. Tonight, though, I just want to love you."

"That sounds nice."

He brushed a kiss against my lips, but when I pressed in for more, he tapped a chiding finger on my nose. "Still not time to be naughty. It's bath time."

I stuck out my lower lip. "And then it will be time to be naughty?"

"We'll see." But he couldn't hide the bulge in his briefs, no matter how patient he pretended to be. So I interpreted his *we'll see* as a definitive *yes*.

• • •

JC ran the bath scalding hot, exactly the way I like it, and added some luxury bubbles that the hotel provided. I got in first and he stepped in behind me. He gave me the royal treatment—washing my body then massaging my back until my muscles loosened. When he finished, I lay back against his chest. He wrapped his arms around me, and we just soaked.

I was relaxed and turned on, the needy buzz between my legs growing with every minute that passed. JC was taking his time with me, though. And I knew the more I fought him, the longer he'd make me wait.

So I found something else to get my mind off my aching desire. I ran my fingers over the words inked on his skin. "I know we're waiting until tomorrow for the sharing stuff, but how about one thing?"

"What do you mean?"

"I mean, we each ask each other one thing and the other has to answer." I felt his body stiffen underneath me, and I amended. "If that's totally not what you want to do, that's fine. I'm just curious about you."

He stroked his hand through my hair. "Hmm. That could work. But you ask first. And I reserve the right to decline to answer."

"That's not really—" I was going to say "fair" and then realized none of it was fair. He'd already said that. "Okay. Fine." I had my question prepared already, had it prepared for weeks. "What does the date on your tattoo mean?"

"Are you serious? You have the chance to ask anything and that's what you choose?" His voice was teasing, but he bent his forearm around my waist, hiding the tattoo, as if I'd forget about it if I couldn't see it.

Lucky for him, it was more cute than frustrating. "It's pretty much the only thing I think you'll answer. Besides, I really want to know. Is it something you can tell me?"

"Did I mention that you're absolutely fucking incredible?" He squeezed his arms around me, putting pressure on my breasts, and making the buzz in my core send a high voltage flash through my veins.

Jesus, I was so lit up, so in need of an orgasm.

But I wanted to know about the tattoo. I had an idea about it, and I was burning to have it confirmed. "Are you stalling?"

"No." His arms loosened, but he kept them around me. "I'm sincerely in awe that you let me keep my secrets. I'm an asshole for expecting you not to pry, and you're amazing because you don't. Thank you."

I sat with that for a second, trying to decide if that was his way of saying, *I'm not answering*. And also, since I didn't really think he was an asshole for keeping his secrets, I wondered if there was something wrong with me. I frowned. "You know, I'm starting to feel like maybe I'm not so amazing but more like an idiot. But you're welcome. I guess. Now are you going to answer my question or not? A flat-out yes or no would help to clarify."

"It was the day Corinne died." Or that. That was definitely clarifying.

It was also what I'd guessed. The minute he'd said he'd been engaged, the minute he said she'd died—it was obvious she haunted him. How much of him was a remnant of her? Was there even any room for me in his world with her ghost?

I hadn't expected more, but he surprised me. "I don't know why I thought I needed to ink it on my skin. It's a date I'll never forget. Maybe that's why I did it. It was already so permanently etched in me that it seemed only appropriate to have it etched *on* me as well."

"You loved her." Stupid. Of course he loved her. He was going to marry her. Saying it, though, helped make it real for me. So that I could look at it and see what his love for her meant about me. Selfish. Self-centered. Also, self-preserving.

"I loved her." His tone was definite. "Now I love you." Just as definite. "There's been no one in between."

"Really?" I twisted to try to see his face. But my nose hit his jaw, and all I could see was the curve of his face, the skin of his neck.

"Nope. Just you."

I nuzzled him with the tip of my nose as I let his revelations settle over me. I was hard—I prided myself on that. But my time with JC had softened me. And I was also just a girl with girly doubts and jealousies. I was envious of this dead woman. There was no denying that. I'd have to deal with that. I imagined it might require time.

Then there was the rest of his admission. *Just you.* He'd said that when he came looking for me at the club, said that there was only me. And that was bigger. That was harder to hold. Because who was I? Out of everyone who must have looked his way, of every woman who slipped him a room key or a phone number, why me?

I had one guess. "Am I like her?"

"Not even a little bit. Well, actually, you're headstrong like she was. But that's where the similarities end."

I sat up and turned to perch on his thigh. Pictures of a woman with dark hair and eyes filled my mind. A woman thin where I was curvy. Warm, friendly. Loveable. "Why me, then?"

"Why not you?" His eyes flicked to my breasts and back to my eyes. "Do I need to remind you that you're absolutely fucking incredible?"

I folded my arms over my chest, wanting to have this conversation without the distraction of arousal. "You didn't know that when you started this arrangement. What did you see in me that made you want to—"

"—have sex with you? Let's see, blonde, perfect, round, full tits, long legs, absolutely flawless face. Did I mention the really perfect tits? I was hard within a minute of first meeting you. Painfully hard."

"And that's what it was? My looks? That's why you pursued me?" I realized it was silly as soon as I'd asked. "I mean, I guess that makes sense. You were looking for a physical relationship. I'm sure you had many of them between Corinne and me." God, I was trying to make myself jealous now.

JC put his hands on the edge of the tub and leaned toward me. "Yes. Many physical relationships between Corinne and you. Not a single one of them had me interested in anything besides where they would let me put my cock."

He settled back, sitting straighter than he had been. "I told myself I was pursuing you for the same reason. Which was bullshit because you were a challenge, and I usually don't like to have to work that hard to get laid." He waited until I delivered a begrudging smile before going on. "Truth was, I saw something familiar in you. After Corinne died, I packed everything inside. I shut down. I stopped living. Then someone—Matt, actually—reminded me that she wouldn't have wanted that. He was right. So I got the other tattoo—the Buddhist tattoo—"

"'The current age is but a brief moment in the greater scope of existence.'"

His expression said he was impressed that I'd remembered. "Yes. And I decided to start living for today. Which didn't work out too well at first because I spent a lot of time drunk and unconscious."

"Waking up in strange places with no memory of the night before." I'd remembered everything he'd ever told me. They were the things I'd clung to in my daydreams.

"Exactly. Not very productive. But when I stopped drinking, I was a lot better. Still sad, but better."

I hated the idea of the JC he was describing. I could see him vividly, though. With eyes that held sorrow. Sitting at the piano in the dark playing mournful melodies. Those were fragments of a grief that had once likely encompassed him.

But I hadn't been grieving when I'd met him. "So what was the familiar thing you saw in me?"

"God, when I saw you…" His face brightened in a way that made my heart pinch. He cupped my face with his hands. "I saw someone who had stopped living."

My eyes started to fill. I blinked to keep any tears from spilling.

"But you were so beautiful, not just with the tits and the legs, but your whole being. You were beautifully strong. And I couldn't stand that you were so absolutely fucking incredible," he paused while I laughed, "and yet just frozen. I wanted to be there when you thawed out. I wanted to be the one to thaw you out. Without being stupid like I'd been. And because you were the first…anything, really…that had intrigued me since Corinne's death, I couldn't get you out of my head."

I'd never been so…noticed. It was overwhelming and breathtaking. If I didn't lighten the mood, the tears would start falling and I really wasn't good with crying. "You know I'm a sure thing tonight, right? You don't need all this poetry to put your cock anywhere in me."

"There's no doubt that I'm putting my cock places in you tonight."

I shivered and JC pulled me closer to kiss my uninjured cheek. "You're also going to have to learn to accept that I love you, Gwen. And my love is big. Now that we're starting to talk about things, you're going to be hearing a lot about it. We'll take it slow, if that's what you need. But it's not going to change what I already feel about you."

I was speechless. It was so much easier to listen to the dirty talk. Like he'd said, guys wanted to fuck the blondes with big tits. Spreading my legs, getting someone off—that, I knew. Big love, on the other hand…

It would take some getting used to. It would take some time.

"Okay, my turn for the question. But let's get out of here first. We're turning into prunes."

I let out a long breath, grateful that JC understood my need for slow love just like I understood his need for slow disclosure. Ironic how I'd been desperate for his affection, and now I didn't know how to accept the whole of it. But I would. I'd learn. He'd teach me.

There's no rush, I reminded myself. *We have time.*

JC got out of the tub first. He wrapped a towel around his waist then, when I got out, he wrapped another around me. "That's better," he said when I was fully covered. "Now I can concentrate on what I want to ask."

I'd rather he couldn't concentrate. I'd rather we were done with the emotion-filled talking. I'd rather he lifted me on the bathroom counter and had his way with me.

But fair was fair. He'd answered mine. "Go ahead. Ask."

He put his hands on his hips where the deep lines disappeared under his towel—Jesus, now I was distracted—and asked, "What's the story with your dad?"

Ah, mood kill.

"You don't go small or anything, do you?" He was asking for a big divulgence. My father's whole story should be saved or something. Shouldn't it?

Or maybe I didn't have to compete with his secrets. "It's probably an appropriate question after today."

JC nodded. Then he shut the toilet lid and sat down, his legs straddling the bowl. He held up a comb and slapped his hand on the spot in front of him. "Tell me while I work on those knots."

More royal treatment. Big love. I could do it.

"Okay." I sat on the small space in front of him. Immediately I realized the benefit of this. I could tell him without looking at him, just as he'd been able to tell me without looking at me. I was beginning to think it was him who was absolutely fucking incredible.

I looked down at my hands as he pulled the comb through my hair. "There's actually not a lot to tell. He worked hard, yet we were always poor. Maybe that's why he was always so angry, I don't know. I'm sure his dad hit him too. Learned behavior. He wasn't so bad when my mother was around. Probably because she let him beat her instead of us."

I still defended him. It was the craziest thing. I wondered if I'd ever get over that.

I closed my eyes. "After she died, Norma tried to take the role of protector. She stood up to him. She also wasn't around a lot. She took odd jobs whenever she could to help put food on the table. Then she graduated with honors and got a full ride to Columbia. She tried to see us whenever she could, but we lived in Jersey. It was hard for her to get over there. So we got hit. A lot. I learned how to avoid his worst moods and how to try to keep him happy, but sometimes there wasn't anything to do but take it."

JC didn't say anything. He just kept combing my hair, tugging when the teeth got caught. I leaned away when he pulled, enjoying the bite of pain. Letting that be where I focused my emotion rather than on the pang in my chest that showed up when I started talking about my family.

"Anyway, when I was seventeen, he beat my brother up so bad he had to go to the hospital. Broke several of his ribs. His nose. Punctured his lung. He was twelve. Know what set him off? He saw Ben checking out a man in a magazine underwear ad. I guess he thought he could beat the gay out of him. There'd been a lot of times that social services had been called in our lifetime and things never happened. But this time they did. And Norma stepped up. She'd graduated and had a good job. She got custody of Ben and me until I was eighteen, and Dad went to jail for ten years. He just got out last week. Today was the first time I'd seen him in a decade."

I don't know when JC had finished with my hair. I only realized when I was done talking that he wasn't moving, that both of his hands were on my upper arms, that the comb was on the floor at our feet.

He wrapped his arms around me completely and pulled me into him, his face pressing against mine. And he rocked me. Just rocked me.

I appreciated his silence. It wasn't pity. It was compassion. It felt good.

I brought my hands up to rest on his arms. "Thank you," I said, my voice tighter than I'd realized.

JC placed his lips at my temple. "I want to kiss every place he ever touched you. Every spot on your skin that was ever bruised or scraped. As many times as he covered you in hurt, I want to cover you in love."

"It would take a lot of kissing."

"I'm up for it."

I had warring emotions. Part of me wanted to break down and sob. The other part of me was still tingling and turned on. I couldn't stand the divisiveness. I needed to pick one and let myself be lost in it. "JC, about that kissing, can we do that sooner rather than later? I'm trying to be patient, but—"

He cut me off. "Yes. You've been a good girl. Get up. Let me drain the tub, and I'll join you in the bedroom."

I meant to head to the bedroom, but my reflection caught my eye as I passed the vanity. I still hadn't looked at my face. Honestly, I'd been avoiding it. Now, I couldn't look away. My cheek was purple and angry. A bluish tint had spread up under my eye and even over to my nose. Three darker black-blue marks sat along my bone, distinct outlines of his knuckles. I raised my finger to trace the edges, testing the pain.

We needed a picture of it. I knew that much. Evidence.

But I didn't care much about practical tasks at the moment. I was swept up in something else. The ugly. That as much as I wanted to forget about the person who gave me half my DNA, as much as I wanted to ignore that he ever existed in my life, he'd always be marked on me. Even when the bruises faded, he'd still be there. He'd still be the source of my ugly.

JC slipped in to face me, blocking me from my reflection. "This is where I'll start." He took my hand from my face and held it in his. Then he leaned in and kissed along the bruises, carefully, tenderly. "Here," he said between kisses, "he touched you here. And here." He didn't stop until he'd covered every tinted spot of flesh.

When he was done, he trailed his lips across the bridge of my nose to my other cheek. "How about here? Did he ever hit you here?"

I nodded, and he placed a kiss there.

"And here?" as he moved under my eye.

"Yes."

Another kiss. "And here?" Above my brow.

"Yes."

So it went until he'd covered my skin from my forehead to my jawline. Each gentle kiss a gesture of love. Each *and here* an acknowledgment of pain. My face was wet from my tears as he moved down my neck, and while I knew that he'd eventually press his lips against every part of my body, there was something else I needed. I needed life breathed into me in a big way. Needed my system jolted.

"JC." I waited until he'd lifted his eyes to mine. "Be rough with me. Please. I need to know I'm real. I need to know you're real."

He hesitated a moment before breaking into a wicked grin. "Thank you, Gwen, for telling me that. You know how hot it makes me when you trust me with your needs."

He proceeded to show me, claiming my lips like a predator, devouring me. Our mouths still locked, he picked me up and spun me around. He set me down on the counter and loosened my towel. This time as he moved his mouth down my body, he didn't ask where I'd been hurt. Instead, he covered all of me. Every inch. Nipping and licking and sucking. He left hickeys on my chest. Bites that would later bruise covered my breasts. He kissed me and he marked me.

He covered me with love.

I was already moaning and writhing when his lips found my clit. My core was tight, high-strung from all his attention. So when he sank to his knees, his nails digging painfully into my thighs, and sucked the swollen bud of nerves into his mouth, I immediately found myself on the brink of orgasm. "Fuck, JC. I'm going to come."

"Good girl. Tell me more." He tipped my hips back and threw my legs over his shoulders, opening me wider to him.

I put my arms back and braced myself on my elbows, searching for the words I knew he liked to hear while he pleasured me. "It's building. I'm getting tighter. God, it feels so good. You make me feel so good. You make me feel so loved."

Fingers plunged into my wet center. The second he hit the sensitive spot against my wall, I went over. I cried out his name, my legs tightening and shaking while my whole body—every nerve ending—ignited and flared with warmth.

My vision was still clearing when he brought his fingers out and used my slick juices to slide a finger into my ass. I was tight and snug, but I opened up easily to him. With his mouth still adoring my clit, and the rush from my first orgasm still clinging to me, the brush of his fingertip against my tender tissues set another climax gathering.

I surrendered then. Completely. Totally, letting the waves crash over me, through me. He was going to love me big, and I was going to resist, but here, under the ministrations of his mouth and tongue and fingers, I could let go. Here, I could let him love me whole and entirely. Here, his love was full, and I knew how to accept it.

• • •

When I was limp and boneless, JC carried me to the bed. "How are you? Can you take more?"

Despite the two overwhelming orgasms that had wrecked through me, he had yet to fill me, and I wanted that. "I can take more."

"Good." He dropped his towel to the floor and my eyes flew to his erection standing thick and ready. Just the sight of it sent another stirring through my veins. It hit me then, how lucky I was to have found him. This creature who could care about my body and my spirit in equal measures. This man who could fuck me and fall for me too. It was absolutely fucking incredible.

Before joining me in bed, he turned the lights down and messed with his phone until music started playing. "Is this okay?"

"I love Maroon 5."

"Listen to the lyrics."

I'd heard it before, but I listened now as JC turned me to my side and slid behind me. The words were about being scared, scared to love. And the singer asks his woman to say yes, to take a chance on their relationship. The title repeated over and over in the refrain—*My Heart is Open.*

Damn, it could have been my song for JC.

Was he trying to tell me he understood how I felt? He was always so in tune with me—it wouldn't surprise me.

He didn't explain the choice. As the song played, he kissed along my back, trailing his lips underneath my shoulders and along my scar there. His cock pressed into the crack of my ass, hot and hard. His hand curled around to my chest and squeezed my breast, then pinched my nipple to the point of pain. I'd thought I was spent, but with the music and his twitching erection and the way he was worshipping me, glorifying me, a new hum began to sing between my legs.

The song was over by the time he'd covered every inch of my backside, but after a second of silence, it started up again.

He rolled me over to my back and nestled between my legs. His cock pressed against my center, and I squirmed, trying to get it in the place I wanted it. But JC held me still.

"I heard it today," he said, his eyes finding mine. "In the cab ride from the airport to the club. I downloaded it immediately. I realized it's everything I want to be with you. I want to tell you yes. I want to be here for you until you tell me yes back. Even with the things I can't share, Gwen, even with the words I can't say yet, my heart is open."

If there were such a thing as an emotional climax, I had one. Something inside me burst and spread through my chest, through my limbs, down to my toes, up to my head. It was hot. Tingly. Bliss.

His gaze still locked on mine, he entered me. In one thrust, he was stretching me, filling me the way he'd filled my heart. Perfecting me.

"Yes," I cried. "Like that. Yes." *Yes, I love the way you feel in me. Yes, give me more. Yes, my heart is open too.*

He moved in and out, not fast, not too slow. He was enjoying me. He was telling me how he loved me. He was proving his yes. His hips circled, nudging my clit. I moaned and sighed. I gasped. I sang.

And he continued to cherish my skin, brushing his fingers across my thighs and hips, finding my scars, caressing them tenderly. "As many times as it takes." His mouth hovered above mine, his breath hot. "I will kiss away your bruises. I'll kiss away your pain."

I wrapped my arms around his neck. His attempts to heal me were valiant, and I appreciated them more than words could say. But he needed to know the process was ongoing. That true healing would take time.

I brushed my lips against his and told him. "Most of the scars are on the inside."

"I can be there too." As if to prove it, he pushed my legs in toward my chest, and on his next stroke, he hit deeper in me, deeper than I thought I'd ever felt him before. Deeper than anyone had ever been inside me before.

He kissed me hungrily, licking into my mouth. Everywhere I felt him—with my lips and tongue, against my skin, inside my pussy, inside my chest and head and limbs. He infiltrated my senses and my soul.

And when his tempo picked up and he pounded into me with sharp, unyielding jabs and the tension pulled tight in my core, I held on. I waited. When we went, we went together, open and free, our climaxes uniting into one glorious, brilliant explosion.

We made love through the night and fell asleep wrapped around each other with the dawn.

I woke midmorning to his voice, harsh and angry. He was on the edge of the bed, the phone at his ear. I'd missed whatever he said, but emotion was written all over his body. He was more than angry. He was completely enraged.

He ended the call without a goodbye, simply letting the phone fall from his hands and to the floor. He stood and paced the room for half a minute before screaming, "Fuck!" and throwing his fist into the wall.

I gasped, both because he'd startled me and because violence in any form made me uneasy.

Still shaking his hand, he spun toward me, his eyes finding mine. Immediately, his face softened, but his body remained tense.

"Wanna talk about it?"

He shook his head.

"Is it one of the things you can't say?"

He didn't answer. His breathing had been fast and heavy, but now he took a deep breath in and let it out slowly.

Then he climbed back on the bed and knelt before me. "I want to talk about us. Let's talk about us." He took my hands in his. "Can we?"

"Yeah. Sure." I was apprehensive. Edgy. Cautious. "What about us?"

He kissed the back of one hand, then the other. "I love you, Gwen. You know that I love you, right?"

"I do."

"And you love me?" His tone was urgent and panicked. Not at all like normal.

Concerned, I shifted so I was kneeling too. "I do. I do love you, JC. What is it?"

"This is good," he said under his breath. "This is going to work." Then he smiled, his grin unsteady but sincere, his hands tightly wrapped around mine. "Gwen. Marry me."

Chapter Seventeen

I laughed.

There was no other appropriate response. It also helped to relieve some of the strange tension building inside of me.

But when I was done laughing, he was still looking at me with earnest, intent eyes. He obviously wasn't joking.

"JC." I sat back on my heels. "Stop being weird and talk to me about what's going on."

He tightened his grip on me. "I'm serious, Gwen. I'm asking you to marry me."

I blinked a few times. I hadn't even had any coffee yet. There should be a universal law that made caffeine a requirement before serious conversations and proposals.

I looked down at our hands joined together and found that the knuckles on his right hand were red and scratched from his punch to the wall. He was lucky he hadn't hit through the sheetrock. "Oh God, honey. Does it hurt?"

He glanced at his hand then returned his attention to me. "I can't feel it. It's numb. Marry me."

This was the third time he'd said those words and the first time that they actually got through to me. My throat and chest tightened and critters began flitting around in my stomach, and while some of the sensation felt pleasant I had no doubt what I needed to say. "I can't marry you, JC."

"Why not?" The response came fast and even. Prepared. As though he'd been expecting my *no*.

I pulled my hands out from his while I tried to come up with the answers that should be completely obvious. "Because it's too soon. Because we don't even know each other. Because we only just said we loved each other." I slid out of the bed, uncomfortable being so near to him while he was acting so off.

"But we've felt things for longer than that. And what does time matter anyway? We love each other and that's what counts. Marry me." He was so confident in his delivery. Each time, two words—*marry me*. As though saying them over and over would make the difference. As though I would be convinced eventually, and he just needed to be patient.

"JC." I found my underwear and put them on, feeling too vulnerable without any clothes on. "I can't—" I took a deep breath.

But maybe I could.

I looked for a shirt to put on while I tested the idea out in my mind. I'd never thought about marrying JC. I never thought I'd marry anyone, actually. So the idea of a union like that at all was peculiar and foreign.

But now that I was thinking about it…

It wouldn't be the worst thing. Having a place to come home to every night—or morning, in my case—a place that was more of a person than a location. A place that was safe. A place that was filled with love. It was a warm thought. One that spread and grew and felt less ridiculous than it should.

I found JC's t-shirt on the floor and pulled it over my head. When I turned around, he was standing not a foot away, expectant. "You can't? Why can't you?"

"I don't know. Maybe I could." *Shit, did I really just say that?*

I wandered into the front room, nervous energy driving me to keep moving.

He followed. "Maybe. You said maybe."

"Maybe," I said again. "I need some time to think about it. Like a lot of time. This is completely out-of-the-blue and crazy, but out-of-the-blue has worked in my favor before." I'd jumped JC that night in the club without any premeditation. "Still. I'd need some time. At least a few weeks. Maybe longer. So my answer is maybe." What the fuck was I saying?

I forced myself to breathe, in and out, instead of having a full-out panic attack like I kind of wanted to have.

Maybe isn't yes, I told myself. *Maybe is fine. Maybe is acceptable.*

Jesus, how could I even be considering this?

I turned to him, hoping he'd be happy that I hadn't exactly said *no*.

He wasn't. He was frowning, shaking his head. "I don't have…" He made an exasperated noise, sort of like a sigh with a little bit of a groan.

"I'm not asking for 'in a few weeks.' Today, Gwen. Marry me today."

"Oh, no. No way." *Hell, no.* In fact, now I might actually have a panic attack because how could he even be thinking that I would marry him *today*? It was ludicrous. It was unfathomable. It was completely and utterly insane.

Had I fallen in love with a lunatic? That would be my luck. And whether or not he was a lunatic, was I ruining everything I had with him by being the only sane one between us?

I took more deep breaths, did more wandering of the hotel suite at a speed that could better be described as pacing, except that it was not in any sort of straight line.

JC was right on my heels. "Stop freaking out. I'm serious. This is good."

I circled around the couch, but he turned so when I got to the other side, he was waiting there. "We'll fly to Vegas and be man and wife before nightfall."

I turned and headed toward the bedroom.

"Think about it, Gwen. We could spend the whole night making love."

I spun around so fast I practically bumped into him. "We can spend the night making love without getting married. Here. In New York City."

He circled his arms around my waist, lacing his hands to hold me still. "I know, but it will be different."

His arms were heaven. His arms were peace. They calmed me and comforted me even though they made me a little bit dizzy at the same time.

Not dizzy enough to think about taking his proposal seriously. But dizzy enough to remember how much I loved being held by him.

"Think about how much better it will be to be married," he said. "We'll be together like this all the time. Together for real. Nothing can come between us."

I put my hands around his neck and placed a kiss on his sternum. "That sounds wonderful, JC. But that's not what marriage means. Those are things you decide in a relationship together, and they don't just happen overnight. They don't just happen with a ring and an *I do*."

He leaned his forehead against mine and rocked us from side to side. "So let's decide to be together all the time. That we're together for real. And that nothing can come between us. And we'll seal the deal with a wedding. I have to go to Vegas anyway."

He was so sincere, so persistent…and he'd been so magnificent to me, especially in the last twenty-four hours. And I loved him.

But that just wasn't enough.

"No." It was enough to make me feel bad though. "I'm sorry. I can't. I can't do that."

He pushed me away, frustrated. He ran a hand through his hair then put it on his hip. "Why not?"

I shook my head, not knowing how to answer anymore.

"Why. Not?" he repeated, separating each word. He placed his palm on his chest. "My heart is open, Gwen. Is yours?"

"This has nothing to do with my heart being open, JC. This is about practicality." I wrapped my arms around myself. I was frustrated now too. I didn't like having my feelings challenged. I had a hard enough time accepting and acknowledging what I felt. To have it then scrutinized and confronted made me very uncomfortable.

He hit the closet with his fist, not as hard as he'd punched the wall, just loud enough to make sound. "Fuck practicality. Marry me."

"I said *no*." My tone was low and stern. Final.

Irritated, I headed to the nightstand and started looking for my phone. I knew I should call Norma soon and find out what she wanted me to do about Dad, but mostly it was an excuse for something to do. Look for my phone so I didn't have to stand there and have a face-off with my one-day boyfriend about whether or not we should get married. Today.

I didn't find it on my side of the bed, so I crossed to the side JC had slept on and found it under the Advil. I took three of those as well, swallowing them without water. I needed them, and not just because my face was throbbing.

JC stood the whole time by the closet, watching me.

When I looked up at him, he took advantage of my gaze to try again. "Tell me why. Give me a good reason why. Do you not really love me?"

How long does it take Advil to start working?

Despite the headache he'd given me, I did love him. I didn't want to lose him. I didn't want to push him away. I wanted him to understand.

I went to him and took his hand in mine. "Of course, I love you. I *really* do. But JC, be real. The only thing we really have between us is sex. I hope—" *That isn't the right word.* "No, I *know* that we have potential for more. For so much more. But that's going to take time to create and

214

work out. We can't get married on the basis of physical compatibility and emotional potential. That's not how you build a great marriage."

He brushed a hand across my cheek. "You're thinking with your head, Gwen. Stop thinking with your head and listen to your heart."

I closed my eyes and tried to understand how we'd gotten to this point. Our entire relationship had been unorthodox, but this was way off course. He was so desperate, like he thought he'd lose me. Had I made him feel like I wasn't going to stick around? Or had something happened to—

It was the phone call. Jesus, of course it was. I'd been so stunned by the proposal I'd almost forgotten the connection. That had been what triggered this...this...whatever this was. Who on earth had he been talking to? And what the hell could inspire this much panic?

I opened my eyes and searched his. "Right now my heart is telling me that there's something else going on, JC, and that you're reacting to it by pulling this crap."

"This isn't crap. This is me saying I want to give my life to you."

His touch on my skin, the affection in his voice—what if he really did just love me *that much*? Was that the most absurd thing in the world?

Yes. It was absurd. And I was losing patience.

I dropped his hand and backed away. "You had a phone call that upset you—upset you enough to punch a freaking hole in the wall—a phone call that you can't tell me anything about but it led you to propose. There's something going on. This is not just a whimsical romantic notion."

His posture changed as he assumed a new tactic. "Marry me, Gwen. And I'll tell you everything. All of it. Every single secret I have."

I suddenly went cold. "That's a pretty shitty ultimatum." Hot rage blew in across my icy veins. "You think I'd marry you just to ease my curiosity?" I hadn't pressed him. I hadn't pressured him in any way to tell me anything, and he came back with this?

He was quick to amend. "I'm sorry. I didn't mean for it to sound like that. It's not an ultimatum. It's just...it's just how it has to be. I wish it were different and it's just not. Because I had obligations. And a road I was taking before I ever met you. I'm bound and it's killing me. You have to hear me—*it's killing me*. I need *you*. I *want* you. I love you. So I'm not suggesting you'd marry me to ease your curiosity, but I wanted you to know that I wouldn't be a husband with secrets."

He pulled me back into his arms. Back into his heaven. "Marry me,

Gwen. Marry me and let me make you feel good. Let me bring you coffee in bed. Let me push your body and show you how beautiful you are. Let me cover you everywhere with love. Let me take care of you and adore you and be with you."

If there were warmer words in the dictionary, I didn't know them. If there were other phrases and sentiments that were capable of melting the most frozen parts of me, I'd never come across them. I'd accepted my role in life. I knew who I was and what my purpose was. I hadn't been made to be noticed or adored. And this man—this man not only noticed and adored, but he *worshipped.*

And he knew how to make me believe that he'd worship me forever.

I let myself kiss him. I let myself feel his urgency and his sincere need for me through the movement of his lips and tongue. I let myself feel worthy of his devotion.

Then I stepped away—out of his heaven, out of his peace. And I prayed that one day, paradise could really be mine. "N-no," I said, my voice catching. "I'm sorry. But I know I'm not wrong. It has to be no."

His whole body fell in defeat.

Like a good dream that fades upon waking, I tried to cling to it, tried to bring some of it back. "Look, we need to spend more time together. Move in, maybe." He was in L.A. more than half the week anyway. It was a compromise that I could agree to, though I had a feeling there wasn't anything that could appease him at this point. He had his mind stuck on this one thing, for some reason, and there was nothing I could do to unstick him.

All animation was gone from his features now. He'd given up. "That won't work. I don't even know when I'll be back in New York."

"Because I won't marry you?" My throat felt like it was closing, and my emotions were warring. Was I pissed at the emotional blackmail? Or was I worried that I was losing him entirely? Maybe a little bit of both.

"No. Because it's not safe."

"It's not *safe?* Why is it not safe?"

He waved his hand. "Forget that." He gathered himself, reigning in all expression. "Please don't ask me to say more. This is how things are right now and I can't change them. I don't know if I'll be able to be back here for a while."

I thought he might have made a slip of some sort, but now I was focused on his last words. *I don't know if I'll be back here for a while.*

He delivered it with such stoicism, and I had to be—*something*—in response. Something that would counterbalance the complete impassiveness that he'd adopted after his stunning display of passion only a moment before.

Had to be something, so I chose pissed. "Okay, let me get this straight. You were going to marry me then abandon me?"

He put a palm up in the air as if he could stop my train of thought with the flash of his hand. "I was going to ask you to come with me." Like that fixed everything. Like that made all the difference.

Like hell it fixed everything. The only difference it made was to make me more irked. "You mean, you were going to ask me to pick up and just leave everything? For you don't know how long?"

His answer came in the form of a guilty smirk.

"Why would you think I'd do that? I can't do that. I have a life here. A job. A sister. I can't just leave." My voice was getting higher and with it probably my blood pressure. I threw my head back like a Pez dispenser, but instead of letting out candy, I was letting out frustration. I couldn't figure out why a normally rational person would be so unreasonable all of a sudden.

Unless I was fooling myself, and I really didn't know enough about JC to know that he was normally rational.

Or maybe...

The comment about safety came back and my head popped back down in place. "JC, are you in trouble?"

He'd been pounding his fist against his forehead but stopped and met my eyes. "Not the kind of trouble you're thinking."

"I'm not thinking anything! I don't have enough information from you to form any sort of thinking at all!"

My phone started ringing in my hand. I ignored it for two rings. Then, cursing under my breath, I glanced down and saw Norma's name as well as the low battery flashing. It wasn't the most appropriate time to take her call, but I needed to talk to her. And I needed a break from the conversation with JC. I needed a moment of levity.

I angled away from him and answered. "Hello?"

"Did I catch you at a good time?"

I stole a glance at JC. "Not really. But my phone's going to die, so go ahead and talk."

"Got it." She was walking as she talked. I could hear her heels clipping along tiled floor. She almost never made a phone call while she was sitting still. It was a waste of time. She was more efficient than that. "Are you doing okay this morning?"

Honestly, I wasn't sure. "That's not really an easy question to answer."

"I understand." She didn't, but I let her believe she did. "I'm sorry to make you do this, but I need to see you."

I'd expected this. She'd need me to fill out my report and to sign it and whatever else the law required to file a charge against him. "Okay. When?"

"Now. I can have a car pick you up in fifteen minutes."

Another glance at JC. I didn't want to leave him this way. There was too much tension between us. "Can we make it a little later?"

"No. We're meeting with an officer from the NYPD. He just called and this is when he's available. We need to get your testimony and that security tape. He needs to see your face. Is it bruised?" She was so matter-of-fact about it. I'd always loved that about her. She wasn't too precious or overly warm. She got things done. She took care of the details.

"Yeah. It's pretty black-and-blue. He got me with his knuckles."

"We'll need to photograph that."

"Right." I took a deep breath in then blew it out. "Okay, then. I'll be ready."

"Four Seasons, right?"

"Yep."

"The car will be there in fifteen."

I held the phone to my ear a few seconds after she'd hung up. My gut had already been in knots about JC. I wasn't ready to deal with my father too. All I really wanted to do was climb back into bed and start the day over again. Better yet, climb back into bed and repeat the night before—making love and whispering sweet nothings into the darkness.

But the sun was up and a car was on its way.

I turned back toward JC. "My sister," I said. He'd watched me the entire call, his face even. "She needs me so we can file the charges against my father. She's picking me up in fifteen. So."

He nodded. Then he closed his eyes and ran his hand roughly across his forehead. He looked lost. Alone.

It broke parts of me that I didn't know I had. I wanted to run to him, wanted to wrap him in my arms and make it better. Wanted to convince him that whatever he was wrestling couldn't defeat him.

But I didn't know that was true. I didn't know anything about him at all, really.

I shook my head, not knowing how to deal with the situation, and definitely not having time for it. "I want to talk about this more later," I said as I gathered my clothes from around the room. "We'll work everything out."

"Uh hmm." He didn't look at me, his thoughts elsewhere.

In the bathroom, I gave myself ten seconds to examine the colorful souvenir my father had given me, then forced myself to ignore it. I cleaned up in the sink and used some of JC's deodorant before trading his shirt for the clothes I'd worn the day before. I brushed my teeth with my finger and his toothpaste. My hair took longer to deal with. It was a tangle of knots again, evidence of having been fucked well all night. Luckily, I found a ponytail holder on the bathroom counter from another visit and was able to fasten a messy bun.

When I came out, JC was dressed and sitting at the front room desk, working on his laptop.

"I'm going now," I said, awkwardly.

He stood and crossed to me. "I heard what you said, Gwen. I want you to know that. But if you change your mind—I booked a room at the Trump Hotel in Vegas. There's a flight at twelve-fifteen out of LaGuardia. I bought my ticket under Alex Mader, and I have another seat on hold for you. You could join me."

My head was spinning. "Alex Mader? Is that your real name?"

"No. It's the name I'm using to travel. Join me."

His words started to hit me with comprehension. He was leaving. He was really leaving. Now. I had to go deal with my fucking father, and the man that I loved was fucking leaving and he didn't know when he'd be back.

I started to tell him not to leave or to wait until I got back from seeing Norma, but he cut me off, pulling me into a tight embrace. "Don't say anything. You have to go. I have to go right now too. I really don't want to go without you. So think about joining me. Please."

He kissed me. Like a last kiss, tasting of all the flavors of goodbye. Longing and sorrow. Melancholy and anguish. Desperation and regret. Finality.

When he broke away, he placed one more kiss on the tip of my nose. "Change your mind, Gwen. Change your mind."

Chapter Eighteen

The car was waiting for me when I got downstairs. It wasn't the usual black generic company car that Norma used on occasion. It was rich and expensive looking. More plush. Had to belong to Hudson Pierce.

Which meant she'd involved him in my drama. Great. How awesome to have random important people know that no matter how strong I appeared on the outside, I was really just a punching bag.

Despite my humiliation, I managed to smile at the driver—a middle-aged white guy with an overzealous moustache and a full head of brown hair. He was new too. His Hawaiian shirt and cargo shorts were definitely not standard uniform. For some reason, the change in routine made me feel even more off-balance.

I climbed into the backseat with a sigh.

Luckily, after he told me where we were headed—to a coffee shop near Pierce Industries—Mr. Moustache didn't try to chat me up. I was grateful. I needed the quiet. I needed peace. What I really needed was a tumbler of bourbon and a few hours of mindless television, but since that wasn't happening anytime soon, I'd take the silence.

My mind was overactive, though, and wouldn't let me rest. Combined with the storm of emotions going on inside me, I felt like a volatile mess. If only JC's farewell hadn't been so cryptic, I wouldn't feel so unsettled. He said he was leaving, and I believed him. But did he really not know when he'd return, or was that a bluff to get me to agree to his ridiculous proposal?

When he'd said it, I'd been mad. Mad that he'd planned to abandon me. Then mad that he wanted to take me away from my life. After that, Norma had called, and I had to leave and it was only now that I was really realizing that he might actually be leaving me. That his invitation to join him at the airport might be my last chance to be with him.

But why on earth would that be true? He acted like he didn't have a say in when he returned to New York City. Did he have a project that had gone awry? Something that would require more of his time and attention? If that was the case, then why did he want to marry me first? So that I'd be tied to him?

The longer we drove, the heavier the ball of dread in my stomach became. The more I believed that JC was actually in trouble. He had to be. It was the only thing that made sense. Was the trouble so bad that he had to run? Did he think that if I knew what it was that I'd not love him anymore? Was that why he wanted to make sure I said *I do* before he told me what the situation was?

Regret began to creep in. I should have told him that I didn't care what he'd done. I should have told him that I'd never judge him for his past. He'd been so amazing about letting me feel loved no matter what. I obviously hadn't done the same.

Why the hell hadn't I done the same?

And was it too late to try?

I tried to check my phone for the time but found it dead. I'd left the hotel around ten. It couldn't be any later than ten-fifteen. If I told the driver to go to the airport right now, I'd make it with plenty of time. He'd probably say no. He got his orders from Norma, not me. But maybe, as soon as I hopped out, I could hail a cab and head straight there. Did I dare bail on my sister like that?

I did dare. Norma and the charges against my father could wait. So I'd inconvenience a police officer. That didn't really bother me too much. I wouldn't have felt the same urgency only six months before, but I was a different person now. A person who cared enough about her happiness to try to do something about it. If this was my only shot with JC, I had to take it. I had to give him another chance to open up to me.

I prepared myself mentally for the rest of the ride, and as we approached Pierce Industries, I was already looking for a place I could hail a cab.

Except, the car stopped *at* Pierce Industries and not at the coffee shop down the block. And not just at Pierce Industries, but in the valet section of the garage. Before I asked, the driver explained as he handed his keys over. "There's no parking at the shop, so we'll walk from here."

We'll walk? He was coming *with* me? Why wasn't he just dropping me off and leaving?

I got out of the car, confused, and followed the driver out to the sidewalk.

"It's at the end of the block to the right." *Ah! Maybe he is leaving me.* "I'll let you lead the way."

Or maybe not.

I took a few tentative steps toward the coffee shop to see if he would follow, all the while keeping my eyes peeled for a taxi. When I was certain he was coming too, I turned back to him. "I can get there from here by myself, thank you. I appreciate you taking me this far."

"I apologize, Ms. Anders, but I've been instructed to escort you directly to your sister."

My body went rigid. "Have I done something wrong? Am I in trouble?"

"Nah. Nothing like that." His eyes scanned everywhere, I realized, without his head moving an inch. "Your sister's concerned for your safety, that's all."

If my levelheaded sister was concerned for my safety, then there was something I didn't know about going on. Something serious.

I stopped looking for a cab.

Norma was easy to spot inside the coffee shop. She was sitting with three men—one in a police uniform, one I didn't recognize, and another with his back to me. Despite what my driver—not only my driver, it seemed, but also security detail—had said, I was still cautious as I walked over to join her. He let me go alone, getting in line to get something at the register. It was nice to have my space, but even though my sister hadn't seen me yet, I no longer had any inclination to go anywhere but directly to her.

"Hey," I said, when I reached their table. Then, when I saw the face of the third man, I screamed.

He shot up out of his chair and pulled me into his arms. "Hey yourself, big sister."

Ben, Ben. I nuzzled into his shirt and held onto him with my life. Held onto him tight enough to hide any wayward tears. So many things I wanted to say, but no words came. I thought them extra hard, hoping he'd hear them anyway. *I've missed you. I love you. I'm so glad you're here. Why are you here?*

"Good to see you too," he said as he held me. Eventually, when the others behind us started to seem restless, I forced myself to pull away. "You look like shit, by the way."

"Gee, thanks," I said, pretending to be shocked. "What are you doing here, anyway?" As overjoyed as I was to see him, I was also afraid that his presence meant there was more that I didn't know was going on.

"I'll get there. Gwen, this is Eric." He nodded to the other plain clothed man. Eric was everything my brother wasn't. He was tall where Ben was on the shorter side, bulky where Ben was thin, light haired where Ben was dark.

"He's cute," I whispered to Ben before bending forward to take Eric's hand.

"This will have to do since I'm trapped behind the table," Eric said, "but later I'm going to have to give you a big hug."

Normally, I'd be hesitant about anyone who thought they were good enough for my brother. Eric was different. He'd gotten my brother through a rough time which earned him points right away, and now, in person, I could instantly tell he was both a protector and a teddy bear.

Good for Ben.

"Gwen, if you don't mind, we don't want to waste the officer's time." Norma smiled up at me, but it didn't feel very welcoming. That phrase "*smile didn't meet her eyes*" came to mind. Her eyes were not shining. Her eyes were serious.

I swallowed, remembering the somberness of the situation, and sat down in the empty chair with a nod. I suddenly wished I'd ordered a coffee first. I had a feeling I needed energy for this conversation.

Norma must have seen me eyeing her latte. She passed it over to me as she said, "This is Officer Taylor. He's handling the case with Dad."

"Hi. And thank you." I took a swallow of the too sweet beverage. At least it wet my dry throat. When I set the drink down, I found everybody's eyes on me.

A chill ran down my spine as a thought suddenly occurred to me. "You didn't confront him already, did you?" If the cops had talked to him, he'd be pissed. Maybe he'd threatened me. Was that why I had the security dude? Had Ben come because of that? Was this why everyone was so anxious about my arrival?

As irrational as it may have been, the thought of angering my father set me into full-fear mode. My hands felt clammy and my stomach churned. I wanted to believe that I was safe. He was on parole, after all. He was in a halfway house. Yet, he'd managed to hit me once already.

Norma put a comforting hand on my knee. "He's not going to hurt you, Gwen. Do you hear me?"

I searched her face, but I wasn't comforted. She was worried and that worried me. I turned to the officer. "What did he say? I need to know." I shifted my eyes to Ben. "And what does it have to do with you being here?"

Ben nudged me with his elbow. "My being here had nothing to do with any of this, but all of this does make me glad that I happened to come when I did. Now let the cop talk before Norma gets her panties in a wad."

I glanced over at Norma in time to see her scowl. "Okay," I conceded. "But you're filling me in on everything later." I returned my attention to Officer Taylor.

"Go ahead," Norma said to him, as if giving permission to talk. Though, from the expression on his face, I was pretty sure he didn't care whether she permitted him or not.

I liked him already.

"We haven't actually spoken to William Anders yet," Officer Taylor said. "We would have, after you filed your report. Or his parole officer would have. But he never came back to his house last night."

"What does that mean?" Every hair stood up on my body in rigid fear, but I had to be sure I understood what I was hearing. I wanted it spelled out.

Now Officer Taylor glanced at Norma before answering. "It's a violation of his parole. With the assault charge you're filing now, in addition to his attempt at extortion, this is enough to see him incarcerated again."

Ben sat forward in his chair. "I'll tell you what it means—it means he's on-the-run. He realized he fucked up with you yesterday, and he's too scared to go back and face the consequences. It means no one is monitoring him. It means the asshole is free."

"It means we aren't safe," Norma added.

Well. I'd wanted it spelled out and I got it. I took another swallow of her latte, wishing it were something stronger. Wishing I were someone stronger.

I placed a hand over the one Norma still had on my knee and squeezed. *She's overreacting*, I told myself. She's being precautious. We're still safe. *I'm* still safe.

But I knew the truth was exactly opposite. She wasn't the type to overreact. I could even imagine the source of the looks between her and the cop. She'd probably told him not to scare me. To keep his details short and concise. She'd either neglected to lecture Ben the same way or he'd ignored her.

I ran my free hand back and forth across my throat, needing something to do with my fingers, and asked the hard question. "You think he'll come looking for me again, don't you?"

"It's hard to say," Officer Taylor said. "He came looking for you once, and that makes us more likely to believe he'd come for you again. Especially since he didn't leave with what he wanted."

I nodded. God, I felt like a bobblehead with all the nodding I was doing, but it was easier than saying the equivalent words. Easier than saying, *I understand what you're getting at.* Easier than acknowledging verbally that I was in full agreement that my father would very possibly come after me again.

A sob caught in the back of my throat. The boogieman of my youth was real and alive and dangerous. How could I not be scared to tears?

And Ben! He had to be as frightened as I was. He'd been even more tormented by my father.

I reached out to take his arm. "You shouldn't be in town right now." Ironic that I'd been the one that had wanted him to come to New York so desperately, and now I was telling him to leave.

Ben patted my hand. "It's scary as all hell, isn't it? But I'm good. Trust me."

Behind him, I saw my driver take a seat a couple of tables away. He barely glanced at us. Was he watching all of us, I wondered? Would that be how we lived now? Covertly watched over by strangers hired by my sister?

I didn't like the idea. Ben was being strong, though, so I decided I needed to be tougher too. I sat up straighter, forcing myself to appear as brave as I wanted to be, refusing to let fear paralyze me. Not like it had in my childhood. "Why is he being so stupid, anyway? I don't get it. He wasn't ever a criminal. He beat his kids. He didn't steal or blackmail. He wasn't a guy who went 'on-the-run'."

"As I explained to your brother and sister before you arrived, prison changes people, Ms. Anders," Officer Taylor said, patiently. "And fellow inmates aren't always very kind to child abusers. Your father wouldn't have had an easy time in there. It seems he developed a drug habit, as well. Crack, I'm guessing. That's not uncommon, and, the strange thing for many of these addicts is that being released becomes more of a burden than a blessing. Their main concern is where to get their next score and they have no contacts, no money, no place to go back and crash afterward."

My father's a crack addict. Great. Should I have been able to tell that when I'd seen him? Had he been shaky? His eyes dilated?

Guilt rattled through me. Guilt—of all things. How fucked up was it that I felt like this was our fault? Like, if we hadn't put him jail, he wouldn't be so messed up. If we hadn't put him in jail, he wouldn't be a threat to me today.

They were bullshit responses, but I couldn't help feeling them. I hated the part of me that cared at all that my father suffered. I hated that I wondered why Ben couldn't just stick it out like I had. Hated that I even thought for a second that my peace of mind now should be any more valuable than my brother's safety was then.

I couldn't look at him.

Norma leaned in. "Whatever you're thinking right now, Gwen, it's natural. Don't beat yourself up over it."

Easier said than done. She didn't know what I was thinking.

As if to remind me what a monster my father was, my face started to throb right then. *Remember this pain,* it told me. *Ben went through this and more. Your father deserves to be a mess.*

Hateful words were no more encouraging than guilty ones. I took my hand from Norma's and crossed a leg over the other. "So what happens now?"

I'd addressed the question to everyone, but it was Office Taylor that answered. "We obviously want to get him where we know he's going to be. Right now, that's at the club tomorrow morning. We've already contacted the owner and the general manager and plan to have a team waiting for him when he shows up."

"Will I need to be there?" I stopped breathing while I waited to be told whether I was going to be bait or not.

Thankfully, the officer shook his head. "We don't think so. We'd prefer that you aren't, actually."

I sighed audibly. "Okay. I prefer that too."

Norma smiled reassuringly. "Matt already said you could take as much time off as you need. He completely understands."

"Thanks. I'll think about that." Really, I couldn't think about anything anymore. My thoughts were a buzz like a radio dial not quite set on a station. For the rest of the interview, while Officer Taylor took down my report, while he photographed my face, while he dotted the *i*'s and crossed the *t*'s, I buzzed. Anything that floated across my mind was lost to the interference. Nothing took hold. Nothing touched me.

I had no idea how much later it was when Officer Taylor made his farewell and Norma and I sat alone with our brother and his boyfriend. At some point, someone had gotten me my own coffee—Eric, maybe—and I warmed my hands around it now. Strange how cold I felt when the shop was stuffy and stifling.

Norma sat back in her seat and studied me for several seconds. Finally she said, "Do me a favor, will you? Take a deep breath. This part is over. Let it go."

I was tempted to argue with her—I needed my tension; it made me feel safe—but my shoulders were beginning to hurt and my jaw had locked from clenching. Maybe trying to relax wasn't such a bad idea.

Somewhat grudgingly, I inhaled and then exhaled. I did it again. After the third time, I actually felt a little less stressed. I rolled my neck from side to side and shook out my arms.

"Better?"

"Yes. Thank you. I needed that."

"I know." She turned to Ben. "How about you? How are you holding up?"

A glance at my brother said that the day hadn't been a picnic for him either. "I don't know," he said. "I really thought when we did this ten years ago that it was going to be the end."

"We all did." Norma's voice sounded tired, and I realized in that moment that even though she'd missed living with the worst of our father, she'd been fighting him most her life just the same. For us. I was amazed she wasn't more exhausted.

Ben shifted in his seat a few times, and I recognized the awkwardness of hard emotions. Ones that were heavy and difficult to carry, let alone talk about. "It's not fair," he said finally, his jaw working. "It's not fair that he still gets to make us scared."

Eric offered his hand and Ben took it, gripping his fingers around his boyfriend's tightly.

"I'm okay." Ben's reassurance was directed to Eric, but I suspected it was for all of us. "Really. Just pissed. Which is much better than feeling ashamed and scared. Trust me."

I didn't need to trust him. I knew firsthand that shame and fear felt pretty damn shitty. I was feeling that way right then.

"Can we be done with Dad? And now can you please tell me what you're both doing here?"

Ben and Eric exchanged a look I couldn't read. "Well," Ben said. "Eric and I have been talking about coming out here for a while now. In my therapy, after the hospital, I realized that I'd been pushing away all reminders of the past, thinking that was the way to get over things. It wasn't, of course. Because the past will always be and I can't change it and I need to learn to accept it, yada yada, mumbo jumbo psychology stuff. But the other part of that is, when I kept things away that I considered reminders, I really was shutting out the things that made me strongest. You guys, for one. This city is another. Meaningful relationships." He smiled at Eric at the last one. "So instead of trying to hide the painful things, I'm working on facing them and living with them. It's really made me a different person."

"That's amazing, Ben. I can tell, and I'm so glad. And I'm really glad that you decided to visit, even though I think you have terrible timing."

Ben let go of Eric's hand and put his arm around the back of his chair. "We were actually planning to come out next month, but when Norma called yesterday, I wanted to be here now. And we're not visiting—we're looking for a place to live."

"You're moving here?" I couldn't have been more surprised if he'd said he was pregnant. "Both of you? But why? I mean, yay! But I'm so confused."

Ben laughed. "I know. It's quite a one-eighty. But I'm telling you, I'm different. I'm not letting Dad scare me away anymore. I've wasted too much time away from my family. From both of you. I want to be here. I *need* to be here. Now that Dad's being an extra special dickwad, I need to be here more. We need to stick together. We work best that way."

I nodded, again with the bobblehead, but this time not saying anything because I was too happy.

"Anyway," Ben went on, "Eric's company is based out of New York, and he can get an easy transfer. I haven't had a job since I took my leave from the movie theater. When Norma offered to help us out, it felt like a good time to come."

I turned to Norma. "You knew about this?"

She shrugged. "We'd talked a little about it. He wanted it to be a surprise."

"It's a really good surprise." *The best surprise.* I beamed, not caring about the pain from my cheek.

"Enough about me," said Ben, which was funny since we'd barely discussed him. "I want to know about you and this guy you're seeing."

The mention of JC brought a new wave of emotions on as I suddenly remembered where I'd left things with him.

"What's wrong?" Norma asked, reading me as she always did. "Are things not going well?"

I took a moment to answer. I'd been so desperate to go after him earlier. Then I'd forgotten it all while I dealt with the more urgent situation regarding my father. Then there was the distraction that Ben's arrival had provided. It wasn't even noon and I'd already been on a rollercoaster of emotions.

Having had a little time away from the morning with JC, I now had some perspective. Perhaps I'd been too dramatic about it.

"Well," I said, trying to decide how to sum everything up. "Things are strange, right now. Actually, most of it's pretty fucking amazing. We just said we loved each other. And he took care of me all night after, well, after the Dad thing. JC was really sweet." I took a sip of my drink, hoping to hide the blush that had crept up as I'd talked.

"That's fabulous!" Ben said.

At the same time, Norma said, "I had a feeling he'd come around."

"Yeah, he came around all right. And it was fabulous. But then he ruined it this morning. He proposed."

Norma perked up, but it was Ben who really reacted. "As in marriage? Get out of town."

"Yep. Wants to go to Vegas and tie the knot. Tonight." Telling it to my siblings this way, leaving out the strange parts like the phone call he'd received and his desperate behavior made the whole thing seem ridiculous again.

Or maybe I wanted it to sound ridiculous so that was how I told it. Because I really didn't want to feel like I'd made the wrong choice.

"Are you going to go?" This came from Norma.

"No! I'm more levelheaded than that. Give me some credit. I don't even know his full name. I really don't even know his first name." Excuses, excuses, excuses. I recognized that I was making them. I wondered if Norma saw through these as easily as she saw through every other part of me.

"Anyway." I picked at the sleeve on my coffee cup. "When I left, he said he was heading to the airport and that he hoped I'd join him. He was so final about his goodbye. Like, if I don't marry him then it's over. Which if that's the case, I definitely don't want to marry him. But also, if that's the case, I'm really going to be sad." My bravado faltered at the end, and I bit my lip to keep from getting any more emotional about it.

I waited for Ben to console me or Norma to lecture me or give me whatever it was that I deserved. I wasn't quite sure what it was. Maybe nothing. Maybe I deserved nothing at all.

I'd shredded most of the coffee sleeve when Norma finally asked, "He's headed to Vegas now?"

"Yeah."

Norma sat back in her chair. "You should go."

"I agree," Ben piped in.

My head flipped up. "I should marry him?"

"No." Norma said at the same time Ben said, "Why not?"

Norma considered. "Well, if you want to. But I meant you should go to Vegas. Join him. Be with him. He obviously needs you. And, right now, I'd be happier if you were out of town. Might as well go and work all this out with him. Forget about everything here. Get to know the guy. If you end up getting married, hey, that's fine too."

"I so appreciate how cavalier you are with the rest of my life." I said it sarcastically, but really, I kind of did appreciate it.

She sat forward and leaned her forearm on the table. "I'm being anything but cavalier about your life. I'm trying to keep you safe from a man who has hurt you over and over. JC, on the other hand, has done nothing but good for you as far as I've seen. If you said it was what you wanted, I'd approve a future with him in a heartbeat."

I gaped. When I realized it, I shut my mouth, but continued to stare at her incredulously. This was not like my sister. She was even more practical than I was. She was grounded and pragmatic. She looked for the best return on investments. She didn't suggest risky ventures. Ever.

Perhaps realizing how out of character she sounded, she backed off a little. "All I'm saying is to go to Vegas. Then figure out the rest when you get there."

"It's a really good plan," Ben added. "I'd certainly feel better if you were out of town right now."

"How is it any different than you being here?" My tone was harsher than I'd intended, but not harsher than I'd meant.

"It's way different," Ben said. "Dad doesn't know I'm here. He doesn't know where to find me. He doesn't care to find me. And I'm not the one who he's already asked to do something for him. Plus I have Eric to protect me." Both men laughed at that like there may have been an inside joke.

Or maybe they were just that happy together.

And Norma had Boyd.

"You're thinking about it." Ben winked. "You're just as easy to read as you always were."

I rolled my eyes. "But you just got here. I can't leave when we haven't had time to catch up."

"I'm going to live here, drama queen. We'll see each other All. The. Time. Besides, Eric and I don't have time for you. We have to see a million places and decide where to live by Sunday when we leave. You'd be in the way."

I was too exhausted to make any more excuses. Ben was right—I'd see him later. I'd also feel better away from my father while he was on the loose. It was a good idea, really.

And I did want to be with JC. I didn't want to marry him, but I wanted things to work out. I needed him to know that I wasn't going to get scared off by whatever trouble he was in.

I picked up Norma's phone sitting in front of her and looked at the time on the screen. It was a quarter to twelve. The bubble of excitement that had started to form fizzled and popped. "There's no way I can make the flight."

Norma shrugged. "Book the next available. Use my credit card. Do you know where he's staying?"

"Yes."

"Good." She looked over at the man who'd driven me there. "You know the man who drove you here?"

"The Tom Selleck wannabe?" I asked.

Ben hit the table with his palm. "That's who he looks like."

She couldn't help but crack a smile at that. "His name is Reynold. He's one of Hudson's staff bodyguards. He loaned him to me for the day. He'll see you home and stay outside the door and then he'll drive you to the airport."

"He'll sit *outside the door*?" I'd figured he was security, but I'd thought he'd be more undercover. "He already looks like Magnum P.I. Isn't that a bit obvious?"

"I'm not trying to be discreet," she said, frustration underlying her words. "I want Dad or any of his friends to know that you are being watched."

"Okay, okay." Honestly, I was tired. I should have simply said okay from the beginning.

Another sudden wave of emotion crashed over me. This particular wave was filled primarily with gratitude.

I reached for Norma's hand with one of mine and one of Ben's with my other. "Thank you, guys. You especially, Sissy. For everything."

Norma put her other hand on top of mine. "I love you, Gwen. There isn't anything I wouldn't do for you." Her delivery was so matter-of-fact. So plain as day that I had no choice but to truly believe it.

She pulled away first, and I knew it was with the sweetest affection that she said, "Now get the hell home and pack."

• • •

The soonest available flight I found to Las Vegas was a red-eye that didn't leave until midnight. The wait didn't bother me much. It gave me time to do what I needed and let my emotions settle a bit. I booked the ticket and packed a bag then called Norma with the details of my plans.

"Good. Do you want to tell Reynold or should I call him?"

Since I wanted to pretend that I had no reason to need a bodyguard, I asked her to call him. "What about you, Sis? I don't want you alone here."

"I'm going to go straight to the boy's after work." She'd taken to calling him "the boy" on our phone calls, in case anyone ever overheard her. "So I won't see you. Have a good trip. Enjoy yourself and call me when you get there, okay?"

"Got it. Love you. Be safe."

We hung up and I called Matt. He didn't answer, and I had to leave him a voicemail telling him I'd be out for at least the next week. I felt a little like an asshole, running away and all. But all I had to do was think of my father with his cocky grin and his upraised hand, and I didn't care anymore if I was running away. It was survival. This was what I needed to do in order to not break down.

As much as I had on my mind, I still was able to get a few hours of a nap in. When I woke up, it was time to go.

By the time I landed in Vegas, I'd managed to put the reason I was running away from New York completely out of my mind. Now that the trip was all about meeting up with JC, I started to get excited. Really excited.

And anxious.

He wouldn't mind if I surprised him like this, would he? It was certainly the most spontaneous thing I'd ever done. It made me feel a little crazy. Crazier was that, at some point on the flight, I'd actually begun contemplating his proposal. Why shouldn't we get married? What could be the worst thing that happened?

I still wasn't convinced, but I'd open the door for it to be an option. Like Norma said, I'd get there and then I'd see what happened. It was enough of a possibility, though, that my stomach remained in a constant flutter long after the descent into McCarren.

I was so abuzz with nervousness and anticipation, in fact, that I didn't realize the major flaw in my plan until I walked through the doors of the Trump Hotel and stood in the lobby—I didn't know what room he was in. And I couldn't ask the front desk since I still didn't know his actual fucking name.

Fighting the distinct urge to crumple to the floor and have an epic cry, I forced myself to think of solutions before giving up entirely. There were only two elevators. I could sit by them and wait until he came down. Which could take days. I let out a heavy breath of frustrated air.

Then I remembered the name he'd booked his flight under.

It was worth a try.

With as much confidence as I could muster, I approached the desk. "Hi, would you happen to have an Alex Mader staying in the hotel?" I wasn't sure the hotel would legally be able to disclose room numbers for registered guests. If that was even the name he'd booked under.

I got hopeful when the desk clerk responded by typing some things into his computer. After a minute of studying his screen, he asked, "Are you Gwen?"

My heart pounded so loudly, I was sure he could hear it. "Yes, I am."

"If you can just show me your ID, Mrs. Mader, I can get you a key to your room."

Mrs. Mader. JC had said he booked the room already before he left New York. He'd been hopeful. I tried not to let that mess with my head too much as I pulled out my card and handed it to the desk clerk. "It, uh, still shows my maiden name. Does that work?" I fought the shiver that threatened to run down my back. It was too easy to enjoy this. Too easy to believe that I was actually on my way to becoming Mrs. Mader.

Or Mrs. Whatever-JC's-Real-Last-Name-Was.

"This should be fine." The clerk scanned the ID then gave me a keycard. "Room four-seventeen."

That was it. I had the key. I had the room number. I was doing this.

The only other time I'd been in Vegas was for a birthday weekend with Norma when she'd turned thirty. We'd stayed at the Venetian, a huge sprawling hotel that could practically call itself a city. The Trump Hotel was nothing like that. It was small and classy. There wasn't even any gambling, which was probably exactly why it was small and classy. While most of Sin City had turned me off on my other visit, I liked this.

What I didn't like was how fast I made it to the fourth floor. I'd barely had time to gather myself, and here I was about to see JC. A string of *I should have's* made their presence in my mind and stalled me for a few minutes after the elevator doors shut behind me. *I should have waited to get here until a decent hour of the day. I should have stopped in the lobby restroom to make sure my hair looked okay. I should have worn sexy lingerie underneath these sweats. I should definitely not have worn sweats at all.*

What the hell had I been thinking?

But sweats or not, messy hair or not, I was eager to see JC. It felt like a week had passed since we'd parted instead of eighteen hours, and I all of a sudden couldn't stand for it to be a minute longer.

With renewed excitement, I followed the signs to room four-seventeen.

I hesitated again at the door. Sure, I had a key, but I didn't want to just walk in unexpected. It would give me a heart attack if someone did that to me. I decided to knock.

It was only seconds before I heard movement and the lock being turned. He hadn't been sleeping then. Had he been missing me? Did he think it would be me waiting on the other side of the door?

When it opened, though, it wasn't JC standing there. I was met by an older woman—well, older than me, anyway. Forties, if I had to guess.

She had strawberry blonde hair and too much makeup and wore nothing but a T-shirt and panties.

I started to panic and then realized I must not have heard right when the clerk gave me the room number. "I'm so sorry for disturbing you," I said. "I have the wrong room."

The woman smiled like it was no big deal. "Who are you looking for?"

"JC." Maybe I should have said Alex Mader. I was so confused.

"Oh no, sweetie. You got the right place. He's here."

"He is?" I was even more confused now. And panicked. It was rude and out of place seeing how it was her room and all, but she was wearing no pants and was supposedly in a hotel room with the man who'd just asked me to marry him not twenty-four hours before—I had to know. "Can I ask, who are you?"

She didn't seem in the least offended. In fact, she brightened. As if answering the door to a strange woman at four in the morning and being interrogated was completely normal.

"I'm Tamara," she said. "I'm his wife."

Chapter Nineteen

The hall tilted. Blood whooshed past my ears, and my toes and fingers instantly went numb. And my chest—it sunk, like an elevator out of control, plummeting to the ground level, ready to crash.

But it was late—or early—and I was tired from traveling and feeling feelings. It was possible I misunderstood or the chick in front of me misunderstood or that somebody somewhere misunderstood.

Then I saw him—behind her, his hair tousled, his chest and feet bare. Somehow seeing him like that, half-dressed and intimate, was worse than simply hearing that the goddamn motherfucker was married. Because, number one—it seemed to prove that he actually was married. Number two—it suggested he'd probably been fucking her earlier that very night while I was rushing to be with him.

And, number three—oh-my-god-I'd-fallen-in-love-with-someone-who-was-fucking-married!

When he realized who I was, his eyes popped open and his face paled. "Gwen!"

I delivered the most scathing glare I could muster and still didn't begin to scratch the surface of what I wanted him to understand from me. "You're a fucking asshole."

Then, since I didn't know how to actually express any more than that, I spun and headed back toward the elevator, dragging my suitcase behind me.

Fuming. I was fuming and raging and red. I was red. All sorts of red. I wanted to scream and yell and hit and throw things. I hated that I felt so violent. So red.

And somewhere under all of that red, there was blue. But I wanted to get out of there before it showed itself with something as weak as tears or blubbering.

"No, no, no, no!" JC must have pushed past his wife—his goddamn fucking *wife*—because he was instantly at my side. "That isn't what it looks like."

"Yep. That's what they say." My words were tight, clipped. Red.

"Hold on. I'll explain." He jogged to get ahead of me then walked backward as he begged me to stop. "Please, you have to let me explain. Don't just leave. I can explain."

I wanted to keep walking. My internal tracking system had locked on the elevators, had locked on escape. It was survival instinct. But I was a reasonable person, a person who relied on more than instincts. I had to give him a chance to clear things up.

God, please let him clear things up!

I stopped, my face hard. My heart, not-so-hard. "Try."

"Okay. I. She." He gave an exasperated tug to a lock of hair at the top of his head. "Jesus, I don't know where to start."

I folded my arms over my chest. "Start wherever. Just start."

He rubbed his palms together. "Okay. Okay."

His difficulty to summarize the situation killed any lingering hope that the whole thing was a misunderstanding. It was only sick curiosity that made me prompt him. "Who's the woman? Start there."

His face scrunched up, as though that question was particularly hard for him to answer. I waited for him to confirm what she'd said. Waited for him to say the words, *she's my wife.*

Instead, he said, "I don't know."

"Yep. Fucking asshole." I would listen if he talked. More evasive answers were all I ever got from him, and they were not going to be good enough. Not this time. I started to go around him.

He spread his arms out, blocking my way around him. "I mean it. I woke up right before you got there. That's when I saw her." He was squinting, I realized, and as he talked he lifted his hand to shield the light coming from the wall sconce. "I went to the bathroom. And I came out. And there you were. I'm sorry, I'm having a hard time gathering my thoughts."

Gathering your lies, more likely.

Except, now that I was adjusting to the haze of red surrounding me, I could see that his skin looked really funky. Pale. Almost green. When I leaned forward, I saw his eyes were bloodshot. And he smelled weird. Like toothpaste and sour.

And the way he was blocking the light... "What the fuck is

wrong with you?"

"Nothing." He shook his head then stopped, seeming to regret it. "I'm. I have a hangover."

"At four in the fucking morning?" It felt surprisingly amazing to swear while angry. I didn't have a lot of experience with the emotion. Anger and its blaring red was too much my father's shade. I avoided it whenever possible, filling my palette with the softer hues of annoyance and irritation.

Today it was not possible. Today was bright red words and bright red volume. "When the fuck did you even start drinking to be hung over at four in the fucking morning?"

"On the plane." He held up a victorious finger in the air. "*That's* what I'm trying to say! Let me go back to then. The airport. I was at the airport and *you didn't come.*" He enunciated the last phrase, pointing his finger now at me.

Oh, hell no. "I was dealing with my fucking father! It's not like you gave me much fucking time in the first place. And I never said I was even coming, so it's your own damn fault for making fucking assumptions."

He waved his hand, as if trying to wave away any wrong implication he'd made. "I know, I know. It wasn't enough time. But it was all I had."

He laced his hands and put them behind his head. "Look, I'm not blaming you." He dropped them again to his sides. "I'm telling you what happened. You didn't come and I got on the plane and I started drinking."

"But you don't drink."

"I was upset. I drink when I'm upset."

Upset because I hadn't come. He didn't come right out and pair the two ideas, but it was understood.

"I was drunk by the time I landed. I remember coming here. Checking in. Then I went to the bar and kept ordering." He wished he hadn't. It was all over his face—the regret, the misery.

Regret didn't fix shit, and frankly, I didn't give a damn if he felt miserable. "And Tamara?"

"Who?"

"Your. Wife?"

He cringed and I wasn't sure if it was because I'd spoken too loudly for his sensitive ears or because he didn't like what I'd said. The door next to us opened long enough for a woman in a bathrobe to glare at us then shut again.

JC lowered his voice. "Can we talk about this somewhere else?"

"I'm not going in that room with that woman."

He let out a small sigh but didn't try to change my mind. After scanning the hallway, he said, "Over here." He reached to grab my arm.

I pulled away. "No. Don't. I can walk on my own."

He frowned, but again, he accepted it.

I followed him down the hallway and stopped at the vending room. He held the door open and gestured for me to go in. It was more private at least. And dark, the only light coming from the soda machine. And where else were we going to go? JC wasn't wearing a shirt or shoes, and I certainly wasn't waiting around for him to get dressed so we could head down to the lobby. I knew that the time I gave him now correlated with how strong my resolve was. Every second that I allowed him weakened my determination.

Leaving my suitcase in the hall, I went in.

He shut the door after him. We stared at each other.

"Well? Tamara?" My voice cracked. Shades of blue slipping in.

"I don't even remember meeting her." His tone was frustrated, but I sensed it was with himself more than with me. "The last thing I can clearly remember is sitting at that bar, thinking about you, thinking that if you would have just married me, it would have solved everything."

The image pinched in my chest.

Then I realized what he was alluding too, and all compassion dissolved. "Are you trying to tell me that you got drunk over me and somehow married someone else?"

He said no words. His expression said it all.

"Jesus fucking Christ. I'm out of here." Nice plan coming in the room first—now he was in front of the only door out. "Let me through."

He didn't move. "It was stupid, Gwen. I know that. I know."

It was more than stupid—it was irresponsible and unbelievable and mean. "Let me through. I need to go." I wanted to get around him but didn't want to touch him. It made for quite the dilemma.

He didn't budge. "No. Listen to me. I'm not trying to excuse what I did. It was fucked up and you have every reason to hate me. But I can undo this. I'll get it annulled. I don't even know that we really got married. It's her saying that we are, that's all. I haven't seen any proof."

"Each thing you say makes it worse." Red faded into purple. I wasn't only fuming anymore. The steam of the rage had cooled and left me hurt. Anguished. "Let me go. Please, let me go."

"I can't. I can't." He reached his hands out toward me, holding them in the air when I flinched away from his grasp. "Ah, Gwen. You and I can still be together. You came. That means something, doesn't it?"

Did my voice sound as desperate as his did? I felt like it should. I was so very desperate. Desperate to leave. Desperate to believe him. Desperate for the whole thing to go away.

"I wish I hadn't come now." Wished it more than anything. "I came because I hated how things were left, not to marry you. And it doesn't matter why I came because now you've been with her." Purple-blue poured out of me, my pain evident in the texture of my words. The image of them together—having sex—it was the worst thing I could imagine. He hadn't said they had, but how could they not? Wasn't that what drunken marriage hook-ups in Vegas were always about?

He could tell what I was thinking. "I haven't. I haven't slept with her. I swear."

"How can you be sure?" If he couldn't remember going to a chapel and tying the knot, how could he expect to remember something as simple as unzipping his pants?

"Because I wouldn't. I couldn't do that to you. I wouldn't. Ever." He was frenzied, frantic for me to believe him. "I woke up dressed. And when I'm drunk, I can't—" He waved his hand, letting silence fill in the blank.

"Can't perform?"

"Exactly."

A weight dissolved from where it had been pressing against my chest. That's how badly I wanted what he said to be true.

Except he wasn't all the way clothed. "Where's your shirt then?"

"I took it off just before you got there." When I gave him a disbelieving glare, he admitted, "I'd thrown up all over it."

"That's what that smell is." That seemed to embarrass him. *Good.* I preferred that it did.

We were quiet for a few seconds, each of us sulking in our misery. I couldn't say why, but I trusted him. He was a fucking irresponsible asshole, but I didn't think he was lying. It didn't make the situation any less painful. It didn't help me figure out what to do or say next.

Eventually, JC spoke. "I told you I do stupid things when I drink."

Stupid didn't begin to cover it. "Did you kiss her?"

He looked away and cursed under his breath. "I don't know. I don't remember. Maybe." His eyes came back to mine. "If I did…if I did, Gwen, it was you. In my head it was you. The whole time. I know this isn't helping. I know I fucked up. I was upset. I wanted you to be with me and I fucked it all up."

He was broken. And I felt so broken myself. If I stood by him any longer, I would try to put him back together. I would fall into his arms and let him put me back together too.

He saved me from my own weakness by stepping away from the door. "Look, go. If you want, you should go. I'm not going to keep you here if you don't want to be here."

He crossed the room to the other wall. I could leave now. There was nothing standing in my way. Well, nothing except everything that pulled me to JC in the first place.

I folded my arms across my chest and leaned against the door behind me. JC leaned against the wall behind him as well, his hands thrust in his jeans pockets. We stared at each other, a silent faceoff. Or maybe a silent agreement. This situation had gotten out of hand, and we both knew it. Problem was, neither of us knew how to correct it now.

"I'll fix it," he said after a few minutes. "I'll undo it. It's not a real marriage. I don't even know her last name."

"I don't know your last name either."

"It's Bruzzo."

Bruzzo. I moved my lips, testing out the feel of his name in my mouth without adding a voice to it. It was a gift. He meant it as a peace offering, and I appreciated it.

But it was too little too late. A trinket given as an afterthought. "Funny how that doesn't change anything. Really, what's the difference between you marrying her or you marrying me? We're both strangers to you."

"We're not. Don't say that. You and I are not strangers. You're right that knowing my name doesn't change anything because it's just a detail. It's not important. We already know everything that matters about each other."

"I don't think that's true. Because whatever this is that's driving you to try to get married and solve everything—I think that probably matters very much in your life, and I know shit about it." My voice cracked, signaling it was time to be done. I refused to break down in front of him.

"This was a bad idea. I shouldn't have come. I need to go now." I turned and grasped the door handle

"You said you could wait. You said you didn't need to know my secrets." They were harsh accusations that were meant to stop me, and they did.

I swiveled back toward him. "That was before *you* made them so important!" I covered my face with my hands. I knew I should go, but I wasn't quite ready. There was too much unsaid, and while I couldn't seem to get anything meaningful from him, I had things I'd meant to say to him. Things I'd have to say if I was ever going to be able to leave without regrets.

I put my arms to my sides and faced him straight on. "I know you're in trouble, JC. I know you think that I won't understand or that I can't handle whatever it is you're hiding, but I would love you anyway. My heart is open, JC. I will love you anyway. I even love you after you—goddammit, I can't believe I'm giving this to you—but I even love you after you fucking married someone else on the same fucking day you proposed to me."

He was in front of me in two strides. Tentatively he put his hands on my upper arms. I let him.

"I'm not in trouble." His thumbs swept over my skin, sending shooting stars of electricity down my arms. "I'm the key witness in an investigation. I'm sworn to secrecy in exchange for government protection. I'm not supposed to say any of that to you. The guy I'm testifying against is not a good guy at all. He's dangerous. He's without morals. I'd thought things were going to be okay when they arrested him. The call I got this morning—yesterday morning, I guess—he made bail. He wasn't supposed to make bail. He doesn't know yet that I'm the key witness, but he will when the prosecutors reveal their evidence. It will be soon. I'll have to be off-the-grid when that happens."

My mouth fell open. I was as stunned by his sudden decision to be honest as I was by what he'd said. Though what he'd said was pretty overwhelming. *Key witness. Dangerous guy. Off-the-grid.* The words spun in my head.

Then c*lick. Click. Click.* Each piece slipped into the puzzle that I called JC. *Why he couldn't talk about things. Why he couldn't come back to New York.* The whole picture began to make sense.

"I didn't tell you earlier because of my oath." He stepped closer so more of our bodies touched, and I put my hands behind me, wedged between the door and my ass, so I wouldn't be tempted to reach out for him. "But I also didn't tell you because I needed you to be safe. Any and all of my personal ties are vulnerable. The less you knew about me, the better. I figured you were safe in the beginning, when our arrangement was so casual. The minute it became more, I couldn't guarantee that."

Why he'd tried to remain distant.

Click. "And the protection I'm offered from the government doesn't extend to love interests."

"No."

Click. "But it extends to wives."

"Right."

Why he wanted to get married so quickly.

"Well, at least Tamara's safe." It was bitchy. I *felt* bitchy. The situation was laughable, really. Someone else looking at it, watching this episode, would get a long hard kick out of it. What would it be called? *The Wednesday I Didn't Get Married. The Wednesday He Married Someone Else.*

JC's hands dropped from my arms. His expression said he didn't find the humor.

"Sorry. I'm still trying to get my head around this." I took a deep breath and wrapped my arms around myself. "So the only way I'll be safe from whoever you're testifying against is to marry you. And then how do they protect us?"

"They'd protect us by hiding us. Making it so no one else can find us."

"Give up our lives, you mean."

JC sighed and leaned heavily against the adjacent wall, as if the whole conversation was a weight that he barely had the strength to carry. Or maybe not the conversation, but the situation he was in. Yes, that.

He ran a hand over his face before tilting his head to look at me. "I don't really have anyone I'd be giving up besides you."

I warmed at that. It was what every woman wanted, wasn't it? To be the only thing that mattered to a man. Why couldn't I give him the same in return? "That's not the case for me. I have Norma. I have Ben." Ben, who was finally moving back to be closer to us—I couldn't leave him now.

However, my brother, of anyone, would understand needing to run away for a bit. "Would I be able to talk to them first?"

"No. I wasn't even supposed to tell you unless we were married. It was why I didn't tell you yesterday."

"So I just disappear and can't tell my family and that's the only way I can be safe from someone that's after you." Marriage for protection—it sounded archaic and not something I ever would have chosen, but I was starting to worry it was my only option.

JC hesitated for a moment.

"Am I in danger if I don't go with you?" I prodded.

"No. If you didn't marry me, you'd be fine. The guy I'm testifying against doesn't know anything about you. It's me who has to leave." He knew as he said it that he was decreasing his chances of convincing me to go. But he was honest. And I appreciated that.

I appreciated it enough to ask more questions. "For how long?"

"I don't know. A few months. Maybe longer. I'm not sure."

"Like how much longer *could* it be? Could it be a year? More than that?" I couldn't decide if I was considering going with him or if I was just desperate to know how long he'd be away from me. Either way, this answer was vital.

"I honestly don't know." He moved in front of me again. "It depends partly on how the trial goes and some other things. But I'm not telling you anymore than that, Gwen, unless you're coming with me." He trailed his thumb down my jawline. "I can't put you at risk. I feel like I'm already putting you at risk just by telling you this much."

His touch made me vulnerable, even in such a small dose. It was both a salve and a poison—healing the wounds between us and killing me at the same time.

I didn't turn away from it, but it did make me bitter. "You could have said some of this earlier, you know. Before you ran off and married someone else."

"Forget about her. She's not part of this. This is about us." JC put his hands on either side of me, surrounding me, caging me. "Yes. I should have told you something at least. I was convinced that you would be safer if I kept all of it from you. And I wanted to honor my agreement with the people I'm cooperating with. Now, I'm not sure what I'm doing. Now, I just want you with me."

I couldn't help myself—I reached up to wrap my hands around his neck. "I want to be with you too. But this? This is big."

"It is. It's not fair to ask you to be part of this. But I'm asking you anyway. Because I haven't cared about anyone or anything for so long. Nothing. Until you. You mean something to me. And I don't have to know when you were born or how many siblings you have or where you grew up to know that I *feel* for you. I can't pretend that isn't just as big as what I'm asking you to do. It's bigger. To me, it is."

He stepped back from me and spread his hands out, pleading. "This is it, Gwen. This is all my cards on the table. My heart is open and I'm seizing the moment. I'm living for now. For you. This is me saying yes. Say yes, Gwen. Tell me you'll say yes."

Yes was on the tip of my tongue. He pulled it from me so easily, like a magician pulling out the never-ending strand of scarves. *Yes, yes, yes, yes, yes, yes.* The list of things drawing me back home was slim, after all. I loved working, but I could get another job. I wanted away from my father as it was. Ben had just come back to town, but he had Eric. And Norma—she had Boyd. They didn't need me, though not being able to tell them where I was going was a definite downside. Was it enough to not follow the man I loved?

Probably not.

But there was something else that was in the way of my acquiescence, and it was most certainly *enough* to make me do or not do almost anything—me. My gut. My instinct.

It said, *you don't know him well enough to marry him.* It said, *you don't know him well enough to run away with him.* It said, *you don't know him well enough to trust him to not break your heart again like he did tonight.*

It said, *you don't know him period.*

He had valid excuses for his secrets, but nevertheless, he'd kept them from me. He'd withdrawn from me and hurt me when he did, and that pain was far too recent. He'd tried to woo me into a marriage without all the details. And he'd married someone else.

They were all things I could forgive—and would—but not overnight. Not in a vending room at the Trump Hotel. Not soon enough to make a *yes* in any way be possible.

So my answer had to be, "No."

JC's entire body sunk. A balloon deflating. I deflated with him, even though I'd been the one who'd made the agonizing decision.

"You're sure?" he asked.

Loaded question since I was anything but sure.

But I didn't have to be sure—I just had to mean it. And I did.

I meant *no*.

I took in a deep breath. "I love you," I said, with every ounce of sincere affection I had in me. "And my heart is open. So much more open than it's been in a long time. But as much as I want to be carefree and spontaneous, I'm still responsible and practical. And practicality says that if this is really something between us—if this is really as big as you think it is, as big as I think it is—then it will last. It will be there when you come back. It will wait. And if it doesn't, then it wasn't meant to be."

"It *is* meant to be." But it didn't sound like he was really fighting me. More like he was throwing in his opinion for the record.

"Then it will last." I held his eyes, memorizing the weight of them on me, and the way they soaked me up and reflected only the very best things. I thought of how it felt to be covered with his lips and his hands. With his love. I memorized that too.

Then I told him again, for my sake as well as his, "No."

"No." When he repeated it, it became real. It was an acknowledgement, not a question. It was the notice of acceptance. It was a white flag, the final surrender in the battle of Prove My Love.

It was his way of saying, *I let you go. I set you free.*

He pulled me into his arms and pressed his forehead against mine. "I love you, Gwen. You brought me meaning again, and I'm so grateful for that. Don't wait for me, okay? When I can come for you—if I can—I'll find you and we'll go from there. But don't wait for me."

My eyes started to burn. "Why? Is there a chance you won't come back?" Then another thought. "Will you be in danger?"

"I'll be fine. I just don't want you to waste any of your life waiting. I've done that. I don't want that for you. I will come for you, but you have to live like I'm not. Promise me."

His tone made me uneasy. I didn't know if he was lying about the danger, and that made me uncomfortable and reaffirmed my decision not to go all at once. But the promise not to wait…

I couldn't do that. I wouldn't. I had too much unresolved with him. Too much undone. I'd invested, and I wanted to collect on the payout. I wanted to discover who he was and show him who I was. I wanted to fall in love, deeply and more certainly. I wanted to go through it all, and then, if I was lucky, get another chance at the question. A chance where I could make a better decision that wasn't based on a crazy timeline or controlled by people outside of us.

They were only words, though, and they were words he wanted to hear, so I promised him.

Then he kissed me, hard and rough, his lips smashing against mine with the force of someone who wanted things to be different. I let him bruise me and mark me with his exertion. It was a kiss that had to last me a long time, and I wanted to be able to remember it well.

• • •

I didn't have any idea where to go when I left the hotel, so I told the driver to take me to the airport. With nothing else to do, I bought a standby ticket on a ten-thirty flight to New York City then wandered around for a while. I felt numb, my mind empty. I watched people hurrying to their gates. I saw an old woman hit a jackpot on a slot machine. I picked up the binky of a mother who hadn't realized the baby had dropped it.

Around nine, I got up the strength to call Norma. "I'm coming home."

"Do you need money for a ticket?" She was brilliant like that, to not ask. To just understand what I needed.

I'd tell her all of it. Later. Not on the phone. "Nope. I already got it."

"I bet that cost a pretty penny. Text me the flight information, and I'll have Reynold meet you. I'll have Boyd order dinner in for all of us at our place. I'm sure Ben and Eric will join us once they're done apartment hunting."

Reynold. I knew in an instant what that meant, the hair on the back of my neck rising. "Dad didn't show up?"

"Nope. Whether he got high and forgot he'd set it up or he sensed a trap, I don't know. There's a warrant out for his arrest, but not much anyone can do now without any leads."

Dad was still out, then. Guilt peeked through the numbness. Guilt for being a problem in the first place. Guilt for coming home and making Norma have to worry. She probably wished I would stay away until he was caught. If she knew JC had offered government security—a secret I would never share—I wondered if she'd wish I'd disappeared with him. It wouldn't surprise me. She was that kind of protector.

Staying with JC hadn't been my choice, though, and I didn't regret the one I'd made. Even if it meant I had to face my demons head on.

I could do it. I was ready.

"Dad isn't going to get to me," I said, only a little more boldly than I felt. I gave myself points for that—feeling brave at all where he was concerned was not easy for me.

"I know. I won't let him." She paused. "Come home."

I'd never heard her say sweeter words.

After I hung up, I found a restroom that wasn't overly crowded. I took the last stall and locked it. Fully clothed, I sat on the toilet and drew my feet up, tucking my knees under my chin.

And I sobbed.

Epilogue

Norma didn't take her eyes off her phone as she quietly scolded me. "Sit still, would you? You're bouncing is giving me the jitters."

"Then sit somewhere else." We'd only checked in with Hudson Pierce's secretary two minutes ago, and she'd told us we'd be seen soon. Norma could deal with my twitching for that long.

She put a hand on my knee, stilling it. "Are you nervous or something?"

"No. I'm anxious in general." It was my latest go-to emotion. Not very comforting but nearly always appropriate.

"And grumpy," Norma muttered under her breath.

I scowled. It wasn't like I didn't have reason. My father still hadn't been apprehended and I wasn't sleeping well. I'd been staying in a room at the Gramercy Park Hotel since I'd returned from Vegas a week before because Norma thought it was safer. She'd wanted to hire a fulltime bodyguard, but I refused to be watched and followed twenty-four/seven. It wasn't like Dad had money or resources. He couldn't hire someone to find me if he couldn't find me himself. I just had to not be any of the places that he might look for me on his own. Our apartment. The Eighty-Eighth Floor. So now I was staying in a hotel and looking for a new job.

My entire life was disrupted. Norma was lucky I was only grumpy.

Then there was JC.

I missed him. I'd been used to only seeing him once a week, but knowing I wouldn't see him anytime soon made me miss him in a way that made my bones and my teeth ache. With the pain and the distance, I'd begun to have doubts, the regret I vowed not to have, sweeping in like high tide. Maybe I should have gone with him. Maybe it didn't matter that I didn't really know him. I'd come home only to go into hiding anyway. Wouldn't I have much rather been hiding with him?

The whole thing left me sullen and surly.

I felt bad about taking it out on Norma, though. Hudson had her working on a project that was taking more of her time than usual, and on top of that, she was dealing with all the bullshit regarding me.

I made an effort to be friendlier. "Have you gotten word on when our apartments will be ready?"

"Just did," she said, closing an email on her phone. "Beginning of next week."

"And it doesn't have my name anywhere on the lease?"

"Nope. It's all under Eric's name."

Eric and Ben moving into the city had made things easier. Unbelievably, they'd found a building that had two apartments available, side-by-side. It was a secured building, and with money from Norma, they'd been able to put a down payment on both of them, stating that they planned to remodel into one in the future. Maybe they would one day, but for now, they would be living in one and I in the other. Well, they would be as soon as they arranged the actual move. It would be a month or so, I suspected.

While the circumstances were not the best, I was actually looking forward to having a place of my own. I'd never lived by myself, and at thirty, I figured it was probably about time. And I'd be next door to my brother. It was perfect and probably the only way things could have worked out that wouldn't have made Norma feel bad for pushing me out.

I had a feeling she still felt bad, and admittedly, I hadn't done much to change that. I'd been too preoccupied with wallowing. God, I was such a shitty sister. I opened my mouth to give her a thank you, at least, when Hudson walked out of his office.

"Norma, I apologize for making you wait. I was on the phone." He saw my sister every day so I wasn't surprised that their greeting wasn't more formal. To me, he held out his hand. "You must be Gwen."

"I am." I took his hand. It was warm and firm. The kind of shake that I expected a man of power to have. "It's nice to finally meet you in person, Mr. Pierce. Norma has told me so much about you."

I swear I felt her kick me even though she only did it in her mind.

"It's Hudson. And likewise. Come on in." He ushered us into his office and gestured for us to take a seat at the armchairs facing his desk while he shut the door. It was a large office—he had a complete sitting area along with his work area. Floor-to-ceiling windows were his walls.

FREE ME

I couldn't help but remember the last time I'd been pressed against windows like that. Naked, panting while JC had showed me how good it could feel to be so exposed.

"Please, sit," Hudson said.

"Sorry. I was just admiring the view." Jesus, I probably looked like an idiot. I hadn't realized I was still standing, staring dumbly out the window, until he'd said something. I sat now, crossing a leg over the other, hoping my blush wasn't too evident.

"It is rather distracting," he said. "That's why my desk faces away from it." He sat at his seat before asking, "Did you two have a nice holiday?"

The day before had been the Fourth of July. I'd spent most of the night walking around the city. While Norma was being spanked by her boyfriend and the rest of the country ooh'd and ah'd over colors in the sky, I'd made my way to the Four Seasons. I'd wanted to just be in a place that we'd been together, JC and me. My key didn't work in the door, and when I went to check on it at the front desk, I was told the room wasn't booked to JC Bruzzo anymore.

It was only then that it truly hit me how gone he was.

"Lovely," Norma said. "Thank you for asking."

I sensed that next she was going to ask him how his holiday was in turn. Since small talk was not my thing, I cut her off before she did. "I really appreciate this opportunity. Norma said she faxed my resume over earlier, so I didn't bring that with me. I'm happy to tell you anything you want to know about my current job duties or my schooling or ideas I might have for The Sky Launch. I think there's a lot of potential to make that club the 'it' place, and I believe I have what it takes to help get it there."

Hudson sat back in his chair. "I did get your resume. I only looked it over briefly, but I'll pass it on to Alayna Withers. I'm sure Norma explained what Alayna's looking for?"

"She did. Is it Alayna that is actually doing the hiring?" I hadn't gotten many details from Norma. She'd simply said it was a job made for me and to show up at two.

"I own the club, but Alayna is the General Manager. I have very little to do with operations. I'm happy to help with anything I can, but hiring you is not my decision. She asked me to find someone capable of running the place with her, though, and I think from what I know about

251

The Eighty-Eighth club and your education, you would be a perfect fit."

A beep sounded, like a notification on a phone. "Excuse me," Hudson said, pulling out his cell from his desk drawer.

As he checked his message, Norma leaned over and whispered, "That's Alayna's ringtone."

"Oh." From only the few things he'd said, I could tell the guy had a total hard-on for his girlfriend. He talked about her with a note of awe and reverence in his tone. I bet he didn't excuse himself to answer just anyone's texts. Hers, though...

For a moment, I let myself be jealous. Until I remembered that I too could have someone loving and adoring everything I did. But I'd told him no.

"It seems Alayna is on her way up now," Hudson said, tucking his phone back into his desk. "She can meet you in a few minutes."

"Perfect timing." Norma smiled stiffly, and it occurred to me that she wasn't that fond of Alayna. Or the idea of Alayna, anyway. Though my sister was happy with Boyd, she'd loved Hudson from afar for too long to easily accept another woman in his life.

The insight made me strangely feel closer to her than I had in a while.

"Hudson." Even the way she said his name had a tenderness to it. "While we wait for her to join us, I have to ask. If you do hire—" She paused. "I mean, if Alayna hires my sister, I'd want to make sure there were certain security precautions taken at The Sky Launch."

"Norma—" I stopped myself before I said something sisterly and inappropriate. I turned to her boss. "Whatever security the club has, I'm sure is fine."

"You'll be happy to know that The Sky Launch has top-notch security." Hudson pinned his focus on Norma. "The thing most precious to me is at that club. Believe me when I say the place is safe."

"Thank you, Hudson, for understanding."

It was irritating that I was being talked about like a weak thing that needed protecting. It really wasn't that dramatic of a situation. "I'm not in any danger or anything. I wouldn't want you to think I'll be a problem in that way. It's just that my father—"

Hudson put up a hand to stop me. "Norma told me that you'd like to keep your reasons for transferring private. If you'd rather not share those reasons with Alayna, I'd prefer not to hear them either. I don't want to keep any secrets from her that aren't absolutely necessary."

There was another exchange of glances between my sister and her boss. Obviously, the two had secrets of their own. Business related, most likely. No wonder she'd had such an epic crush on him—the two of them were tied together through the jobs that they both loved. I wondered if either of them realized exactly how tied they were.

"I believe I just heard the elevator." Hudson stood from his desk and crossed to his office door. As soon as he opened it, a woman walked in. He cupped his hands around her face. "I got your text. What's wrong? Are you hurt?"

"No, not hurt." She was shaking. She was scared. I could sense that kind of fear a mile away. It was familiar.

Immediately, I felt bonded to her. Even if Norma didn't like her, I did. While her focus was elsewhere, I studied her. She was quite attractive—thin, brunette, dressed well.

"Alayna, what is it?" The way Hudson looked at her with such affection and concern...it was too sweet. It pulled at something in me. Made my chest throb. Made me a little bit bitter.

I turned away.

"I need to show you something. Can I—" Alayna cut off when Norma stood up.

"Oh, I'm sorry." Alayna gathered herself, masking her previous emotion. "I didn't realize you weren't alone."

"Alayna, you remember Norma," Hudson said.

"Yeah, I do. Norma Anders. We met at the Botanic Gardens event." Her tone was tight. There wasn't any wonder as to why—my sister wasn't very gracious to her.

"We did meet then. It's good to see you again, Alayna." Norma focused on Hudson. "If you two need to talk alone, we can step out."

"No, no. I apologize for bursting in. It's not like me to interrupt." Alayna sounded embarrassed.

I twisted again to look at them just as Hudson said, "Actually, Alayna, this is perfect timing." He nodded at me so I stood. "This is Norma's sister, Gwen. She's one of the managers at The Eighty-Eighth Floor."

"Oh." Alayna's expression was unreadable. Then her eyes lit up. "Oh!" She crossed to me, her hand out. "Alayna Withers."

I smiled, genuinely. "Nice to meet you." She scanned me over the way someone does when they meet someone they are looking to work with. The way I'd scanned her a moment before.

I imagined it then—working with another woman. Managing a club side-by-side. Sharing ideas, building a better business. Becoming friends, even. I'd been too occupied with the need for the job to think about what possibilities could be in store for me in a new place. It was exciting.

"Alayna's currently the Promotions Manager at The Sky Launch, but as I told you, she'll become the General Manager once the current manager leaves." Hudson had actually suggested she was already the General Manager. I sensed he was appeasing her by referring to her as Promotions Manager now. He saw her at her fullest potential.

It made me feel like I could see it too. "Hudson told me you're looking for an Operations Manager."

She nodded. "Is that something you might be interested in?"

"Definitely."

We arranged for me to come into The Sky Launch the next evening for an interview. She'd been concerned about working around my schedule at Eighty-Eighth, but I told her I had the day off to make things easier. I didn't want to explain that I hadn't been able to return to my club since I'd had the encounter with my father. It was why I hadn't argued about finding a new job when Norma suggested it—even thinking about returning to the old one sent me into an embarrassing spiral of fear that I hadn't felt since growing up.

Based on how frightened she'd seemed when she arrived, I wondered if Alayna might have understood my own fears.

Maybe I'd tell her. One day.

Hudson escorted us to the waiting room where Norma thanked him profusely. I'd thanked him for the opportunity earlier—I thought it was enough, especially considering how he wasn't the one I needed to thank if I got the job, but Alayna.

When he closed the door to his office, Norma turned to me, obviously relieved. "That went well. You were surprisingly pleasant. I'm impressed."

Her comment stung. "Yeah, well, she'll find out soon enough that I'm a cold-hearted bitch." I started toward the elevator then turned back to Norma. "I'm going through a tough time. It doesn't mean I'm not going to be professional."

"That was patronizing, wasn't it? I'm sorry." She was motherly now, her business self put away. She walked the few steps to me and put a hand on mine. "I know this is hard. Are you sure this is what you want to do? We could hire security. You could stay at Eighty-Eighth."

I shook my head. "You know I can't go back there."

"I know you don't want to go back there. I think you can do anything you set your mind to." She meant it to be supportive and empowering— and it was—but also it made me roll my eyes internally.

I did appreciate her effort. I rewarded her with one of the insights I'd gleaned from our meeting. "Alayna's totally jealous of you and Hudson, you know."

"That's hilarious considering that he's never given me the time of day. Thank God I'm not hung up on that anymore." But she couldn't fool me—she liked hearing what I'd said. "Are you going straight down? I'll wait for the elevator with you."

I ran my hands through my hair as we walked. I'd had it cut and dyed only the day before and was still getting used to the shorter length.

"I like it." Norma gestured to my hair. "It's a good color on you."

"You think so?" I pulled a lock out to study the dirty blonde shade that seemed so different from my natural lighter hue.

"I do." She pushed the down button on the call panel. "Why did you dye it, anyway? To hide from Dad?"

"Nah. I wanted a change. Isn't that what a girl does when she breaks up with a guy—gets her hair done?"

"You didn't break up. He's coming back for you."

I'd told Norma everything about JC except his last name and the reason he was leaving town. I also didn't tell her that if I'd married him, I would have disappeared indefinitely. It was impossible to explain without telling her the whole story, and besides, I didn't want her to realize how close I'd been to leaving her without a word.

She'd listened. She'd nodded. At first she'd been quite upset about his marriage to Tamara, almost madder than I'd been, but she calmed down about it eventually, saying that she understood the crazy things people did because of heartache. Maybe she'd forgiven him entirely, I wasn't sure, but I suspected that her latest cheerleading and upbeat remarks regarding him and our relationship were meant to cheer me up rather than as a reflection of her true opinion on the man.

Whatever it was meant as, I wanted to believe it. Wanted to believe he was coming back for me. But there was a big obstacle standing in the way of that, that I'd only acknowledged to myself so far. It was the one and only downside to me taking a job with Alayna Withers. It was the only thing that made me hate myself for not being able to go back to my old job.

"What is it?" Norma prodded, reading my distress. "Don't you think he's coming?"

"No. I do. Well, just. I don't know when he'll come back, for one. And he told me not to wait, which I'm ignoring. But I'll no longer work at the one place that he knows to look for me. He doesn't have my full name or my number. How is he supposed to get to me?"

"Hmm." She thought about it for a moment. "JC strikes me as a very resourceful man. I'm not worried."

I stopped chewing the inside of my lip and decided it didn't matter if she was right or not. Fretting about it wouldn't change anything, and the fear of not being there for JC's return wasn't enough for me to stay working someplace that made me uncomfortable. Especially when I had an even better opportunity now at The Sky Launch.

And JC *was* resourceful. With all the things I didn't know about him, I did know that. He could make things happen. He could stay committed to a task. He could follow through.

If he really loved me as he said he did, he'd do anything it took to find me.

END OF BOOK ONE

Find Me

BOOK TWO IN THE FOUND DUET
A FIXED TRILOGY
SPINOFF SERIES

He left his life to keep me safe from one danger. I left my life to feel safe from another. Some days I regret the choices I made when we parted. Other days I'm convinced there was no other way.

Everyday, I wait.

I wait for him to find me.

JC and Gwen's story concludes with FIND ME.

Acknowledgments

Ah, fun. We're at this part. This part that I both dread and look forward to. There are so many people that I am dying to express gratitude for, but I always feel inadequate about how I say it. And I'll probably forget someone and feel like crap on a stick about it. Maybe this will be the book I get everyone in.

Enough stalling. On with it.

To Tom who frees me in more ways than he knows. Thank you for being my husband, my caretaker, my research assistant, my graphic designer, my children's father, my lover, and my friend.

To my girls who will one day realize what it is Mommy writes and will be proud anyway. (If you're not, pretend.) Thank you for being patient with my parenting skills and please know that I love you more than there are words in my books.

To my mother who maybe doesn't even read these. I'm only who I am because of you. Thank you for the freedom you've given me to live my life. It's made for the best life ever.

To Bethany Hagen, my beloved editor, book fairy, and best friend that the Internet has ever given me. And this is where my words feel inadequate. This book was so tough at the end. If not for you, for me. I am unfathomably grateful for your faithfulness. You stayed with me when you had every reason to let this project finish without you. You cannot know how much that has meant to me. I will try to make it up to you with talk of beaches and moors and Fassy and priests and tarot and Mozart and anal and gummies and Scotch.

And, also, I appear to be a crier now. Well, that's new.

To Rebecca Friedman for being someone I enjoy working with, talking with, scheming with, plotting with, and making deals with. Let's go to Italy and spend a few weeks, shall we? I bet we'd talk about work the whole time.

To Shanyn Day for putting up with me and doing all the things I hate as well as pretending I'm still a decent person, even though you see me when I'm really not. And for all that job stuff you do—publicity, assisting. That's good too.

To Kayti McGee for being my work wife. You are strong and wise and witty and creative in ways that blow my mind. You're there when I need a fresh dose of snark and an ear to hear my judgies. If you put out more, you'd be perfect.

To the best band ever, the NAturals—Gennifer Albin, Sierra Simone, Melanie Harlow, Kayti McGee, and Tamara Mataya. You ladies are my safe place. Thank you for letting me be part of you.

To Eileen Rothschild for giving me enough flexibility to be able to write All. The. Things. And for being cool and giving me contracts and marketing support and all that.

To Kimberly Brower for the audio deal (and for being a reader), and to Flavia Viotti for all the foreign deals you're going to make for me as well as the ones you already have.

To Lauren Blakely and CD Reiss for your ideas, brainstorming and friendship on the way to world domination. You both poop gold. I'm so lucky to be able to get to sniff some of it.

To Cait Petersen for keeping me formatted and within regulation at all the vendors without ever batting an eye. To Kari March for the most beautiful teasers—and such a quick turnaround! To Jenna Tyler for eyes that miss nothing—you make me look flawless.

To Josh Taylor for the unsolicited but very welcome law advice. I'll try to frustrate you less in book two.

To Letty Caporusso, Roxie Madar, and Melanie Cesa for the early feedback. Your notes were priceless and so very appreciated. To Angela McLain for being the first to read the final version. Did you even know that? Surprise!

To Brandie Zuckerman who named Gwen and I forgot to credit her. It's been so long now that even you have a new name. Hope your life is going as beautifully as it looks on Facebook.

To the groups I have found myself in—the women who keep me in Order (you know who you are), the women who tell me to FYW (you know who you are), and the women who write at home like me and are wildly entertained by Hiddles and dinoporn (you know who you are). When I say *I've found myself*, I don't just mean that I ended up with you accidentally I mean that I have found my true self amongst your company. You're beautiful people and I'm lucky to know you all.

To the amazing industry friends I've made along the way (this is where I'll forget peeps)—Kristen Proby, Emma Hart, Trish Mint, Amy McAvoy, Jesey Newman, Claire Contreras, Kristy Bromberg, M. Pierce, Kyla Linde, Lisa Otto, Pepper Winters, Rachel Brookes, Melody Grace, and so many more that I can't possibly name them all. It's thrilling to be able to work in a field with so many people I admire. You make the daily commute from my bed to my desk worth it.

Thank you to the bloggers who support and promote and give their time and Facebook/Twitter feeds to my stories and me.

Thank you to the Free Me Street Team and the Obsessed with the Paige girls and the Hudson! Fixed Trilogy fans. I lurk in your groups way more than you realize. Thank you for the continued love, even when I'm not around.

Thank you to the READERS! Every single one of you who picked up my book when there are so many books to choose from—I am so indebted to each of you for your time and your purchase or borrow and your word-of-mouth. You have transformed my life. I am overwhelmed by you daily. DAILY. Thank you from the absolute bottom of my very filled heart.

And above all, to my God who has given me the ultimate freedom. I am awed by your plans for me and ever grateful. Thank you for seeing my beautiful soul underneath my wounds.

If you liked FREE ME, please consider supporting the author by telling your friends and/or leaving a review.

To keep up-to-date with all of Laurelin Paige book releases, visit www.laurelinpaige.com, and sign up for new release newsletters. Emails only go out every couple of months.

Twitter: @laurelinpaige
Facebook: www.facebook.com/laurelinpaige
Pinterest: www.pinterest.com/laurelinpaige

Are you a fan of Hudson Pierce? Join the Hudson Pierce fan group on Facebook: www.facebook.com/groups/HudsonPierce

COMING DECEMBER 29, 2015 FROM LAURELIN
PAIGE, THE FIRST BOOK IN A TWO-PART SERIES:

First Touch

Early praise for *First Touch*:

"Paige is unflinching in her depiction of a complicated relationship, and the results are explosive." —*Kirkus Reviews*

"Edgy sex and pulsating mystery make this fast paced and sensual story impossible to put down." —Jay Crownover, *New York Times* bestselling author of *The Marked Men* series

"Laurelin creates a romance that comes in many touches…Each chapter leads you deeper into mystery, twisting what you knew, making you love who you're meant to hate. A fascinating read!" —Pepper Winters, *New York Times* bestselling author

"Dark, intense, and incredibly sexy, *First Touch* kept me on the edge of my seat from page one up to the very last word." —Shameless Book Club Blog

"Gritty, edgy, dark and compelling, *First Touch* pulls no punches and just might leave you reeling." —Megan Hart, *NYT* and *USA Today* bestselling author of *Tear You Apart*

"*First Touch* is her best work to date… it smolders, captivates, & rips you to pieces… we're obsessed!" —Rock Stars of Romance Blog

"This spellbinding story will have you glued to the pages from the first page to the last. Paige's best work yet. Thrilling, captivating, sexy, and shocking. I am in love with this story." —Claire Contreras, *New York Times* bestselling author of *Kaleidoscope Hearts*

"*First Touch* is shocking, stunning, and intense with a heat level that can only be measured on the Kelvin scale." —CD Reiss, *USA Today* bestselling author of *Shuttergirl*

"*First Touch*…will leave you on pins and needles, breathless and begging for more. Laurelin Paige has delivered her finest work yet." —Jen McCoy, Literary Gossip Book Blog

"A beautifully executed maze of suspense, seduction, and ridiculously hot sex." —Alessandra Torres, *New York Times* bestselling author

"A dazzling mystery to unravel … wicked and yet sensual. Decadent in her ability to weave a captivating story from beginning to end, Laurelin Paige has another hit on her hands." —Kendall Ryan, *New York Times* bestselling author

"*First Touch* is a heart chilling page-turner from a master storyteller – and the hottest thing I've read this year, hands down." —M. Pierce, bestselling author of the *Night Owl Trilogy*

"Laurelin Paige writes an addictive mix of emotion and sexy that draws the reader in and doesn't let go until long after the last page is read." —K. Bromberg, *New York Times* bestselling author of the Driven Series

"*First Touch* is a deliciously dark and sinfully sexy story that had me up way past bedtime. Laurelin Paige knows exactly what a woman craves, and I'm craving more Reeve." —Geneva Lee, *New York Times* bestselling author

ALSO BY LAURELIN PAIGE

Alayna Withers and Hudson Pierce defeat all odds as they find love in the *New York Times* bestselling

Fixed Trilogy

Fixed on You (Fixed #1)
Found in You (Fixed #2)
Forever with You (Fixed #3)
Fixed Trilogy Bundle (all three Fixed books in one bundle)
Hudson (a companion novel)
Chandler (Coming Soon)
Falling Under You (Coming Soon)

AN EXCERPT FROM *FIXED ON YOU*:

I finished the transaction with Regular and slid down the bar to take care of the suit at the end of the counter.

"Now what can I get…you…?" My words trailed off as my eyes met the suit's, the air leaving my lungs, suddenly sucked out by the sight that met me. The man…he was…*gorgeous.*

Incredibly gorgeous.

I couldn't look away, his appearance magnetizing. Which meant he was exactly the type of man I should avoid.

After the numerous heartaches that had dotted my past, I'd discovered that I could divide the men I was attracted to into two categories. The first category could be described as fuck and forget. These were the men that got me going in the bedroom, but were easy to leave behind if necessary. It was the only group I bothered with anymore. They were the safe ones. David fell into this category.

Then there were the men that were anything but safe. They weren't fuck and forget—they were, "Oh, fuck!" They drew me to them so intensely that I became consumed by them, absolutely focused on everything they did, said and were. I ran from these men, far and fast.

Two seconds after locking eyes with this man, I knew I should be running.

He seemed familiar—he must have been in the club before. But if he had been, I couldn't imagine that I'd have forgotten. He was the most breathtaking man on the planet—his chiseled cheekbones and strong jaw sat beneath perfectly floppy brown hair and the most intense gray eyes I'd ever seen. His five o'clock shadow made my skin itch, yearning to feel the burn of it against my face—against my inner thighs. From what I could see, his expensive three-piece navy suit was fitted and of excellent taste. And his smell—a distinct fragrance of unscented soap and aftershave and pure male goodness—nearly had me sniffing at the air in front of him like a dog in heat.

But it wasn't just his incomparable beauty and exquisite display of male sex that had me burning between my legs and searching for the nearest exit. It was how he looked at me, in a way that no man had ever looked at me, a hungry possessiveness present in his stare as if he not only had undressed me in his mind, but had claimed me to be sated by no one ever again except him.

I wanted him instantly, a prickle of fixation taking root in my belly—an old familiar feeling. But that I desired him didn't matter. The expression on his face said that he would have me whether I wanted it or not, that it was as inevitable as if it had already happened.

It scared the hell out of me. The hair on my skin stood up as witness to my fear.

Or perhaps it rose in delight.

Oh, fuck.

ALSO BY LAURELIN PAIGE

Lights, Camera...

Take Two

Star Struck

AN EXCERPT FROM *TAKE TWO*:

She sat back, attempting to put everything in perspective. He was a player. A self-declared gigolo. At least he didn't deny it.

And she couldn't deny that she was mildly interested. More than mildly. More like wildly.

But she knew herself. She was too into him already. It wouldn't take much to make her fall for him. As Bree had said, he would make her cry.

She sighed then leveled an even stare at him. "I can't date you, Micah."

His eyes hinted amusement. "Who said anything about dating?"

"And I definitely can't do that with you."

He leaned forward, challenge written all over his face. "Why not?"

"Are you serious? To just be a random number in a group of women? A notch in your bedpost that doesn't mean anything?"

Micah put his hand over hers. His touch burned like fire on her skin. "You wouldn't be random. You're Maddie from the party."

"God, Micah, that's just...gross." She slid her hand out from under his. "I'm not against one-night stands in general, but you said it before. You're different. You'd be different."

Micah leaned forward and placed his hand on her leg under the table, sending electric shocks throughout her body. "If by different you mean the most insanely hot, wicked pleasure you've ever felt, then yes, I'll agree."

His fingers moved in circles on her leg, and her mind filled with unwanted images of the insanely hot wicked pleasure Micah promised.

Shaking the fantasies out of her head, she removed his hand from her thigh. "Though I imagine what you say is true..." He winked at her and she had to look away. "That's not what I meant. Most hookups you can love and leave. But not you. I'd see you everywhere after and I'm not talking about in person. And it would make me a major hypocrite. I don't approve of how you use women like Kleenex—"

"Hey, no one's ever complained."

"I'm sure they haven't." His cavalier attitude about the whole thing just reinforced her decision. "And I'm sure you aren't used to hearing those words, but I'm not interested, Micah. Not in the least."

Okay, that was a lie, but he didn't need to know that.

WRITTEN WITH KAYTI MCGEE UNDER
THE NAME LAURELIN MCGEE

Miss Match

Love Struck

MisTaken

ABOUT *MISS MATCH*:

Welcome to the sexy, crazy, wildly unpredictable world of modern matchmaking, where fixing up strangers is part of the job—but falling in love is an occupational hazard...

HE'S THE PERFECT CATCH.

Blake Donovan is tall, handsome, rich, and successful—so why would a guy like him need a matchmaker? Andréa Grayson has no idea, but a job is a job. After being blackballed from a career in marketing, Andréa agreed to use her unique profiling skills to play matchmaker out of pure desperation.. But when she meets her highly eligible—and particular—first client face to face, she wonders what she's gotten herself into...

IS SHE HIS PERFECT MATCH?

Blake knows exactly the kind of woman he's looking for—and it's the total opposite of Andréa. Though smart and undeniably sexy, she is simply too headstrong for a man who's used to being in charge. Still, Blake's blood pressure rises whenever she's near him. How can he explain the smoldering attraction that sizzles between them? And how can Andréa deny she's feeling it, too? Maybe, just maybe, they've finally met their match...

About the Author

Laurelin Paige is the *NY Times*, *Wall Street Journal*, and *USA Today* Bestselling Author of the Fixed Trilogy. She's a sucker for a good romance and gets giddy any time there's kissing, much to the embarrassment of her three daughters. Her husband doesn't seem to complain, however. When she isn't reading or writing sexy stories, she's probably singing, watching *Game of Thrones* and *The Walking Dead*, or dreaming of Michael Fassbender. She's also a proud member of Mensa International, though she doesn't do anything with the organization except use it as material for her bio.

CPSIA information can be obtained
at www.ICGtesting.com
Printed in the USA
BVHW031646100320
574626BV00001B/32